Conor Brady is the forr
Garda Ombudsman comr
and teaching fellowships
University College Dublin. *In the Dark River* is the fourth novel in the Joe Swallow series. He lives and works in Dublin.

Praise for *A June of Ordinary Murders*

'A vivid and crafty whodunit ... Fans of mysteries that capture the flavour of the past will hope that Swallow has a long literary life.' – *Publishers Weekly, Starred Review*

'Brady's powerful first mystery novel is evocative of the period. The many aspects of life in 19th-century Dublin are cleverly woven through a baffling mystery.' – *Kirkus Reviews*

'Swallow is an increasingly interesting protagonist who is left to face the realities of his professional future and his closest personal relationship; readers will want to see more of him.' – *Booklist*

'Making his mystery debut, former *Irish Times* editor Brady presents a fascinating and in-depth historical peek at crime solving in a bygone era when it took more than a few keystrokes and a phone call to catch a perp. Swallow is a complicated, earnest hero with just enough flaws to make him endearingly sympathetic.' – *Library Journal*

'Conor Brady's debut novel is a slice of history about Dublin, Ireland, and the Dublin Metropolitan police, intertwined with a first-rate murder mystery, and peopled by characters both complex and realistic.' – *NY Journal of Books*

'Like all great historical fiction, *A June of Ordinary Murders* stuns us into fresh recognition of a period we thought we knew – and as if that weren't enough, hides all of its meticulous research inside a superbly engaging mystery. Get in on the ground floor. Conor Brady is the real deal.' – *Charles Finch*, bestselling author of *The Laws of Murder*

'Brady weaves a police procedural that does full justice to the complex nature of the social, political and criminal labyrinth that was Dublin in the summer of 1887. He paints a vivid picture of the city ... Swallow himself is very much in the mould of the classic fictional policeman, a man ostensibly dedicated to upholding law and order and seeking out justice …' – *The Irish Times*

'As in the best crime fiction, the city itself is here a kind of character – and it's a Dublin we haven't seen a great deal of in recent fiction … An absorbing read, cleanly written, beautifully structured and thrillingly vivid … Brady has done an excellent job of conjuring the febrile atmosphere of the city as it lurches and stumbles its way towards the War of Independence.' – *Sunday Business Post*

'Delivers a thrilling sense of the familiar, lit with the profane … the pace raises the novel above the period pastiche.' – *Sunday Independent*

'Brady handles the political atmosphere of the time with aplomb. *A June Of Ordinary Murders* pulsates with a vivid sense of a country on edge as the land wars rage and preparations get under way for a royal visit.' – *Irish Independent*

Praise for *The Eloquence of the Dead*

'In Brady's stellar second whodunit set in Victorian Dublin … the astute Swallow is a particularly well-rounded lead, and he's matched with a complex, but logical, page-turner of a plot.' – *Publishers Weekly*

'The second case for the talented, complicated Swallow again spins a fine mystery out of political corruption in 1880s Dublin.' – *Kirkus Reviews*

'If intricate plotting and journalistic descriptions of time and place pique your fancy, Brady is your man.' – Historical Novel Society

'He has given us a compelling and memorable central character in the shape of Detective Swallow … If the RTÉ drama department are looking for something to fill a *Love/Hate*-sized hole in next year's schedule, they could do worse than look at the continuing development, and adventures, of Detective Joe Swallow.' – *Irish Independent*

'Swallow, a keen amateur painter, brings a sharp eye to bear on his surroundings, which in turn allows Brady to give us a vivid account of late Victorian Dublin in all its squalid glory. The result is a very satisfying police procedural/mystery and an equally fine historical novel.' – *The Irish Times*

Praise for *A Hunt in Winter*

'Interesting and daring.' – *Irish Examiner*

'A cracker of a book and very enjoyable.' – *Hotpress*

'A rattling tale which draws in real-life historical events, a multi-strand thriller plot, the complex web of personal relationships … an entertaining read … many mystery fans love to follow the hero on his journey through life, book after book. In Joe Swallow, they have an interesting and agreeable travel companion.' – *Irish Independent*

'The window Brady provides into the everyday lives of ordinary Irishmen caught in a dramatic moment gives his third entry a combination of the best elements of police procedurals and historical mysteries.' – *Kirkus Reviews*

'The story is engaging, and Brady does an excellent job in characterization of Swallow and the lesser players. Readers will bond with the Irishman from the beginning and care about his personal triumphs and losses. The author's mastery of setting makes late 19th-century Dublin come alive … an enjoyable read.' – Historical Novel Society

'Brady's strong third whodunit set in Victorian Ireland … seamlessly integrates the political tensions of the day into the plot … the series' historical backdrop should continue to prove a rich source for future entries.' – *Publishers Weekly*

In the Dark River

In the Dark River

Conor Brady

IN THE DARK RIVER
First published in 2018 by
New Island Books
16 Priory Hall Office Park
Stillorgan
County Dublin
Republic of Ireland

www.newisland.ie

Print ISBN: 978-1-84840-702-2
Epub ISBN: 978-1-84840-703-9
Mobi ISBN: 978-1-84840-704-6

A CIP catalogue record for this book is available from the British Library.

Typeset by JVR Creative India
Cover design by Nina Lyons
Printed by

New Island received financial assistance from The Arts Council (An Chomhairle Ealaíon), 70 Merrion Square, Dublin 2, Ireland.

New Island Books is a member of Publishing Ireland.

That was the end of the woman in the wood
Weela, weela waile
That was the end of the woman in the wood
*Down by the river Saile**

*Saile – 'Saileach' (Irish, Adj.: Dirty, foul, filthy)

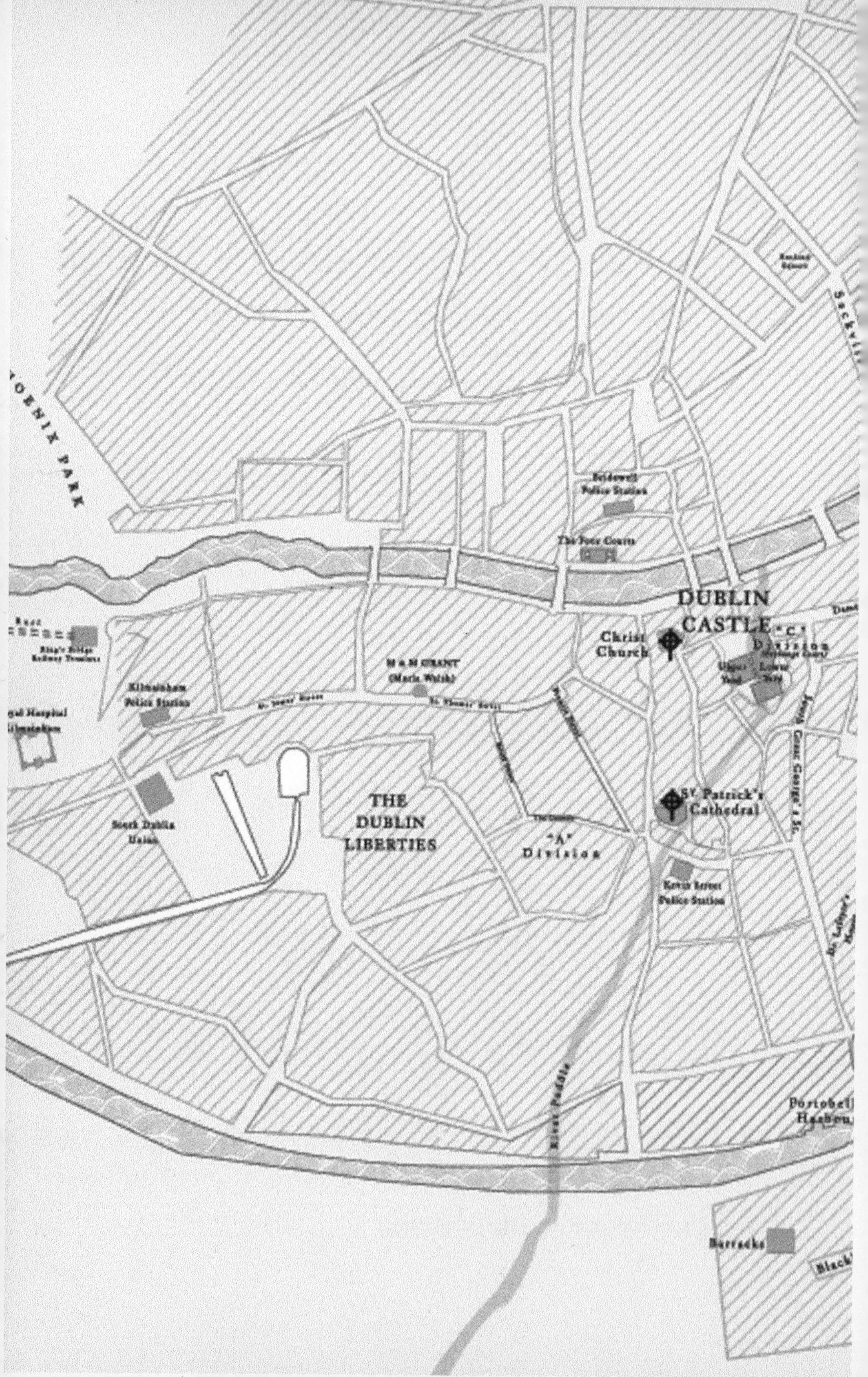

PHOENIX PARK
Bridewell Police Station
The Four Courts
DUBLIN CASTLE
Christ Church
"C" Division
Upper Yard
Lower Yard
Kilmainham Police Station
THE DUBLIN LIBERTIES
St. Patrick's Cathedral
"A" Division
Kevin Street Police Station
South Dublin Union
Great George's St.
River Poddle
Barracks

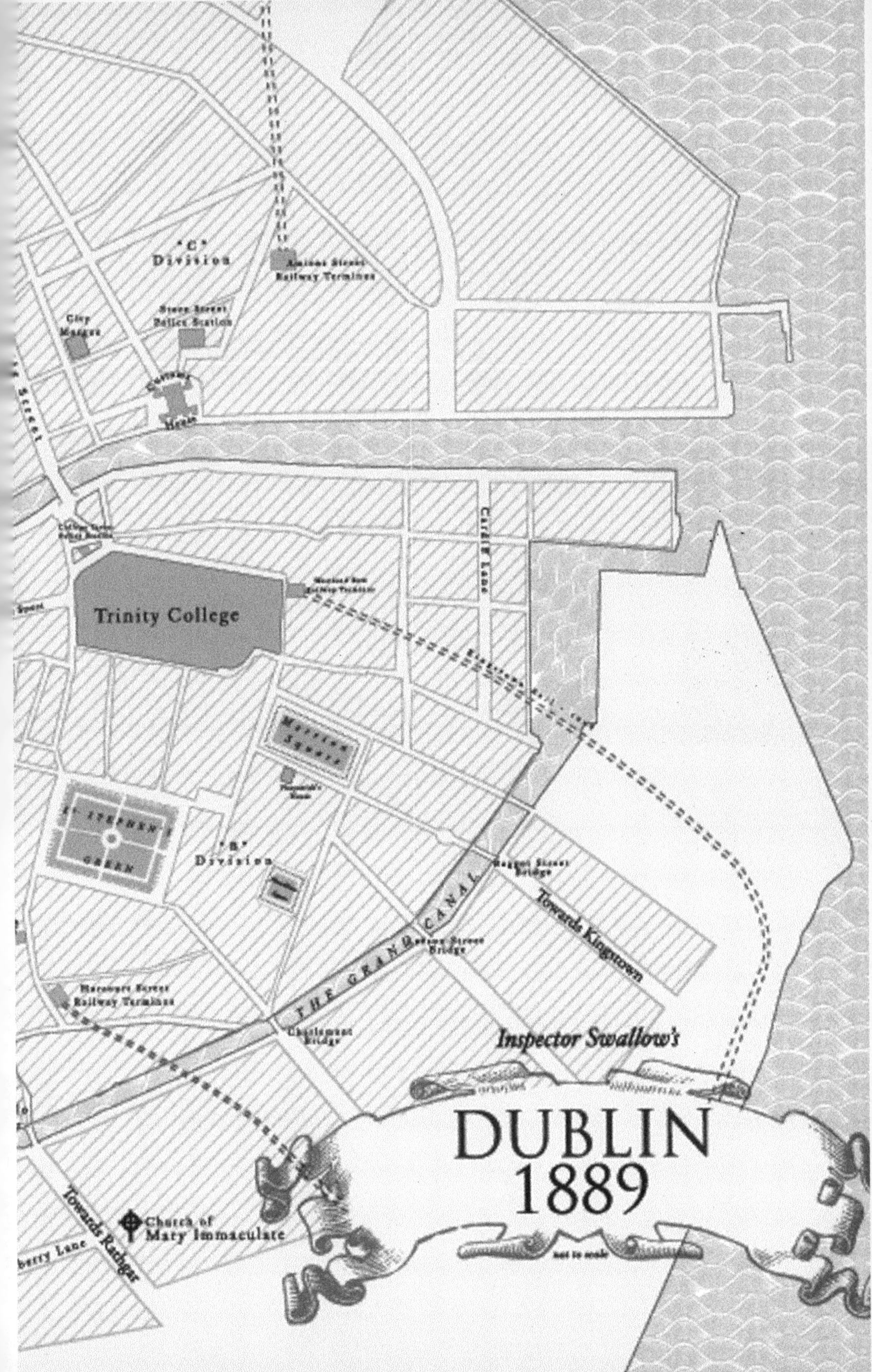

"C"
Division
Amiens Street
Railway Terminus
Store Street
Police Station
City
Morgue
Custom
House
Trinity College
Cardiff Lane
Merrion
Square
St. Stephen's
Green
"B"
Division
Baggot Street
Bridge
Towards Kingstown
THE GRAND CANAL
Leeson Street
Bridge
Harcourt Street
Railway Terminus
Charlemont
Bridge
Inspector Swallow's
DUBLIN
1889
not to scale
Towards Rathgar
Church of
Mary Immaculate

Prologue

Hotel Los Embajadores, Madrid, March 1st, 1889

The grey streets that he had walked since morning had been scoured by a dry, cutting wind.

'*Altitud*,' the waiter had told him curtly an hour ago when he shivered, complaining, in the café. It blew all afternoon, rising up from the Castilian plain beyond the city. He had sought unsuccessfully to attain oblivion with as much cheap Spanish brandy as his dwindling *pesetas* would allow. But when the last of the oily spirit was gone, he would have to make his way back to his hotel room. There might be money from Paris or London in the morning, he told himself. Even if there was, he knew it would not be a lot. But with any luck it might be enough to enable him to stay ahead of his pursuers for another while.

'*Altitud*.' He remembered reading somewhere about the Moors, building their stronghold, *Majrit*, high on the central plateau of the Iberian Peninsula so that it baked in summer and froze in winter. That was the problem with being a journalist. One collected enormous amounts of useless information in one's head. Then some Christian king corrupted the Arab name and called it Madrid. Bloody awful place to put a city, he reflected. Dublin or London might be damp and chilly in March. But they would not have this scourging *sirocco* wind from Africa. The pier at Kingstown had been positively balmy when he walked it with his two boys a month ago.

Was it only a month? The brandy had him addled. It was probably less, he reckoned, since everything had started to fall asunder that morning of the commission at Westminster. One minute he was being lionised and courted by the men from *The Times*. They assured him he would be their star witness before the Royal Commission of Inquiry. They had billed his appearance at the top of their news column.

DUBLIN EDITOR TO PRODUCE LETTERS
Mr Richard Pigott to take the Stand
COMMISSION TO HEAR FROM DISTINGUISHED JOURNALIST

He had the evidence they needed in the letters he held, linking Charles Stewart Parnell, the leader of Irish nationalism, the 'uncrowned king' of Ireland, to Fenian violence and even to murder. The next minute, he was being torn to shreds in the witness box in St Stephen's Hall by that clever little Catholic lawyer from Newry, Charles Russell.

He had underestimated the lawyer and had made stupid mistakes himself. Everything had happened quickly once Russell identified the spelling mistakes in the letters, challenging him to spell the key words. When he made the same misspellings the lawyer had successfully branded him a rogue and a liar. The hall had filled with guffaws and catcalls. Even the three judges in their scarlet robes struggled to contain their amusement.

Russell had started his cross-examination with deceptive courtesy. But within half an hour he was tearing at him like a terrier savaging a rat. He tried unsuccessfully to stutter out the evidence that he had so carefully rehearsed beforehand, coached by the men from *The Times*. He realised he was babbling incoherently, the perspiration breaking out all over his body, matting his hair and beard and staining his waistcoat and suit. The presiding judge sympathetically announced an adjournment. The rest of Richard Pigott's evidence would be taken tomorrow.

Suddenly the men from *The Times* and the security detectives who drank with them in the pubs in the evenings were no longer his friends. There was anger in their eyes and in their voices. They had turned on him as a pack. There was no more back-slapping or jolly quips. There was no talk of the evening's promised dinner at Simpsons-in-the-Strand with its exquisite food and wines. A security agent he knew simply as 'The Captain' had pulled him aside and tapped him angrily on the chest as witnesses, lawyers, officials and the public gallery had spilled out into the Palace Yard, making for the nearby public houses and coffee shops to dissect the morning's dramatic collapse.

'Take a bit of advice now, Paddy,' he hissed, 'make yourself scarce. Their Lordships have a distinct aversion to perjury. Make no error, there'll be a warrant for your arrest within a day or two. Maybe even this afternoon. And none of us wants to hear you in the witness box explaining how you came into possession of evidence that turns out to be a forgery. It wouldn't be good for any of us, would it? So, come back here in the morning and we'll have a little present to help you take a nice holiday in Paris.'

He drank heavily that evening, on his own in a noisy saloon bar by the river. He took the furthest corner of the bar, sinking back into the shadows in case he might be recognised. He thought he heard his name being mentioned more than once in the raucous conversations going on around him. The thought of going back to the commission in the morning for more punishment filled him with dread. But he would have to turn up to get the money promised by the security agent. He slept in his clothes at the Aldwych hotel room provided by *The Times*, mercifully anaesthetised by the alcohol and coming to an unwelcome wakefulness around dawn. Before leaving for Westminster he packed the smaller of his two suitcases, carefully placing the Webley revolver provided by his security mentors – for 'his own protection,' as they had said – among the jumbled garments and other paraphernalia. After the chamber-maid had brought the morning jug of warm water, he made a desultory attempt to smarten his appearance for the witness stand. But when he saw his haggard face, crumpled suit and bloodshot eyes in the mirror, he realised it was futile.

In the event, the cross-examination by counsel representing *The Times* was brief and painless. Russell had destroyed him the previous day and the newspaper's case was hopeless. In its detestation of Parnell and its visceral opposition to his campaign to secure Home Rule for Ireland, it had backed a dud, a forger and a perjurer. *The Times'* counsel had nothing to argue with. Russell needed no more from this discredited witness, although the public gallery was eagerly anticipating more sport. As he made his way clumsily towards the stand that morning, Pigott saw a man in the public seating – he had no idea who he was – pound a fist into the palm of his other hand, mouthing the word 'smashed' at him. It was exactly how he felt.

When the commission adjourned early for lunch, The Captain was waiting for him in the Palace Yard.

'Here's fifty pounds,' he said, pressing an envelope into his hand. 'There'll be more when you get to the other side. There's tickets in there as well for Dover and on to Paris, and a set of travel documents authorised by the Foreign Office in the name of Roland Ponsonby. Just get on the next train for Dover and talk to nobody. Understand?'

'But I thought I'd go back directly to Dublin. I've got two young sons there to look after.'

'I don't think you quite understand,' the Captain said testily. 'You're going to be a wanted fugitive anywhere in the United Kingdom. And if you go back to Dublin they'll probably shoot you anyway. The newspapers are baying for your blood. At least the Fenian rags are.'

He knew he had no choice but to do what he was told. It was a hurried cab ride to the hotel to collect the case he had packed the night before and then another to Victoria to catch the Dover train. The weather for the crossing to Calais was calm and uneventful. But he was sick with anxiety. His travel documents got no more than a cursory glance from a French official on the quayside. He breathed a little easier when he boarded the night train to Paris. It was warm and comfortable. He ordered a bottle of claret in the buffet car and calmed a little as its warmth spread through his vitals. At the Gare du Nord in the morning a man wearing a Derby hat and a Harris tweed coat stopped him just beyond the barrier and handed him a ticket.

'You're a marked man.' The accent was broad, strong, Scottish. 'The powers-that-be want to make an example of you. They want to jail you for perjury. You've made them look bad. So we don't know how long we can protect you for. Our advice to you is to keep moving. Take the train for Barcelona at the Gare d'Austerlitz. I have tickets here for you. It's departing in an hour. You'll cross the Spanish border at Port Bou and then continue on to Girona. Change trains at Girona and take the first service you can get aboard to Madrid. We'll be in contact there. Don't worry, we look after our own.'

The Scotsman led him to a cab outside the station. He muttered instructions in French to the driver and walked away without a word to Pigott.

The train to Barcelona was overcrowded, noisy and dirty. The ticket was ostensibly for a first class carriage but when he tried to secure a seat he discovered that every one had been reserved. Eventually, having walked the length of the train three times, he squeezed into a banquette seat in a second class carriage between an overweight Catalan salesman who, he discovered, dealt in olive oil and a middle-aged French woman dressed in widow's black.

After some desultory conversation in English, the Catalan salesman fell asleep. The French widow stared silently through the window at the darkened countryside. There were frequent stops at cities and towns, one more uninviting than the other in the gloom of the night. He would have liked to go to the dining car for some refreshments but dared not leave his place which would certainly be taken by someone condemned to stand in the crowded corridors. At some point he fell asleep. When he woke it was morning, with a bright sun rising over the countryside. Green fields and meadows had given way to brown earth, with terraces of what he guessed were vines. The houses were roofed with red terracotta. Here and there in the landscape he could make out sizeable buildings, but whether these were fine dwelling houses or more utilitarian constructions, he could not tell.

All passengers had to alight after Port Bou to be cleared by Spanish border officials. A small, swarthy officer, in a green uniform and a tri-cornered hat examined his travel document, scowled and stamped it aggressively, muttering just one word.

'*Ingles.*'

A great many passengers had already disembarked at Perpignan and Port Vendres. So by the time the train had crossed into Spain it was pleasantly uncrowded. He was able to claim a comfortable seat for himself in first class and he breakfasted on coffee, some cheese and cured ham and a small loaf of fresh bread in the dining car. The Mediterranean sparkled to the south and the Albères, the foothills of the Pyrenees, were green and verdant to the north. He began to feel better about things, relaxed even. It would all blow over in time, he told himself.

He disembarked at Girona and took the next train to Madrid. It was comfortable, clean and well provided with a decent dining car and a choice of good wines at very reasonable prices. The journey passed quickly and pleasantly as he dined on fresh sea-bass and sampled the excellent Riojas offered by the railway company.

At Madrid's Estación de Mediodía, another man, younger than the fellow in Paris and grinning cheerily, dressed in what might have been the pavilion outfit of a cricket club, greeted him on the platform. Notwithstanding the good wine and food on the journey from Girona, he was tired and dishevelled after more than two days travelling without proper sleep or ablutions and without a change of clothing.

'You are Mr Roland Ponsonby, of course.' The young man clapped him on the shoulder and smiled broadly.'I've been waiting for you. Welcome to Madrid. I'm sure it will be a very successful visit for your business.'

Pigott disliked him instantly.

'And what business am I supposed to be in … exactly?'

'Oh, that's a matter for yourself, Roland.'

The grin broadened.

'I'd say you'd easily pass as a buyer. A merchant. Let's say you're here to find suppliers for good wine. You'd know a bit about that, wouldn't you?'

He winked knowingly.

'Who are you? Who do you work for?' Pigott asked testily. He found himself greatly irritated by the young man's tone of familiarity.

'Oh, call me Brown or Black or White or Grey, perhaps. Any one of them will do. And I work for the same people you do. Or did, in London, until the other day. We … ah … solve problems for Her Majesty's government, as you've gathered. And just now, Roland, you're a problem.'

He led Pigott to a waiting cab.

'The hotel we've got for you is comfortable enough. It's not the very best. But we don't want you running into anyone who might recognise you. Just keep out of sight until we know it's safe to show yourself. They've issued a warrant in London for your arrest and they're very serious about finding you. With any luck, they think you're still in Paris.'

'I want to get back to Dublin as soon as I can,' Pigott said quietly. 'I've two young boys who need their father. And I have business interests …'

The young man's grin had vanished. His expression was tense.

'Look, I'm only a small cog in a very big wheel, Mr … ah … Ponsonby. But I think you'd better understand the trouble you're in. As I read the wires, you led the government to believe you had evidence that would fix this fellow Parnell. They want him dealt with. You took their money, even though they'll always deny that, of course. They looked after you, and then it turns out that what you've sold them is a pathetic forgery. So, they're going to throw you to the wolves. They have to. They can't be seen to be complicit in perjury. So your goose is cooked, Roland. And if you go back to Ireland they'll nab you in an instant. That wouldn't suit you and it wouldn't suit my bosses either.'

He opened the cab door.

Pigott stepped up to the footplate and took his seat. The man did not attempt to join him but leaned through the lowered window.

'Now, we know that the last thing my bosses want is for you to be brought back in handcuffs to give evidence that would embarrass them. So, my job, along with my colleagues, is to keep you out of reach. You'd be best to accept that you won't see Dublin for a long time. And if you do, it'll be through the bars of a prison van. Now, we'll get you settled into your hotel. The driver knows where you're going. We'll take care of the charges for your room and your meals and here's some pesetas to allow you to have a little drink or whatever you like.'

He handed Pigott an envelope through the window.

'Good day, Mr Ponsonby. Enjoy your visit.'

The Hotel Los Embajadores was a parody of its pretentious name. The tiny room he was allocated on the third floor was dingy and dark with an odour of decay. The fare in the dining room was plentiful but consisted mainly of stewed vegetables and pork, with cured fish as an occasional alternative. The wine was dry and vinegary. None of the staff and none of his fellow guests who seemed to be, in the main, commercial travellers, could speak any English. Since the only thing to do was to drink in one or other of the bars or cafes nearby, his funds had run low very quickly.

He was too drowsy from the brandy to notice the two men sitting in the lobby when he got back to the hotel that afternoon. They stood, hats in hand, as he came towards them.

'Señor … Pon … son … bee? A word with you please, if we may.'

The man's English was heavily accented and each syllable was articulated slowly and deliberately.

Pigott's fuddled brain told him this was not good news.

'Yes … that is my name … Ponsonby … of course.'

His companion dug in his pocket and produced a folded sheet of off-white paper. He dangled it in front of Pigott's face. He could see a crown embossed at the top of the page.

The first man cleared his throat.

'Señor Pon … son … bee, I am Subteniente Vargo of the Guardia Civil,' he said slowly, as if remembering lines he had rehearsed very carefully. 'I am to ask that you will accompany us to our headquarters.'

'May I … may I inquire why?'

'I am not at liberty, Señor, to discuss this. All I can tell you is that my superiors are acting on a request from the Embassy of Great Britain here in Madrid. Can you please now step outside? We have a carriage in the street.'

Suddenly the fog of alcohol was gone and Pigott understood with immediate clarity. The unhappy freedom that he had travelled so far to secure was threatened. This was not what his protectors at the Special Irish office in Scotland Yard had promised him. If the British Embassy was involved it meant that a decision had been taken at the highest levels to bring him back to punish him in public. It was decision time.

'Very well,' he told Vargo. 'But I would like to shave and put on a fresh shirt. May I have a few minutes?'

The policeman nodded.

'Of course. We shall wait here.'

He climbed the stairs to his room to where he knew the Webley lay in the drawer by the bedside. There was no need to check it. He had kept it loaded since leaving London.

He sat on the side of the bed. He had the gun. He had just a little money. It was decision time. His mind went to Dublin. To his two sons. To the better days and the nights of good food and drink with roistering friends. He could probably find a way out through the back of the hotel. But what then? Where would he go? How could he survive without money or friends to rely on?

A floorboard squeaked noisily outside his door. He heard men speaking softly but urgently in the corridor. One voice was English. Maybe two. He thought he could hear a key being slipped into the door lock.

The clerk on duty downstairs at the reception had served as a non-commissioned officer in the Spanish infantry. Conditioned to observe and take note, he was aware that there were men in the lobby waiting for one of the guests. They had been there since mid-morning. It was not his business to know who they were or why they were waiting for Mr Ponsonby, but he had little doubt that they were men of authority rather than Mr Ponsonby's friends. Earlier, when one of them had yawned and stretched his arms in boredom, he had caught sight of a pistol under the man's coat. And because he had been a military man himself, when he heard a sharp, reverberating retort from the floor above, the clerk knew that somebody had fired a shot.

Chapter 1

Dublin, Tuesday, June 4th, 1889

Swallow liked June. It was the best-behaved month of the year, he reckoned. Summer in Dublin was generally a travesty of its own name. In more than three decades living in the city he could only remember one summer that had lived up to expectations of blue skies and sunny days. That was two years previously when the golden jubilee of Queen Victoria's coronation was marked by her loyal Irish subjects, a cohort that by no means extended to the entire population. June 1887 was so hot that the tram tracks buckled outside the Shelbourne Hotel on St Stephen's Green. But mostly his memories of July and August in Dublin were of hanging grey clouds over the Castle's Lower Yard or, in the days when he was a young constable in uniform, of rain streaming from the rim of his helmet, on to his blue cape.

The morning was proof that June was the best of it. Maria was still sleeping in their bedroom above Grant's public house when he left Thomas Street for the Castle just before eight o'clock. The streets were bathed in pale, lemon light, spilling over the rooftops as the sun gained height out on the bay. Unlike other Victorian cities, Dublin had little manufacturing industry, so the air was pure and fresh apart from the faintest tang of hops from the Guinness brewery at St James's Gate. The various bells in the cathedrals and churches began tolling the hour as he passed the Augustinian Friary at John's Lane. He could tell them individually and in their sequence. The deep, sonorous peals of Christ Church, the tinny ring of the two St Audoen's, the metallic thump of St Nicholas', the flat tone of St Catherine's, the melodious harmony of St Patrick's. Christ Church started a moment before the others as if to assert its senior cathedral status. St Patrick's always seemed to be a chime or two behind. Or was it perhaps that it took the sound a little time to travel up the rising ground?

The city streets were quiet. No Dublin shop opened its doors before nine o'clock. Business houses and professional offices rarely started their day before ten, while the judges and lawyers across the river in the Four Courts only got down to business at eleven. But since his promotion to detective inspector the previous year, Swallow had adopted a strict regime that would always have him at his desk in the detective office at Exchange Court by half eight. The morning shifts across Dublin's six uniformed divisions, from the crowded A, around the Liberties, to the comfortable, affluent F, along the southern side of the bay, started at six o'clock. So the sergeants' reports from the night before would be on his desk. By nine o'clock, when John Mallon, the chief of the detective force, G-division, would arrive, Swallow could fully brief his boss on the state of crime and subversion in the second city of the Empire.

Although the wealthy south city suburbs of Ballsbridge, Donnybrook, Rathmines and Rathgar had been experiencing an unusual wave of aggravated burglaries and housebreakings over the previous twelve months or so, there was rarely much serious crime. The streets were well supervised by the 1,800 uniformed members of the Dublin Metropolitan Police, meticulously patrolling their beats in eight-hour shifts. But there was always plenty of political subversion. The bulk of G-division's work was taken up with surveillance, gathering intelligence and countering the activities of Fenians, dynamiters, land agitators and radicals, as well as protecting important persons and buildings. The uniformed DMP men went about their patrolling unarmed apart from a short wooden baton. Each of the eighty or so members of G-division however, carried a standard .44 Bulldog Webley revolver at all times.

He crossed Cornmarket and High Street into Lord Edward Street. After the City Hall, the seat of Dublin Corporation, he turned out of Dame Street into the gloomy alleyway that was Exchange Court. Huddled in against the northern flank of Dublin Castle, the sun never touched its black cobbles or its dull redbrick walls. It was probably the coldest and dampest building in Dublin with an extraordinarily high frequency of respiratory complaints and illnesses among its occupants.

Pat Mossop, the duty sergeant for the previous night, was sifting a sheaf of papers on the wooden countertop in the public office.

'Morning, Pat. Anything strange or dramatic?'

Mossop looked tired. The Belfast man had taken a revolver bullet in the chest two years previously while making an arrest on Ormond Quay. Only the speedy action of his colleagues, Swallow among them, in getting him to the nearby Jervis Infirmary had saved his life. His recovery was slow and something less than complete although the police surgeon at the Kevin Street Depot had eventually declared him fit for duty. Swallow's plan now was to find him a quiet desk job with regular hours to make life easier. But so far, no opportunity had come up. As a fall-back position, he tried to have him rostered as frequently as possible for indoor duty in the public office.

'There's another aggravated burglary at a big house out in the countryside beyond Rathgar,' Mossop told him. 'A place called Templeogue Hill. It's just in the city area, apparently. Another hundred yards and it wouldn't be our problem.'

The boundaries of the Metropolitan policing area had been expanded in the past year as the city suburbs grew. The E-division, headquartered at Rathmines, had been given responsibility for several townlands that had heretofore been policed by the Royal Irish Constabulary, the armed body which formed the model for most of the police forces of the Empire.

'The lads are out there now,' Mossop said. 'I've only got a preliminary report so far. The house of a Mr and Mrs McCartan. He's a lawyer and I think he's involved in various businesses as well. The wife is some sort of an invalid, I gather. According to the sergeant from Rathmines, there were three, maybe four in the job. At least one had a gun. Some sort of revolver, "a big gun," the maid says. But then again, nobody ever seems to see a small gun.'

He glanced at his notes.

'They got in the back door around ten o'clock and the intruders roughed them up. The man seems to be fairly badly injured. They kicked the housemaid around but she's only bruised. They hit the man a few wallops on the head with some sort of a metal bar. He's not in any danger but the doctor sent him down to Baggot Street Hospital for stitching. There's a safe in the house and these fellows seemed to be able to pick it or break it easily enough. The lads are trying to get a fix on what was taken but it seems there was a fair bit of cash and jewellery. The householders are fairly shocked, according to the sergeant, not too coherent. The man of the house seems to be in a spitting rage about the local bobbies falling down on their duty and so on. Hard to blame them, I suppose.'

'That's the tenth one of these jobs now in a year,' Swallow mused. 'And the second in, what, three weeks? Second appearance of a gun too.'

'Not even three weeks. More like two and a half since the one down on Anglesea Road.'

G-division still had no success in identifying a group of three men who had broken into the home of John Healy, an elderly, retired and almost blind businessman in Ballsbridge, threatened him with a gun and knives before making off with cash, silver plate and jewellery.

'Who went out to the scene?' Swallow asked.

'Shanahan and Keogh. They knocked off duty at ten o'clock but they were having a pint or two in The Brazen Head. They were less than happy to be pulled out and put back to work after a full day shift. But I made it clear I wasn't asking. I was telling them.'

It was an all-too-familiar story in G-division. In spite of personnel numbers being increased since the savage murders of the Chief Secretary for Ireland and his Undersecretary in the Phoenix Park seven years previously, G-men were frequently obliged to work extra shifts. Rising political tension demanded extra surveillance and protection duty.

'Have they any leads?'

Mossop shrugged.

'It's too early, Boss. You know we've been watching the gangs closely since these jobs started. The Vanucchis, the Cussens and the Downses mainly. We've put a hell of a lot of hours into surveillance and a fair bit of money has gone out to informers, but none of them seem to be involved.'

Swallow nodded. The Vanucchi gang, headed by Charlie Vanucchi, operated from The Liberties area and were involved in crime that ranged from selling illegal whiskey to organised, large-scale theft on and around the Dublin docks. Vanucchi had inherited most of the criminal empire once controlled by Cecilia Downes, better known as 'Pisspot Cess,' who had been the queen of crime in the city for more than twenty years until her death two years previously. She had acquired her unflattering soubriquet due to the fact that as a young girl she had battered the skull of her employer, who had caught her stealing, with a metal chamber pot. A smaller number of her followers had refused to accept Charlie Vanucchi as their boss after her death, so they had reorganised at the western end of The Liberties, under the leadership of Vinnie Cussen, a criminal with a long record for violence. They operated around the Coombe area and had a presence across the river in the red-light district, centred on Montgomery Street. A smaller gang, including two nephews of Cess Downes, had established themselves around the Stoneybatter area.

'I think some of the lads have even put a few bob of their own out to the snouts,' Mossop added. 'But they're hearing nothing on the street. And none of the old lags have been much on the move. Besides, none of the usual clients carry guns and mostly they aren't the kind to go lashing out with iron bars unless they had to. Could be there's some new operators in town, maybe coming in every few weeks from God knows where.'

Dublin criminals rarely had access to firearms, even though Fenians and other agitators had guns aplenty and usually had no qualms about using them, even against fellow-Irishmen, if they happened to be in the police, the military or the magistracy. By and large the criminal gangs in the inner city tried to avoid the use of violence in their activities. The new suburbs however, now rapidly developing outside the city's canals, offered tempting targets for housebreakers and burglars. With the City Corporation now firmly in the control of Catholic merchants and tradesmen, affluent Protestants, all strong Loyalists, many of them bankers, businessmen and wealthy professionals, preferred to move out to Rathmines, Ballsbridge, Clontarf, Glasnevin or Drumcondra. They could more happily reside in the new suburbs under town councils that were more likely to be influenced if not wholly controlled by like-minded men.

'Have we any description of these fellows?' Swallow asked. 'Height, age, dress, accents?'

'Not yet, Boss. Like I said, the man and the woman are badly shocked. And the maid says they wore masks. But when they've recovered a bit and if they think they can remember anything, I'll arrange for photographs from DCR and we'll get them to have a look.'

DCR – the Dublin Criminal Registry – was a showpiece of modern policing methods for the Dublin Metropolitan Police. Housed at Ship Street, behind the Castle, it contained upwards of ten thousand records of persons convicted or suspected of crime. Organised using the new Dewey Decimal system along the lines of a modern library, the staff could locate and retrieve the file of a named suspect in half a minute. Almost all the files opened since 1883 contained photographic images of suspects as well. In the aftermath of the Phoenix Park murders, the DMP and the Royal Irish Constabulary had been among the first police forces in the United Kingdom to be supplied with photographic equipment and with trained staff to operate it.

'Anything else happening?' Swallow asked.

'Apart from that, just a few drunks from a Dutch ship down on the North Wall got into a row with the locals at McDonagh's up on Gloucester Street. A few black eyes and broken noses but no worse than that. The head man at McDonagh's saw it brewing and sent the cellar lad running down to Store Street. The bobbies were up there in force fairly quickly and got things under control. The four Dutchmen and three of the local heroes will be in the Bridewell court later. And a bit of traffic from around the country. I was just going to put the routes on your desk.'

The printed 'routes' came through the ABC police telegraph that connected the DMP's twenty-five stations. It was the most modern communications technology, another beneficial by-product of the Phoenix Park murders.

The assassins had been under surveillance by G-division earlier in the week of the murders, but information on their plans and their movements had not been circulated through the wider police network. No expense had been spared in strengthening or resourcing the Dublin police in the aftermath of the murders. Extra men were appointed to G-division. More money was made available to recruit informers. The best of equipment, including the ABC system, field cameras and typewriting machines had been provided.

'Anything happening in security or intelligence?' Swallow asked.

'There is, actually,' Mossop tapped a file on his desk. 'Two of the intelligence fellows from the Upper Yard took Dunlop of *The Irish Times* for dinner at the Burlington last night to pump him for what he knew about Mr Parnell and Mrs O'Shea. He conveniently stopped in and briefed me afterwards.'

Any mention of the security section that operated from within the office of the Permanent Under-Secretary in the Castle's Upper Yard, set Swallow's alarm bells ringing. It had been gradually built up over the past two years as a special agency, separate from the police and G-division, working directly for Charles Smith-Berry, the Assistant Under-Secretary for Security, a man with experience in locations as diverse as Egypt, Mesopotamia and Palestine.

The English-born Smith-Berry did not conceal his disdain and his distrust of G-division in general and its chief, John Mallon, in particular. He was blunt in his frequent clashes with Mallon, the most celebrated detective in Dublin. He believed that the G-men's loyalties, as Irishmen on the Crown payroll, were divided. And he believed it was necessary to have a separate cadre of intelligence officers, English, Scottish or perhaps Ulster loyalist, and preferably with a military background, operating as a counterweight to G-division and reporting directly to his office.

In reality, Mallon acknowledged privately to his senior confidantes, including Swallow, that Smith-Berry was right. The security service saw itself as the instrument of the government's will. G-division, or at least its senior members, had a different perspective.

It was the objective of the Westminster government to destroy Parnell and to kill off the campaign to establish Home Rule for Ireland. If Ireland got its own parliament, the logic went, it would split the United Kingdom. And if the United Kingdom split, it would be the beginning of the end for the Empire. Great Britain was the richest nation on the earth because of the profits it made from that empire. From the royal family down to the working men in the industrial cities, its people enjoyed the highest standards of living of any people anywhere on the planet. Smith-Berry's department in the Upper Yard of Dublin Castle was committed to achieving the aims of its political masters.

Mallon, on the other hand, took the view that if Parnell were to fall, Ireland would descend into unprecedented violence. As long as the people could be persuaded to believe in political action, the great majority would not want to take up the message of the gunmen and the bombers. But if Parnell's steadying influence were to be removed, the way would be open for the men of violence to take centre stage. It was a scenario that no committed police officer could countenance. Both as an Irishman and as a policeman, Mallon cared less for the Empire than for the peace and welfare of his own countrymen. And that put G-division and the security department in the Upper Yard at loggerheads.

The men of G-division were reciprocally disdainful and mistrustful of Smith-Berry's agents. Mallon ensured that his informants around the city were well rewarded for information about them. Who they were. Where they were billeted. Where they ate and drank. Who they endeavoured to cultivate as their contacts and habitués. Some of them lived in rooms in the Upper Yard. Others stayed in hotels or boarding houses around the Castle. They were tough men, hard drinkers for the most part, keeping to themselves. When they made contacts among the population, they appeared to have access to almost limitless funds to recruit informants. But their understanding of Irish politics and of Irish ways was abysmal. Swallow knew most of them by sight and by the names they used.

'Which of them was it?' he asked Mossop.

'Reggie Polson and a fellow called McKitterick.'

Smith-Berry's men habitually adopted false names. Swallow knew the two agents calling themselves Polson and McKitterick from earlier, terse encounters in joint operations with G-division. Reggie Polson, as he called himself, was ex-army, Swallow could tell. He had an ear for accents. He placed Polson's origins somewhere in the Home Counties, possibly Berkshire or Buckinghamshire. He guessed him to be about his own age, surmising that he was probably a replacement for the senior agent who called himself Captain Kelly before he was moved out of the security department the previous year. He reckoned that McKitterick was a junior member of the department, probably a former non-commissioned officer.

Mossop pushed the file across the desk.

'I've written it up for you, Boss. It's all in there, at least as much as I was told earlier.'

Swallow took the papers and climbed the stairs to the second floor. His rank gave him the privilege of a modest office with a twelve-paned window that afforded a view across the roofs of South Great George's Street. Apart from the robbery at Templeogue Hill, the crime reports were routine, as Mossop had indicated. But the intelligence of the meeting between Andrew Dunlop of *The Irish Times* and two security agents from the Upper Yard was disquieting.

Swallow had collaborated with Dunlop a number of times, as policemen and journalists often did but seldom acknowledged. Even though he worked for the pro-unionist *Irish Times,* Dunlop's sympathies lay with the cause of Irish Home Rule and with the man who was leading the struggle to secure it, Charles Stewart Parnell. He was a highly respected journalist, on intimate terms, it was said, with the highest officials of the administration, right up to the Marquess of Londonderry, whom as the Lord Lieutenant, was the Monarch's representative in Ireland. It was a measure of the naivety of the English intelligence agents working for the Assistant Under-Secretary that they assumed Dunlop had to espouse the same political values as his employers.

Dunlop had first voiced his political opinions to Swallow at the time of the Maamstrasna murders, the bloody mass-killing of a family named Joyce in Connemara at the height of the Land War. Reporter and policeman had been drinking in a shebeen near Leenaun after the funerals of the five murder victims. The investigation of crime outside of Dublin was the responsibility of the Royal Irish Constabulary. But experienced Dublin crime detectives often travelled to give support to their less-experienced rural colleagues.

'Neither the people who pay you nor those who pay me seem to grasp the reality that if it wasn't for Parnell there'd be scenes like this every second week in every county across Ireland,' Dunlop told him, as they drank the rough, illicit whiskey or *poitin* that was the house's staple. 'Politics is a dirty game, but it's infinitely preferable to the sort of savagery that's happened here.'

Dunlop was a Scot, with inherited family memories of the Highland Clearances. He had come to *The Irish Times* after a successful career in Scottish journalism and then in Fleet Street. He understood the land-hunger that could drive men and women to terrible deeds. And he had grown weary, over many years as a journalist, of reporting on the blunders and failures of the authorities in trying to pacify rural Ireland. He was happy to share information with Swallow if he thought it helped G-division to stay a step ahead of the Castle's intelligence department.

Swallow opened the intelligence file to read Mossop's note. Every contact or agent had a code name, so Dunlop's identity would not appear in the written record. Mossop had, not very imaginatively, allocated Dunlop the name 'Horseman' for his long-jawed features.

Swallow spread the flimsy sheet on the desk.

To: D/Insp Swallow

Report from informant 'Horseman.' Note taken at Exchange Court, 11.30pm Tuesday, June 4th 1889.

Informant states he was invited to dine at Burlington Hotel, Trinity Street, this evening by two gentlemen whom he knows to be attached to the security section at the office of the Assistant Under-Secretary at the Upper Yard. They use the names Reggie Polson and Jack McKitterick but H believes these to be aliases. He believes them to be military rather than police. Both speak with English accents.

They expressed frustration at the difficulties of securing publication of damaging information against Mr Parnell since the suicide of Richard Pigott and his exposure as a perjurer and forger at the Westminster commission last year.

They invited H to give his views on Mr Parnell's private life and in particular his relationship with Katharine O'Shea, the wife of Captain O'Shea, formerly Member of Parliament for Clare. The man calling himself Reggie Polson said he was angry at seeing a brother officer humiliated by his wife's open adultery with Mr Parnell. When H said he had no knowledge of such matters, they offered to furnish him with information that might be published in his newspaper. H said he would be interested to receive such information but he doubted if his editor would allow it to be published on grounds of propriety and that it was not the policy of his newspaper to promulgate scandal.

Polson said that was all the more reason they wanted this information published in his newspaper. It had a high reputation and what it printed would not be lightly dismissed as a fiction or an invention.

H asked if they were certain that it would be in the authorities' best interests to see Mr Parnell destroyed in his reputation. They said it remained the firm conviction of their superiors that if Mr Parnell succeeds in securing Home Rule for Ireland this would be the first break in the structure of the British Empire and that it must be prevented at all costs.

Polson said it was believed that Captain O'Shea was thinking about breaking his silence on this scandal which had endured for many years. He had told friends that he could not indefinitely tolerate Mr Parnell's behaviour or his wife's infidelity. Polson said that if the newspapers were to indicate a wider public knowledge of the scandal, this might encourage Captain O'Shea to act decisively and to seek a divorce through the courts.

Informant agreed to meet these gentlemen again next week.

Informant departed Exchange Court at 11.55pm.

The above for your information.

Respectfully,
Patrick Mossop D/Sgt

Swallow initialled the sheet to indicate that he had read it and returned it to the file folder. When his boss, John Mallon, read it later in the morning he would want to discuss it. Mallon would be unhappy with this development, he knew. The chief of G-division knew very well of the illicit relationship between Parnell and Mrs O'Shea. He knew that when in London or attending Westminster, they lived as man and wife at Eltham, in Kent. That they had three children together and that Katharine's husband had grudgingly but silently accepted the situation for years, content to hold his seat in parliament, first for County Clare and later for Galway Borough.

Mallon strongly disapproved of Parnell's relationship with Mrs O'Shea. As a devout Catholic, he told Swallow more than once, he could not do otherwise. But he also understood that it was the influence of the haughty, Wicklow land-owner that kept violence and outrage in check across the country.

'Murder and adultery are both grave sins,' Mallon had told Swallow solemnly. 'Our job is to prevent the first one. It's down to the bishops and the priests to deal with the other. But they support us in what we do. So they're entitled to expect our support in what they do.'

Swallow chose diplomatically not to argue. He too was Catholic, but he was not particularly concerned at Parnell's domestic arrangements. Or anybody else's for that matter. He had been quite relaxed about living intimately for three years with his landlady, the young widow Maria Walsh, above her public house on Thomas Street, in contravention of church teaching as well as police regulations. Mallon turned a blind eye to the breach of regulation but he had been palpably pleased when the union was regularised with their marriage a year previously, after Maria had become pregnant.

Mallon would be disquieted, Swallow knew, to learn that Captain O'Shea was restive. The newspapers knew about Parnell's relationship with Katharine O'Shea, of course. So did almost everybody in public life both in Dublin and London. But for as long as O'Shea chose not to make an issue of his wife's infidelity there was no public scandal and the leadership of the Irish Parliamentary Party was safe. If O'Shea were to come out publicly, however, it might be a very different matter. The churches would have to condemn Parnell and urge their flocks to shun him. Respectable society would repudiate him. His power base would collapse and with it the campaign to give Ireland political independence. Nobody could fully envisage what would follow, but Swallow shared Mallon's conviction that it would be bloody and uncontrollable.

The immediate task of the morning however was to chair the crime conference in the day room at Exchange Court, allocating jobs and responsibilities. Pat Mossop was already there ahead of him, with a jobs roster spread out on the desk.

The twenty or so detectives rostered for duty had arrived in generally cheerful mood. The robbery at Templeogue Hill, near Rathgar, had not been reported in time for any account to appear in the morning newspapers so that even those who had already picked up their *Freeman's Journal* or *Irish Times* were anticipating nothing too challenging in their working day. It would mostly be outdoors duty, under a pleasant, warm sun. Some might be on plainclothes watch around the fashionable thoroughfares, Grafton Street, Wicklow Street, Dawson Street, on the alert for pickpockets and shoplifters. Others would be on surveillance or protection, including a detail of three men who would have the pleasure of attending a cricket match at Clontarf, discreetly guarding the Viceroy, Marquess of Londonderry. Two or three even luckier ones would be assigned to monitor passenger traffic at the Mail Boat Pier at Kingstown. A lazy day, taking the air by the sea would include a substantial mid-day dinner, compliments of the harbour company, in the restaurant it provided for its clerical staff.

Swallow's summary of the previous night's attack and his instructions for follow-up dissolved the prospect of a lazy summer's day.

'Housebreaking is bad enough. And we're having too many of them. But this sort of brutality is another. And there's a gun, maybe more than one, somewhere out there in the wrong hands. There's probably something or somebody new in this picture,' he told the rapidly-sobering assembly of G-men.

'This is the second aggravated burglary we've had now in three weeks in the E-division. They've both been in the hours of darkness. The victims in both cases have been threatened and put in fear of their lives. The man attacked last night was treated in hospital. His wife is invalided and is in a state of shock. Next time this happens we could be talking about a murder.'

A murmur of acknowledgment went around the day room. Men's expressions began to change. The atmosphere became business-like.

'We're going to put everything we can into these cases. So we're not doing any street patrols or surveillance today. I'm suspending the mail boat detail and I'm bringing the Lord Lieutenant's detail down to two men. I want everyone working the informants list. We've heard nothing from any of them, even though we've had four big jobs now in three weeks. Either some of our own clients have decided to change the rules of the game or we've got some new operators on the scene.'

Heads nodded in agreement across the room.

'If there are new players, they must be staying somewhere, eating somewhere, drinking somewhere, whoring somewhere. They could be English or Scottish or even from Belfast or Cork. So I want all the boarding houses and the doss houses checked. There's three, maybe four in this gang. Later today, we'll have more detailed descriptions.'

'Is there any hard evidence these two cases are linked, Sir?' It was Detective Johnny Vizzard, lately promoted from uniform duties to G-division. 'Maybe there's more than one gang at work here.'

'It could be,' Swallow shrugged. 'But there are similarities.'

'There could be some inside knowledge involved here,' Vizzard suggested eagerly. 'No criminal just picks houses like Anglesea Road or Templeogue Hill at random. Besides, those two areas are covered by the beat-men out of Rathmines and Donnybrook. Have we checked out the servants in those houses?'

'I think that was being done in the attack on old Healy by some of the local beat-men,' Mossop intervened. 'They've got more local knowledge. But we'll double check.'

'There's another strange thing about this job last night, Sir.'

An older, uniformed sergeant from Rathmines stood up. Swallow brought his name out of the recesses of his memory from some long-forgotten investigation.

'What's that, Ned?'

'I was beat-sergeant up there in that area a couple of years back. There was always a couple of big dogs at the McCartan house. I mean really big fellas. Irish wolfhounds, I believe they were. I'd have thought they'd have been great guard-dogs. But I'm not hearing anything about them.'

Pat Mossop gestured helplessly to the file on the desk.

'There's no mention of any dogs in this report, Ned. Maybe they got rid of them?'

The sergeant shrugged.

'I dunno. I just thought to mention it.'

His voice trailed off.

There were no further interventions from the floor. Mossop ticked off each G-man's detail for the day. They would start working through the inner city divisions, A, B, C and D, calling on informants at their usual haunts and checking the guests in the boarding houses and less salubrious establishments. If the men who had attacked the McCartans were lodging somewhere in the city, G-division would find them. Swallow left him to the task and set off down the Castle Yard to report to Mallon.

Mallon's main office was in the Lower Yard, rather than at Exchange Court itself. So vital was his role in the eyes of the Castle authorities that it was considered necessary to have him located immediately at hand to the Commissioner's headquarters. The allocation to the chief of G-division of a fine, three storey house, also in the Lower Yard, close to the Palace Street gate, was further confirmation of his importance. Having breakfasted with his family there, he would invariably cross the Yard, under the shadow of the Chapel Royal, in time to be at his desk by nine o'clock sharp.

Mallon glared at him before he had an opportunity to open his mouth about the aggravated burglary.

'This isn't good news, Swallow.'

Mallon stabbed at Mossop's one-sheet report of his conversation with Andrew Dunlop on his table.

'No Sir.'

Swallow knew his boss's temperament too well. There were no pleasantries about the fine June morning or the balmy air. Mallon's mouth made sharp grimaces between staccato sentences, delivered in his sharp, South Armagh accent.

'First, they try to destroy the man with forged letters, to tar him as an instigator of violence around the country. Then they try to use us to blacken his character. Now they're going to traduce him in the newspapers. Villains.'

Swallow winced at the recollection of repeated confrontations during the previous year between G-men and security agents employed in the Under-Secretary's department. In one incident, security agents had raided his own home, searching for files that might give them evidence to compromise Parnell. Swallow had been in Germany pursuing investigations into the murder of Alice Flannery near Rathmines. Maria had confronted the agents and in the ensuing melee, had lost the baby she was carrying. She and Swallow were still dealing with a heavy loss.

'You know that you don't have to persuade me about their villainy, Sir. My wife and I are still mourning the unborn child they snatched away from us.'

Mallon nodded sympathetically.

'I know, Swallow. I'm conscious of that. I'd have thought by now they'd have given up though. I've come across this fellow

Reggie Polson at a meeting up at the Under-Secretary's office a couple of weeks back. A nasty, condescending piece of work. Smith-Berry wanted me to be impressed. He told me this 'Mr Polson' had done great work for Her Majesty's government in all sorts of exotic places. So, I asked him had he seen much of Ireland. He told me he hadn't stirred out of Dublin. Can you imagine? The great security hero who's never gone out to have a look at what's going on around this country. They're a bloody menace. As thick as planks.'

Swallow had made it his business to get to know most of the security agents by sight. When he knew where they drank and dined he would discreetly pass through the bar or the dining room, noting details of height, clothing, appearance and so on.

'I think I know him. What does he look like, Chief?'

'Tall. Over six feet. Athletic build. Fair haired. Thin moustache. Carries himself well. I'd bet he's military and fairly senior at that. There's a scar on his left cheek. Quite a deep cut, three or four inches long. Probably found himself on the wrong side of a sabre or a bayonet.'

Swallow placed him immediately. He had seen him drinking at the bar with some of his colleagues in the Burlington Hotel on Dame Street a week previously. The Burlington was favoured by bankers and financiers as well as senior military and high-ranking civil servants. There had been something about the man that put Swallow on guard. There was a disquieting restlessness about the way he paced around among his fellow-drinkers, whiskey in one hand, cigar in the other, while his eyes roved the bar and its customers.

'It's probably just as well they're so badly informed, Chief.'

'What do you mean?'

'If they were smarter they'd know that Andrew Dunlop is sympathetic to Mr Parnell and they'd have brought their business to a journalist with different loyalties. There's a lot of that type around. If they'd done that, we wouldn't know about this scheme.'

Mallon nodded again.

'Or maybe they'd have gone to a journalist with an eye for ready cash, like Pigott.'

'Fair enough, Chief. Though we were doubly blest in Pigott. He was greedy for money and he was stupid as well.'

Mallon permitted himself a smile.

Richard Pigott had been bribed by the Castle authorities more times than Mallon could remember. Whether it was a question of planting an alarming report in his newspaper or spreading a helpful rumour among the city's pressmen, Pigott was always for sale. But when a commission had been established at Westminster to examine alleged links between Parnell and Fenian extremists, Pigott's supposed documentary evidence was shown to be forged by his own hand. There was a noticeable lull in anti-Parnell propaganda in the newspapers in the months after his death in Madrid, where he had fled after his forgery had been exposed.

'You're right, Swallow. But of course, when these fellows find that Dunlop won't publish what they want they'll try elsewhere. It's only a matter of time until they find some hack in some printing house willing to do their dirty work.'

'That's very likely,' Swallow agreed. 'Although if Dunlop is willing to … ah … co-operate, maybe we could put them on the wrong track. Gain some time if nothing else.'

Mallon looked glum.

'It's probably inevitable that the scandal will come out anyway. Does the name Mrs Benjamin Wood mean anything to you?'

'No Chief.'

'A very wealthy but recently deceased lady in Kent. She was Mrs O'Shea's aunt and from what I gather she's been the main source of the family income for many years. She's also funded Captain O'Shea's high-living, to a considerable degree. Those who know him say the only reason he has kept up appearances with his wife is to ensure that money keeps coming in. But 'Aunt Ben,' as it appears she was known, is no more, and apparently, she's left her estate in trust for the children. There's a lot of money involved but now it seems Willie won't get his hands on a bob. So he's telling friends he's being short-changed for his forbearance and he hasn't a reason any longer to keep up the appearances of marriage. If he enters a petition for divorce, that's going to be a matter of public record. They won't even need the newspapers to blow the story.'

That put a new and worrying slant on the situation, Swallow realised. Money could be a great means of getting information. But it could also be used to buy silence as it had with Captain Willie O'Shea up to now. Equally, the realisation that one's expectations and hopes, financial or otherwise, are not going to be met could be a grievous provocation. He felt a slight twinge of sympathy for O'Shea, despite himself, even though he had never met the man.

Mallon stood from the desk and looked down into the now sun-filled Lower Yard. A platoon of young constables, recruits from the training depot at Kevin Street on a familiarisation march, were standing to attention, listening attentively to their sergeant-instructor, as he pointed out the important offices of state from which the government of Ireland operated and whose dictates they would enforce. Even from a distance, he could see them starting to perspire in their heavy, buttoned-up tunics.

'I've got to do some preparation for a meeting up the Yard with Smith-Berry and some of his acolytes,' Mallon said. 'Let's put this aside for the moment and come back to it later. If you think you have a way to even delay what these fellows have in mind, I'd be glad to hear it.'

Swallow realised he had not had the opportunity to report on the attack at Templeogue Hill. It was probably better to let it pass, at this stage, he reckoned. John Mallon's mind was on bigger things than an aggravated burglary, even when it involved the use of guns.

Mallon waved towards the door, indicating to Swallow that he should go. Then he turned back to the window.

'You know, Swallow, I'd say it's going to be a hot sort of a summer.'

Chapter 2

At first, the men working on the tunnel thought the bones were probably those of an animal. It was common enough, deep down in the caves and fissures through which the underground River Poddle flowed, to come across the remains of dogs or cats or larger creatures that had drowned in the current that flowed into the River Liffey from under the Castle. Sometimes there might be farm animals, goats or sheep, that found their way into the water where it rose to open ground in the countryside between Cookstown, near Tallaght, and the city itself. There might even be human babies from time to time, sometimes not fully formed, sometimes newly-born, consigned to the dark waters of the Poddle for whatever reason, unwanted or unable to survive in the world.

There were three men in the working party today. They had chiselled and dug their way through the black clay and the rock below Lord Edward Street and Essex Street for over three months to connect the new sewer from the Upper Castle Yard to the river below. Latterly, they had opened a trap, removing a few square yards of cobble, in Essex Street, outside the Dolphin Hotel, facilitating access to their task.

The Castle's inhabitants had used the Poddle to carry away human waste and other detritus since King John fortified the site of *Dubh Linn,* the 'black pool' on the Liffey in the 13th century. In the Irish language it was called the *Saileach, or Saile,* meaning dirty. But the development of the piped water supply from the Vartry Reservoir in the Wicklow Hills over the previous two decades had enabled the installation of modern sanitary facilities in much of the city centre that could flush everything away underground and thence to the sea.

Sometimes men working on the new sewers or on foundations under the Castle found bones that were not those of animals. The Normans often buried their dead within the curtilage of the Castle, especially at times of conflict with the native Irish when it was particularly dangerous to venture outside the wall. The Vikings had burial sites around the 'black pool' where they anchored their long-ships. Even so, a man who wanted to keep his job at a shilling a day did not raise an issue that could bring down a foreman's wrath by delaying the work. Bones and skulls might be given a cursory examination but then swiftly knocked aside and deftly buried with a few, swift shovelfuls of damp earth. Of course, there was always the hope of finding something valuable, even an old sword or a helmet, although it was rare enough.

This time, the jumbled fragments that caught the light from the carbide lamp seemed to be trapped in a crevice where the watercourse turned downward for its final fall into the Liffey. The long bones might have belonged to a smaller farm animal, a calf or a sheep perhaps, but the skull was unmistakably human. Some fragments of what might be a thin cloth, each one some inches long, were trapped in the ribcage.

The front man raised the hissing Carbide gas lamp and called over his shoulder to the foreman.

'What are we goin' to do about this so?'

The foreman pushed forward, taking the lamp and bringing it over the tangled skeleton.

'Ah, Christ. Sure, we'll be here for a week.'

It would be an easy thing to dislodge the remains from the shallow crevice and topple them into the stream.

'Give us the crow-bar there.'

The third member of the work-party stepped forward, boots sloshing against the flow. He handed the foreman the heavy bar, clawed at both ends.

The foreman had wedged one end under the spine and was about to press down on the other to prize out the tangled assemblage when he saw the dark, matted hair at the back of the skull and the rope twisted around the neck.

'Christ.'

He stepped back alarmed, almost losing his balance in the stony bed of the stream underfoot.

'There's dirty work here.'

He brought the lamp down to the skull. Even to an untrained eye this was no Viking or Norman. The two rows of teeth in the jaw were complete and perfect, still in their sockets. This was a young person, no relict from medieval times but someone whose life had been much more recently, and probably violently, brought to its end.

'D'ye see that?'

He gestured to the back of the skull.

The others peered forward, straining to take in the detail under the faint glow of the burning carbide.

'What are we goin' to do, so?' one of them finally asked.

'We'll do what we have to,' the foreman answered slowly. 'We'll go back up and tell them who needs tellin' about this. That's our Christian duty to this poor soul.'

Chapter 3

The first time that Swallow crossed to England, he was working on the murder of Ambrose Pollock, the Lamb Alley pawnbroker, with the Special Irish Branch at Scotland Yard. He learned on that visit that a great city like London was differentiated from a smaller one like Dublin by its dinner arrangements.

In Dublin, men other than lowly labourers and porters, generally went home in the middle of the day to eat their dinner. Business houses usually afforded employees an hour and a half. Professional men might allow themselves two hours.

The various tram services were regular, reliable and inexpensive. A man could be at his house in Rathmines or Phibsborough, fifteen minutes after leaving his place of employment. He could linger over the table with his wife, enjoying his soup, mutton chops and perhaps a custard pudding and still be back at work within the stipulated time.

But London was on a different scale. People took their mid-day meal at or near their workplace. Many business houses operated canteens. Scotland Yard had its own mess, or rather, three messes, serving good food (and inexpensive alcohol) to different ranks. Swallow observed that there were many more teashops on the business streets in London than in Dublin. And some public houses and taverns offered basic foods like bread, cheese or sausage. They all seemed to do good trade in the middle of the day, but he learned that men usually took their main meal of the day at home in the evenings.

Before he had married, Swallow dined, if that was the word, perhaps twice a day at the police canteen in the Lower Yard at the Castle. It was simple, nutritious fare, yet it was predictable and repetitive. Vegetables were invariably boiled to mush. Meat tended to be burned. The one positive constant was good bread, freshly delivered every morning from Johnston's bakery in Ringsend. However, since he and Maria had become man and wife, he felt he should get home to Thomas Street for mid-day dinner if he could. The early weeks of her pregnancy had been trying physically and emotionally and by late morning, having set the staff to their tasks, putting order on the two bars on the ground floor, she needed to go upstairs to rest. By one o'clock, Carrie, the cook, would have dinner ready to be served in the dining room looking down over Thomas Street. Even on days when he was unable to leave the Castle, or when he was engaged in police duty elsewhere, the table would always be set for two.

But so far, the day had proven amenable to his domestic commitments. By midday he had completed the necessary paperwork around the divisional crime reports. Dunlop's account of his meeting with the agents from the Security Secretary's office was disquieting, as was Mallon's corroborative intelligence concerning Willie O'Shea's intention to petition for divorce from his wife. He would try to arrange a meeting with Dunlop later to see if it might be possible somehow to throw the security men off the scent. Newspapermen worked late and were rarely to be encountered around the city in the earlier part of the day. There was nothing he could do immediately. So, there was no reason that he should not go home to Maria for an hour.

It was a fifteen-minute walk from the Castle to M&M Grant's licensed premises on Thomas Street. Swallow often reflected that the short journey perfectly encapsulated the spirit of the city, with numerous buildings dedicated either to religion or alcohol.

After Christ Church there were the two St Audoen's, one for the Protestants, the other for the Roman Catholics. Then St Augustine's, with its enclosed community, and St John the Baptist, maintained by the Franciscan friars. Then St James's, on the corner of Echlin Street, from where, since medieval days, pilgrims had begun their long journey to Santiago de Compostela in Spain. Somewhere under Meath Street, he knew, were the buried foundations of the once-powerful abbey dedicated to St Thomas Becket, so expansive that its buildings reportedly stretched all the way down to present-day Pimlico. Finally, almost directly opposite from Grant's, St Catherine's, outside of which the patriot Robert Emmet was executed in 1803 after his failed insurrection against English rule.

There were two busy distilleries. John Power's was located behind the Franciscan church, on John's Lane. Henry Roe's was on Thomas Street itself. Grant's stood almost in the shadow of Arthur Guinness's great brewery at St James's Gate, and the public houses along his route could be numbered in dozens, ranging from scabrous taverns to salubrious select bars. Grant's was firmly in the latter category. Swallow's family had operated their own public house near the Curragh of Kildare for three generations, so he understood the licensed trade. He reckoned that Grant's was one of the finest premises in Dublin and certainly the leading house in and around the Liberties area.

Maria had inherited the business in the female line. Its two bars faced the street with spacious living quarters spanning the two upper storeys. When she had accepted a proposal of marriage from a charming merchant seaman, Jack Walsh, she had made it clear that although she would be Mrs Walsh, the Grant name would stay over the door. When her husband's vessel went down with all hands in a violent storm off the Welsh coast three years later, she dealt with her grief, at least partially, by throwing herself into a programme of steady improvements in the business. She was a progressive landlady in charge of an already successful house and she eagerly embraced new ideas. She invested carefully in M&M Grant's, bringing running water to the two bars, as well as flushing toilets and purpose-built urinals at the back. The windows that opened on to Thomas Street were widened, bringing more light into the interior. In the public bar, plain forms had been replaced with solid, oak benches. Rickety high-stools that had served in the select bar were gone. In their place, she had installed high-backed swivel seats, upholstered in heavy, brown leather. One of the first improvements she had undertaken was to have the house connected to the city's expanding gas supply, enabling the smoky oil lamps that had hung on the bar walls for generations to be taken down and replaced with mantles that shed a soft, warm light with a gentle hissing sound. Being a prudent woman, however, she had not immediately extended the gas supply to the living quarters which still depended on oil lamps and candles for illumination.

After she had the three good bedrooms on the second floor refurbished and redecorated, she advertised in *The Evening Mail* for a lodger who might occupy one of them. She had been doubtful at first when she learned that the Mr Swallow who had replied to the advertisement, was a detective sergeant in G-division at Dublin Castle. It would be against police regulations, she knew, for an officer to lodge on licensed premises. But that was his problem, she reasoned. There could be advantages in having a G-man around the place. It could offer security and reassurance in a house where a woman lived alone and conducted a business. Besides, she thought, even if he was perhaps ten years her senior, he was rather handsome.

Swallow was also accustomed to dealing with some of the less pleasant aspects of the bar business. One night when Grant's was unusually busy he came downstairs to deal with some noisy and unruly customers. There was an exchange of words after which one of the troublemakers, a strong cooper from the brewery, threw a punch at him. Swallow avoided it easily and retaliated with a swift right hook that sent the man flying backward across a table to collapse on the floor. Swallow lifted him by the collar and propelled him through the door into Thomas Street.

Thereafter, when he would come off duty, he would sometimes saunter through the bars, exchanging a greeting here and there with customers that he had come to know. It was a way of sending a message to would-be troublemakers and of reassuring the regulars who wanted to enjoy a well-ordered venue. After closing-time he and Maria might take a drink together and talk about the day's business and about his police work in the first-floor parlour. He liked a mellow Tullamore whiskey. She enjoyed a fortified sherry or sometimes a port.

Gradually, the conversations moved from business to more personal matters. She spoke of the loneliness she had learned to cope with by immersing herself in the business. He told her how his medical studies at the Catholic University in Cecilia Street had foundered on the rock of his drinking, leaving him with the choice of emigration or joining the police. He expressed his frustration and resentment to her. In spite of his successes in police work in general and in crime detection in particular, his Roman Catholic background multiplied the odds against his getting promotion in a force dominated by Protestants and Freemasons.

Without either of them consciously working towards it, the relationship between landlady and lodger quickly moved to affection and then to intimacy, although for appearances' sake, 'Mr Swallow's Room' was meticulously maintained by Maria's housemaid. There was fresh water and clean towels on the washstand each night and his shirts and collars were set out on the bed. The sheets, although unused, would be changed regularly and the pillow cases would be re-arranged each morning.

Things might have remained so for a long time were it not for Maria's discovery in December that she was pregnant. They were married the next Saturday, at the Franciscan friary of Adam and Eve, on Merchant's Quay, with the ceremony performed by their old friend, Friar Lawrence. Afterwards, there was a fine reception for their friends and families and some of Swallow's colleagues at Mr Gresham's Royal Marine Hotel in Kingstown. A magnificent meal and lively entertainment had been marred only by the need for John Mallon and his wife to return urgently to

Dublin Castle in response to the discovery of a young woman's dead body near Montgomery Street. The celebrations continued nonetheless and the following day Swallow and Maria returned to Thomas Street as man and wife.

He had never known such happiness since his childhood, he realised, in those short months before catastrophe struck. That he could ever be a husband and a father, engaged in establishing a family home, had simply not been within the compass of his thinking. But now its imminence was exhilarating. The conversations after closing-time in the first-floor parlour became less about her business and his police work and more about future dreams and questions. Would the baby be a boy or a girl? Who would it be like? What names could they choose?

Maria would not be a very young mother, no more than Swallow was going to be a young father. Her future brother-in-law, Harry Lafeyre, who served as the Dublin City Medical Examiner, had referred her to an eminent consultant at the Rotunda Lying-In Hospital. He had pronounced her strong and well, and said he could anticipate no difficulties in the delivery when it came.

Everything had changed however, since the miscarriage. It had been brought on by a violent fall when she had angrily confronted security agents who had raided their home, searching for G-division surveillance files they believed Swallow had secreted at the house. It had taken only a few weeks for Maria to recover her physical strength after losing the baby, but her emotional state remained fragile. She preferred to stay in the first-floor parlour much of the time, rather than busying herself downstairs, supervising the staff or conversing with the regular customers as had been her habit.

The easy conversations that had been a feature of their relationship became more infrequent and strained. Maria never directly blamed him or his work for the baby's loss. She did not have to. Had he and Mallon not defied the demands of their political masters by refusing to hand over the surveillance files on Mr Parnell, the security agents from the Under-Secretary's department would never have come to search for them. There would never have been the confrontation with the odious Major Kelly, who had led the raiding party, swearing that he would see Swallow in jail for treason. There would have been no fall on the stairs, no miscarriage, no shattering of the happy world that had been in the making.

It might have been easier, Swallow reckoned, had Maria come out directly to blame him. The sorrowful silence and the avoidance of the subject were harder to bear. She had asked him repeatedly to take a reduced pension, to leave the police and to come into the business with her as a full partner. But he had been unwilling, whether because he feared losing his freedom or because he actually liked the work he did, he was unsure himself. Now she was silent on the idea of retirement. He wondered if he should raise it himself.

He sought Harry Lafeyre's advice.

'As a doctor, I'd say leave well enough alone,' Lafeyre had told him. 'Maria's not the first woman in Dublin to lose a baby. She's had the best of medical care and she'll recover in time. But as a friend to both of you, I'd also say be very caring of her for the next few weeks and months. The emotional effects of a violent miscarriage can be very powerful.'

He followed Lafeyre's advice as best he could, spending as much time as possible at Thomas Street, sometimes when he should have been at work with an important investigation in hand. Mallon understood what was happening and quietly allocated some of the detective office workload to junior officers in Swallow's place.

'It's good experience for young lads,' he had replied gruffly when Swallow queried some of the job-sheets. But he knew that arrangements were being made to help him and Maria through difficult circumstances.

He tried to avail of the long evenings and the balmy summer weather to get Maria out of the house and into the open air, especially on Sundays, when she normally absented herself from the business. They would cross the river at Kingsbridge to the Phoenix Park and walk the length of Chesterfield Avenue to the Castleknock Gate, sometimes stopping to watch the deer cropping the summer grass. One clear August evening they took the tram to Howth at the far extremity of the bay. It took them all the way to the summit of Howth Hill from where they could gaze back at the city and across the blue water to where the mountains ringed the bay. But their conversation on these occasions became increasingly spare. As he looked past her to where the sun was preparing to set that evening, he saw a tear course silently down her face.

When he reached Grant's, Maria had already gone upstairs to the dining room, leaving Dan Daly, the senior barman to tend to the few customers in the two bars below. He thought she looked rested and well as she sat to table. The sash windows looking on to Thomas Street were raised a little, allowing a gentle current of warm June air into the room.

'It's a beautiful day out there,' he told her cheerily as he took his chair. 'You should get out for an hour or two in the sunshine. Maybe take the tram out to Sandymount and take some sea air.'

She frowned.

'Thanks, Joe. But I'd prefer to rest.'

She remained silent as Tess, the maid, came in with a soup tureen from the kitchen downstairs.

When Tess had served the light chicken consommé and left the room, he tried again.

'It would do you good. You might even call on Lily, take the train and have afternoon tea at the Salthill Hotel or the Royal Marine?' Maria's sister Lily, engaged to be married to Harry Lafeyre, was her closest confidante. He always sensed that her spirits recovered somewhat when they spent time together.

He knew what her likely answer would be. It was almost always the same sort of response now.

'I might be needed here,' she said without apparent conviction.

'Ah, no you wouldn't. The day is slow and Dan's well able to manage on his own. Maybe you might call by Harriet's lodgings either? She's finished school now and she's busy marking end-of-term examination papers. She'd probably relish a break from that. And it's only a short distance away.'

Swallow's sister, Harriet, taught at a primary school on South Circular Road and stayed in lodgings nearby.

She shook her head silently and stared down at her soup.

'I don't think I'd like to interrupt Harriet. And, anyway, Lily is still at work.'

Lily was an art teacher at Alexandra College on Earlsfort Terrace. Swallow knew that the school term had ended and that without classes to be taught she would be mistress of her own time. He was about to press the point when Tess knocked and put her head around the door.

'Pardon me Ma'm … but there's a young *polisman* below at the side door, lookin' to talk to th' inspector. He says 'tis important … very important altogether.'

He felt silently guilty, realising that he was relieved to have an excuse to be taken away from the table.

Chapter 4

'There's no way I'm going down there into the shit with this machine. If it falls over or gets wet, it'll be ruined. It'll cost a fortune to have it replaced and I'll get disciplined for damaging official property. Anyway, there's no light down there, all I'd get would be a blur.'

Swallow knew that Tim Hogan, the photographic technician was right. Getting a man in and out of the narrow trap from the cobbled surface of Essex Street to the river below would be a challenge. Trying to manoeuvre the bulky camera with its tripod through the opening would be next to impossible. Besides, from what the agitated foreman told him they had seen twenty feet under the ground, there would probably be little of evidential value in photographs.

The young constable sent to fetch Swallow from his dinner at Grant's knew only that something – or somebody – had been found in the underground river. When the workmen had regained the surface, they hurried to tell the constable on duty at the gate of the Castle's Upper Yard. He called out his sergeant and the sergeant, in turn, had sent a fit young constable with a Bullseye lantern back to the scene to climb down through the trap to verify what the workmen claimed to have seen. When he came back to the top, his uniform wet and smeared with mud, he confirmed that there were what seemed to be human remains below. The sergeant then notified the duty officer at the Detective Office in Exchange Court.

Pat Mossop was at the scene before him. So too was Stephen Doolan, a veteran, uniformed sergeant from Kevin Street with four constables. Hogan was standing patiently by the open police car that had brought him with his equipment from the Royal Irish Constabulary Depot in the Phoenix Park.

'No point going down, Tim,' Swallow agreed. He had worked on many occasions with Hogan. The photographer knew his craft well, understanding both its capabilities and its limitations. Like Swallow himself, he was a Kildare man so they had an affinity that sometimes extended into sinking a few pints or whiskies together at one or other of the public houses that Depot personnel frequented on Parkgate Street. 'But stand by until we get this body up. I'll need you to take your pictures then.'

He beckoned to the foreman.

'How far in is it? What's the depth and the direction down there.'

'The water's about twenty foot under the ground. It's not too deep, maybe a foot and a half though there's probably pools that'd be deeper. A man would want to be careful. The body's downstream of the trap. I'd say it's about thirty foot along. Caught on a rock ledge to the right as you'd move towards the river.'

He would make a good witness, Swallow thought to himself.

'We'll need to get some sort of a sack or a bag to get it to the surface,' Doolan said. 'An ordinary stretcher wouldn't work. Then we'll go down with the lads and do a search, maybe a hundred feet in each direction for a start.'

Doolan was reliable, one of the most experienced officers in the force in conducting scene searches.

Swallow nodded.

'I'll go down myself first, Stephen. I'd like to see whatever there is before it's moved.'

Two constables were sent to the Barrack-Master's stores at Kevin Street to get pairs of waterproof waders and oilskins along with Bullseye lanterns, ropes and field haversacks.

'Get a couple of lengths of tent canvas too,' Swallow told them. 'We can make a hoist to get this poor devil up. And bring half a dozen screens and poles to give us a bit of privacy.'

A small crowd of curious pedestrians and passers-by had already formed on the pavement watching the knot of policemen and workers gathered around the manhole in the cobbled street. Half a dozen diners had emerged from the nearby Dolphin Hotel to see what was going on, one portly gentleman with a white linen napkin still conspicuously stuffed in his waistband. He thought that he got the aroma of roasting beef from the hotel kitchens. When he looked up at the hotel's higher windows he saw guests and staff peering down at the street scene below. There was nothing like a bit of street drama to get the attention of Dubliners, he told himself.

When the constables came back from Kevin Street, pushing the equipment in a handcart, the workmen helped them to erect the canvas screens, shutting off the view. Swallow stripped off his suit and boots and donned a set of oilskins and waders. Doolan did the same, before each man took a haversack, attaching its straps behind his shoulders so that it fell on his chest. Pat Mossop looped two ropes around their torsos and checked that the Bullseye lanterns were working properly.

'I'll go down first Stephen,' Swallow said. 'Give me about ten feet before you follow and then stay within arm's reach when we're below.'

He lowered himself over the edge of the trap with two of the constables and a workman taking the strain on the rope. The cold air below the surface of the street, contrasting with the warmth of the summer day above, caught his breath at first. Behind the chill he could smell the dirt and waste of the sewage that the underground flow carried to the Liffey. Then the men above started to pay out the rope and the sunlight faded as he went down towards the flowing water below. His eyes adjusted to the darkness as the lantern's beam seemed to strengthen. He sensed his feet touching ground and the water rushing against his waders.

When he looked up he could see Stephen Doolan's bulk descending after him, his lantern playing small, yellow shapes on the walls.

The cavern itself was surprisingly wide, with brown-yellow brick forming an arched tunnel. Swallow knew the Poddle ran under the Castle, but always imagined it as a narrow stream. Here, however, the flow was shallow, wide and sluggish. Even as he raised his lantern to throw a thin light downstream he could make out quantities of bodily waste, whether animal or human, bobbing along the surface.

'Keep your hand on my shoulder,' he told Doolan. 'Let's get this done and be out of here.'

There was movement to his left just at the waterline. In the corner of his eye the light picked up three or four sleek, scurrying creatures, squealing with alarm.

He started to inch forward, holding the lantern out in front, cautiously feeling the uneven rock and silt under his waders, counting the small steps. If the foreman's estimate was accurate they should find what they were looking for fairly quickly. With Doolan's hand on his shoulder, he could feel the other man's breath on his neck and hear the sloshing of his waders in the filthy water. The air was putrid, stinking of decay and animal waste. With every cautious breath he felt that his mouth, throat and lungs were being coated in filth.

He had counted just fifty steps when the Bullseye caught a white gleam to his right, perhaps half his own height above the surface of the water. A few shuffling, cautious steps through the flowing water and the light picked out the skull and jumbled bones.

He heard Doolan behind him.

'Jesus!'

Doolan's hand dropped from his shoulder as he moved forward, joining his lantern with Swallow's to illuminate the macabre presentation on the rocky shelf. Swallow could see the long leg bones, crazily askew beneath the pelvis. The bones of the right arm were thrown across the rib-cage almost in a defensive pose. The skull lolled to the right as if the skeleton was exhausted, positioning itself in repose. The light clearly picked out the length of rope around the neck.

'Dirty work, alright,' Doolan said softly. 'I wonder who this poor creature might have been.'

'And who decided he or she would end up like this,' Swallow added.

'It could have come from anywhere,' Doolan said. 'The river goes out into Dublin county.'

'That's true,' Swallow said. 'But the skeleton looks pretty well intact and complete. All the big bones are present. If it travelled far in the current I'd have thought there'd be bones broken away all along the course of the river. I'd say he – or she – was put in somewhere not too far away from where we are.'

Doolan laughed mirthlessly.

'I forget you're a medical man, Joe. More or less. But I daresay I've taken more bodies out of rivers in my career than you have. Water is a funny element. It's very hard to learn much that can be relied on. Can you see anything else that might tell us a bit more?'

'You can see that ligature around the neck?'

'I can.'

'How would you describe it?'

'About the width of a bootlace. Knotted tight. A thin rope. Could be used for something like a washing line.'

'I agree,' Swallow said.

He moved a few steps through the swirling water, past the jumble of bones and played the beam of his lantern on the rocky outcrops beyond the skeleton.

The light caught the outline of what might have been a length of mud-caked rope snagged on an outcrop of black shale just above the waterline. He reached to touch it and followed it with his right hand into a fissure in the shale. Where it ended, his fingers closed on something hard and cold with sharp edges. He realised that he was touching a bunch of keys, held in a ring at the end of some sort of lanyard or belt.

'Look at this, Stephen,' he called to Doolan.

Doolan peered into the cleft.

'God leave you your eyesight, Joe. I don't know that I'd have spotted that.'

Swallow drew it slowly from the rocky fissure and held it up in the beam of his lantern. Then he placed it carefully in the haversack on his chest.

Chapter 5

It was past four o'clock by the time Doolan's constables had retrieved the remains from the Poddle. With the dark water swirling around their knees, they had dislodged the bones carefully from the rocky ledge, placing them in a makeshift sling fashioned from army canvas, before raising them slowly to the street through the sewer trap and onto the back of a covered police car.

Swallow, rid of his stinking waders and oilskins and relieved to be back in his own clothes, stepped forward to lift up the canvas cover. He nodded to Tim Hogan who had been waiting patiently beside his photographic equipment.

'You can take your pictures now, Tim. Just make sure you get everything into the frame.'

'I've done this before, you know,' Hogan replied testily, as he trundled the camera and tripod into position.

Swallow knew that the instruction was unnecessary. Hogan was a professional. There would be pictures from every angle and of every bony part, this was just part of the standard banter between them.

'Did you remember to put a plate in the camera, Tim?' he jibed.

Hogan affected a thick rural accent.

'Jaysus, thanks for remindin' me, Joe. Sure, I'd be lost without you. And me, just a slow ould bobby up here outta the plains o' Kildare.'

'You see the ligature around the neck?' he queried Hogan.

'I'm not blind.' Hogan's tone was serious now. 'And you don't need to tell me you want it close up.'

It was down to business now.

'Good man, Tim. There are some traces of clothing there, around the rib cage. Can you make sure you get those?'

Hogan grimaced an affirmation.

'Sure. They're very small but I'll get up close with a magnifying lens. You'll be able to see every strand.'

When Swallow and Doolan had regained the surface, they found that the group assembled around the trap had been augmented by a couple of important-looking officials from the Dublin Corporation as well as a uniformed inspector and a superintendent.

Swallow's heart sank as he recognised the corpulent superintendent, bulging in his braided tunic, as Maurice Boyle, his former boss at G-division. Universally known as 'Duck,' from his distinctive waddling gait, Boyle had gone on promotion a year previously to E-division, covering the affluent southern suburbs of Rathmines, Rathgar and Ballsbridge. He had recently been appointed to take charge of the even more prestigious B-division, covering the south city centre. Lord Edward Street was just within the boundaries of the B, in the Duck's area of jurisdiction. His advancement was a mystery to his colleagues who knew that he had little skill as a detective. Swallow had a strong hunch it had something to do with the Freemasons and with Boyle's brother, a canon of the Church of Ireland who was reportedly spoken of in church circles as a future bishop.

'Jaysus, Swalla', yer not smellin' like a bunch o' roses.'

Boyle's porcine nose wrinkled over his drooping moustache. He bulged in his uniform, perspiring in the heat of the day.

'What's goin' on down there?'

He wagged his ebony cane towards the trap.

Swallow resisted an urge to tell him to jump in and find out for himself. It was, after all, his division. Any criminal business would ultimately be his responsibility as divisional officer.

'Nothing good, anyway,' Swallow answered. 'There's a body, or what's left of one after the fish and the rats have done their work.'

'Ah, sure it's probably some oul' fella who fell in after a feed o' drink.'

Swallow pulled off his oilskin jacket. It felt good to breathe fresh air and have the cleansing sun on his face.

'I wouldn't think so. It's foul play.'

'Ah, there ye go, Swalla', always makin' things worse than they are. Yer a fierce pessimist. Why are ye sayin' that?'

'There's a rope looped around the neck. That might be a clue.'

If Boyle picked up the sarcasm, he pretended otherwise. He gestured with his cane towards the side of the street. Swallow could see that the crowd gathered on the pavement, straining to see what was going on behind the police screens, had grown in numbers. It was the nearest thing that poor people were likely to get to entertainment on a midsummer afternoon.

'Well, in that case I'd better address myself to the gentlemen of the press beyond on the footpath,' Boyle announced. 'I'll have t' advise them that I'm in charge of th' investigation of a possible case o' murder.'

Swallow was relieved to see him waddle across the street to where a group of three or four reporters from the Dublin newspapers stood, smoking and laughing. Swallow recognised most of them and knew them by name. Geary from *The Freeman's Journal,* Hall from *The Mercury* and Carberry from *The Irish Times.* Another dead body was just another story in the working day to the hard-bitten gentlemen of the press. But Duck Boyle was always drawn to the journalists, as a moth to a candle.

Doolan's constables, kitted out in waders and oilskins were lowered into the cavern, looped in pairs with lines and buckles and connected to the surface by long ropes, knotted every three feet to measure distance. Two pairs moved upstream towards where the Poddle flowed under the Castle itself. Two others followed the flow downstream towards where it entered the Liffey. One man in each pair held a lantern while his fellow probed the water and the riverbed with a short steel-tipped pike. Doolan's instructions were to search a hundred feet in either direction and to retrieve anything of possible evidential interest. Each man had strapped on a canvas haversack as he and Swallow had done earlier.

'You're looking for clothing, boots, shoes, and anything that might be a possible weapon,' he told them. 'Anything you find, put it in the haversack. If it's too big, note the location on the rope and we'll try to find a way of getting it out. If you do locate anything, Detective Sergeant Mossop here has to log it in the book.'

Pat Mossop was the best Bookman in G-division. The Bookman was the keeper of details and records, the careful note-taker, the repository of knowledge in any criminal investigation. He activated the required processes, in accordance with the dictates of the Police Manual and ensured that all physical evidence was tagged and secured. Every member of the investigation team had to report progress to the Bookman when each job, however insignificant, was completed. Without having to be told, Mossop had assumed the familiar role from the moment he had reached the scene, even before Swallow had been summoned from his dinner-table.

'I notified Dr Lafeyre,' he told Swallow. 'He wants the remains sent to the city morgue at Marlborough Street and I'm to send a man to advise him when that's in hand. He's at his rooms in Harcourt Street but he can be down there later.'

'Good work, Pat. Anything else?'

Mossop gestured to his notebook.

'I've got everything that can be known at this stage. Time of discovery, names and addresses of the workmen, all the usual stuff. There's a few big-wigs from the Corporation here too so I've got their details in case we need more information about the engineering and that kind of thing. And I sent down to

Merchant's Quay to get a priest to give last rites to this poor unfortunate.'

Swallow nodded. Mossop was a Belfast Protestant but the gesture of sending for the priest was characteristically conscientious. If there were more Pat Mossops and fewer Duck Boyles in the job, he frequently told himself, the ratepayers of Dublin would get better value for the money they put into the city's policing service.

He drew his half-hunter to check the hour. Harry Lafeyre's post as city medical examiner was a part-time one. As events might demand, he would either work at the new, well-equipped morgue in Marlborough Street or, if requested by the authorities, at locations where persons might be found deceased in suspicious circumstances. Otherwise, he conducted a private medical practice from rooms at his house on Harcourt Street. Ordinarily, he would see his last private patient at around five o'clock.

'Send a message to Lafeyre to say we'll be at Marlborough Street by six o'clock, so. But before you do that, I want you to have a look at this, tell me what you think it is and put a description in the book.'

He reached into the haversack, drew out what he had found and laid it on the running board of the photographic technician's open car.

In the sunlight he saw that what he had thought to be some sort of rope in the dark of the cavern was a broad, leather belt, perhaps three feet long, swollen and distorted by immersion in the water. At two or three places, where the swelling had burst, he could see that it comprised two strips of leather, laid back to back and closely stitched. The stitching at the end which would have held the buckle had rotted away. But midway along, caught between two swellings in the leather was a bunch of keys, held on a ring with a diameter that Swallow estimated at about three inches.

'Was that with the body?' Mossop asked.

'Close enough. You couldn't say for certain that there's any connection. But there might be.'

Swallow gingerly probed the bunch of keys with the blade of his pen-knife, scraping away mud and slime and spreading them out fan-like in a three-quarter circle. There were twenty-five in all, of varying sizes, some big enough to fit a heavy door lock, others likely to fit smaller locks, perhaps on cupboards or cabinets.

'The metal isn't heavily corroded,' Mossop observed. 'How long would you think they're in the water?'

'Impossible to say, but they're not there for years. They were caught on a ledge maybe four or five feet from the body. Let's assume they belonged to whoever the body is, or was, what would that tell us?'

Swallow knew that Mossop's answer would be the right one.

'That we need a locksmith to tell us where they might have come from.'

Chapter 6

The Dublin Castle authorities had spared no expense in the construction and equipping of the Marlborough Street morgue.

Harry Lafeyre was proud of his 'Palace of the Dead,' as he sometimes referred to it in black humour. It boasted new electric lights. It had an insulated ice house in the basement. There were four dissecting tables, manufactured in stainless steel. There was running water throughout, connected to the Vartry Supply. There was even running hot water in the dissecting area, with pipes connecting to a furnace at the back of the building.

Swallow worked confidently and easily with Lafeyre. They were, in a sense, complementary opposites. Lafeyre had worked as a field surgeon with the Natal Mounted Police in southern Africa. He had shared the hardships and dangers of police work in the *veld*, learning the use of the Winchester saddle carbine and the long-barrelled Colt .45 revolver. Although Swallow's time at the Catholic Medical School in Cecilia Street had been cut short by alcohol before he could qualify as a doctor, he still remembered enough from his anatomy lectures to follow Lafeyre's commentaries with ease. And there was the happy coincidence that Maria's sister, Lily, was Lafeyre's fiancée.

Doolan's men were still at work underground at Essex Street when Swallow and Mossop left to walk the mile or so across the city to Marlborough Street. Swallow was glad to be able to get away from the putrescence of the air that permeated the space around the trap leading down to the stinking Poddle.

The evening sun shed an ebbing warmth over the city as it moved behind the tower of Christ Church, getting ready to sink away to the west. They walked down Parliament Street and crossed the Liffey at Grattan Bridge. Swallow drew the fresh, salty air, coming up the river from the bay, deep into his lungs. He could feel it cleansing his innards, dissipating the cloying stink that had seemed to form an outer skin around his hands and face since he had gone underground.

The shops on Capel Street were preparing to shut at the end of the business day. Young counter assistants were rolling in the blinds that had been dropped down to protect the merchandise in the windows against the sun. At Greenberg's, the art dealers and jewellers, a dark-haired woman in a long, pleated dress was taking trays of rings from the front window, carefully passing them to a helper who was invisible from the street but whose hands could be seen rising to receive the precious jewellery that would be lodged for the night in the strong Milner safe behind the shop.

The woman raised her eyes from her task and smiled as the detectives walked by. Swallow smiled back at Katherine Greenberg. She had taken over most of the running of the family business since her father's ill-health had begun to get the better of him. Just months previously, Swallow had fortuitously come on the scene at Greenberg's as two London-based criminals attempted a robbery. Her father, Old Ephram, had been injured, however Swallow had captured one of the robbers while the other was subsequently apprehended in London.

Like most business families on Capel Street, the Greenbergs lived over the shop. Capel Street had lost much of its lustre. In years gone by, before fashion dictated that smart shops and wealthy people should locate themselves south of the river, it had been a premier street for business and for residence. Its buildings were tall and spacious, with fine craftsmanship in their walls, ceilings and woodwork.

Swallow had been a welcome and frequent visitor to the Greenberg house since his days as a young constable on the beat along Capel Street. He was entitled to thirty minutes rest half way through an eight-hour tour of duty. So he would climb the side stairs to the Greenbergs' living quarters over the shop. Katherine would bring honeyed almonds and *speck* as he sat drinking coffee, or sometimes a strong Lebanese wine from the Bekaa Valley, with her father, his Roman-style police helmet on the table between them. Although he was fifteen years her senior, he knew she had always carried something of a flame for him. Now she was past the age at which a Jewish girl should have been married. After her mother's death a decade earlier she had devoted her energies to looking after Ephram and becoming more involved in the business. Swallow's visits to the Greenberg house were rare enough now since he no longer pounded the beat on Capel Street, although he met Katherine regularly at the painting class they both attended on Thursday afternoons at the Municipal School of Art on Thomas Street.

The evening air became sweet with the scent of fruit as they turned into Lower Abbey Street. The stalls at the nearby Smithfield Fruit Market, behind Mary's Abbey, were shutting too and tired fruit-mongers were loading their unsold produce into barrows. He realised he had not eaten since breakfast time, having left his dinner untouched on Maria's table to attend at the scene in Essex Street. Now the scents of apples, pears and soft fruits set off pangs of hunger.

He stopped a thin-faced lad pushing his barrow along the pavement and dug into his pocket for a penny. He held it out to the boy.

'Will you give me two apples there, Son?'

'They're three a penny, Sir.'

'Two will do.'

He pressed the coin in an eagerly outstretched palm and then bit into the crisp flesh of the Pearmain Pippin. Its taste in his mouth after breathing the foul air of the underground river was delicious, nutty and aromatic. He handed the second apple to Mossop.

'Here, Pat. Keep your strength up.'

They crossed Sackville Street, now busy with clanging trams, boarding the thousands of workers coming from the offices and shops. The flower sellers at Nelson's Pillar were packing up for the evening too, filling their baskets with the blooms they had been unable to sell during the day. A couple of young men seemed to be haggling with them over last-minute purchases. Prices were always reduced at the end of the day and there were bargains to be had for blooms that would certainly be unsaleable tomorrow.

Harry Lafeyre's brougham carriage was drawn into the stable lane at Marlborough Street. There was no sign of his surly coachman, Scollan, who doubled as his general assistant and his porter at the morgue. That told Swallow that the city medical examiner was already at work inside for some time.

'Gentlemen,' Lafeyre greeted them cheerily as they came into the examination room. It smelled, as it always did, of disinfectant and rubber.

'Your timing is good. I've had a look at what's left of this poor woman, which isn't much, I'm afraid. So I'm ready to tell you what I know – which actually isn't a whole lot either.'

The jumble of bones that had been loaded onto the police open car earlier at Essex Street had been assembled in what Swallow could see was their correct order on one of the examination room's steel tables.

'Well, that's a start,' Swallow said, drawing a tall stool under himself beside the examination table. 'You've determined the sex?'

Lafeyre pulled off his heavy rubber gloves and apron and took another stool. He waited until Pat Mossop had positioned his pencil above his notebook.

'Yes, the pelvis tells me it's a mature female, maybe thirty-five to forty years. She was five feet tall, average build, I'd say. No signs of any ill-health. She seems to have been well-developed and well-nourished. The pelvic structure suggests she might have borne a child or children.'

'Cause of death, Doctor?' Mossop asked.

Lafeyre shrugged.

'There's nothing clinical to help us there. Almost all of the flesh is gone. There's no internal organs left. I assume you've drawn some conclusions from the rope around the neck?'

Swallow grimaced.

'Tentatively. She wasn't wearing it as a piece of jewellery.'

'Agreed,' Lafeyre nodded. 'Then asphyxia would be the likely cause. But we'll never get an answer from what's there on the table.'

He gestured to the skeletal remains, gleaming under the examination room's strong lights.

'There's a few other things. There's a little portion of the scalp with a few strands of hair still attaching. I took it off and Scollan's putting it in formaldehyde to preserve it. The hair is dark but it could be dyed so I've taken a small amount to test it. I should be able to tell you what colour it was originally.'

Mossop busily worked his pencil across the page.

'There were some fragments of cloth along the left rib cage,' Lafeyre went on. 'I saved them and I have them on slides. I couldn't guess what the material is. But I'll put them under the microscope when they're dried out. The teeth are good. She has two small fillings in gold in the maxillary molars. The fillings are well done, so she had enough money to get professional attention.'

Swallow nodded.

'She wasn't the poorest of the poor,' Mossop said sympathetically.

'Probably not,' Swallow said. 'But she wasn't the most fortunate either, was she?'

'Any thoughts about the ligature?' He directed the question to Lafeyre.

'You can see that it's been tied in a slip knot. I'll open the knot later and see what I can learn about it, if anything, under the microscope.'

'Is there any way you can tell how long ago she died, or how long she was in the water?' Mossop asked hopefully.

Lafeyre shook his head.

'More than days. Weeks anyway. Maybe even months. But not too many months. There are so many variables. All the soft tissue is gone except for that small area on the scalp. Even that wouldn't be left if she was down there for a year, let's say. And the skeleton was pretty well intact. Apart from a couple of ribs all of the bones are there. And there's none of the big bones missing.'

He glanced at the wall clock.

'I've a dinner engagement at my club, so I'm going to leave it at that for the present. I'll follow up on the hair and on the rope tomorrow. We'll put the remains in the ice-room even though there isn't much need. I assume you'll notify the coroner?'

'I'll take care of that,' Mossop said.

'There's one other thing I'd like you to have a look at when you're setting up the microscope,' Swallow said.

He reached into the haversack and drew out the leather belt with the bunch of keys that he had recovered from the river.

'We found these not far from the remains. They may or may not be connected, but I'd like you to see what can be learned from them, if anything.'

Lafeyre took the leather strip with a small, steel tongs and spread it along the steel table.

'It's reasonably intact, isn't it? If it did belong to the deceased it would suggest she's been down there a few weeks, not much more, not less. Leather is fairly resilient for a while but once the outer surface is broken it can start to deteriorate quite quickly.'

He reached for a cardboard evidence box on the work-shelf.

'We'll store it and I'll examine it tomorrow.'

'So,' Lafeyre inquired, 'on the basis of what we know, are you calling this a murder inquiry?'

Swallow hesitated. The evidence was strong but it was less than absolutely conclusive. A full-blown murder inquiry would put considerable extra demands on an already stretched G-division. He could report the case to John Mallon in terms that would leave it an open matter. A file could be opened and quietly closed without too much effort going into it. It was tempting. He would need a lot of thinking space and time to deal with the threat to Parnell from Willie O'Shea's planned divorce petition and the plan by the security service to leak it to the newspapers. But there was something compelling about the sad bundle of bones on the steel table behind Lafeyre. Once, he knew, this had been somebody's daughter, or sister, or mother, or wife, who deserved better than being flung underground, to rot in the dark, dirty waters of the Poddle.

'It's a murder inquiry,' he said after a moment. 'We can't ignore that length of rope around the neck. 'We'll have the case conference at Exchange Court in the morning.'

Chapter 7

Hall's Palace Bar in Fleet Street was a favourite with the reporters and editors from *The Irish Times.* They shared its fine mahogany counters and polished leather seating with clerks from the Bank of Ireland and other financial institutions on Dame Street and College Green, as well as some senior policemen from the headquarters of the B-division at nearby College Street Station.

Swallow ordered a Tullamore and installed himself in one of the booths near the door. The whiskey was mellow and smooth and curiously cooling after the heat of the day. The bar was quiet. The bankers who came for a couple of drinks after work had departed. The reporters across on Westmoreland Street were at their busiest at this hour. The police shifts at College Street would not change until ten o'clock. It was slow business at the Palace with just one barman on duty.

Mossop had walked with him to Westmoreland Street after they had finished at the morgue. They parted outside *The Irish Times* and Mossop continued to Exchange Court to send notification to the coroner and to put a report out on the ABC telegraph to all stations. Then he would hand-deliver a copy of the report to John Mallon's house in the Lower Yard. The provision of official lodgings for the head of G-division and his family within the Castle represented a significant saving on the Mallon household budget, while the Castle authorities had the comforting knowledge that their chief of detectives was always available around the clock.

Swallow turned into the newspaper's front office. He could smell newsprint and ink from the printing press, located at the back of the public office. A couple of clerks were still at work, taking in the classified advertisements which constituted a significant part of the newspaper's income and for which it had something of a reputation. He knew them both by sight.

'Do you know if Mr Dunlop is in the building?' he asked the more senior-looking of the two.

The clerk recognised him too.

'I believe so, Mr Swallow. I saw him walk up the stairs an hour ago.'

'Would you ask him to join me across at the Palace if it's not inconvenient?'

The clerk knew that even the busiest journalist, working against a deadline, would find time to share a drink with a senior G-man who wanted to talk.

He nodded towards a young copy-boy, lounging on a cane chair behind the counter.

'I'll send the message up straight away. You go ahead. If there's any problem, I'll send the lad across to you with word.'

He did not have long to wait in the booth. He had taken a second sip of Tullamore when Andrew Dunlop came through the door. He moved into the booth, pulling a chair behind him.

'Swallow,' he nodded, signalling to the barman, 'an unexpected pleasure.'

Swallow smiled.

'Thanks for taking the time, Mr Dunlop. Is it a busy evening?'

Police guidelines recommended the use of code-names when in contact with informants. But it would have been a nonsense. They had known each other for years before Dunlop had agreed to act as an agent for G-division, using the soubriquet 'Horseman'. Besides, if anyone saw detective and journalist meeting or overheard their conversation, the use of coded language would simply raise suspicions.

'Nah. Nothing dramatic going on at all. Westminster is having a dull day. There's very little happening in the courts. It's good to get out of the place.'

The barman placed a Bushmills on the table in front of him. Dunlop shared John Mallon's taste for the Ulster whiskey that was darker than Swallow's pale Tullamore, and more pungent.

'That's very disturbing news you picked up about Captain O'Shea and his wife,' Swallow said.

Dunlop nodded.

'These two fellows from the security service are pretty well out of their depth politically. But they know that if they can get the knowledge of Parnell's relationship with Mrs O'Shea into the public domain, it's going to damage his political support very severely.'

They clinked glasses.

'Sláinte.'

'Good luck.'

Dunlop put back half his Bushmills in a gulp.

'Had you met these two, Polson and McKitterick, before they took you to dinner at the Burlington?' Swallow asked.

'I'd never met McKitterick, but I knew about Polson from Madrid. Of course, he wasn't calling himself Polson. He was John Smith.'

'What was he doing in Madrid? What were you doing there, for that matter?'

'The newspaper sent me out there, along with our best foreign correspondent, Cornelius Clarke, in March when Richard Pigott fled after he'd been exposed by the Westminster commission. He was holed up in a hotel but we didn't know its name. They wanted us to see if he would tell us who had put him up to the forgeries. He didn't do it just for the fun of it. He had to have been bribed and put up to it by some person or persons in or close to the authorities. But he was dead by the time we located him. Clarke is a stringer for *The Daily Telegraph* in London and they've got first-rate contacts with the British intelligence services. Some contact there enabled him to identify Pigott's hotel. But Polson was there, when Clarke arrived. He found him searching through Pigott's belongings with the man's body still warm on the floor. There were some Spanish detectives there and they seemed to be operating under Polson's direction. It turned out then that Clarke recognised him from an earlier encounter in Cairo.'

'Cairo?'

'Yes, the British secret service maintains a big operation there, covering all of the Middle-East and bits of North Africa. That whole region is crucially important to the security of the Empire. Keeping trade routes open, all that sort of stuff. He had agreed to meet Clarke in Madrid a couple of times, trying to pass himself off as a diplomat. But everyone apparently knew he was secret service. Diplomats don't usually carry revolvers as he did. He was a hard drinker too, shot out the chandeliers one night in the Gran Hotel Ingles.'

Swallow nodded. G-division's knowledge of the Upper Yard's secret service personnel rarely extended to having the detail of their previous assignments.

'You didn't meet him yourself?'

'No. My job would have been to interview Pigott. But with him dead, the newspaper wasn't going to add to its costs by keeping me on the continent any longer than was necessary. I was on the next train to Paris and then across the Channel to England and then home to Dublin. Clarke stayed on to do a series of articles about Spanish politics, why the country is losing its overseas possessions, all that kind of thing. They're just a few decades ahead of us, you know. It's all fallen apart. The politicians can't agree on anything. And there'll probably be war with America over what's left of the once-mighty Spanish Empire. The Americans want to get hold of Cuba, the Philippines and a few more places. They need military and naval bases. And they see money-making opportunities.'

'John Smith wasn't a very imaginative alias,' he grinned. 'Did you know he'd been transferred to Dublin?'

'No. The last I heard of him, he was briefing the local press in Madrid and pouring drink into them, explaining why Pigott had shot himself. They believed him, it seems.'

'So how did he make contact with you here?'

'He just called to the newspaper, asked for me by name and when I came downstairs he introduced himself. He told me he'd been transferred to Dublin to the Under-Secretary's security office and they'd appreciate it if I'd join him and a colleague for dinner that evening at the Burlington. I didn't know him from Adam.'

'So you thought you'd have a decent dinner at Her Majesty's expense?'

Dunlop grinned.

'Quite. But as it happened, Cornelius Clarke was in the Burlington when I arrived. He'd had a long and late lunch with some visiting French correspondents. I was a bit early so we went for a drink. He was just leaving the bar when he saw Polson and McKitterick coming in. He recognised Polson from Madrid of course, and the next morning at the office he told me about their previous encounter. They hadn't seen him so Polson, or Smith, or whoever he is didn't know he'd been recognised. He still doesn't, I'm sure.'

'That could be very fortuitous,' Swallow said.

'I told your sergeant at Exchange Court they had identified themselves as Reggie Polson and Jack McKitterick, but names mean nothing because they work under aliases. John Smith is as good as Reggie Polson or any other name he chooses to give himself,' Dunlop added.

Swallow nodded his understanding. The security agent who had brutalised Maria in the raid on their home identified himself as Major Nigel Kelly. But Swallow could find no Major Nigel Kelly in the Army List. He had never been able to ascertain his true identity. It was probably just as well, he told himself. If he knew who he was and where he could be found, he would almost certainly seek him out and kill him.

'Did he tell you what his role is here at the security office?'

'No. But he didn't have to. Every government has fellows like him. They've usually got a made-up title and they're on the payroll of some department or office that nobody has ever heard of. But they're spies and *agents provocateurs* really. Mostly they've got military service behind them. Any half-competent journalist can spot them a mile off.'

'So how did the conversation go?' Swallow asked. 'There doesn't seem to have been much subtlety.'

'No, there wasn't. Polson is evidently the more senior of the two. He actually talked briefly about his time in Madrid, not knowing I'd been there with Clarke at the time of Pigott's death. I led him on, probing him a bit. I said I'd known Pigott, which I had, and that I was interested in the details of what happened to him. He said he arranged for Pigott to get a decent burial and got his few belongings back to Ireland. Pigott was widowed and he left two young sons, it appears. He told me that arrangements had been made for their welfare, whatever that means. He said he had left no money or estate and that some charity in Kingstown had stepped up to assist the young fellows.'

'Tell me what he had to say about Captain O'Shea.'

'He asked me first if I knew him. I said I only knew him as any political journalist would know any Irish member of the Westminster parliament. I wasn't socially acquainted with him.'

'Did he tell you how he knew O'Shea was planning to petition for divorce?'

'Not specifically. But he says he served for a while with O'Shea as an officer in the Hussars, said he'd kept in touch with him after they had resigned their commissions and that they remained friends. He said he knew that a good journalist never turned away from an important story so he wanted me to know that O'Shea was thinking about filing for divorce on the grounds of his wife's adultery with Parnell. He said they could give me a lot of detail that would enable *The Irish Times* to publish the facts ahead of anyone else.'

'They seem to think that O'Shea is dithering though?'

'Yes, it might be that he's hopeful even yet of getting a share of his wife's inheritance from her aunt. The old lady put everything in trust for Mrs O'Shea's children. But they think they can use *The Irish Times* to force his hand. I should add they told me there'd be a hundred pounds in it for me if their material gets published.'

Swallow raised an eyebrow.

'That's a great deal of money. Would you not be tempted?'

Dunlop smiled and sipped at his Bushmills.

'It is three months' salary, but no, not all journalists are like the late Mr Pigott. And you know my politics, Swallow, just as I know yours. If O'Shea files for divorce, citing Parnell as the respondent, it'll cut the ground out from under the Home Rule campaign. That'll probably be the end of Parnell, as we know.'

Swallow tasted his Tullamore.

'Probably. And that'll be followed by chaos, with an open field for the bomber, the assassin and the gunman.'

Dunlop laughed.

'You're very lyrical this evening, Swallow. That's the sort of stuff I'm supposed to say … or write.'

'I'm not wrong,' Swallow said quietly.

'No, you're not,' Dunlop answered, after a moment.

He signalled to the barman to repeat the orders on the table.

'Is there any way this can be averted?' Swallow asked.

Dunlop shrugged.

'The real problem is that if I don't co-operate with them and publish the story, they'll simply go elsewhere. There's half a dozen newspapers around the city that would be more than willing to run with it. They'd prefer it in *The Irish Times* because it's the most reliable and influential. They know enough to know that. They said so. But *The Mail* or *The Journal* or *The Express* would serve their purposes almost as well.'

The barman placed two more whiskies on the table, deftly lifting the empty glasses with his other hand.

That made sense, Swallow reckoned. Once a sensational matter like this moved into the public domain it would be taken up instantly in every publication across the Kingdom. He had experience of the press in full, collective pursuit of a victim or victims, when the Invincibles were arrested for the murders of Cavendish and Burke. Whatever restraint they might exercise individually, they abandoned totally when operating in a pack.

'If it can't be prevented, could it be delayed perhaps?' he asked.

Dunlop sipped his Bushmills again.

'A little perhaps, but not for very long. What have you in mind, Swallow?' he asked eventually.

Swallow reached for his whiskey.

'Where did you leave matters with these two fellows?'

'I told them I'd need time to brief my editor, Mr Scott, and get his agreement to publish. I explained that Scott is utterly punctilious and thorough. He won't be rushed into anything and certainly not into something of this magnitude. Polson seemed to understand that and to accept it. So, he said they'd call by my office again to get an answer. They might even be there as we speak.'

'Then it's best if you pretend to go along with them. Tell them you think *The Irish Times* will publish the story and they're to give you every scrap of documentation or other evidence that they have. Let's at least see how much they know and what they're trying to peddle. How long do you think you can stall them? What sort of interval could there be between you getting the paperwork and going to press?'

'Maybe a couple of days. I can tell them we'll need to verify and check the facts. We'll have to decide if we want to put questions to O'Shea ourselves and indeed to Mr Parnell, and we'll need to engage the newspaper's legal advisors. But that's about it. Where's the possible advantage in delay?'

'I don't know, frankly. But I'd like to discuss this with Chief Mallon. He's close to Parnell and he has a great deal of influence in political and governmental quarters. Tell me, do you think Mr Parnell is aware of what Captain O'Shea says he's going to do?'

'I don't know that.'

'If nothing else, Mallon will be able to give him advance notice of what's coming up. And if Parnell is alerted, he might even be able to persuade Captain O'Shea not to go ahead with the divorce. Parnell and Mrs O'Shea probably managed to buy him off in the past when he was able to benefit from her aunt's wealth.'

Dunlop drained his whiskey and looked ruefully into the bottom of the glass.

'It'll be a day of sorrow and grief for Ireland if this goes ahead.'

He stood from the table to leave.

'One of the reporters back at the office told me earlier you had Essex Street cordoned off and that you were down in the Poddle with a squad of bobbies, looking for something. We've got a report about it in tomorrow's editions. What was all that about?'

Swallow drained his own glass and stood as well.

'I suppose it was about sorrow and grief, too. It comes in varying shapes and guises, as we both know, Mr Dunlop.'

He realised he had hardly thought about Maria all day.

Chapter 8

John Mallon's house faced across the Lower Yard to Francis Johnston's architectural triumph, the Chapel Royal, where monarchs and their representatives came on Sundays and other special occasions to pay reverence to the Almighty who, so it was understood, had anointed them for their high places. Swallow sometimes marvelled at the reassuring simplicity of this arrangement. He served the Commissioner of the Dublin Metropolitan Police. The commissioner served the government. The government served the Queen. The Queen served God.

Darkness was settling over the Lower Yard when he came back to the Castle through the Palace Street gate. The gas lamps were lit and the constable on duty had fastened on his night cape to counter the damp evening air coming up from the river. In the Yard, the last of the setting sun was throwing fantastic shadows from Johnston's spires and buttresses across the ground, giving it the appearance of a crazy chess-board. He remembered that under the cobbles on which he was walking, the dark Poddle to which he had descended earlier in the day was flowing to its rendezvous with the Liffey. Somewhere he had read that the ground here was so soggy and porous that Johnston had used a wooden frame to build his beautiful chapel in order to lessen the weight on its foundations.

John Mallon answered the door to Swallow's pull on the bell-cord and led him into the small parlour at the front of the house where he always conducted official business. If the Mallon family had the privilege of a spacious home, paid for and maintained by the Crown, the price the family paid was the daily intrusion of their privacy by Mallon's various underlings, reporting, seeking advice or instruction or sometimes with documents to be signed.

Mallon's wife dealt with these undoubted inconveniences by maintaining the family's domestic locus in a second, somewhat larger, parlour at the end of the ground floor corridor. Swallow had never been in there, but when he visited he could sometimes hear children's voices, laughter and the sounds of crockery being used.

'You'll take something?' Mallon's greeting for Swallow was always the same out of office hours.

So was the answer.

'If you're having one yourself, Chief.'

Mallon poured two measures of Bushmills from the bottle on the sideboard. He handed one to Swallow and gestured to a water jug on the table.

'Help yourself.'

They sat. The Bushmills was strong to Swallow's taste and he always half-filled Mallon's tumbler glasses to mitigate its peaty tang. He would have been content to go without it, having already taken two drinks with Dunlop at the Palace, but it would have seemed ungracious.

'You didn't tell me about the attack on a Queen's Counsel earlier,' Mallon said a little sharply, dropping himself into his customary armchair.

Swallow was momentarily at a loss.

'Sir?'

'Sir John McCartan and his wife. The Templeogue Hill robbery. I've received a minute from the commissioner directing us to throw everything we have at it. I gather there's one coming from the Lord Mayor too.'

Swallow groaned silently. It was unlike Mossop to leave him short on important detail. But in fairness to him he had made it clear that the initial report that came in from the crime scene was brief and preliminary.

'I didn't make the connection, Chief. I'm sorry. I just had the family name. I know Sir John McCartan, of course. He's cross-examined me a couple of times in court.'

'Not only a QC, but a member of the Corporation too. And the chairman of the Dublin and Leinster Bank. As if that wasn't enough, his wife is invalided. She's been a recluse for years. She's had to be attended this morning by various medical men to try to calm her panic.'

He read from what Swallow took to be the commissioner's note.

'Prominent citizen, leading legal and business figure, etcetera, etcetera, nobody safe in their beds. Threatened with a gun and beaten with some sort of a club or bar. Where were the police? Why isn't there anyone in custody? Dastardly outrage. I don't have to spell it out.'

'No, Chief. I can imagine there'll be a fair stink over it. But we're stretched now with the body in the Poddle and all the protection details. I've just warned the lads at the conference that we can't wait around until someone gets killed in one of these robberies. I've put Shanahan and Keogh full time on them and they can get all the support they need from the divisions. We're taking all the usual steps. There's nothing in from the informants and we've been watching the Downes and the Vanucchi and the Cussen gangs. I think we've to consider that there might be some new operators at work, so I've ordered a check on all the hotels and lodging houses to see if we have any out-of-town criminal types.'

Mallon sipped his whiskey.

'I know you've a lot on your plate, but there's a lot of potential trouble around. Not least this problem with the O'Shea divorce and Mr Parnell. But we'll need to show cause on this one. The Commissioner has ordered the night beats to be doubled in the E-division. There's men being drafted in for the ten o'clock shift tonight. I think you'd best go out to the McCartan house yourself and see the great man and his lady. Expression of concern. Reassurance. No stone being left unturned. You know the line.'

Swallow groaned inwardly. He had a full work schedule and a distressed wife.

'Fair enough, Chief. I'll get out there this evening or tomorrow at the latest.'

Mallon nodded.

'And what's the story with the body in the Poddle? I've been through Mossop's report.'

'There's not a lot to report, Chief. It's early days. Dr Lafeyre says it's a female, around thirty years maybe. There's nothing to identify the remains. If it wasn't for the ligature around the neck we could put it down as some sort of misadventure but I don't think we can ignore it.'

'I agree,' Mallon said. 'Although I'd prefer not to. At all events that fool Boyle has told the newspapers that it's murder and that he's in charge of the investigation. But true to form, we know that if it isn't cleared up , he'll shift responsibility back to us.'

'We'll try not to let that happen, Chief. Like I said, it's early days.'

Mallon sighed.

'Yeah, I know that. So, to other business. Have you done any thinking about the Willie O'Shea problem?'

'I have, Chief. I've just come from talking to Andrew Dunlop. The story with Captain O'Shea is serious. He's briefed his solicitors. Dunlop says the fellows from the Upper Yard have him more or less persuaded to go ahead with the divorce. But here's an interesting thing, Dunlop knows Reggie Polson from Madrid when he was sent out by *The Irish Times* to interview Pigott. Polson, or whatever his real name is, was there for the secret service. He tells Dunlop he was in the army with O'Shea and knows him well. But O'Shea seems to be dithering a bit. He seems to think he might still have a chance of getting hold of some of his wife's aunt's money. So they want *The Irish Times* to report that he's briefed his lawyers. They're passing all the details to Dunlop, probably tonight. They reckon if *The Irish Times* publishes the story that'll get him across the line.

Mallon frowned.

'Will *The Irish Times* run with the report?'

'Dunlop's been clever. He's played along, telling them he needs some evidence, documents or whatever. Then he'll need to clear it with his editor, Scott. He can slow things up, maybe for a couple of days, he's agreed to do so as much as he can. But, as he says, if *The Irish Times* doesn't publish the story, they'll simply bring it to another newspaper that won't bother to wait for corroboration. At best, we can delay things for a bit.'

'Does Mr Parnell know about O'Shea's intentions?'

'We don't know for certain. But Dunlop thinks not.'

'I suppose it's possible that he could still persuade O'Shea to stay his hand,' Mallon said. 'O'Shea has always been overawed by him. Maybe he could offer him some inducement to leave well enough alone. Like money, for example.'

Swallow nodded.

'From what we know of O'Shea, throwing money at him might work. Do you think Mr Parnell could pay him off, so to speak?'

Mallon drew his pocket watch and checked the hour.

'I don't know. But in my experience of politics and police work, money is usually the surest way of getting the result you want. Now, Parnell is due at Westminster tomorrow night. He's crossing from Kingstown on the morning mail packet. If we move fast, we'll catch him before he retires for the night. I'll message ahead.'

Swallow knew it was Parnell's habit invariably to overnight at the Salthill Hotel, close by Kingstown Harbour, before travelling to London. It was the favoured location for members of the Irish Party at Westminster, being a little away from the bustle of the harbour itself. Two G-men were routinely assigned to protection duty there. He had allocated the protection details for the week and he knew that Mick Feore and Johnny Vizzard were rostered for the job.

'Get the telegraph room to notify the night sergeant at Kingstown. He's to send a constable on the double to the G-men at the Salthill. Whoever is there on duty needs to tell Mr Parnell that I'm on my way to meet him and that it's urgent. We'll be there at eleven o'clock.'

Five minutes later, they were in a closed police car, drawn by a matching pair of black horses, with a rough-rider constable, hastily summoned from a card game in the Castle stables, at the reins. A skilled rough-rider, usually a man with cavalry experience, could coax his horses to a sustained speed of perhaps fifteen miles an hour through city streets. Travelling in darkness would slow the pace but they would be in Kingstown before the last of the summer evening light would have faded. It would have been more convenient and even perhaps faster to take one of the trams that connected the city centre to Kingstown and the village of Dalkey beyond, but the last service back to the city departed at half-past ten.

They swung out of the Palace Street gate and along Dame Street, passing the Bank of Ireland and Trinity College. The college windows blazed with lights. Swallow surmised there was some event taking place, probably a splendid dinner. Trinity had the reputation of doing fine banquets. He imagined the fellows drinking and dining heartily at laden tables and realised he had eaten nothing but an apple since breakfast. Now he suddenly felt ravenous. He might have done better, he told himself, to have found some solid sustenance rather than the three whiskies he had consumed.

They followed the coast road, through the fishing village of Ringsend, leaving the darkening bay to their left and travelling parallel to the railway that connected Kingstown and the Mail Boat Pier to Westland Row terminus. Soon they were in open country. High walls with impressive gates at intervals marked the boundaries of the wealthy estates, stretching down towards the sea from their owners' mansions on the higher ground to the south. Montrose, Mount Merrion, Frescati. At Blackrock, the falling darkness was briefly challenged by the glow of gas lamps, recently installed along the village street. Once through

Blackrock it was open country again with more modest villas perched here and there on the cliffs above the shoreline.

Soon the hotel, imposing and bulking on the Dunleary promontory, was in sight. Elegant terraces, lining the road past Seapoint, signalled to them that they were in the affluent suburbs of Kingstown. The driver swung the car through pillared gates, across the gravelled forecourt and reined the horses to a halt at the granite steps leading to the hotel's main entrance.

Feore and Vizzard were in the shadows by the doorway, stepping forward as Mallon and Swallow ascended the steps.

'Good evening, Sir.' Feore was the senior man. 'Mr Parnell has your message and he's expecting you. He's upstairs in his suite. If you'll follow me, Sir.'

He led them across the carpeted lobby and signalled to a boy, dressed in a green uniform, standing by a baized door. The boy pulled the door open to reveal what looked to Swallow like a narrow metal cage. He had heard or read somewhere that the Salthill had installed one of the first elevators, or human lifts, invented by Mr Otis in America. No other hotel in Ireland or England, it was said, could boast of this modern convenience. It shuddered and swayed a little as it ascended to the hotel's top floor. The sensation of being lifted against the force of gravity was novel but not unpleasant. When the machine stopped, the boy drew back the metal gate and they stepped out into the corridor.

Feore pointed wordlessly to a door opposite.

'You can go back down, Men,' Mallon told the two detectives. 'Mr Swallow and I could be here for a while.'

The door was opened almost immediately in response to Mallon's knock. Swallow recognised TD Sullivan, formerly Lord Mayor of Dublin and one of Parnell's senior lieutenants at the Westminster parliament. He greeted Mallon.

'Mr Mallon. A pleasure to see you, as always. The Chief is inside.'

Swallow knew that Mallon had visited Parnell here at the Salthill Hotel before on more than one occasion. Now he led the way into a comfortably furnished sitting room, with high windows facing out towards the sea. Sullivan did not attempt to follow.

Parnell, wearing a dark blue dressing gown, rose from an armchair by the window and reached out in a handshake to the man who had once arrested him and conveyed him to Kilmainham Jail on government instructions. That was eight years previously. He had gone cheerfully and without resistance. Both of them had known that the arrest, rather than disabling his campaign for tenants' rights, would serve better than anything else to strengthen his leadership.

'What brings you out at this late hour, Mr Mallon? It must be important.'

He gestured to a long settee.

'Please, Gentlemen. Take a seat.'

The Salthill Hotel was supplied with electricity but just one lamp burned on a small table beside Parnell. Swallow had seen him many times but never at close quarters. He thought he looked tired and drawn in the lamplight.

'This is Detective Inspector Swallow, Mr Parnell,' Mallon nodded towards him. 'He is my trusted colleague at G-division. He has received intelligence that I believe necessary to convey to you. As you know, I cannot involve myself in political matters, but when I become aware of something that threatens such stability as we have in the country, I am obliged to act on it.'

Parnell smiled thinly.

'You were ever a police officer of absolute probity, Mr Mallon. And I know that you have your country's best interests at heart. So you have no need to convince me of your bona fides. Now, tell me the nature of this threat.'

'It's a very delicate matter, Sir,' Mallon began. 'It concerns your … ah … personal circumstances and I hesitate to broach it. However, the intelligence that Inspector Swallow has received indicates that Captain William O'Shea, lately member of parliament for Clare and then the Borough of Galway, is about to petition the courts for a divorce.'

He hesitated briefly. There was no flicker of reaction on Parnell's face.

'The grounds for divorce, to be pleaded to the court, are that his wife, Katharine, has been engaged in an adulterous relationship with you. I have every reason to believe the accuracy of Inspector Swallow's intelligence, Sir. And there is more. Details of Captain O'Shea's instructions to his lawyers are being passed to the newspapers, specifically to *The Irish Times*, possibly this evening.'

Mallon fell silent. Parnell's features remained passive, but Swallow heard him sigh gently.

'This is a serious development, Mr Mallon,' Parnell said after an interval. 'I had thought that Captain O'Shea was, shall we say, at ease with the fact that his wife, whom he never loved and who was never in love with him, had found that happy and contented state with me.'

'My information is that his motivation would be financial, Sir,' Swallow said cautiously.

'Financial?' Parnell suddenly flared. 'Financial? He's had his parliamentary seat and its salary all along on my say-so. Is it to do with Katharine's inheritance?'

Swallow knew enough about politics to know that what Parnell said about O'Shea holding his seat on his say-so was not quite true. O'Shea had supported Parnell and the Irish Party at Westminster but was not a member of it. He had taken two seats more or less on his own account although the voters would certainly have known where his sympathies lay.

'I believe so, Sir.' Mallon said.

'I knew he'd be angry about the decision by Katharine's aunt to put her estate in trust for the children, but how can petitioning for divorce benefit him financially?'

'It's not impossible that somebody could have offered him an inducement, knowing that a petition for divorce, naming you as the respondent, would do you enormous damage politically,' Mallon answered. 'There are men in the employment of the government who would consider it a service to the Crown and a good use of the Exchequer's funds.'

Parnell rose from his chair, paced to the window and stared thoughtfully out at the now darkened sea.

'It might not be such a bad thing,' he said, still facing the window. 'Mrs O'Shea and I have never hidden our relationship but it's never been public either. There would be considerable freedom in it. And there are those in the parliamentary party who would stand by me.'

'I'd suggest, Sir,' Mallon said, 'that there are also those who would be delighted to have an opportunity to drag you down.'

'The people would not allow that. They know that I'm the reason they're getting ownership of their farms. And they know that without me the cause of Home Rule will be put back for at least a generation.'

'Mr Parnell,' Mallon's tone was patient and respectful. 'The people have short and selective memories. They're also susceptible to propaganda from the Fenians and other extremists who characterise you as a member of the landlord class, not of their religion and with different loyalties. I'd say that it could be a serious mistake to over-estimate your support, especially once the Catholic bishops weigh in against you, as they undoubtedly would.'

Parnell resumed his armchair.

'The Roman Catholic bishops are very supportive of me, Mr Mallon. I am not of their church certainly but they know I stand for order and that I am implacably opposed to violence. They certainly don't want the country taken over by extremists who reject their authority and who do not baulk at murder.'

'I'm afraid I have to disagree, Sir,' Mallon was firm. 'Of course, the bishops recognise your moderating influence, but they couldn't possibly stay silent, much less offer support, to someone who is – forgive me for being so blunt – a public sinner. They would be obliged to condemn you as being morally unfit to be the political leader of their flock.'

'But if the worst comes to the worst and O'Shea gets his divorce, then that would enable Katharine and me to marry. All would be regularised,' Parnell answered.

Mallon shook his head.

'No, Sir. That is not how their lordships would view it. They would see remarriage after a divorce as simple adultery. Worse, it would be adultery under a veneer or a pretence. I'm afraid that's the reality.'

Parnell was silent for a long moment.

'I can try to avert this, perhaps. How long before the newspapers will publish?' he asked Swallow.

'A couple of days, at best, Sir. I don't believe *The Irish Times* will run with the story. But for the moment, the security agents who are peddling it believe that it will. When they realise that isn't happening, they'll go to some other newspaper or periodical that perhaps won't be so careful.'

Parnell grimaced.

'*The Irish Times* is far from being a friend to my cause. It has condemned me in the most unforgiving terms more than once. It's rather ironic that I'm counting on its forbearance to gain a little time.'

He stood again.

'I'm travelling to London in the morning. I happen to know that Captain O'Shea is staying at his club there. I'll arrange to see him and hopefully I might be able to change his mind about this. But if, as you say, Inspector Swallow, it's about money, I'm not really in a position to satisfy his needs on that front. I have an estate and a house in Wicklow, but I don't have much in ready funds.'

He laughed but it was not a laugh that bespoke amusement. Swallow could not be sure if he picked up just a hint of self-pity.

'I'm a fairly typical Irish landlord. A lot of acres, but not a lot of pounds.'

'I daresay that if this matter can be settled with money, I might know people who would willingly come to your assistance,

Sir,' Mallon said. 'It would take some little time, of course. But there are wealthy people in this city who understand very well that if you were to be unmade, what would follow would be disastrous.'

'You never cease to amaze me, Mr Mallon,' Parnell said. 'But I would hope it will not come to that. I'll arrange a telegram to you with a simple message advising if I've been successful in trying to persuade Captain O'Shea to abandon his plan. I'll use a code name. Shall we say "Salthill"?'

He extended a hand to Mallon and then to Swallow.

'Good night, Gentlemen. Thank you both for your concern.'

As they left Parnell's suite to take the elevator back to the lobby, Swallow told himself that he too never ceased to be amazed by John Mallon.

Chapter 9

Dublin, Wednesday, June 5th, 1889

The dayroom at Exchange Court was abuzz with conversation when Swallow arrived for the crime conference in the morning. A dozen G-men were dispersed around the chairs and benches, chatting and smoking. Some were reading various morning newspapers. A larger contingent of uniformed constables and a couple of sergeants were formed into smaller groups, some sitting, others lounging against the dayroom's oily green walls. Although it was not yet nine o'clock, the early sun had already warmed the space uncomfortably and the air was heavy with tobacco and the smell of cooked breakfasts from the adjoining canteen.

Duck Boyle was seated in full uniform behind a trestle table at the top of the room with Pat Mossop sitting to his left. Swallow took the seat at Boyle's right. Mossop had a stack of papers on the table as well as the heavy, bound murder book. Boyle had *The Weekly Racing Gazette* spread in front of him.

After a few moments he banged the table with his cane, calling the room to order. The policemen's conversations dwindled and died.

He slowly turned his corpulent bulk to look at the wall clock behind his head. It showed two minutes past nine o'clock.

'Good mornin' Gintlemin. We're a bit late startin' but now that Inspector Swalla' is here we can proceed.'

It had been midnight by the time Swallow and Mallon left the Salthill Hotel to make their way back to the Castle and an hour later when Swallow got home to Thomas Street. The public house was silent and shuttered and there was no light in the upper floors. He surmised that Maria had retired for the night. That assumption was confirmed with a pencilled note on the table, beside the cold supper of ham and hard-boiled eggs, along with a glass of milk, put out for his return. He was gone beyond hunger but he finished the food and the milk and made his way quietly upstairs to the single bedroom which he had originally occupied as Maria's lodger. He had slept badly and struggled to respond to the Thomas mechanical alarm clock when it woke him at eight o'clock, falling back into a doze and wakening again at half past the hour. With a quick splash of cold water from the ewer on the washstand, he knew he had to hurry to get to Exchange Court for the conference. But he paused momentarily to listen outside the door of the bedroom where Maria was still sleeping. The house was silent but he could hear her breathing through the door she had left slightly ajar.

As the senior officer, it was Boyle's place to run the first conference of the inquiry.

'We have a case o' murder on our hands,' he intoned solemnly, as he folded the *Racing Gazette* away. 'Naturally, I have familiarised meself with all of th' available evidence and as an experienced detective, I have me own theories and insights into the case. But we'll start with Detective Sergeant Mossop's review of the known facts as they are.'

Mossop cleared his throat and started to read from the murder book.

'The discovery of human remains in the River Poddle, flowing under Essex Street, was in the early afternoon of yesterday, at approximately one o'clock. The informants were Patrick Byrne, a works foreman employed by Dublin Corporation and two labouring men. None of these have been known to the police in any adverse way.

'There was a rope ligature tied around the neck which is the basis for designating this as a murder inquiry. There is nothing to indicate the identity of the deceased. Scarcely any soft tissue remained. There were some small fragments of fabric attaching to the ribs. These may have been from the deceased's clothing or they may have adhered to the skeleton in the flow of the water.'

He looked up from his notes.

'The remains were conveyed to the morgue where Dr Lafeyre conducted a preliminary examination. Detective Inspector Swallow and I attended yesterday afternoon as he did so. So I'll ask the Inspector to outline what the examiner could tell us.'

Swallow placed his own notebook on the table.

'Dr Lafeyre believes the remains to be female. A mature woman, probably somewhere in her mid-thirties. She seemed healthy enough. Just five feet tall. He couldn't be certain, but she may have borne a child or children. He couldn't offer anything firm on date of death, but he thinks the body was in the Poddle, and I'm quoting him directly now, 'longer than days, probably weeks, possibly months but not for many months.'

He looked around at the conference.

'Rodents, fishes and the flow of river water had done their work. Probably the only reason we found a reasonably intact skeleton was because it had been snagged on an outcropping rock down there. The teeth were all pretty well intact in the mouth and there was some dental work done on two molars using gold filling.'

A murmur of surprise went across the conference.

'That tells us, perhaps, that this was a woman of at least some modest financial means. Dr Lafeyre says the dental work was of a high standard.

'Dr Lafeyre can't offer anything on the cause of death unfortunately. But he's assuming strangulation with the rope that Sergeant Mossop has described. He's going to put it under the microscope today to see if he can tell us anything useful about its composition and possible use or origin.

'Now,' he glanced towards Mossop, 'an interesting item was located in the river close to the remains.'

Mossop displayed an enlarged photograph of the leather belt and the bunch of keys that had been retrieved from the river.

'This was located in the Poddle, a few feet from where the remains were found,' Swallow explained.

Heads were craned forward as the men sought to get a closer view.

'There'll be copies available,' Swallow said. 'So everyone can see it close up. It's a belt, as you'll have gathered. It appears to be made of leather and there are twenty-five keys of various sizes in the bunch.'

Mick Feore, who had been on protection detail with Parnell the previous night, raised a hand. Swallow surmised that he must have had, at best, three or four hours sleep in the detectives' dormitory overhead.

'But we've no way of knowing if it's connected to the remains, Inspector. That river is full of stuff, carried from God knows where. I've been down there myself on a couple of cases.'

'Correct,' Swallow nodded. 'But it might be, and since we haven't any identification for the victim so far, it could be the best clue we'll have to finding out who she is.'

'Ye see, if we kin find the locks them keys fit into,' Duck Boyle interjected, 'we kin prob'ly establish who they belonged to. An' that might be the deceased.'

There was a momentary, embarrassed silence as the conference absorbed this deductive insight by the most senior officer present.

'Dr Lafeyre is examining them with the microscope this morning,' Mossop added quickly. 'Once he's finished, I'll bring them to Donaldson's, the locksmiths, to get their opinion on what their uses would have been.'

'There's a number of things we need to get started on right away,' Swallow said.

He beckoned to Feore.

'Mick, I want you to take a couple of men and get back through the records to give us a list of all the women gone missing in Dublin over the past twelve months. Start with any from their mid-twenties through around forty and give us a list of the ones still missing.'

Feore nodded.

'I'm on that, Sir.'

Swallow turned to Stephen Doolan.

'Stephen, you've done more ground searches than anyone else in the room. I want you to get a map of the Poddle's course from the City Engineering Office and trace it out to its source in the country. I believe it rises out near the village of Tallaght. I need a list of all the points where it's above ground and then also a list of the traps or openings where there's access from the surface to the watercourse.'

'That's understood,' Doolan said. 'But it'll take time and a lot of manpower, Joe. I happen to know that the Poddle's got smaller tributaries as well. There's one that comes in from under the Liberties, joining the river just under the Lower Yard. It's called The Coombe Tributary. So we'll need to follow its course as well.'

'I think that's about everything we can do at this stage,' Swallow said.

Respect for rank required that it be left to Duck Boyle to have the final word and to bring the conference to a close.

'Superintendent?'

Boyle inclined his head in acknowledgment.

'Thank you Inspector Swalla'. I do believe, as th'Inspector has said, that we've covered all th' important aspects o' the matter for the present. You'll report any developments to me, immediately, I know.'

Swallow had long developed a technique of pragmatic obsequiousness in dealing with Duck Boyle. Now he was just thankful that he was not to be detained from his breakfast by a lengthy exposition of criminological theory from his one-time direct superior in G-division.

'Indeed. That will be done for your information, Superintendent, and in order to have the benefit of your guidance for the investigation.'

One of Boyle's more consistent qualities, he reminded himself, was that he wouldn't recognise irony if it came up and bit him on the leg.

Chapter 10

He had decided to stop in at the public bar at Grant's before going upstairs to their private quarters. Ordinarily, he would walk through the bar and be a presence for a little while each evening or perhaps in the afternoon. He was 'showing the flag,' he told Maria. It was a way of reminding both customers and the staff that he was there in support of his wife and that he was never too far away.

The bar was quiet, with just two customers, contemplating their pints of porter on a side table. Dan Daly, Maria's head barman, whom she had inherited along with the public house, was behind the counter, hands in pockets, staring through the frosted window giving out on to Thomas Street. He seemed not to notice Swallow coming in. That in itself was unusual.

'Afternoon, Dan. How are things with you?'

'Ah, Mr Swallow, I didn't see you there at all. I'm sorry.'

The grey-haired barman shook himself out of his trance, drew his hands from his pockets and started to shine a glass tankard that was already gleaming.

Swallow laughed.

'You were away with the fairies there for a bit, I think, Dan.'

'Ah, I was I suppose, Mr Swallow. Don't mind me.'

Something told Swallow that the barman had not been idly day-dreaming. There was a look of worry, preoccupation perhaps, on his normally untroubled face.

'Come on. Tell me. There's something not right. Is there a problem?'

'Ah, 'tis nothing you need to worry about, Mr Swallow.'

Swallow perched himself on a bar stool.

'We've known each other for a few years now, Dan. I know when you're happy and I know when you're out of sorts. So, what's bothering you?'

The barman replaced the tankard on the shelf and threw his polishing cloth on the counter.

'Truth to tell, Mr Swallow, I'm thinking it might be time for me to move on. I've been here twenty years. I'm not getting any younger and I'm not sure I'm up to the job anymore.'

'That isn't the way I see it, Dan,' Swallow said quietly. 'You're the head man here. You were head man before Mrs Swallow took over. You know every customer. You keep the place like a palace. Grant's couldn't manage without you. And I know I speak for Mrs Swallow too when I say that.'

'Ah, I don't know about that now.'

'What do you mean?'

'About Mrs Swallow, I suppose. I think she's not happy with the way things are being done here anymore.'

'I don't think that's so, Dan,' Swallow answered. 'She always says how much the place depends on you. You're on top of everything here. You're looked up to with respect by the staff. Every single apprentice we've ever had here has praised you for the way you've taught them the trade.'

Dan shrugged.

'Maybe that was the case in earlier times, but Mrs Swallow doesn't seem to think so now. She's … well … as likely to find fault now whenever she's in the place.'

'For example?'

'Ah, I don't want to make anything of it … but this morning she said the countertops were filthy. They weren't. I wiped them down with carbolic and hot water and dried them myself, same as I do every morning. You could eat your dinner off them.'

Swallow nodded.

'I understand. I know you scrub every square inch of them. Look, don't make too much of it. She's not in the best of order since she lost the baby. We've all got to be a bit patient for a while.'

Dan reached for another tankard and started to polish it with his cloth.

'Maybe you're right, Mr Swallow. She's always been a lady to me. I know it's not been an easy time for her. Or for you either, I'm sure.'

'No, Dan. You're right there. It's been a difficult time. She's had a lot to deal with. And I'm not always the best one to rely on for sailing in troubled waters.'

When he went upstairs, Maria was in the dining room.

'I didn't hear you come in last night,' she greeted him. 'You must have been very tired after such a long day.'

She took her seat at the table as Tess came in with the soup tureen.

Swallow sat opposite and reached for a glass of water. He was still perspiring from the walk in the heat of the day from Exchange Court. There was still work to be done on the night's crime reports from the divisions, but he told himself it was important to be home to take his mid-day meal with Maria after the previous day's hasty departure and last night's late return.

'I read in the newspaper about finding that poor creature's remains down in the underground river,' Maria said. 'What a terrible thing to contemplate. I hope that you'll be able to find out what happened. It must be dreadful for her family.'

The vegetable soup was thick and very hot, an unappetising choice on a warm, summer day. But there would be no profit to complaining to Tess. He made a pretence of liking it and refilled his glass with cool water.

'Of course. But I wouldn't even be sure that we'll be able to say who she is. We're trying to check the missing persons lists.'

He sipped his water and smiled at Maria.

'It's not really table talk, let's leave it. I'm sorry I was so late last night. I had to go out to Kingstown with Mallon to meet Mr Parnell at the Salthill Hotel. Did you sleep well? I could hear your breathing this morning as I left.'

She raised an eyebrow in surprise.

'Mr Parnell? That must have been interesting. Has something important happened?'

For a moment he was going to tell her about Captain O'Shea's proposed divorce suit, then he checked himself. It was not that Maria could not be trusted to keep a confidence concerning police business. But she did not need to be burdened with knowledge of other people's problems or distress. He sidestepped the question.

'No, it was to advise him of some threats we'd learned of, it's routine. The man has a lot of enemies. But, yes, it was interesting. I'd seen him many times and I'd heard him address meetings, but I'd never spoken with him before. He has a very strong presence. Mallon and he have known each other a long time.'

Maria stiffened slightly.

'If it was just routine, why did you have to travel out to Kingstown in the middle of the night? Couldn't you just as easily have been at home and left whatever business had to be done to Mr Mallon?'

He stopped pretending he was enjoying the soup, dropping his spoon noisily into the bowl.

'Please don't try to interrogate me, Maria. My duty makes a great many demands on me, you know that. I won't be answerable for my every action in discharging it. Suffice it to say that it was necessary to do my duty.'

She was silent for a moment. He saw her eyes moisten.

'I waited until midnight,' she said quietly. 'It's not easy sitting here on my own, you know. I just wish that …'

Her voice trailed off.

He knew that at this point he had to be patient and gentle. He choked back a rising sense of impatience.

'I appreciate that. And I know that every day and every night is difficult since … the baby. I've tried to convince you to get out more, enjoy the summer days. I'm sure that would help.'

'You know I'm needed here. I can't just take off … to the waters … or wherever,' she answered sharply.

'Dan Daly can manage for a few hours if you're not there.'

'He's slowing down. I have to stand behind him now to get anything done. And when it's done it's often not done right. Everybody seems to depend on me.'

'I think he believes he's doing his best and that you're criticising him.'

Maria's eyes blazed.

'Are you telling me that you've been discussing me with my employees?'

The sharpness in her voice had switched to full-blown anger.

'I'd remind you that although I am your wife, I remain the proprietor and the licensee of this house. I will not have my staff discussing the running of this business with my husband. And I expect more of my husband than to have him discussing me with them.'

'It wasn't like that, Maria,' he said evenly. 'The man was upset and confused. I simply reassured him that he's well thought of. There wasn't any discussion, as such.'

Tess appeared at the dining room door, carrying the main course on a tray. Maria swung around to her.

'Go away, please, Tess. Mr Swallow and I need to have a private conversation.'

'Now,' she slapped the table with an outstretched palm, 'I have offered you, more than once, the opportunity to come into this business with me on an equal basis. But you wouldn't do it. So, having that decision, you have no say in how I run it or how I deal with my employees. You've refused an offer that most men would jump at because you want to stick with your wretched police work … and we've seen the unhappy results of that selfish, stupid decision.'

She hesitated for a moment, drawing breath. Swallow knew what was coming.

'That decision cost the life of our child,' she sobbed. 'Our beautiful child.'

It was a monstrous charge. And yet, he knew, there was truth to it. If he had left G-division, as Maria had wanted, he would not have been in conflict with the security department. There would have been no raid on the house by Smith-Berry's agents. There would have been no confrontation between Maria and the agent known as Major Kelly. No fall on the stairs. No miscarriage. No lost baby.

He felt angry and empty all at once. Now Maria had her head in her hands and had started to sob openly. A gentle, sorrowful sobbing, as she rocked forward and back over the table.

He had no answer to give and he could think of nothing to say that might alleviate her distress.

'I'm going back to work,' he said, quietly, after a few moments.

Chapter 11

'Two developments while you were out, Boss,' Pat Mossop was waiting for him on the first floor of Exchange Court before he got to his office. Swallow could see he wanted to impart whatever news he had as quickly as possible.

He gestured to Mossop to follow him inside and closed the door behind them.

'There's a note from Dunlop,' Mossop said, handing him an envelope and a single sheet of plain paper. 'It arrived in the post an hour ago.'

Dublin's postal delivery system was so efficient that correspondents might send letters and receive replies to them up to three times in any one day. The franking on the envelope told him it had been posted at the General Post Office in Sackville Street before half-ten that morning. It was addressed to Mossop and marked 'private and confidential'.

Swallow placed the single, typewritten sheet on the desk. Dunlop had chosen his language with care so that anyone intercepting the letter could not possibly understand its references.

> *The goods that were expected have arrived and are currently being examined. They would appear to be as described and of the declared quality. However it is apparent from my superiors' initial reaction that they are unlikely to be suitable. They will not meet the needs of this firm and will be returned, probably on the day after tomorrow.*

It is likely that a new buyer will be found very swiftly with the goods on the market and that a completed sale will be announced within days if not hours.

Horseman.

'I suppose that means more to you, Boss, than it does to me,' Mossop said, looking quizzically at him.

'I had a meeting with Dunlop and I briefed Chief Mallon. He and I went out to the Salthill Hotel last night to see Mr Parnell and we told him what we knew. He's going to see if he can persuade O'Shea to drop the divorce suit. Dunlop is trying to play Polson along for a few days to give us a bit of time. Whether it will work, I don't know.'

Mossop shrugged.

'Well, it's good that Mr Parnell will try at least. I imagine he can be fairly persuasive when he wants to be.'

'There was something else, Pat?' Swallow queried him.

'Yes, Boss. Dr Lafeyre sent a message to meet him at Marlborough Street as soon as you can. He's going to be there for the next few hours.'

'I'll go across there immediately. Copy that note over to Chief Mallon and I'll see you here later.'

He stopped at the Palace Bar on Fleet Street as he made his way to Marlborough Street and ordered a pork pie and a glass of ale. He was hungry, having abandoned his dinner and he needed something to wash away the taste of Tess's heavy soup. The bar was quiet. There were no pressmen from *The Irish Times*. They were at work, reporting the courts and the other business of the city. It would be different in the evening time when they would have completed their work, but for the moment he was happy to enjoy the calm of the empty bar without company.

A cooling wind came up the river from the bay and stirred the city air as he crossed the bridge to Sackville Street. He grinned at the sight of the seagulls sitting atop John Henry Foley's monument honouring the Liberator, Daniel O'Connell. It was too imperial in its tone, he always thought, presenting the acknowledged leader of the common people and the author of Catholic Emancipation in the style of an emperor. Foley had died before it was completed a few years previously. Swallow reckoned he would have been unhappy to see it become a favoured target for defecation by the big, raucous sea birds. Perhaps one day, he thought, there would be a statue to Charles Stewart Parnell as well. In his quest for Home Rule he was following in the footsteps of the Liberator. However, that likelihood would be considerably diminished if he became the object of condemnation as an adulterer. That would be ironic, he told himself, given O'Connell's reputation as a prodigious begetter of children out of wedlock. Some wag had it that one could hardly throw a stone anywhere in Kerry without hitting one of O'Connell's offspring.

When he got to Marlborough Street, Harry Lafeyre was just finishing a post mortem in the examination room.

'An eejit of a baker's lad above in Stoneybatter that got his shirt caught in the dough mixer,' the surly Scollan informed him, jerking his thumb towards where the city medical examiner was bent over a corpse on one of the steel tables. 'Broke his neck, I'd say … don't know why the doctor is takin' so long about it. But he'll be done in a couple o' minutes.'

Lafeyre removed his heavy rubber gloves and apron, washed his hands with carbolic soap and led Swallow into the smaller of the morgue's two laboratories.

'There's some very interesting material here, Joe,' he smiled, emphasising each word very slowly. That smile always told Swallow that Lafeyre had important information and he was going to enjoy imparting it.

'First, let me tell you about the ligature.'

He took a rectangular, glass container from the shelf and laid in on the bench. Swallow could see the thin rope, now washed and clean and lying in a short loop.

'This,' Lafeyre tapped the box two or three times, 'is somewhat surprising.'

'Could we skip the theatrics, Harry, and tell me what it is?'

Lafeyre's grin was somewhere between self-satisfied and triumphant.

'This, my dear Detective Inspector, I believe to be part of a restraint used for an animal. In simple terms, an animal's tether or lead.'

He tipped the thin rope out of the glass box and placed one end of it under the Grubb microscope.

'You can see it's very tightly woven but also that the fibres have been strained. They're stretched. But if you look in there between the fibres you can see strands of hair. It's a coarse, tough, wiry hair. It could be from a lot of animals, I suppose. Maybe a horse or a goat or a dog.'

Swallow put his eye to the glass. He could clearly see the hairs between the fibres. He nodded approvingly to Lafeyre.

'I don't suppose you can tell me what breed of goat they came from?'

Lafeyre knew the question was facetious.

'Ah, you're being smart. You should be kneeling down in admiration and thanking me.'

Swallow laughed.

'Good work, Harry. You're right. But give me a guess.'

'Ah, you need a specialist in veterinary medicine, I'd say. There aren't many of those around although there's talk of establishing a college to train people in animal medicine. I'm only a doctor for humans.'

'You should have been a *polisman,* Harry.' Swallow laughed again. 'You're far too smart for doctoring.'

'You've seen nothing yet, my friend,' Lafeyre ignored the jibe and reached for a second, larger glass box. Swallow could see that it contained the leather belt he had retrieved from the Poddle as well as a small metal box, perhaps three inches cubed.

Lafeyre spread the belt on the workbench, placing a glass evaporating dish beside it. The belt had cracked and blistered along its length as it had dried out. Swallow could see that Lafeyre had unpicked much of the stitching that had held the two layers of leather together.

'The belt itself tells us nothing of significance,' Lafeyre said. 'The leather seems to be cowhide but if it's American, for example, it could be bison. It's impossible for me to tell. But now, here's the real find.'

He reached for the metal box, lifted the lid and turned it upside down on the dish.

'What do you think of that, Inspector Swallow?'

Swallow found himself looking at a collection of glittering coins. Gold half sovereigns. And scattered among the brilliant discs, perhaps a score of bright, sparkling stones, flashing white and blue.

'Jesus Christ, Harry. Are those what I think they are?'

Lafeyre picked up one of the stones between thumb and forefinger and held it to the light streaming through the window.

'I'm not an expert but I saw a lot of these in my time in southern Africa. I even bought a few, straight out of the mines in the East Rand. There's a couple of them in the ring I gave to Lily when we became engaged. I'd say these are good quality diamonds. They're not the very best but they've got good light. Very little colouring, and they've been expertly cut and polished.'

'Where did they come from?' Swallow asked.

'The coins and the stones were stitched into the belt, between the two layers of leather. Whoever had them obviously wanted to keep them safe and reckoned that the best place was around their waist.'

'Any idea of what the whole lot is worth?'

'There are twenty-three stones. They're high carat so you'd really need a skilled jeweller to say what the monetary value might be, but you're talking about some hundreds of pounds. And, of course, there's the sovereigns. These are all 1874 or 1859. I think that 1859 is rather rare. Again, you'd need professional advice on that.'

Swallow scribbled details silently in his notebook for a few moments.

'Right,' he nodded to Lafeyre, 'let's hypothesise that the dead woman was wearing the belt. And that she was garrotted with the rope. What sort of conclusions can we draw from what we know so far?'

Lafeyre grimaced.

'You're the detective. I'm only the technical consultant here. But I suppose we can say she was a woman who had some means of acquiring these valuable goods. And I suppose we can surmise that whoever killed her didn't realise that belt she was wearing had all this loot in it, otherwise it wouldn't have gone into the Poddle with her, would it?'

'Anything else?'

'The gold fillings in her teeth tell us she wasn't poverty-stricken, so maybe – just maybe – she was a woman of means. Not a housemaid or a washerwoman.'

'She could have been a prostitute. Maybe she took her fees in diamonds or gold.'

Lafeyre laughed.

'Not to denigrate the ladies of the night here in our fair city, but not too many Dublin prostitutes can command a diamond or a half sovereign for their services. I believe the standard rate charged in the brothels in Monto now is a shilling. And I don't find any evidence of syphilis in the bones, it's usually apparent.'

Swallow gestured to the stones and the half sovereigns.

'Will you put those in a secure container for me and I'll sign a receipt for you. Like you say, I'll need expert advice about them and I think I know where to go for it.'

A strong cautionary instinct told Swallow that it would be counter-productive for too many people to know about the diamonds and half sovereigns. Apart from any other consideration, if news got out it would result in a flood of applications from imposters and chancers claiming ownership.

'Can we keep this between ourselves for the moment, Harry?' he asked Lafeyre. 'I'll brief Mallon and Pat Mossop but nobody else.'

Lafeyre nodded.

'Of course, I can understand you'd not want to set off a stampede of treasure-hunters.'

He took a small wooden evidence box with a hinged lid from a drawer under the workbench.

'You might learn something with an expert about where they came from by the cutting on the stones, and depending on the rarity of the coins you might be able to establish something about their history. Where will you take them?'

'The best authority on jewellery and precious objects that I know is old Ephram Greenberg over on Capel Street,' Swallow told him. 'I'll see what he makes of them.'

'He must be a great age now.' Lafeyre carefully counted the stones into the box. He took a second box from the drawer and laid the coins in it. 'I thought his daughter, Katherine, had more or less taken over the running of the business. Lily tells me she doesn't come to her class anymore because she's too busy with work.'

In addition to her teaching post at Alexandra College, Lafeyre's fiancée, Lily, taught a painting class at the Municipal School of Art on Thomas Street. Swallow himself had been enrolled in it for two years now, even though it was invariably a struggle to set aside two hours from his work every Thursday afternoon.

'Yes, I haven't seen her there for a while.'

'A pity,' Lafeyre said. 'Lily says she's an extremely talented painter. She was honoured last year by the Royal Dublin Society.'

Swallow was silent for a moment. Both Lafeyre and he well understood that the day Katherine Greenberg left the class was the day that Lily announced to her pupils that Mr Swallow was going to marry her sister, Maria.

'Yes,' he said eventually, 'she's the best of Lily's pupils, very definitely. She's missed from the class, I think.'

Chapter 12

In the way that news of any occurrence out of the ordinary will circulate in a small city, the citizenry of Dublin had become aware that something was astir. Sergeants and constables were knocking on doors at addresses from which women had been reported as having gone missing over the previous year. Mostly, they were informed, by families or landlords or neighbours, that they had either returned or been located. Some were reported to have left Dublin, mainly for England. Others were deceased. One was said to have been relocated to the Richmond Asylum for the Insane at Grangegorman.

Other policemen were visiting locksmiths and hardware shops, showing photographs of a bunch of keys. Did any tradesman or assistant think they might be familiar? Failing that, did they have any suggestions as to what purposes the different keys might have served? Mostly, it was agreed, they were fairly standard, run-of-the-mill specimens, likely to be used for interior doors in dwelling houses or offices. One long key looked as if it might be used to operate a heavier lock such as might secure a large external door or perhaps a safe or strongbox.

'You can tell by the bitings, the teeth as some call 'em, that you'd be using that in a lock with prob'ly six levers,' the locksmith John Donaldson of Townsend Street, told Pat Mossop, who showed him the black and white image. 'That shank is, what, three inches? So, it's for a good lock on a heavy, thick door or maybe a safe. And it's got a big bow there to give you leverage when you want to turn it. I can't tell about the metal from just looking at your picture but it's probably an alloy. They're tougher when they're made out of an alloy rather than just brass or iron.'

In the narrow streets of the south inner city and in the open countryside to the west, parties of constables were to be seen around the locations where there was access to the underground Poddle. Metal grids and covers on culverts and drains were being examined to see if there were signs of having recently been opened or removed. Further out in Dublin county, towards where the river rose, close to the village of Tallaght, officers with their tunics off, to alleviate the heat from the summer sun, searched along its narrow banks, up to the point where it turned downward into the earth and out of sight.

In the hotels and the cheaper boarding houses around the city centre, G-division detectives were checking registers and questioning owners and staff. Who was newly-arrived in Dublin? Were there any doubtful characters showing a bit of money? Had anybody, a snooping maid or a curious porter, perhaps seen someone with a gun or a knife or a club? Were there crowbars or jemmies under a bed anywhere or concealed in a cupboard?

For those who failed to observe the police activity at first hand, the newspapers had gleaned more than enough intelligence to compensate. Swallow left Lafeyre at the Marlborough Street morgue and bought an *Evening Mail* from a paperboy at the corner of North Earl Street. He moved to the inside of the pavement to scan the headlines in the main news page inside.

REMAINS DISCOVERED IN RIVER
Police busy at Essex Street
SUPERINTENDENT BOYLE IN CHARGE
MANY POLICE SEARCHES

He grinned mirthlessly. Somehow, Duck Boyle was always able to get his name linked to important cases. If the investigation led nowhere, of course, any mention of his name would fade from the narrative. It was well known that he was always ready to pass police information to selected reporters in return for favourable publicity. Conversely, when something went wrong, his name was nowhere to be seen.

The attack on Sir John and Lady McCartan was reported in the adjoining news column.

OUTRAGE NEAR TEMPLEOGUE
Prominent Queen's Counsel and his wife attacked
Maid in house beaten and threatened
A GUN AND KNIVES USED BY ROBBERS

The report below detailed Sir John's legal career, his diverse business interests, as well as his distinguished place in politics and in municipal affairs, before going on to express the sense of outrage 'welling in the hearts of all of Dublin's right-thinking citizens' at the audacious crime. The narrative reminded readers that this was the second such dastardly and violent assault in the respectable suburbs of the city in less than two weeks and the sixth or seventh in a period of just three or four months. At the conclusion of the report, the fervent hope was expressed that the police would meet with early success in identifying and arresting the perpetrators of these vicious crimes. Remarkably, although Superintendent Maurice Boyle had been in charge of the E-division at the time of the still unsolved attack on the elderly businessman, John Healy, at Anglesea Road, having been transferred to B-division only days ago, his name did not appear anywhere in the column. In police work, as in other walks of life, Swallow reflected, success had many fathers but failure usually remained an orphan.

He crossed Sackville Street at Nelson's Pillar. The sun had started its slow descent as the afternoon gave way to evening but the streets were still fetid. Two lines of steam trams had formed, one outside the GPO on the western side, the other outside the Imperial Hotel on the eastern side. Soon they would be filling with passengers at the end of their working day, heading homeward to the suburbs. In the middle of the broad thoroughfare, behind the Pillar, cabmen and their horses, drawn up in file, were equally dozy in the heat. He was glad of the shade as he passed into Henry Street.

Goldberg's jewellers and fine art dealers on Capel Street had been established by old Ephram Goldberg when he came to Dublin from Manchester more than fifty years previously. It was a regular port of call for Swallow in his days as a beat constable in the Bridewell. There was always fragrant, black coffee and yeasty bread with *speck* or sweet cake, in the family parlour over the shop. Later, when he had moved to G-division, and he would visit old Ephram Goldberg, perhaps for advice on items of value that might have come into police possession, the coffee gave way to wine, red and strong. What Ephram Goldberg did not know about gold, silver, precious stones and *objets d'art* was not worth knowing. Possibly more important, he always knew what was being offered or traded around the city, and by whom, whether in the jewellers, the fine furniture dealers or the lowly pawn shops.

Nowadays, unsteady on his feet and able to move about only with difficulty, Ephram kept himself mainly to the back office while Katherine dealt with customers at the counter in the front. Ever since the attempted robbery a year previously, in which Swallow had fortuitously intervened, the door to the street was latched and locked and visitors now had to pull on a bell-cord to gain admission.

Katherine opened the door a moment after he had rung and gestured him inside. She was, as always, business-like in a severe, black dress without adornment. There were no customers in the shop but he could see Ephram's grey head through the glass partition that separated the public area of the shop from the office at the back.

'Mr Swallow. It's not often that we see you nowadays.'

She smiled but there was chiding in her tone.

'Hello, Katherine. How are you?'

'I'm very well, thank you. You're looking for my father, I assume.'

'Yes, I am.'

'He'll always be glad to see you, as you know' she said, a little more softly, leading the way across the shop-floor.

'It's a pity you stopped coming to Lily's art class,' he said. 'Are you very busy here in the shop?'

She stopped in her stride.

'My father isn't able to run the business any more,' she said. 'I'm needed here and I don't have time for hobbies.'

He smiled.

'I understand. But you're without doubt the best talent in the class. You're missed, you know.'

Her expression hardened again.

'Well, you'll all have to get on without me, I'm afraid. I should have asked, by the way, how is your wife? I hope she is well. I heard about her unfortunate mishap.'

'It wasn't a mishap, Katherine,' he said, just a little more sharply than he had intended. 'She was assaulted in her own home.'

She hesitated for a moment. Just as she was about to reply, the office door opened and Ephram Greenberg peered out into the shop.

'Joseph.' His face, bearded and lined with age, broke into a smile. 'I knew I heard voices out here. Come, come in and sit down with me.'

Swallow and Katherine followed him as he shuffled back into the office and lowered himself into a padded chair beside a long, mahogany table, laden with pictures in gilt frames, marble statuettes, mantle-clocks and other items of his trade.

'Sit down, Joseph. It's been a long time since we talked. I want to hear all the news from the famous Detective Inspector Swallow.'

He gestured towards his daughter as she started to leave.

'No, my dear. The wine, bring the wine. We must attend to our guest.'

Katherine nodded in silent assent to the old man's request. She crossed the room to a tall, double-fronted cabinet.

Ephram Greenberg reached across the table and touched Swallow's hand.

'How are you, Joseph? I know that you have had to contend with a great sorrow. You and your wife have been in my thoughts. I have prayed for you both in the synagogue.'

Swallow nodded.

'I'm managing to get along, Ephram. As you say, it's been a great sorrow. A very great sorrow indeed. My wife, Maria, remains deeply troubled. The loss of the baby has hit her very hard.'

Katherine put two crystal goblets on the table and started to open the bottle of Burgundy she had selected from the wine rack below the cabinet.

Ephram squinted at the label on the bottle and grimaced.

'Unfortunately our usual delight from Bekaa is out of stock. We shall have to make do with this poor French substitute.'

'Bring another glass, my dear, and sit with us,' Ephram told her. 'The business day is almost over and we can just leave the door locked.'

She seemed to hesitate. For a moment Swallow thought that she was about to demur, but when she had poured for both of them, she crossed the room again to take another glass from the cabinet.

Ephram raised his glass.

'I understand, Joseph. I have known great loss and sorrow in my life too. It does not simply disappear but with the help of the Almighty one can learn to deal better with it as time goes by, I think. Fate can be hard. We are often denied what we want the most. Life is like a river. When the sun shines, the water looks bright. When the sun goes out of our lives, the water becomes dark. I learned that when I lost my beloved wife.'

Katherine silently sipped her glass of Burgundy.

'Those are very wise words, Ephram,' Swallow said, raising his glass in response.

He placed the two evidence boxes from Lafeyre's morgue on Ephram's mahogany table.

'I've something here that I need your help on.'

The old man nodded.

'Of course, Joseph. If I can assist you, I will always do so.'

Swallow carefully opened the box of precious stones on the green baize square between them on the table. Then he placed them, one by one, in a straight, glittering line. He heard Katherine's slight intake of breath as she realised what she was looking at.

'I'd like you to look at these, Ephram, and tell me what you can about them. Where they might have come from. What kind of person might have them. Perhaps what they might be worth.'

Ephram sighed gently.

'These are valuable. I can say that even without a closer examination. But you probably know this anyway.'

He took one of the stones in his jeweller's tweezers, placed it under the lens of his loupe and peered down through the eyepiece. Then he turned the stone over and back, viewing its cut from different sides. He repeated the process with each of the others before turning to his daughter.

'Katherine, my dear. Would you please look at these and tell us what you think?'

She moved to the other side of the table and did as he had done with each of the diamonds. She took a longer time than her father, moving the loupe from one eye to the other while deftly manoeuvring each of the carbons with the tweezers.

When she had finished, she returned to where she had been sitting and stared hard at Swallow.

'These are mostly fine stones,' she said. 'Some are better than others. None of them are absolutely perfect. But absolute perfection in diamonds is probably as rare as it is in humans.'

Ephram looked quizzically at his daughter for a moment.

'Joseph is not looking for philosophy, my dear. He wants to know what we can tell him about these. Where they might have come from? Who might have worked upon them?'

She shrugged.

'They are very varied in colour. Two are near colourless. There are three or four that are light yellow. The others have a faint tint. So, they must come from various sources. There are various shapes too and quite different cuts. Mostly they seem to be European cut.'

'What do you mean by "various sources", Katherine?' Swallow asked.

'That they're not all cut from one bigger stone.'

'And when you say they are "European cut", is it possible to say where they might have been finished? What country or city?'

She shrugged.

'Possibly London or Amsterdam. It would be impossible to be more precise.'

Swallow saw that Ephram was smiling.

'My daughter has learned her trade very well,' the old jeweller said with pride. 'I can add very little to what she has told you. Apart, that is, from one very small detail.'

It was difficult to tell whether the brief cloud that crossed Katherine's face showed either annoyance or embarrassment.

She recovered immediately and gracefully.

'I doubt that I will ever know as much about the jewellery business as my dear father,' she smiled. 'But I am trying hard. And I'm sure I will always have more to learn.'

'Come, Joseph,' Ephram beckoned to Swallow to put his eye to the loupe.

He selected one of the larger stones he had examined earlier and used the tweezers to place it under the lens.

'This is what is called a Princess Cut. It's a perfect square. Beautifully cut and quite brilliant. But if you look to the horizontal point on the left side as you look at it, you will see a very tiny adhesion. It looks like a pin-head.'

Swallow pressed his right eye socket down on the loupe. Sure enough, he could see a small grey point on the surface of the diamond. Then he realised there was another. And on the opposite side of the gem there was a third, slightly bigger than the first two.

'Those are small fragments of whatever metal the diamond would have been set in,' Ephram said. 'It was probably silver. They're on three other stones as well. This tells us that they were formerly set in metal. Possibly in rings, or in a tiara such as might be worn by a wealthy lady. They would probably have been removed with some force, I think. An expert would have opened the clasps so that the diamonds could literally fall out. Whoever freed these stones from whatever they were set in was no professional.'

Katherine left her seat, walked back around the table and when Swallow had done, put her head down to the loupe again.

After a moment, she nodded in agreement.

'I'm sure my father is correct. I saw something, but I thought it was dust. One can actually see the jagged edge on the fragment.'

She looked at her father.

'I'm sorry. I know I missed that. As I said, I'm still learning.'

Ephram waved a hand dismissively.

'Are you going to tell us how these came to be in police possession, Joseph?' he asked. 'Or is that confidential?'

'No. I'll tell you that in absolute confidence in a moment. But first, I want you to look at something else.'

He carefully replaced the diamonds, one by one, in the first evidence box. Then he took the second box from his pocket, opened it on the table and placed the gold sovereigns on the green baize.

Ephram took each coin in turn, noting the detail and then tapping it lightly with a jeweller's hammer, so small, Swallow thought, that it might have been a child's toy.

'These are genuine,' he said finally. 'Worth a nice sum. The dates are good, in the sense that relatively few sovereigns were minted in these years. None of them is worth a fortune. But if they came in to my shop, I would buy them for a good price.'

'How much would the whole lot be worth?' Swallow asked. 'The diamonds and the coins?'

The old man turned to his daughter.

'What do you think, my dear?'

'The gems vary in their quality and I would need to examine each one very carefully. But I would think the total value might be around £500. And maybe £50 for the sovereigns. So the total would be perhaps £550, maybe more.'

'I think my daughter's estimate is very accurate,' Ephram said.

Katherine poured more Burgundy.

'You have excited our curiosity now, Joseph,' she said, smiling a little for the first time since he had entered the shop.

'I'm not sure that there's a whole lot that I actually know,' he said. 'You may be aware that human remains were found in the river running under Dublin Castle yesterday.'

Ephram nodded.

'Yes, I read about it in the newspaper this morning. It says in the newspaper that this is a case of murder. Truly terrible. Are these connected with whoever was found in the river?'

'They could be. We found these stitched into a leather belt close by the location in which the body was recovered. In fact, there were only bones, a skeleton. But the city medical examiner, Dr Lafeyre, is able to tell us that they're the remains of a woman, probably in her thirties. There was a bunch of keys attached to the belt as well.'

Ephram nodded again.

'Aha, so you think if you can identify the provenance of the diamonds and the coins it may help to identify this poor woman.'

'We have other lines of inquiry, of course. But I know that you deal with many persons who have precious things to sell. What sort of woman do you think would have this amount of wealth secreted away in a leather belt that she wore around her body?'

The old man sipped his wine and thought silently for a moment.

'That is not an easy question to answer, Joseph,' he said finally. 'She would not be a dealer because she would require easier access to her valuables than if they were stitched away in a belt. And she obviously did not have a safe hiding place or a secure location, like a bank, or even a safe. These diamonds have come from a variety of sources. They could be stolen from different places or people over time. Or she might have invested in them, using money she received. But I do not think that any of these gems is sufficiently rare or outstanding to be particularly remembered by a jeweller or dealer if he handled them or worked on them. I'm sorry, that isn't very helpful to you, I'm sure.'

It wasn't, Swallow reflected silently. But courtesy required that he deny it.

'No, on the contrary. Thank you, Ephram. That's very useful information. It will help to narrow the field of our inquiries. The first thing in almost any murder investigation is to identify the victim. After that, you can start looking for the perpetrator.'

They finished the wine and Swallow stood to go. Katherine led him back through the shop and opened the door to the street, quiet now, with the day's business over and the sunshades rolled in for the night.

'Thank you for your help,' he said, stepping out into the fading light. 'It's good to see your father well. He's lost none of his sharpness.'

She smiled for the second time in the evening.

'He is happy to see you. There will always be a welcome here for you, Joseph. Remember that.'

'Yes, Katherine, I will. Is there any possibility we might see you again at the painting class?'

'Who knows?' she said, still smiling. 'I'm a woman who rarely rules out any possibility.'

Chapter 13

Swallow had four choices.

The light of the midsummer evening was still sufficiently strong when he stepped out into Capel Street to enable him to read the time on his half-hunter. He stood on the pavement outside Greenbergs to consider his options.

He could, and possibly should, go back to the Castle to brief John Mallon on Lafeyre's discovery of the gems and half sovereigns, stitched into the belt they had retrieved from the Poddle. It was an intriguing development, but it did not necessarily advance the investigation. It was sometimes a finely balanced thing, whether to intrude upon the little domestic privacy the Mallon family were allowed to enjoy in the Lower Yard or to ensure that the chief of G-division was kept fully up to date on developments. Mallon always insisted that if the G-men were to err in that judgment it should be on the latter side. But, Swallow told himself, there was nothing to be done immediately about Lafeyre's find. He had followed it up with his visit and inquiry with Ephram Goldberg. It would be sufficient, he decided, to provide his boss with details in the morning.

He could go home to Thomas Street to Maria. Perhaps she would be downstairs in the bar. She always made an evening appearance there, however brief it might be. She did not serve the customers herself, that was the responsibility of Dan Daly and the other barmen. Rather, she presided. Sometimes standing at the end of the bar, acknowledging the greetings of the clientele, sometimes moving easily among the tables, bestowing a welcoming word here or a smile there.

But equally, she might be sitting in the parlour upstairs, possibly reading but more likely, as of late, simply staring at the window in silence. He could see the picture in his mind's eye and sense the atmosphere in the room and he could not look forward to returning to them.

Or he could go somewhere for a few quiet drinks. Ephram's Burgundy had given him a lift. A drop of Tullamore on top of it would complete the job. Perhaps he might drop into The Brazen Head, or the Dolphin Hotel? Or maybe the Burlington? A couple of whiskies in the cool of the Burlington's airy bar would be just right.

Or he could take a tram to the McCartan house at Templeogue Hill to visit the crime scene and to impress upon Sir John and Lady McCartan the vigour and diligence with which the burglary and assault upon them and their servant were being pursued by the police, as he had promised Mallon he would do. But there was another possibility. Why not combine his options, he asked himself? The pocket watch told him it was not yet half-past seven. He could have a drink at the Burlington and then stroll around the corner to South Great George's Street to catch a tram for Rathgar. From there it would be no more than a ten minute walk through the countryside to Templeogue Hill.

Billy Gough, the manager of the Burlington, greeted him in the lobby. Gough's late father had been a G-man who used his modest influence to get his son taken on as a trainee waiter at the Shelbourne twenty years previously. Young Billy, however, was not content to be a waiter. He had ambition and ability to match. He took every training opportunity he could get and worked hard to become first a dining room supervisor and then, a front-of-the-house trainee manager. Once into management he had transferred to Brown's Hotel in London, rising to the post of assistant general manager. From there he had returned to Dublin to run the prestigious Burlington.

'Very good to see you, as always, Mr Swallow.'

Billy always maintained an appropriate degree of formality when working at the front of the house. But in the privacy of his well-appointed office on the second floor, over some excellent whiskey or cognac, he was a reliable confidant who could always be counted upon to keep his G-division contacts in the picture if anyone or anything suspicious came into his purview at the hotel.

A year previously, a quiet word in Swallow's ear had led to the arrest of an American arms dealer with a score of Navy Colts and five thousand rounds of ammunition in two trunks under his bed. They would have been for sale to the highest bidder, whether to ordinary criminals or to political extremists. In turn for Billy's goodwill and co-operation, G-men maintained a low-key, occasional presence at the Burlington, and in the event of any trouble or threat around the place, there would always be a swift police response.

'Are you dining or just joining us for a drink?' Billy beamed, extending a manicured hand in greeting.

'Just a quiet drink in a busy day,' Swallow grinned, returning the manager's handshake.

'Ah, yes. I saw about that gruesome find in the river. Pure chance that those workmen came across it, I gather. Have you hopes of clearing it up fairly quickly?'

Swallow shook his head.

'We haven't even identified the poor woman yet. But it's early days.'

The manager nodded sympathetically.

'I'd say you need something to refresh you. Go on inside, make yourself comfortable and they'll look after you in the bar as usual.'

It was a standing courtesy to favoured customers at the Burlington that their first drink would be on the house. It was a small strategic investment that paid handsome dividends from the bankers and brokers and wealthy business professionals who were the habitués of the elegant hotel.

It being midweek, the bar was not over-busy. The bankers and brokers would dine well during the week but they would tend to leave their serious drinking until Saturday when the commerce of the week would have finished, with profits and dividends accumulated and calculated. Three or four tables were occupied and one group of five middle-aged men were standing at the bar, laughing, smoking and drinking champagne. Swallow surmised that some deal had been closed so successfully that celebration could not be postponed to the end of the business week.

A solitary drinker sat slumped at the end of the bar, his whiskey glass and a soda syphon on the counter in front of him. He was surveying the room through the engraved mirror that ran the length of the wall behind the bar with the unfocused gaze of a man who had drunk too much. Swallow wondered if he knew that the mirror was also a one-way window through which staff, or on occasion a G-man on surveillance, could observe customers, with the co-operation of Billy Gough and his staff.

His eyes and Swallow's locked in a moment of mutual recognition and then fixed. Neither man would break the stare. Now there was only one way to handle the situation. Swallow walked across the bar and took the adjoining stool.

He signalled to the barman and called, 'Tullamore.'

Then he nodded to his neighbour.

'Mr Polson, I believe.'

There was a thin, hesitant smile.

'I've … I've been waiting to meet you, Inspector Swallow,' he slurred. 'My colleagues have told me a great deal about you. I believe I've seen you here … before.'

He waved a limp hand towards the room.

'And my colleagues have told me a great deal about you, Mr Polson. And I've seen you too, of course. You're not inconspicuous.'

'Aha. So, the sleepy G-division isn't entirely … devoid of powers of observation.'

'It's hard to miss so many drunken Englishmen wandering around the city.'

Polson raised his glass.

'Touché.'

The barman placed Swallow's Tullamore on the counter.

'Compliments of Mr Gough, Sir.'

Swallow raised the glass, nodding to Polson.

'I'll have a splash of that soda, if I may.'

Polson tried to reach for the soda syphon but clutched thin air instead. Swallow leaned across him, thumbed the pressure lever and directed a short jet of sparkling bubbles into the whiskey.

'So how do you find Dublin, Mr Polson?'

'To be absolutely honest … now … to be very honest, Inspector, it's rather dull.'

More often, Swallow believed, a detective would acquire knowledge by pretending to know little. But sometimes, he might learn more by letting a subject understand that he already had a lot of knowledge. This was probably one of those latter situations, he told himself.

'After Madrid, I suppose it's a bit quiet, alright.'

If Polson was surprised by the reference, his face did not show it.

'I had work to do in Madrid. Work, ye know. Real work,' he said after a moment.

'It seems to have cost a man his life.'

'Wha' … what are you referring to?'

Swallow realised that the security agent was more than just a little drunk.

'Richard Pigott.'

Polson raised his glass to drink but it missed his mouth on the first try.

'Pigott? That … fat bas … bastard? Don't tell me you'd weep for him. He squealed like … like … a pig … for mercy in the hotel room.'

Swallow froze. The implications of what the drunken security agent was saying were explosive. The official version of events at the Hotel Los Embajadores in March was that Pigott had been told by Spanish police that he was to be deported to England, that he had gone to his room under the pretence of getting his things and shot himself there. Now he was being told that he had been shot, begging for mercy, probably by the man sitting opposite him.

'You were in the room when he died.'

It was a statement more than a question.

Polson seemed to become suddenly alert.

'Aha, you'll not hear any more … from me, Mr … Swallow. You think you can trick me? Well … well, you can't. Better men than you have tried.'

He called to the barman.

'Scotch. A double.'

'Now, let us get back to … matters here in your unfortunate country,' he wagged a finger. 'I'd been given to understand … that you were up against it here. Fenians, bombers, dynamiters and so on. I was looking forward to some … action, since your fellows seem to have no appetite for the job. Getting to grips with the murdering bas …. bastards, you know.'

'There's a few of those, alright. But mostly they're people who're angry for one reason or another. Like somebody has stolen their land or humiliated their families over generations. Or robbed them with extortionate rents. And sometimes they get led astray by smarter people.'

Polson shrugged.

'It's an unjus … unjust world, you know. Some people are meant to ru … rule. Others are meant to be ruled.'

Swallow pointed to the scar on Polson's face.

'Who were you getting to grips with when that happened?'

Polson took his double scotch in two gulps. Swallow noticed that he had not added any soda water this time. He grimaced as the raw spirit hit the back of his throat. But remarkably the alcohol somehow seemed to restore him to some coherence.

'A Boer Kommando was foolish enough to take us on. We just took a few scratches. They left a dozen dead. And God-knows-how-many wounded.'

'We? What regiment?'

'You're very curious. Did you see service yourself?'

'No. But it's usually informative to know what company a man chooses to keep when he decides to go into uniform.'

Polson seemed momentarily uncomfortable. Swallow could see the alcohol starting to cloud his eyes again.

'Eighteenth Huzz … Huzzars, if … if you must know. The Princess of Wales's Own.'

'Eighteenth Huzzars? Isn't that Captain Willie O'Shea's old regiment?'

'You're bloody well … well … inf … informed, Inspector.'

Swallow nodded.

'Probably a lot better than you might imagine, Mr Polson. Tell me, do you know the captain?'

Polson signalled the barman again.

'Anor' Scotch. An' a Tullamore, here.'

His expression hardened. Any remaining trace of the earlier, forced smile faded.

'Now, Inspector Swallow, the intell'gence service knows … knows all about you and all … all … 'bout your politics. We're not very surprised by any of it. You and your … your G-men are Irish. You can't help that, and you can't be expected to think or to act like Englishmen. Tha's simply a fact … and tha's why we've been … brought in.'

The barman put their drinks on the counter.

'So,' Polson raised his glass, 'I'm not going to give you any information about who I know and who I don' know. Because we don' trust you … people an' we've got very … very good reason not to. My advice, Inspec'or, is to … stick to burglaries and bits o' bodies in the river and leave s'curity work to those who're good at it. You're just bobbies in suits. We work directly for the gov'ment.'

Swallow threw back his drink in one gulp.

'And my advice to you, Mr Polson, is to try to remember that this isn't Africa. You're not at war here. Getting to grips with the bastards, as you put it so eloquently, is not what this is all about.'

He stood to go.

'Thanks for the drink. I'll return it another time.'

He pointed again to the scar on Polson's cheek.

'You can tell me the real story about that when we meet again. I have friends who served in South Africa and I happen to know that the Eighteenth Huzzars weren't anywhere near it when the fighting was going on with the Boers.'

Chapter 14

The Rathgar tram was almost empty at this hour of the evening. His fellow-passengers were four or five tired-looking men, travelling homeward, as he surmised, from their extended working day in city-centre offices or shops. The last of them stepped off outside Findlater's grocery in Rathmines and he was left quite alone in the saloon, apart from the elderly conductor, as the vehicle steamed slowly towards its terminus.

As soon as he had taken his seat he had reached for his notebook. Not the police-issue one but the one he always carried to record information that would, in all probability, never form part of any official report. He used the twenty-minute journey to record in full detail what Polson had told him about his presence in Madrid and the death of Richard Pigott there. Swallow had known Pigott, as he knew many of the editors and journalists around the city. He was not a man to be trusted, selling his skills corruptly to the highest bidder. And Swallow had not been particularly surprised when the Newry-born barrister, Charles Russell, had exposed him for a forger and a perjurer at the Westminster commission.

It was possible that the drunken Polson had simply spun a story to impress him, or to lay a false trail. His explanation for the scar on his face was a fabrication. Perhaps he was a fantasist. Or simply a blow-hard. But if what he had told him was true, the official version of Pigott's death was a fabrication, probably put into circulation with the complicity of equally corrupt journalists and security or police operatives. He had not taken his own life. He had been murdered, probably to prevent him revealing who had put him up to forging the letters, supposedly written by Parnell. The political ramifications would be more than far-reaching if it became known or even suspected that Pigott's death was not suicide but the work of government agents. What Polson had told him in drink was dangerous to know. Men had been killed in Ireland for a lot less.

He had filled four pages by the time the tram turned along the Rathgar Road. He descended at the first stop after the Church of the Three Patrons, sometimes referred to disparagingly as 'the servants' church.' It had been built, it was said, on the instructions of the Roman Catholic Archbishop of Dublin, William Walsh, to cater to the spiritual needs of the Catholic servants working in the newly-built homes of the wealthy, predominantly Protestant, residents of this affluent suburb.

It was a brisk ten-minute walk along Garville Avenue, through Brighton Square and across the Blessington Road. The open countryside began here. The light was fading now, and the lamps had started to come on in the front rooms of the fine, redbrick residences that lined the road. Here and there, behind granite-trimmed garden walls and cast-iron gates, he could hear noisy children, making the most of the extra playtime afforded by the long, summer evening. The thought of his own lost child saddened him as they called and laughed at their games in the gloaming.

He had located the McCartan house, Templeogue Hill, on the ordinance survey map. Surrounded by mature oak and beech, it was approached by a short, gravelled drive, fronted by granite pillars and iron gates. It was a solid, three storey building, probably built originally to be a family home for a wealthy local farmer. There were many houses rather like it in his native rural Kildare, Swallow thought, as he mounted the steps to haul on the front door bell. Waiting for a response, he could see that there were lights burning in the front room on the middle floor, in the hallway and downstairs in what would be the kitchens and probably the servants' quarters.

The tiny maid who opened the door looked terrified. She could be no more than sixteen or seventeen, he reckoned.

Now he could see the bruising on her face and neck.

'I'm Detective Inspector Swallow, from Dublin Castle,' he said gently.

She seemed frozen. Unable to speak.

'I'm from the police. Could you tell Sir John I'd like to have a word with him, if it's convenient.'

'Police … wait there,' she said after a pause, before turning back into the house.

For a moment he thought she was about to close the door in his face or redirect him downstairs as she was undoubtedly required to do with functionaries and messengers. He stepped across the threshold and stood in the hallway.

After perhaps a minute, a grey-haired man, tall but somewhat bent, came slowly down the staircase. His right hand was heavily bandaged and his forehead was masked with adhesive medical plaster. The expression on his face was somewhere between anger and distress.

'What's this about? I'm very tired and so is everyone in this house. Why are you here?'

'I'm Detective Inspector Swallow, Sir John. I'm the crime inspector at G-division.'

The man paused on the bottom step. He stared at Swallow for a moment and then glared disapprovingly.

'I know you, don't I?'

'I've given evidence at a couple of trials where you were for the defence, Sir.'

The glare intensified.

'Yes, I remember you.'

It was clear that his recollection was not a positive one. Swallow recalled that their exchanges during cross-examination had been less than cordial. At one point when Swallow had skilfully rebuffed the lawyer, McCartan had told him he was impertinent.

'So now you're a detective inspector? About time I heard from someone of appropriate rank. Yes, I remember you alright. I hope you're here to tell me you've apprehended the ruffians who broke in here last night. My poor wife has been in delicate health for years and she's been in a state of hysteria since last night. I've had to call out two eminent medical specialists to calm her. Thankfully she's physically unharmed. This is what they did to me.'

He jabbed a finger towards his bandaged forehead.

'That required six stitches this morning at the Royal Hospital.'

'I'm afraid we haven't got that far, Sir. I've come to express my regret and the regret of the entire detective division at these events. And I want to assure you that we are leaving no stone unturned in our investigation. I would be grateful if you could give me a little more information about what happened.'

McCartan's expression became more angry.

'Empty words, Inspector. I spent more than an hour already telling two of your detectives everything I know. To be frank, they both seemed rather slow on the uptake. If you people were doing the job you're paid for and if the city was properly policed this sort of outrage wouldn't happen. Surely you must know who's responsible.'

He raised his voice to a shout.

'All you need to do is go out and arrest them. I'll give you all the evidence you need to put them into Maryborough until they rot.'

Was it possible that the man was still in shock, Swallow wondered? He was not young and he had been through an ordeal. He trembled and shook as he shouted again.

'Useless, damned useless. The whole bloody lot of you. You have no business here.'

It would be pointless to try to engage in any conversation that might yield useful information. Swallow realised it was better to make a tactical withdrawal.

'I'm sorry you feel that way, Sir. I'll go now. But I'll ensure that you're kept fully informed of any developments. I know that this has been a shocking experience for you and your wife. And I hope that you might see your way to having a longer conversation with me in due course.'

McCartan suddenly stepped off the staircase and stood in front of him. He wrinkled his nose, sniffing.

'You've been drinking, Inspector. I can smell whiskey.'

Swallow felt himself blush.

'Yes, Sir. I had a drink earlier in the course of a meeting. Police business.'

'How dare you come to my house in this condition and under these circumstances? I'll report you to the Commissioner. I know him very well.'

He turned and shouted the length of the hallway.

'Cathleen. Come here at once.'

The young maid who had admitted him appeared from the return stairs.

'Yes, Sir.'

'This man is under the influence of alcohol. He's drunk. You should have been able to see that. He should never have crossed the threshold.'

'I'm sorry, Sir. I didn't realise.'

McCartan groaned loudly.

'At times like this I wish Mrs Bradley was still here. She would have used her wits. You're a useless girl. Go back downstairs.'

Swallow raised a hand, indicating to the girl to stay. It was his turn to raise his voice now.

'There's no need for that, Sir. I'm not drunk, or anything like it,' he said sharply.

'Are there no police regulations anymore?' McCartan snapped.

'Indeed, there are, Sir. They permit members of the detective office to consume alcohol while on duty in certain circumstances. So don't threaten me and don't be abusive to the girl. She's done nothing wrong. Now, if you want the men who broke in here to be made amenable, I suggest that you start helping me by giving me the information I need. I can see, however, that you are in a distressed state at this time and I can understand that. I can come back at a time when we are more composed, but for this evening, I would like to ask your servants some questions.'

After a moment, McCartan appeared to deflate. His shoulders slumped. He stepped back towards the stairs and put his hand to the newel post to steady himself.

'I'm extremely tired so I'm going back upstairs. If you think it could be useful to talk to the girl, I have no objection. The other servants are not here. The cook leaves once our dinner is prepared, my coachman is gone to County Cork to bury his mother, and our housekeeper left recently without notice. Lady McCartan hasn't been able to find a suitable replacement yet.'

He turned to ascend the stairs.

'You can use the day parlour, if you want. But you may feel more comfortable downstairs. Cathleen can make you some tea. She can just about do that.'

Chapter 15

He was glad of the tea. More than he realised, he needed refreshment other than alcohol. It was sweet and strong but curiously cooling in the warm night air.

Cathleen seemed to know what she was doing. But she was nervous, moving about the spacious, downstairs kitchen. He sat at the long, scrubbed table as she took the steaming, metal teapot from the range and placed it down in front of him. He saw that her hands trembled as she brought a cup and saucer, milk jug and sugar bowl, all in blue willow, from the dresser. Then she stood facing him, hands clasped in front of her, across the table.

'Won't you sit down, Cathleen? I need to ask you a few questions.'

The bruising was dark on her neck and face, but he could see that she was a pretty young woman, well-nourished and healthy. After a moment's hesitation, she lowered herself slowly on to a wooden chair. She bowed her head slightly and fixed her eyes on the table top.

'Thank you, Sir.'

'Are those bruises sore?'

'They are … a bit, Sir. Thank you.'

'Did you have them looked at?'

'I did, Sir. One of the doctors that came examined me and said I'd be alright. He gev me some pills for the pain.'

'So, tell me about yourself. What's your name and where are you from?'

It took a few moments, as if she had to concentrate, to get her answer.

'It's Cathleen, Sir … Cathleen Cummins. Them's the names I was gave.'

'And where are you from, Cathleen?'

'I kem from the country, Sir. From the school where childer live that don't have any people o' their own.'

'Ah, do you know what school that is? What county is it in?'

There was a long moment as she concentrated.

'St Mary's 'tis called … 'tis a long way away. In the county Wexford. That's all I know, Sir.'

'Do you like it, working here?'

She raised her eyes, looking quizzically at him.

'I don't mind it, Sir. 'Tis that I'm well fed, and I have a little room to meself at the back. And 'tis better here for me since Mrs Bradley went.'

'Mrs Bradley?'

'Aye, Sir. She was the house-keeper but she left.'

'Why is it better for you with her gone?'

She cast her eyes down to the table top again.

'She'd be cross with me … very angry. She'd give out that I wasn't doin' me work proper, like.'

'How long is Mrs Bradley gone, Cathleen?'

'A good spell now, Sir. T'would be a while.'

'A long while?'

'A good spell, Sir.'

The girl wasn't being evasive, he reckoned. She just seemed to have no sense of time. Perhaps it had something to do with being raised in an institution where the routine of the day, the week and even the year was set and regulated by those in authority.

He tried once more.

'And how long are you working here in this house?'

'A while now, Sir.'

'Weeks? Months? Years?'

'I … I can't count them things terrible well, Sir.'

'Well, let me see. Were you here at Christmas time?'

'I … I'd say I was, Sir.'

'Do you remember Christmas, Cathleen?'

'I'm not sure I do, Sir.'

He realised it was not the smartest question to ask. There was probably very little in Cathleen Cummins's unhappy life to make Christmas memorable. But he began to understand but not excuse why McCartan was brusque and impatient with the girl. She was borderline intelligent.

He topped up his teacup and added a little milk. Interviewing Cathleen was hard going.

'So, tell me what happened here last night.'

The girl's eyes filled with tears and she put her hand to her bruised neck.

'Them men kem in the back door. I was sittin' here on me own and one o' them just grabbed me be the neck and he hit me a few times, tellin' me to be quiet. I suppose I was screamin' or makin' noise. I was terrible frightened, Sir.'

'How many men, Cathleen?'

'There was three or four, I'd say.'

'Would you recognise any of them if you saw them again?'

The girl shuddered.

'Oh, I wouldn't want to see them men agin.'

'I understand that, but if you did, do you think you'd recognise them? Would you know their faces?

'I don't think so, Sir. 'Twas that they had masks, cloths like, over their faces. There was one o' them seemed to be givin' orders to t'others. I heard one o' them call him "Sir", I think.'

'And what happened then?'

'They ran upstairs, for the master was gone to bed. The lady doesn't very much come downstairs anyways. She's delicate. So I'd say she was asleep too. Then I heard shoutin' and roarin'. Then I heard the master shoutin' and there was bangin' whin they dragged him down the stairs into his office there. Wan o' them held me be the neck here all the time so I couldn't see anythin'. He had a big knife wit' a white handle an' he tol' me that if I made another sound he'd cut me throat. Then after a while they all wint out the back door agin. The man holdin' me threw me on the floor and kicked me legs a few times. And the master kem down here into the kitchen an' he covered in blood and his clothes all tore.'

'So, it all happened fairly quickly?'

'I suppose so. But it felt a long, long time, Sir. I was in fear o' me life.'

'I'm sure you were, Cathleen,' Swallow said gently. 'But don't worry now, they won't be back. Tell me what happened then.'

'Then the lady appeared on the stairs. She's not a well woman an' she can't use the stairs. But she kem down to the hallway be holdin' on to the rail an' draggin' herself along. She was screechin' and tryin' to wipe the blood off of the master. An' she said to me go to the next house down the road and get help straight away. An' I did an' one of the young lads in there ran down to the village to get the *polis* and the doctor.'

She started to sob loudly.

'I don' think it would have happened if Bran an' Rua hadda' been here still.'

'Who?' Swallow asked.

'Them's the two big dogs the master had here when I started work. I got on great with them. They'd a' kept the house safe. But they died.'

'What happened to them, Cathleen?'

'I don't know, Sir. It's just what the master tol' me.'

There was nothing significant in the girl's account that had not been in the initial report by Shanahan and Keogh, the G-men who had attended the scene. And there was little point in pressing her memories of what would have been a terrifying ordeal even for someone stronger and more mature.

'That's fine for now, Cathleen,' he said, draining the last of his tea. 'I'm sorry the dogs weren't here to keep the robbers away. So would you show me where the men came into the house?'

She led him to the end of the kitchen and opened a door to a short, narrow passageway. The end of the passage, perhaps ten feet away, framed a solid wooden door with a handle at its centre and two six-inch metal bolts. Neither of the bolts was in its shackle. When Swallow stepped closer he saw that there was also a keyhole set in a small metal plate, with MILNER stamped on it in capital letters.

'Who has the key for this lock, Cathleen?' he asked.

'I think it must be the master, Sir.'

'And you're sure this is how the men came in last night?'

'I … I think it must be, Sir.'

'Would those bolts not be locked across at night?'

She hesitated, confused and frightened.

'That wouldn't be my job, Sir.'

'No, Cathleen, I'm not asking that. I'm asking is it usual to have them open or locked?'

'I couldn't rightly say, Sir.'

'That's alright. But this would have been locked?'

He pointed to the keyhole.

'Yes, Sir.'

If the girl's information was correct, he realised, there had been no forced entry at the house. The door showed no sign of having been damaged. The mortice lock was a Milner, one of the best, and could not have been easily picked. The men who had robbed Sir John and Lady McCartan had either been admitted by someone inside the house or they had a key. There could be no other explanation.

Chapter 16

Thursday, June 6th, 1889

The spell of fine weather started to break in the morning. The sun started its ascent over the bay into a clear sky at dawn. But by nine o'clock, as the crime conference assembled at Exchange Court, grey clouds were coming in over the city from the west.

'There'll be rain runnin' down there before the Angelus bell,' Pat Mossop nodded towards the grimy windows facing into the Lower Yard, as the dayroom filled with G-men and uniformed constables.

Duck Boyle had sent word that he would not be present because he was due in the Magistrates' Court. The courts did not begin until eleven o'clock and Swallow surmised that he was probably enjoying the benefit of a lie-on in bed. So he took the rostrum at the top of the room himself as the others settled on chairs and desks or propped themselves against the walls. There was little of the easy relaxation of the early week. It was as if the darkening day was a metaphor for two investigations that seemed to be going nowhere.

His own mood reflected it too. He had slept badly after returning from Templeogue Hill to Thomas Street. For the second night in succession, Maria had retired to bed before his arrival just before midnight. But this time there was no supper, cold or otherwise, awaiting him in the parlour. He wondered if Carrie, the housekeeper, had simply forgotten to provide for him or if he was being sent a deliberate message.

The public house was closed but he could hear the sounds of the staff cleaning and readying the bars downstairs before locking up. He went down the back stairs and into the public bar.

'I'll take a Tullamore, there,' he called to Dan Daly, across the counter.

Dan looked tired and displeased.

'You're late, Mr Swallow,' he observed, reaching for the bottle behind him.

'I am that, Dan. It's been a long day.'

Daly put the whiskey in front of him.

'It wasn't a great time here either.'

Swallow took a mouthful of the Tullamore.

'I don't really want to know about business matters here, Dan. It's more trouble than it's worth.'

'Fair enough, Mr Swallow. But don't say I didn't try to mark your cards in time.'

He finished his drink and retraced his way upstairs to bed alone in what had been his rented room. He could see that Dan Daly was troubled and he did not doubt that it was on account of some difficulty with Maria, but there was no reason to believe he could do anything about her deteriorating relationships with her staff. He had tried and been rebuffed. He did not intend to put himself in a position where that would happen again or where he could be accused of interfering in her business.

He put his head to the pillow and slept, but it was a troubled and uneasy sleep, with his subconscious turning over what Polson had told him in the Burlington as well as what he had seen and heard at the McCartan house at Templeogue Hill. The night of supposed rest did not refresh him. He woke with a pounding head and a dry mouth. It was difficult to concentrate. As a precaution, he jotted down a list of possible inquiries and actions for review at the crime conference.

Now he cleared his throat that still tasted of last night's whiskies.

'We'll deal with the murder case first, Gentlemen. Pat, would you bring us up to date please?'

Mossop opened the murder book and started leafing through the loose-page job reports that he had collected before the conference from the investigation teams.

'There's three, maybe four, possible matches on the missing persons list on the basis that they lived somewhere close to the river. Mary Dunne is around thirty. Hasn't been seen since Christmas. She has a husband and five children in Pimlico. Reported missing by the eldest child, a girl who's just twelve, at Kevin Street. And there's Matilda Evans, also around thirty, from Dean Court, on Patrick Street. She disappeared early in May. Also reported at Kevin Street, in this case by the husband.'

He turned the page.

'Out at Portobello, there's Mary Nelson. She's been missing since April. She's aged thirty-five, with six children. She's widowed. Reported missing by her brother at College Street. The children have been taken into care by the sisters out at Goldenbridge. And there's Anne or Annie Boland, she's single, aged around twenty-five, no children and worked in a dairy at Rathfarnham. But she lodged with cousins out by Crumlin, close to where the Poddle flows overground. She was reported to Rathmines at the end of April by her employer when she didn't come collect her wages. It's too early to rule any of them in or rule them out.'

'Fair enough,' Swallow said. 'Anything significant to be learned from talking to the locksmiths?'

'I went to Donaldson's myself,' Mossop told the room. 'There isn't anything particularly unusual about any of the keys recovered from the river. They could be for use either in a domestic building or a place of business. Donaldson says most of them are copies rather than originals that would have come with the locks when they were installed. One in particular seems to be for a heavy-duty lock, perhaps a strong door or maybe even a safe, they told me.'

'Any point in trying some of the other locksmiths around town?' Swallow asked. 'Presumably some of them are more knowledgeable than others.'

'Donaldson's are probably the best,' Stephen Doolan said. 'But there'd be no harm in trying a few of the others too.'

Swallow gestured to Doolan.

'Since you have the floor, Stephen, what about the examination along the course of the river itself? Anything to suggest where the body might have been put into the water?'

Mossop nodded to Stephen Doolan, sitting in the front row of the conference.

'Sergeant Doolan, would you tell us how your searches are going?'

Doolan stood to face the group.

'We've covered all the stretches of the river that are open and above ground, from out near Fettercairn, through the countryside to the crossroads of Templeogue. Both banks. We've found nothing beyond a dead badger and a bag of drowned kittens. According to the City Engineers there's about a score of traps and access points where it's underground, between the canal and the Liffey. But the truth is there may be some that aren't on their maps. So, we're following our own course and we've got about half of them done. The rest we'll do today.'

'What are you looking for, Stephen?'

The question came from Detective Mick Feore.

'Any signs of recent disturbance, mainly. Broken locks or grates, maybe drag marks in the earth. If we find anything of note, we'll have to go down below at that spot.'

Doolan had extensive experience in searches. He and his team of hand-picked constables had a good record in recovering both missing people and missing goods in the city's waterways, in the sewers, in cellars and attics, in gardens and backyards, even in the city's public parks.

'There's a few tributaries to the river as well,' he added. 'If we don't find anything along the main watercourse, we'll have to start checking them as well. But the body could have been put in anywhere. It could have been close enough to where the skeleton was found. It was more or less intact and that might suggest it hadn't been carried very far by the water. But the flow of that river is slow and easy. So it could have been carried a distance without being broken up, I'd say.'

Swallow knew Doolan and his squad could be left alone to do what they did best. However, he would need men with detective experience to follow up on the four missing women. Their families and acquaintances would have to be questioned carefully and skilfully. If there was any foul play, or even secret tales of unhappiness behind the disappearances, individuals with important knowledge could be evasive and resistant.

He nodded to Feore.

'Mick, pick anyone you want from the day's roster and start on the four women. Their families, friends, neighbours. See does anyone know anything about that collection of keys. But the fact that she had some gold in her teeth is about the most likely lead. Don't be too direct about it. Come at it indirectly, if you can.'

The advice to Mick Feore was unnecessary, he knew. It was delivered for the benefit of the wider audience of less experienced crime investigators. He had learned early in his career as a detective that if a policeman suggests details to potential witnesses or informants they will sometimes agree or concur with the questioner in order to give a good impression or sometimes simply in an effort to please.

'I understand, Sir,' Feore grinned. 'I'll aim for gentle extraction on the teeth.'

It was a poor joke, but it drew a brief ripple of laughter from an otherwise sombre group.

'So,' Swallow stepped back to the rostrum, 'we need to talk about the Templeogue Hill robbery. I went out there myself last night. Chief Mallon wanted me to reassure Sir John McCartan and his wife that we were doing everything in our power to track down the perpetrators.'

Somewhere down the room there was a short, hollow laugh.

'Yes, I know we're stretched and we're struggling to do what we're required to do. But a lot of what us *polismen* do these days is just maintaining public confidence. Even if we're in the dark, we've got to make people believe that we can see what we're at.'

Pat Mossop pointed to two sheets of foolscap on the desk.

'I have a fuller report from Shanahan and Keogh on Templeogue Hill, Boss.'

'Best take us through it, then, Pat.'

'There's not a lot that's new. The statements from Sir John McCartan and his wife and from the maid don't give us anything much on the identification of the attackers. They kept their faces concealed. Sir John says the man who seemed to be the ring-leader shouted in a "rural" accent but that could mean anything. They're not even agreed on the number of attackers. He says four, she says three. The maid says three or four. She also says one of them seemed to be the gang leader and she heard another one call him "Sir" a couple of times.'

Shanahan, seated by the wall, raised a hand.

'The maid, Cathleen Cummins, was held downstairs in the kitchen so she didn't see very much. And she's not a great witness. She's a timid little thing and it's hard getting any information out of her.'

'Have we an inventory of what was taken from the house?' Swallow directed the question to Shanahan.

'We have, Sir. What we were told by Sir John himself is there in the report. But in truth he was so agitated and angry that it was difficult to get clear information out of him as well. In fairness, he's not a young man and he got a fair going-over from these fellows, whoever they were.'

Mossop read aloud from the file.

'Cash in banknotes, approximately two hundred pounds, mainly in one or five-pound notes. Cash in coin, approximately, ten pounds. A solid silver jewellery box, containing eight rings belonging to Lady McCartan. Estimated value of box one hundred pounds. Estimated value of rings, two thousand pounds. A necklace in pearls, strung on gold and a bracelet to match. Estimated value five hundred pounds. Other items of importance but without saleable value were left in the safe. These included property deeds, share certificates and two cheque books.'

'They seem to be smart enough to leave what they can't get any value for,' Swallow observed. 'But it's a very big haul, around two thousand eight hundred pounds based on McCartan's account.'

'Do we know how they got the safe open?' he asked Shanahan.

'It isn't a safe in the real sense, Sir. It's more a strong-box, and not very strong, at that. I'd say it's more tin than steel. So a few bangs of a lump hammer or a bit of leverage with a jemmy and it'd open like a can of sardines. What's puzzling though, is that they seemed to know it was there in the first place. It was concealed behind a wall panel in McCartan's study.'

'How did they get into the house in the first place?' Swallow asked.

'They forced the back door, Sir.'

'Did you examine it?'

Shanahan paused.

'I … I thought someone else did that. Maybe the uniformed men, they were first on the scene.'

Shanahan was a careful, conscientious detective, but like every man in G-division he was working long hours and extra shifts in an effort to meet its workload. He looked tired and crestfallen and Swallow had no wish to embarrass him by highlighting an obvious omission.

'Maybe they did,' he said without conviction. 'I had a look myself earlier when I was out there, but I didn't see any signs of damage. They might have been let in or they might have had a key for the door. There are two big six-inch bolts on it, but they may not have been left open.'

'They could have had inside help, do you think?' Mossop asked.

'It's beginning to look like it,' Swallow answered. 'It's at least a possibility. So we need to find out about the servants, who they are and if there's any with doubtful connections. And maybe also any tradesmen or workmen through the house in the recent past.'

'I've got names for the servants and some other information on them,' Shanahan said, brightening as he flipped the pages of his notebook.

'Tell us,' Swallow said. Around the room, pencils were poised to take down the details.

'The coachman and groom is Timothy or Thady Spencer, aged thirty-five years, a native of Benson Street, Cork city,' Shanahan read slowly. 'He was away last night, gone to Cork to bury his mother, according to the McCartans. The cook is Nora Cahill, aged fifty-five years or so, from the village of Terenure. She had left the house around half-past six after she had prepared dinner. The maid is Cathleen Cummins, from Tipperary, aged seventeen. She served dinner to the McCartans around seven o'clock. That's them all.'

A well-built young constable with a head of thick, black hair, perched on a window-sill half way down the room, raised a hand.

'Wit' your permission, Sir,' he called to Swallow, 'I can tell you about Timmy Spencer.'

The constable's sing-song accent was unmistakably Cork.

Swallow nodded.

'Go ahead. Identify yourself.'

'Constable Dunphy, Sir, 126B. I'm from near to Benson Street in Cork meself and if it's the same Timmy Spencer as sat in school with me, he's a bad one. There's a whole family o' them. Thieves and gougers and troublemakers. If he's been workin' in this house, I'd say that someone should find out who he's associatin' with here in Dublin. Because I can tell you, they won't be annythin' but trouble. He likes to pretend he's with the Fenians but that's only an excuse for crime.'

Swallow acknowledged the young constable's information with an upturned thumb.

'Good man. We'll start by checking the criminal registry and we'll contact the RIC in Cork straight away. And if he's been holding himself out as political that should be in their security records too.'

'I think we'd better check the other servants against the records as well, Pat,' he told Mossop. 'They're probably harmless. But you'd just never know.'

He checked his own notes. The pounding in his head was receding and his concentration seemed to be restored. But there was a comforting reassurance in having the written checklist.

'Nothing significant from the registers in the boarding houses or hotels, I assume.'

Mossop shook his head.

'Nothing out of the usual. There's a few places yet to be visited today. None of the lads on surveillance with the Vanucchis, the Cussens and the Downes outfits have noticed anything out of the ordinary.'

The wall clock showed half-past nine. Time for the investigation teams to be about their tasks.

'Alright, Men,' Swallow closed his notebook. 'I think we've covered all we can for this morning. If anyone turns up anything that might seem even marginally significant on either the murder or the robbery, I'm to be informed immediately and the information logged with Sergeant Mossop, needless to say. We'll meet again in the morning.'

Now he could see the rain streaking down the day room windows.

'Take your coats and hats, Gentlemen. That's going to be down for the day.'

Chapter 17

The young G-man on duty in the public office appeared to be struggling over the occurrence book as he took details across the counter from a well-dressed but angry lady whose pedigree dog, from what Swallow could hear, had been stolen from her garden somewhere.

The officer called over her shoulder as Swallow started up the stairs to his room.

'Chief Mallon wants you in his office down the Yard as soon as you've finished the conference.'

He made a mental note to have Mossop or a senior man take the novice officer through the proprieties of dealing with distressed lady complainants. He could start with offering them a seat in the waiting room rather than having them stand at the counter. He might also be firmly reminded that a senior officer was always addressed by rank in public.

John Mallon worked mainly from the DMP headquarters building at the end of the Lower Yard. His principal office was beside that of the Chief Commissioner, Sir David Harrel, although he also had a secondary office on the first floor of Exchange Court. The distance from the back entrance of Exchange Court to the police headquarters was no more than a hundred yards. But it was sufficient for the rain to give Swallow a wetting as he traversed it.

'I think your warm summer is gone for a bit, Chief.'

He grimaced as he shook water from his head before taking a chair in front of Mallon's heavy oak desk.

'We've got worse news than the weather,' Mallon said tersely. 'But first, tell me, did you go to see Sir John McCartan?'

'I did, Chief. In truth it didn't go very well. In fact it may have made things worse.'

'What happened?'

'He was still angry and I'd say probably in shock from what happened. He threw out a lot of abuse about the police not doing their job, about the G-men who'd attended the scene. And he accused me of being drunk. He's going to make a complaint to the Chief Commissioner.'

Mallon groaned.

'How did you handle it?'

'I gave as good as I got, Chief. I said that, yes, I'd had a drink. In connection with my duty and that it wasn't against regulations. In the end I told him I was sorry to see him so upset and that I'd come back when he might be feeling better.'

'He's got the reputation of being a difficult man at the best of times,' Mallon mused. 'I'll have a word later with the Chief Commissioner and try to deflect any trouble. Did you learn anything useful?'

'I did, actually. It looks as if the gang had a key or some other means of opening the back door. It wasn't forced. So there's the possibility of it being an inside job. It turns out there's a coachman at the house, Timmy Spencer. According to McCartan he's gone to Cork to bury his mother, but one of the lads at the crime conference earlier said he knew Timmy Spencer from Cork. If it's the same fellow, he's a bad one, it seems. He's on the fringes of the Fenians too, or at least he claims he's a patriot. So we're checking with the Cork RIC and in DCR to see if they're one and the same. If they are, we might be on the right track fairly quickly.'

Swallow saw as a small degree of satisfaction register in Mallon's eyes.

'That's not bad. Any developments on the woman in the Poddle?'

Swallow recounted his visit to Lafeyre's morgue, the discovery of the diamonds and half sovereigns, and his inquiries with Ephram Greenberg.

'Ephram's as good an authority as you'll get on that sort of thing,' Mallon said. 'It's unusual to say the least. Very few corpses turn up with five hundred pounds' worth of gems and gold strapped around them.'

'Well, we're not sure we can connect it to the body, or what's left of it. But it's a fair supposition.'

'You're wise to keep this to yourself and myself for the present,' Mallon said. 'If it got out, we'd have every lunatic in Dublin claiming he dropped his grandmother's life savings into the Poddle. But just to be on the safe side, I'll minute the details in my journal and I'll advise Commissioner Harrel. We've got to protect ourselves against any accusation of trying to keep the lid on this. The boys in the Upper Yard would be very happy if they thought they could pinch us for trying to line our own pockets.'

He reached across the desk and lifted a Royal Mail telegram. 'Have a look at that.'

He pushed it across the desk and turned it for Swallow to read.

DISCUSSED WITH INDIVIDUAL INVOLVED STOP
PERHAPS WILLING CO-OPERATE FOR FINANCIAL CONSIDERATION STOP
TIME NEEDED TO SECURE FUNDS STOP MAY NOT EVEN BE POSSIBLE STOP
PLEASE TRY DELAY ALL THERE STOP
SALTHILL

Mallon jabbed at the end of the telegram.

'He's obviously talked with O'Shea and asked him to drop or at least to stall the divorce petition, as he said he would. Like most things in politics and police work, it seems that money could do the trick here if he can raise it. Have you heard anything further from Dunlop about what's happening at *The Irish Times*?'

'I got a message yesterday to say that "the goods had arrived" and were being examined. But they'd probably be returned in a couple of days. That's tomorrow. He said he thought they'd be offered elsewhere and he expected them to "go on the market," as he put it, very quickly. That's to say that the details of O'Shea's petition would be published without delay. "Within days, if not hours" as he put it.'

Swallow had rarely seen John Mallon despondent. But now he saw him drop his shoulders and bring his hands, palms-first, to his face, while uttering something between a sigh and a groan.

'Hours? Not even days? That doesn't give us much of a chance, does it?'

'No, Chief. Even if we could somehow delay the publication of this stuff it'd only gain a bit of time if Mr Parnell can't raise the money to quieten O'Shea.'

Mallon waved a hand expressively. He seemed to brighten.

'I've been working on the money problem and I think I can raise enough to keep O'Shea quiet for a while. But there's not much point if it's all going to be in the newspapers anyway. Even if O'Shea decides not to go ahead with the divorce petition, the papers will be able to say he'd been planning it and cite the reasons why.'

This was the first time Swallow had heard anything about Mallon raising money for Parnell. His mind ran through various possibilities. The chief of G-division had a good salary and probably some savings. But the requirement of satisfying O'Shea would go far beyond his capacities. The intelligence fund? He had access to money for informants. But he had never known it to run to more than a couple of hundred pounds, spread among perhaps dozens of informants, at any time. It would hardly cover O'Shea's dining bills for a month.

'Are you serious, Chief? It would take thousands to solve this problem. We know that O'Shea squanders money like a drunken sailor. He's on tick at every club and restaurant in London. If Parnell himself can't raise enough, what can you do, with respect?'

'You'd be surprised,' Mallon grinned knowingly. 'But I sometimes mix with a lot of very wealthy people in this city who'd happily sacrifice a little portion of their fortunes to keep Parnell in position.'

'For political reasons?' Swallow was puzzled. 'The people who follow Parnell aren't people with money. They're farmers or ordinary salaried folk, trying to make ends meet.'

'That's true,' Mallon said. 'But the people who have most to lose if the country descends into chaos are the wealthy business families. They've got the biggest stake in keeping things steady and they understand that if Parnell falls, what follows won't serve their interests or be to their liking.'

'There's quite a few wealthy people and there's a lot of wealth piled up all over this city,' Mallon gestured with both hands towards the ceiling. 'There's the distillers, the brewers, the railway owners, the people who run the big stores, the families that own those fine ships you see lined up by the Custom House, the people who own the big estates we passed two nights ago, going out to speak with Mr Parnell at Salthill. I've put some feelers out already to the Guinnesses, the Jamesons and the Arnotts. They're all people who love their country even if they don't go around waving green banners and carrying pikes. The money is there if it's needed.'

It made sense, Swallow told himself. There seemed no known limits to John Mallon's circles of influence or to his connections. But if Mallon could arrange for the financial problem to be solved, it might just be possible that he could deal with the newspapers, or more precisely, the potential source of their information.

'I wouldn't want to raise hopes unreasonably, Chief,' he said cautiously. 'But it could be that our friends in the security section might be persuaded not to put the details of O'Shea's intended petition into the public domain if *The Irish Times* refuses to run with the story.'

Mallon straightened up in his chair.

'Christ, how would we do that? You know that they won't listen to us up there. The assistant under-secretary for security thinks we're Fenians and dynamiters that can't be trusted.'

The disciplined, policing part of Swallow's brain told him that his boss had a right to know what he had been told by Polson the previous evening in the Burlington. Something else, perhaps, the free-thinking, independent part urged caution. It might simply be a policeman's instinct to keep some information in reserve or at least to put some of it in separate boxes. More might be achieved by keeping things to himself for the moment. Occasionally, there were things to be done that the chief of G-division was better off not knowing about.

One of those things was going to be done very shortly. And he would be the one doing it. Or attempting to.

He stood.

'I think I might have a way of making those fellows listen on this occasion, Chief. If you can find the money Mr Parnell needs, I can probably do the rest.'

Chapter 18

First, he needed to talk urgently to Andrew Dunlop. He despatched a constable to *The Irish Times* office with a letter, addressed to the journalist, to be handed in at the newspaper's public office on Westmoreland Street.

Sir,

Important that I see you urgently. Please advise bearer, in writing, of earliest suitable time and location.

Yours faithfully,
JS.

'Wait until you have a response to this from Mr Dunlop,' he told the constable. 'If he isn't at the office, find out where he is now and at what time he's expected back.'

He spent the rest of the morning scrupulously reviewing the files on the murder inquiry and the follow up on the robbery at the McCartan house at Templeogue Hill. Mallon had not asked him for any update on either, being clearly preoccupied with the problem of Captain O'Shea and the likely consequences if he went ahead with his divorce petition. At all events, any new information on important cases would be relayed to the chief of detectives in the regular reports that were compiled by the clerical staff at the crime office.

The rain started to ease off around noon and by one o'clock there were patches of blue over the city again. He began to feel more at ease with the day, doing what he was most comfortable with and what he was good at. But he could find nothing significant in the reports so far of the various detectives and constables whom he had set to their tasks. There were no tantalising leads, no trailing strings, no unexplored angles. It was generally the way with crime investigations. At first, there was usually nothing beyond a victim and a crime scene. Then, as the slow-moving gears of the police machine engaged, some useful information should start to come in. And in time, a picture would be formed that would hopefully present more detail and point the way for further inquiries.

The constable was back from *The Irish Times* within the hour. Mr Dunlop was in Belfast, he reported, conducting interviews with political figures there, so he had been told. He would be on the three o'clock train out of Belfast to Dublin and was expected at the office by six. A clerk has assured the constable that he would be given the letter immediately upon his arrival. How long would Mr Dunlop be likely to remain at the office upon his return, the constable had inquired? Swallow noted the constable's initiative. Mr Dunlop would reportedly be at *The Irish Times* all evening after his return, typing up his copy in the reporters' room.

There was little more Swallow could do until Dunlop got back to town, he reasoned. But there was one important arrangement to be put in place for the plan he had in mind. It involved both Tim Hogan, the photographic technician from the RIC Depot, and Billy Gough, the manager at the Burlington. He wrote two short notes, sealed and addressed them and sent for the messenger-constable again. This time the job was to be simple delivery to the addressees.

His immediate tasks and routines complete, he leaned back in his chair to get the measure of the day. For the first time in the week, he could do some thinking on those parts of his life that had nothing to do with police work or crime. The moment his mind turned from these, however, it engaged with the unhappiness that now permeated his personal life. He felt himself becoming weighed down and helpless. Better to shut it out for the moment.

He realised, with something close to pleasure that today was Thursday. Lily Grant's painting class would be starting at two o'clock at the Municipal School of Art on Thomas Street. There was no reason he could not be there for an hour in the afternoon. He had missed the class over the previous three weeks and he was well behind on his assignment, painting a seascape of his choosing in watercolours. He had abandoned an earlier attempt to depict a stormy sea, battering the cliffs at Howth Head, with dark, lowering clouds above. No matter how often he mixed and remixed his blues and blacks and vermilions, he was unable to find the right combination to capture the anger and power he wanted the elements to express in the scene.

Instead he had chosen a tranquil view of the Shelley Banks, the cockle-strewn beach that stretched between the South Wall and the village of Ringsend. He was much more successful, he believed, contrasting the pale sand with strong blues and whites for the sky. He wanted to put some children and beach-strollers into the scene, but would that simply clutter a beautiful seascape? It was a dilemma, but it was an enjoyable one.

It was much more enjoyable than agonising on whether he could summon up the will to go back to Grant's and to Maria for his mid-day meal. There was time enough to get there, to be fed and then to walk down to the art school for the start of Lily's class. That would be the right thing. But the thought of having to engage now with Maria's anxieties and unhappiness was too much. He was too tired to take on her sorrow and her unhappiness just at this time. He would feel better after the relaxation of the painting class. It was always a calming experience. If he were to go back to Grant's now there was every likelihood of further unpleasantness. There would probably be, at best, an uneasy, tense silence. One or other, or maybe both of them, might say things they would later regret. That would only make matters worse.

He went downstairs and crossed the Lower Yard to the canteen instead. He was early. It would be a while before the various offices would start to shut for the dinner break. Many of the clerks would go home to be fed but it was well patronised by detectives with more predictable hours and uniformed men not working on the regular shift system. There was only a handful of diners when he got there so he had his choice of thick, corned-beef or steamed cod with jacket potatoes, carrots and cabbage. He took the corned-beef. There was porter on draught too, but he rarely touched it and never during the day, maintaining his loyalty to Tullamore, if the occasion for drinking presented itself.

The corned-beef was good, lean and not too salty. He had almost cleared his plate when he saw Pat Mossop at the door, scanning the canteen. He located Swallow and almost sprinted across the room.

'We've found McCartan's coachman, Timmy Spencer, in DCR,' he said urgently. 'He's all over the system. Robbery, larceny, assault. How in God's name he ever got work from anyone in the city, much less a Queen's Counsel, I don't know.'

He dropped a bulky file from the Crime Registry on the table.

'Have a look there yourself, Boss. He's been in and out of Cork jail so often they should name a cell after him. Maybe even a whole wing of the place.'

Swallow opened the file and flicked through the pages. Tim Spencer was just thirty-four years of age. The photograph showed a clean-shaven young man with strong, handsome features but with hard, defiant eyes. At a quick glance it appeared that all of his adult life, apart from a few years in the army, had been punctuated by spells behind bars. He had convictions in Cork, Limerick and Galway. There were six convictions for burglary or housebreaking, three for assault, three for handling stolen property and three for being found in possession of housebreaking implements, with innumerable charges of loitering, trespass and being found on enclosed premises. There was no record of any political convictions. But there were a few intelligence mentions of his being in company with Fenian activists, mainly in low-class public houses in Cork.

He found the charge sheet, for Spencer's initial conviction for possession of housebreaking implements, dated for five years previously. Spencer had been apprehended by RIC officers at night in the grounds of a private house near Bishopstown, outside Cork city. In a canvas bag he was carrying, the RIC men had found two crowbars, a glass cutter, suction cap and a wax mould kit, along with six blank mortice-type keys.

Clipped to the back of the DCR file he found a copy of Spencer's discharge from the army along with his service record. He had been stood down from the cavalry two years ago. His discharge was honourable even though the record disclosed a number of Glasshouse detentions for insubordination, brawling and drunkenness.

'And there's more, Boss,' Mossop said, once Swallow had run through the file. 'We sent an ABC to the crime office at Union Quay, asking for any up-to-date intelligence on Spencer and giving them his registry number. We said we understood he might be in Cork for his mother's obsequies. Union Quay just telegraphed back to say they know him of old. They say he doesn't live in Cork now. He visits his family from time to time, goes drinking with his pals but stays out of trouble. What's particularly interesting, however, is that they say his mother is very well. They seem to know her also.'

Swallow felt a small surge of satisfaction. He always enjoyed the sense of tentative achievement when the parts of an investigation started to come together. Wherever Sir John McCartan's coachman had got to, it appeared that he had certainly not gone to bury his mother in Cork.

He passed the file back to Mossop.

'We need to find this fellow, Pat, don't we?'

Mossop nodded.

'I'll get his photograph out to all stations immediately and we'll ask Cork for any information they have on his three H's. Haunts, habits and hoors.'

'Get the photograph circulated to the railway staff at Kingsbridge too,' Swallow told him. 'Platform porters, conductors, barmen at the stations. Start with the men who've been working on the Cork trains over the past two or three days. He's not gone to Cork to bury his mother but he might be gone there for some other reason. He seems to go back like a homing pigeon at intervals.'

He finished his dinner and took a mug of strong tea from the big, steaming dispenser on the canteen counter. Through the canteen windows he could see that the earlier rain had dried off and the sun was back, slanting across the yard, catching the turrets of the Birmingham Tower and the spires of the Chapel Royal. He took his tea outside and sat quietly on a window sill for perhaps a quarter of an hour, taking in the warmth. It would be a pleasant stroll to the art school. He finished his tea, returned his mug to the canteen and departed the Castle by the Ship Street Gate.

Chapter 19

Years of police work had brought him to an understanding that there could be many different and contradictory aspects to any individual and that character was a complex thing. Experience had taught him that sometimes in order to relate successfully to people, one had to put different parts of their lives into different spaces. The most brutal and determined criminal could turn out to be a loving spouse or caring parent. The most dedicated professional man could be cold and uncaring to his own flesh and blood. Thus, when he was in the art school in Thomas Street, Swallow thought only of Lily Grant as the class teacher. It was as if she ceased to be Maria's sister and thus his sister-in-law. He became oblivious of the fact that she was Harry Lafeyre's fiancée, and that they were to be married in the autumn. His relationship with her in the art school classroom was that between a willing, if average, pupil and a patient, talented teacher.

He had expected that when he would re-appear at the painting class, after an absence of almost a month, there would be something of a welcome from his teacher. But the moment he saw Lily's unsmiling face he realised that the woman now glaring at him was not looking upon him as a returned prodigal but as her troubled sister's neglectful husband.

'Mr Swallow. We haven't seen you here for a while.'

Her tone was curt. Cold almost.

'I've been busy, Lily. Professionally, I mean.'

She smiled in greeting as other members of the class assembled, taking their work and settling in at their accustomed places.

'So I've heard,' she answered him. 'You've had difficulties getting home to your wife at any reasonable hour.'

Clearly, she had been in recent conversation with Maria. He knew that was perfectly reasonable, but it irritated him. Notwithstanding, he decided to ignore the implied reprimand.

'I hope you can help me to make up for lost time with my assignment,' he said evenly.

Lily effected a sorrowful sigh.

'Oh, we've moved on from the seascape assignments. Yours is over there on the bench.'

She nodded to the other side of the room.

'We're doing the human form again this week and next. I was too ambitious in moving the class on from it earlier in the year.'

He was disappointed. He believed he had made progress with the seascape depicting the Shelley Banks. He disliked working on the human form because he was not very good at it. But there might be an advantage to be gained if the class was to focus on the human form. The man who modelled for the class was none other than Charlie Vanucchi, the leader of the city crime gang of that name.

Swallow needed to talk to Charlie Vanucchi.

'I was hoping you might give me some help with the seascape,' he said to Lily.

She stepped to the window, away from the others and beckoned to him to follow.

'Really, Joe, I think you'd make better use of your time today caring for Maria than being here. The fact is that her spirits are quite low.'

'You know that I care for her very well,' he said coolly. 'I've tried very hard to help restore her in every way that I can. But she's quite unresponsive. I'm not sure there's much more I can do until she decides to help herself or at least allow others to help her.'

'I know she's difficult just now,' Lily answered. 'She's even snappy with me, but she's been through such a lot. You have to understand how these things affect a woman. She's not chosen to be melancholic, you know.'

Before he could respond, Charlie Vanucchi came through the door, shrouded in a heavy, grey blanket that covered him from shoulder to ankle. He made his way, smiling, through the class, to the model's seat at the centre of the circle of student painters. He caught Swallow's eye and grinned cheerily.

'Ah, Mister Swalla' isn't it won'erful how we're brung together be the love of art?'

Lily had once shown Swallow some of Vanucchi's own sketches in charcoal. He had to admit grudgingly that the gangster had a certain, primitive talent, probably superior to his own. He often wondered if Vanucchi's decision to enroll in the class had been a calculated taunt. The relationship between detective and criminal was complex. Vanucchi sometimes acted as Swallow's informant when he picked up information about Fenians and other political extremists. And on occasion, when other detectives were on Vanucchi's trail for some crime, Swallow had marked his cards, enabling him to stay in the clear. Charlie Vanucchi was useful to Swallow on the streets of Dublin. He was no use to him behind bars.

At some stage, Vanucchi had also realised that the physiognomy he had inherited from his Neapolitan ancestors, with dark features, sallow skin and a lean, muscular body, made him a suitable subject for student groups like this. Swallow reckoned he enjoyed the element of self-exhibition involved. The attraction in posing nude for up to two hours in a frequently cold and draughty classroom was hardly the shilling fee he received from the Municipal School of Art.

He nodded in response, pointing to the clock and then to the door, indicating to Vanucchi that he wanted to talk to him when the class had ended. Vanucchi confirmed his understanding with a wink. Then he let the blanket fall to the ground and with a broad grin to the class, assumed his classic pose, legs slightly bent, torso forward and chin resting on an upturned palm, imitating some classical statue from antiquity.

Lily said a few, brief words of welcome and thanked the model, as convention required.

'Pencil or charcoal sketch only, please, ladies and gentlemen,' she told the class. 'We'll take, say forty-five minutes and then see how we're doing. I'd be particularly happy for you to focus on the model's facial structure and muscles as well as the neck and shoulders. But you may prefer to work on other parts of the anatomy. It's up to yourselves.'

The door opened again just as the students' pencils and charcoal sticks started to move across their drawing pads.

Katherine Greenberg stepped into the classroom, mouthed an apology and started to make her way towards her customary place at the side of the circle, next to Swallow.

'Well, Miss Greenberg,' Lily exclaimed. 'This seems to be the day we welcome back all of our lost lambs.'

Katherine smiled at her just a little too sweetly as she opened her portfolio.

'Thank you, Miss Grant. I'm sorry I'm a little late.'

'You can see what we're at, Miss Greenberg?'

Swallow smothered a grin. Katherine was by far the best talent in the class. Two of her watercolours had been accepted for showing in the spring by the Royal Dublin Society. And she had been singled out for mention in the quarterly report of the art school's council. Lily was thus obliged to treat her with a degree of respect that belied a conviction that her star-pupil had romantic feelings towards Joe Swallow. The fact that they long pre-dated his marriage to her sister was beside the point.

'Thank you, Miss Grant,' Katherine dropped her voice, not to disturb the others. 'I'll just carry on here with the subject, if that's suitable.'

She gestured to Vanucchi, reclining in his natural state.

Lily inclined her head in polite acknowledgement.

'Of course.'

The class worked on steadily for about three quarters of an hour. The only sounds disturbing the quiet of the room were the scratching of pencils and charcoals and an occasional murmured comment or observation from Lily as she moved behind each of the students, appraising their work. When she called the break, just before three o'clock, most of the students adjourned, as usual, to the canteen for a cup of tea.

Katherine stayed at her place and turned to Swallow.

'So, we've both decided to stop playing truant and get back to pursuing our muses,' she smiled. 'I didn't really expect to see you, after what you told us the other evening when you came to visit. And what with all these other crimes being reported in the newspapers. I feel so sorry for those people attacked in their home out at Templeogue Hill.'

'I just got an unplanned break from things. And I'd fallen behind on my seascape. I hadn't even realised the class had moved on from that project,' he shrugged. 'I didn't expect to see you either. You seemed to be very busy with the business.'

'Ah,' she waved a hand theatrically. 'You gave me the encouragement. Besides, my father says he thinks he might have some useful information for you on those items you brought in to us. He'd like you to come by to talk to you again when you can.'

She paused momentarily.

'I could have some supper for you, if you'd like.'

'Thank you. Tell him I'll do that just as soon as I can. I doubt it'll be this evening though. I've got a lot of police business in hand. Speaking of which, I need to have a word with our model.'

He consciously did not respond to her offer of supper. He hoped that perhaps she would think he had not heard.

Charlie Vanucchi had re-appeared in the room, swathed in his woollen blanket, a steaming mug of tea clutched in his hand.

He followed Swallow out into the corridor.

Swallow indicated a quiet alcove off the classroom corridor.

'Now, Charlie, I want you to do a little favour for me.'

Chapter 20

Mossop had set up a review meeting at Exchange Court for six o'clock. In addition to himself as bookman, it comprised Swallow, with Mick Feore, Eddie Shanahan and Stephen Doolan. A review meeting was just that. Most of the detectives and uniformed officers would still be out on inquiries, trying to complete their jobs list. The known results of the day's work, such as they were, would be considered briefly and the bookman would prepare reports for a full case conference in the morning.

Feore was dejected. His men had drawn blanks everywhere in their efforts to identify the woman in the river from the missing persons list .

'She's none of the four we've been trying to trace,' he said wearily. 'Mary Dunne turns out to have gone home to her mother in Galway to get away from her husband. Matilda Evans went out to Kingstown to get a job as a kitchen-maid. She likes the sea air so she didn't come back to Dean Court and didn't tell anyone. Mary Nelson from Portobello is deceased. She died of tuberculosis in the North Dublin Union but the family were ashamed to tell anyone. Annie Boland from Rathfarnham turns out to have run away with a farmer's son from out by Firhouse. They didn't think she was good enough for their darling heir. His family thinks they went to Scotland.'

Eddie Shanahan's inquiries on the McCartan robbery had borne no fruit either. Nothing of significance had turned up in the checks on the hotels and guesthouses. No informants or friendly sources in bars or doss-houses or in the brothels at

Monto had anything unusual to pass on. There was no word of unusually large sums of money being flashed anywhere.

'We've got Spencer's likeness out to every station, with spare copies for beat-men to show around,' he told the group. 'But there's nothing back yet from the lads checking the trains.'

Stephen Doolan reported that his teams had completed their searches along the Poddle and its underground tributaries. They had collected a great variety of old clothes and footwear, empty bottles, broken crockery, tin cans and pieces of sacking, bits of rope and twine along the river bank. These were now stored in the Kevin Street depot but there was nothing to connect any of the items to a crime.

'We checked the access points in the city as well, right down to the culvert in the Upper Yard,' he said. 'None of them is really secure. Locks are broken. Hinges gone. Bars rusted away. If someone wanted to drop a body through and into the water it would have been no trouble. All I can say is that we didn't spot anything suspicious.'

'So we've still no idea how or where she got into the river?' Swallow asked.

Doolan shrugged.

'I'm afraid not. It could have been anywhere between the Upper Yard of Dublin Castle and Tallaght.'

There was nothing more to consider. Mossop took his murder book and files and withdrew to the crime office to prepare his paperwork for the morning conference. Swallow did a final check on the correspondence of the day that had accumulated on his desk and locked his office.

The young G-man still on duty in the public office looked up as he came down the stairs.

'There y'are, Inspector. I was just about to go up to you. A young lad just dropped this in for you. Said it's urgent.'

He noted with satisfaction that the novice officer had picked up some manners since earlier, addressing him by rank. Perhaps someone else had checked him during the day.

He took the plain white envelope and withdrew the single sheet inside. The message was signed 'HORSEMAN' and comprised just one line.

2 AT 9

Number 2 was the location code for The Brazen Head public house. Number 9 was the hour at which Dunlop would be there.

He guessed that Dunlop needed time at the newspaper office to type up his reports after his return from Belfast, and he probably didn't particularly want to meet Swallow at any of the public houses where other reporters would be drinking at the end of the working day. That suited him fine. The Brazen Head on Merchant's Quay was convenient and he liked its dark snugs and aged wooden counters, polished to a shine by the elbows of generations of Dublin drinkers.

He left the building and crossed Dame Street into Parliament Street. He had time in hand so he decided to walk along the quays. He liked this closing time of day in the city, particularly in the summer. The sun was low to the west, streaking distant clouds with red. The sky over the city was clear and the air was balmy, as it usually is when the meteorological phenomenon that is the 'evening temperature inversion' occurs over Dublin Bay.

Unusually, the Liffey was being pushed back upstream by a high tide from the bay, its salty freshness dissipating the river's customary odours of sludge and mud. He crossed the quay to the footpath alongside the granite embankment wall, stepping smartly to avoid a steam tram, hissing and clanging its way towards the Phoenix Park. The still, evening air carried the laughter of the young couples on the vehicle's open deck, making their way to stroll in the Park's rolling acres, or perhaps by Islandbridge, where the river left the city behind and started to flow through wooded countryside.

It seemed an eternity since he and Maria had done the same as these happy couples, walking and talking and making plans for when the baby would arrive. When Swallow came home, leaving his police work behind him, Maria would hand over the running of Grant's to Dan Daly and the staff and they would take the tram to Parkgate Street. They usually went to The People's Gardens, between Chesterfield Avenue and the RIC Depot, so that Maria did not have to walk too far from the tram stop to enjoy its array of plants and shrubs. It was said that there was at least one thing growing in the gardens from every country in the Empire. They would sit by the little ornamental lake, watching the water-fowl, the swooping swallows chasing insects in the warm evening air and even the occasional deer, coming in from the open park for a cooling drink.

Everything was right then. They were happy in their marriage, living in the spacious accommodation over Grant's. Maria had already started to convert one of the bedrooms to be a nursery. She had moved the bed and the furniture out to make way for a cradle and had the walls hung with special wallpaper, printed with soft animal faces, from the Arnott's store on Henry Street. When the baby would be born, they had agreed, Maria would withdraw, at least for a while, from the day-to-day running of Grant's. That might be the right time, perhaps, for him to take his pension, step out of the police and become a full partner with her in the running of the business.

It all seemed so long ago now, although it was less than a year. It had been a happy interlude that he had never expected to enjoy, in a life that was otherwise largely marked by disappointment, failure and loss. The only success he could point to in his life was as a police detective. Not bad, it might be said. Some might even envy it. Passable pay. Plenty of variety. Security. A pension at the end of it. He was good at what he did. Was not his promotion the evidence of that? He even liked the work. So why did it all taste like so much dust in his mouth?

He wondered what Maria would be doing at that moment. Grant's should be picking up as the evening closed in. But it would not be overflowing with custom. It was Thursday, almost the end of the week, when the meagre wages paid out to Dublin workers on the previous Friday would be spent, for the most part. That was why Thursday was the pawnbrokers' busiest day. A good proportion of the money crossing the counters in the city's pubs this evening would have been raised on the back of humble goods put into hock by their owners for a shilling or two.

He hoped Maria would be downstairs in the select bar, presiding as she always did, coiffed and formal and very much in charge of her house. Perhaps he should divert to James's Street on his way to The Brazen Head to see. He could check by looking through the window from the street without having to go inside. But if she was not on the floor, he knew, she would in all probability be in the first-floor parlour, sitting, sad and silent in the dusk. And on this occasion, he knew, he had to be elsewhere. He could not go upstairs to comfort her. Not now. So what would be the point of knowing, he asked himself.

Sooner or later, he knew, they would have to resume their conversation and he would try to bring the pieces of their relationship back together again. Either that or it would wither and die. Neither of them wanted that, he believed. Perhaps the price he would have to pay would be to get out of the police and commit to working with Maria on the business. She was not a very young woman but she was not past child-bearing. The doctors agreed there was no reason why she could not have another child. Perhaps it might be possible to get back to where it had been before and retrieve the happiness. But he could not start down that road this evening.

The Brazen Head was not as quiet as he had expected. Two parties of naval ratings had somehow found their way there from their frigates, moored at the North Wall, evidently with money to spend. He liked to quote an observation once offered by John Mallon, that publicans along the river owed a great debt of gratitude to Her Majesty's Exchequer and the Royal Navy. Moreover, he reasoned, members of the Dublin police should be thankful that rowdy sailors helped to keep them busy and in their jobs.

In the event, these young Tars in their baggy trousers and white caps seemed to be well-enough behaved, beyond a lot of raucous singing and bawdy laughter. He surmised they had not been on the town for very long and had not yet consumed the quantities of alcohol to which they aspired. In all probability they would shortly migrate across the river to sample the wares on offer in the red-light district around Montgomery Street.

He took a vacant snug at the end of the house and ordered a large Tullamore from the barman. The singing and shouting outside in the bar faded and died, confirming that the roistering sailors had gone on their way. Then he settled down to await Andrew Dunlop's arrival and to tell him what he needed him to do.

Chapter 21

Friday, June 7th, 1889

It was nothing short of extraordinary, Swallow had to acknowledge, that Duck Boyle could come up with information about persons of interest to the police, from the lowest to the highest in the land. Since Boyle was a total stranger to hard work, it defied the odds and seemed contrary to all natural justice, he told himself.

More than once in the past, Boyle's extraordinary range of contacts, from the lowest scavengers in the slums, to those in the most privileged and elite circles of society, had enabled him to turn up a missing piece of information that could bring an investigation to a successful conclusion.

The corpulent former G-man, notwithstanding his aggrandisement in rank, was perfectly comfortable drinking in low dives with the kind of people who were shunned even by the city's criminal confraternity. Equally, he mixed with businessmen, high officials of Dublin Corporation and wealthy professionals. He particularly made a point of cultivating the acquaintance of as many publicans, hoteliers and restaurateurs as possible and made it his business to call upon them frequently. Good food and plentiful drink, free of charge, of course, helped greatly to cement these relationships.

In no small part, Swallow knew, Boyle's profitable connectedness with these elite circles was facilitated by his membership of the Brotherhood of Freemasons, otherwise known as the Ancient,

Free and Accepted Masons of Ireland. He frequented the Grand Lodge at Molesworth Street, close to Leinster House, the home of the powerful Fitzgerald family, the highest-ranking in Ireland's peerage. Policemen were prohibited from joining any secret or oath-bound society, but the Masons were an exception, representing as they did a network of Protestant influence that ran through the business, professions, clergy, civil service and even the police forces. Roman Catholics were forbidden by their church from being Masons so the majority of the rank-and-file in both the Dublin Metropolitan Police and the Royal Irish Constabulary could not join the brotherhood.

However, a high proportion of Protestant officers were members of various Lodges. It was commonly understood that being a Mason could help greatly in a policeman's quest for promotion or some other preferment. Duck Boyle's brother, an archdeacon somewhere in Ulster, was reputed to be highly placed in the brotherhood. He was certain to be a bishop, it was said, in knowledgeable circles. So it was not surprising that some of the benefits of his connection and influence might fall to other members of his family.

The morning conference at Exchange Court had not been encouraging. There was no progress on either the Poddle murder inquiry or the investigation into the Rathgar robbery.

'Ye may stand down yer search teams, so, Sergeant,' Duck Boyle had told Stephen Doolan when he reported that the last stretches of the Poddle tributaries had yielded no clues.

Pat Mossop had unearthed potentially useful information on Timmy Spencer's associates. Cross-checks in the Dublin Crime Registry had yielded half a dozen names of other criminals with whom he was suspected of orchestrating robberies in Cork, Limerick and Galway. The photographic section was at work turning out copies of their likenesses for circulation to both DMP and RIC.

'Every man without an assigned duty can just keep workin' around the city, showin' the likeness of this Spencer character,'

Boyle announced. 'As soon as we have pictures of his associates we'll have them out t'every station too. We'll find him sooner or later.'

Eddie Shanahan's team had been hampered in their task of interviewing railway personnel by the effects of a minor epidemic of summer influenza among workers on both the Great Southern and Western line and the Midland Great Western line; of the thirty or so men they wanted to interview, up to a dozen were officially on sick-leave.

'It is me understandin' from me inquiries with eminent medical men of me acquaintance that illnesses of the respiratory system, that is to say, the lungs an' chest, are more common among men whose workin' lives are spint in engines and carriages affected be steam an' fumes,' Boyle solemnly told the conference.

Shanahan nodded in polite assent.

'It's true. There's a whole lot of drivers, stokers, conductors and guards gone off sick on the Southern and Western and on the Midland Great Western. Some of them would have been working on trains between Dublin and Cork over the past week, so we haven't been able to talk to them yet. We're getting home addresses from the railway companies and we'll go to them wherever they are. Mostly they're at their dwelling places but one or two might be in hospital.'

'You'll probably find a few of them out playing football,' Stephen Doolan said cynically. 'The railways are notorious for absenteeism. I've a neighbour on the Great Southern and Western. When you ask him how many men are working there, he says "about half." And he's not embarrassed by it.'

There was brief laughter at Doolan's anecdote before the conference broke up and the various teams went about their tasks for the day. As the last of the G-men filed out of the room, Boyle put a pudgy finger to his mouth to indicate silence and nodded to Swallow.

'Could we have a private word, Swalla'? Somethin' kem me way that might be of interest to ye.'

They climbed the stairs to the detective inspector's private office. Boyle dropped himself into a padded chair by the desk and Swallow took his customary seat opposite. Boyle looked up and down the room and then at the ceiling.

'Ah, begod, this takes me back to whin I was in your job, Swalla'. Them were grand, aisy days.'

They were, Swallow thought silently to himself. Because when Boyle was the senior detective inspector at Exchange Court, most of the hard work was done for him by his then detective sergeant, one Joseph Swallow.

'Now,' Boyle leaned forward conspiratorially. 'There's a thing I want to tell ye about. It mighn't have a bearin' on the robbery, as such. But I picked up a little bit of a whisper. I'm not sayin' it's goin' to solve the case for you. But I heard that McCartan was threatenin' to report ye to the Chief Commissioner for havin' drink taken when ye went to see him. There's a bit of information you might find useful if he started makin' trouble for ye.'

Swallow found himself marvelling at Boyle's ability to source information. There was no official complaint, certainly not yet. So the word could not have spread through the police grapevine. He himself had told nobody of his exchanges with McCartan at his home. Was it possible that McCartan had told somebody else, perhaps even Boyle himself?

'It's true he threatened to complain about me,' he said. 'But I'm not concerned. I was perfectly sober and he was distressed and angry. You couldn't blame him really after what he and his wife had been through. It won't come to anything.'

Boyle shrugged.

'Yer probably right. But he might try to make trouble for ye. And us *polismen* has to stick together when we can. You an' I don't always agree on everythin', Swalla'. But we're in this job together and we have to look out fer each other.'

He chuckled.

'If *polismen* were to go worryin' every time some fella in a stiff collar says he saw them takin' some light refreshments, there'd be none of us left in the job. No, what I want to tell you has to do with McCartan himself. Personal details, if you know what I mean. He's not known as the most reasonable of men.'

'That wouldn't surprise me. So what should I know?'

Boyle dropped his voice to a whisper.

'I have certain contacts ... acquaintances ... if you know what I mean, who have a lot of dealin's with him. Business people who'd move in the same circles with him.'

Swallow arched an eyebrow.

'You mean your brothers in the lodge, or the coven or whatever it's called, where you all dress up in your fancy costumes and give each other funny handshakes?'

'Please, Swalla', let's have some respect for a very upright and very necessary institution. An' I have to tell ye that I can't impart annything of what I learn in lodge to someone who isn't a brother. So don't jump t'any conclusions about where I get me information from.'

'Alright, go on,' Swallow said amiably. 'You know I'm only trying to take a rise out of you.'

'Now, here's the situation,' Boyle whispered. 'There's been bad blood between that man McCartan and his wife for a long time. For most of that she's more or less locked herself away upstairs in the house.'

'When I visited the house, I gathered that his wife was invalided. She didn't appear at all.' Swallow said. 'There's no great news in that.'

'Ah, but there's more. A good bit more, in fact. They have a housekeeper. She's from Belfast too. Brought down specially by Lady McCartan to be her companion and to run the house for her. Well, now, accordin' to my information, this housekeeper lady has, so to speak, got above her station. She's makin' life miserable for t'other servants and takin' her meals with the master o' the house, if ye don't mind.'

He paused.

'There's strong suggestions that she's sharin' more than her meals wid 'im, if you get my meanin', Swalla'. He's not a young man. But there could be life in him yet.'

Swallow tried not to appear surprised. McCartan had made a brief, irritated reference to his housekeeper having gone away without notice. And Cathleen Cummins, the maid, had described her unhappiness at how she had been treated by her. It took him a moment to recall the name. Mrs Bradley. He wondered how much more Boyle might know.

'It wouldn't be the first time that kind of thing might happen, even in respectable Rathgar or Templeogue,' he grinned. 'Tell me about this housekeeper. Does she have a name?'

It was usually safer, he had learned, to give Duck Boyle only the information that was absolutely necessary. He traded in knowledge. And Swallow knew from experience that what Boyle learned from police colleagues was sometimes put into the wrong ears. If he told Boyle that the housekeeper had left the McCartan home, that would probably go straight back to his informant.

'Nah. I wasn't given a name or any details, just that she's from Belfast. Th' individual who gev me th' information believes that Lady McCartan wanted a housekeeper of her own particular faith, whatever that is, and she had t'advertise in the Belfast *News Letter* to find one.'

He pulled himself up from the armchair and made for the door.

'Like I said, Swalla', it won't solve the case for ye. But ye have somethin' there now to use agin' that fella McCartan if he tries to make trouble for ye.'

Swallow knew he was expected to respond gratefully. He forced a smile that he hoped looked sufficiently amiable.

'You're a good friend, Super. A brick.'

Bricks being heavy and dense, he told himself, he had no need to reproach himself for insincerity.

Chapter 22

Swallow had learned at an early stage in his police career that it was important to be on good terms with the clerks. It was arguably more important than being on good terms with the high potentates whom they served, the superintendents in charge of the divisions, perhaps even more important than knowing the two or three men of commissioner rank who were set above the superintendents. The truth was that very few rank and file knew these elite holders of high office, beyond perhaps exchanging a word at a formal inspection or ceremonial parade.

The clerk's job was to know everything on behalf of his master. He had to know every regulation and procedure so that he could deal with all administrative matters as well as handling incoming correspondence and preparing suitable replies to be sent out over his boss's signature.

Swallow crossed the Lower Yard and climbed the stairs to the offices occupied by the Chief Commissioner, Sir David Harrel, and his staff. Harrel's chief clerk, Sergeant Tony Bruton, had served with Swallow when they were both young constables at the Bridewell, in D-division. Every communication of any importance to the Chief Commissioner would pass through Bruton's hands. That would certainly include any complaint made against a policeman from a leading businessman and a QC.

'You could smell the tea from the Yard, if I know you, Joe,' Bruton laughed as Swallow stepped into the office. 'Take a seat and have a cuppa. It's just delivered fresh from the kitchen.'

The Chief Commissioner's offices had their own dining facilities with a cook, a waiter and a porter tending to his needs. As such, his immediate staff had no need either to visit the canteen or brew their own light refreshments.

It was good quality tea too, Swallow thought, as he sipped the hot, fragrant beverage.

'I need you to mark my cards on something, Tony,' he told Bruton.

'If I can, I will, Joe. You know that.'

Swallow recounted his visit to the McCartan house two evenings previously. Not surprisingly, Bruton knew most of the details of the robbery and the steps being taken in its investigation. Any crime or outrage affecting a pillar of society and a QC would have the direct attention of the Chief Commissioner's office and the investigation would be monitored carefully.

'McCartan accused me of being under the influence. I had a couple of drinks but I was perfectly sober. He said he was going to report me to the Commissioner. It might have been empty talk but I need to know because I want to go out to interview him again.'

Bruton nodded.

'Sure, if there's a complaint in, you'd probably be in more trouble by going to talk to him again. But there isn't. Nothing has come to this office, so you're in the clear.'

Bruton poured more tea.

'But since you're dealing with the McCartans, I can tell you a bit more about them. They're bloody difficult people. After my time in the Bridewell my promotion was to E-division, Rathmines. I was beat-sergeant there and the McCartans were a constant source of trouble. They weren't in the big house on Templeogue Hill then. They were in Garville Avenue.'

He laughed.

'They seemed to have a mission to persecute the *polis.* If a tramp called to the door there'd be a hullabaloo. There'd be a complaint at the station that the beat-man wasn't doing his job. One day a carter's horse answered a call of nature and dropped his manure on the street outside the house. They wanted the poor devil of a cartman prosecuted. It never stopped. That was typical. So the old super out in the E, Tom McKenna, the lord be good to him, was in and out of the house all the time, trying to placate them. He told me he figured that she was the real trouble because she was the one with the money there. Her family are big mill-owners in Belfast and that's how he got himself set up in business. His law practice is a bit of a sham really, so Tom believed. He's not making much of a living out of the Four Courts.'

He finished his tea and left Bruton to his files and correspondence. He had learned little that he had not already known about McCartan's irascible temperament. But it was helpful to understand a bit more about the family's inherited wealth. People born to money, in Swallow's experience, could be particularly intolerant towards those they perceived as the serving classes. That included policemen.

Half an hour later, sitting on the upper deck of the tram, making his way to Rathgar, he realised he was unsure precisely why he wanted to interview McCartan again. In part, it was in the hope that the passage of time would have cooled his temper and perhaps enabled him to recall some more detail about the robbery itself. And he wanted to know more about McCartan's coachman, Timmy Spencer, now gone missing. How did a young man with a serious criminal record land a nice job working for a wealthy public representative and a QC?

There was something more than that too, however. Boyle's gossip about McCartan's personal life, and the role of Mrs Bradley in it, might be of no significance. Neither might Tony Bruton's intelligence about the source of the family's wealth. Yet he sensed that there was something missing from the picture, something that he was not seeing and that these might be part of it. The more he turned the details over in his head, the more his instinct told him that what had happened at the McCartan home was no ordinary robbery.

He alighted, as before, after the Church of the Three Patrons and crossed to Garville Avenue. The facades of the solid, redbrick villas, fronted by well-tended lawns, were pristine in the June sunshine. A nurse was playing with two small girls in one front garden, their dolls' tea-set sitting daintily on a tartan rug, spread across the grass. At Brighton Square, the scent of summer flowers wafted out to the pavement as he made his way. Roses, hyacinth and, perhaps lily of the valley?

His reception at the McCartan house took him by surprise. Cathleen Cummins opened the door in answer to his ring. The bruises on her neck were now scarcely visible but she managed a hesitant smile in recognition.

'Good mornin', Sir.'

'Hello, Cathleen. I'd like to see Sir John if he's at home, please.'

'Oh, indeed 'n' he is, Sir. An' he told me if you came back I was to take you straight to him. He's in the drawin' room.'

That was quite a change, he thought, from his previous relegation to the kitchen.

She showed him into the room.

McCartan, wearing a barrister's formal morning dress but with his forehead still plastered, rose from a winged armchair, a sheaf of documents in one hand.

'Ah, Mr Swallow. I believed I would probably see you soon again. Please, take a seat.'

'Thank you. I hope you're feeling better after what happened. And Lady McCartan too.'

McCartan resumed his seat and placed his papers on a low table beside him.

'Your concern is appreciated, Mr Swallow. We're both recovered quite well, apart from my feeling a bit bruised and sore still. These stitches will have to stay in for perhaps a week, I'm told.'

He gestured to the plaster on his forehead.

'I'm glad you're here. I fear I was very intemperate the other night. I can only plead that I was still in shock to a degree. The whole experience was terrible. Terrifying. But it was wrong of me to vent it on you. Unfortunately, I can be rather short with people at the best of times. I understand that you have a job to do. It would please me if we could just put aside what I said, forget about it and go forward.'

Swallow always told himself he could sense insincerity or dissembling in others, but he picked up none of these in McCartan's words or tone.

'I'm sure that's right, Sir John,' he said cautiously. 'I can imagine the upset when something like this happens in your own home. I've actually experienced something not entirely dissimilar myself. What do they say, every man's house is his castle?'

'I'm sorry to know that, Mr Swallow. I hope there were no lasting ill-effects for you and your family. You are a married man, I think.'

Swallow sensed that this could turn into a long conversation if he were to recount what had happened to Maria and caused the loss of their child.

'We managed to deal with it, Sir. Thank you.'

McCartan smiled.

'I'm glad. Now, how can I help? Have there been any developments in your inquiries?'

'There have indeed, I'm glad to say. Although the investigation is far from being complete and we've not made any arrests as of yet. One of the things we've learned is that your coachman, Timothy Spencer, whom you believed gone to Cork to bury his mother, has a lengthy criminal record. He also likes to claim that he's involved with the Fenian Brotherhood. Oh, and his mother, according to the police in Cork, is hale and hearty.'

McCartan's look of astonishment was genuine, Swallow reckoned.

'Spencer? But he had impeccable references. I certainly wouldn't have employed him otherwise.'

'Forgeries, at a guess. There's a big trade in it. You'd be surprised at the people who decide to make a few pounds from being able to write flowery language with a good hand. Would it be possible to see them?'

'Certainly, they're in my study. If you'll excuse me for a couple of minutes, I'll locate them.'

When McCartan left, Swallow surveyed the high-ceilinged drawing room with its Italian mantle in white marble, fine furniture and generous windows opening on to the square, decorated with rich, damask drapes. An elaborate ormolu clock with matching vases sat atop the mantle. An elegant pianoforte filled the window bay. The room and its contents spoke of comfort and wealth.

McCartan came back and handed him three letters.

They read well enough. Conveniently, the referees were not located in Dublin. Two were in Cork city, one supposedly a priest, the other a medical doctor. The third referee was purportedly a landed gentleman in rural Galway. But even to Swallow's inexpert eye, there was a sameness about the writing in all three, albeit with unconvincing attempts to vary the ascenders and descenders.

'If I could borrow these,' he told McCartan, 'we have a handwriting expert available to us who might be able to tell us quite a bit about the author or authors of these. He might even be able to tell us his identity. Most of the forgers doing jobs of this kind will have come to our notice before.'

'Yes, please take them.'

Swallow placed the letters in his pocket.

'Did you know he had served in the cavalry?'

'I knew he'd had army service. But I didn't know any details.'

'Did you ask to see his service discharge?'

'He showed it to me, yes. He told me he'd been in a few scrapes but nothing too serious. I took him at his word. If they'd been of much significance he'd have had a dishonourable discharge.'

That was true enough, Swallow thought to himself.

'We have notified all police stations across the country that we want to locate Spencer. There may be a relatively innocent explanation for his disappearance and for inventing a story for you about his mother having died. But it's suspicious, to say the least. And his criminal record includes housebreaking, robbery and assault.'

McCartan nodded slowly.

'I'm very shocked, Mr Swallow. He has been an efficient and obliging employee. A good driver and a good man with the horses. Do you believe he might have somehow set up the robbery? I've done a little bit of criminal practice, as you know. I believe the term is "an inside job" when someone within a house or a business is complicit in a crime.'

'I think there's a real possibility of something like that,' Swallow said. 'The damage to your back door is superficial and wouldn't have been sufficient to force it open. You have two bolts on the door but it seems that neither of them was in the locked position. They may have had a key or a copy of a key. Would Spencer have access to a key to that door?'

'Certainly not. His quarters are in the coach house. He would have his meals in the kitchen with the maid and the cook. They would have to admit him. So there's a bell hanging inside the door and he'd ring on that to get in.'

'So who would have a key, then?'

'The cook, to get in when she arrives in the morning. The housekeeper, Mrs Bradley, would have had one but she left without giving proper notice. Lady McCartan and I are less than pleased about that, I can tell you. I have a full set of house keys, naturally.'

Swallow flicked the pages of his notebook.

'The cook is Nora Cahill, if I'm correct?'

'Yes, Inspector. But Mrs Cahill has been working here for maybe fifteen years. She's a respectable woman from the village – from Terenure that is – it's inconceivable that she could be complicit in anything like this.'

'And the housekeeper? A Mrs Bradley, I believe.'

'I'm certain if she were here the house would have been secure. She was nothing if not efficient about things like that. But there's no use regretting that now.'

Swallow tried to sound nonchalant.

'Regretting what, Sir?'

'Oh, that she left so suddenly. I … we thought she was quite happy here. But then she just cleared off. She told Lady McCartan she had personal reasons for wanting to go. I assume she went back to Belfast.'

'She didn't leave a forwarding address?'

'No.'

'A bit unusual, I'd say.'

'Yes, I agree. But my wife gave her the pay she was due.'

'How long ago was this, Sir?'

'Almost two months ago, Inspector. It was about a week before Easter. April twelfth, I believe.'

Swallow poised his pencil over the notebook.

'I don't believe we got full details about Mrs Bradley, Sir. Could we start with her full name, age, place of origin? Just basic details.'

McCartan seemed to pause for thought for a moment. But there was no hesitation in his voice once he started to describe the former housekeeper.

'Sarah Bradley. She's a native of Belfast. A member of the Presbyterian faith. She would be aged around thirty-five or thirty-six, I imagine. I believe her to be widowed with two young children who are being brought up by her sister, somewhere in Ulster. Her husband's death left the family unprovided for so she has been obliged to go into service.'

Swallow scribbled across the page, jotting the information as McCartan talked.

'May I inquire if she was satisfactory in her work, Sir?' he asked.

'Yes, I believe so. Although I had little direct contact with her. My wife has always been active as mistress of her house and has directed the staff. She placed an advertisement in the *News Letter* for a Protestant housekeeper and she chose Sarah … Mrs Bradley, that is, having satisfied herself as to her suitability.'

'So how long was Mrs Bradley employed by you here, Sir?'

McCartan suddenly seemed to become irritated.

'About two years, Inspector. But look here, none of this has any relevance to what happened here on Monday night. Mrs Bradley has been long gone. I think the man you want is Spencer. And he's obviously got a gang of associates as well.'

Swallow guessed it was time to show some appropriate humility.

'I'm sure you're right, Sir. It's just a matter of getting as much detail as possible. As a legal man, you'll know that some police work can, unfortunately, be less than thorough on occasion. I don't want that to happen in this important case.'

'Hmmm … well, that's very true,' McCartan's tone was more conciliatory.

'One thing that the local police at Rathmines mentioned was that you had a couple of dogs here at the house. Wolfhounds, I think. They'd have been a good deterrent to robbers, I'd have thought. But I understand they died. I'd be interested to know what happened.'

McCartan nodded.

'Yes, unfortunately. They died within a couple of days of each other. I believe they were probably poisoned.'

'Do you know who would do such a thing?'

'I've no idea. But I'd suspect now that it was connected to the robbery. Professional robbers would have known that the dogs would raise an alarm.'

'Did you report it to the police?'

'No, unfortunately. I wish I had. My wife had been particularly unwell over those days and I had an important case in court. I put it out of mind although I did wonder if some local farmer out here might have done it. My dogs were always well controlled, but there can be problems with sheep and livestock being attacked. We're just on the edge of the city here, with farmland all around. '

John McCartan was a complex man, Swallow told himself. If he was dissembling about the relationship with Sarah

Bradley and her place in the household, he was doing so with great skill. And he seemed to be able to be move from being choleric and angry to being charming and almost warm, with great ease.

'Now, is there anything further I can help you with, Mr Swallow? I've got some important briefs to work on here.'

He pointed to the files on the table.

'Of course. Thank you for your valuable time, Sir John,' Swallow said. 'You've filled in some important gaps in my knowledge. All that remains, for completeness at this stage, would be to speak briefly to Lady McCartan.'

McCartan thrust his hands deep into the pockets of his morning suit, stared Swallow direct in the eyes and shook his head slowly and gravely from side to side.

'I'm afraid that's out of the question, Inspector. Completely so. My wife is a very delicate woman who has already been subjected to a terrible ordeal. She is under the care of two experienced medical men who have ordered complete rest. The notion that she should be questioned by a police officer is simply not in the realm of possibility.'

It was clear that an unbreachable boundary line was being laid down. McCartan's tone was icy again. Swallow had no doubt that his request to speak with Lady McCartan had been anticipated and that every word of her husband's response had been carefully considered and rehearsed. It was time for a diplomatic retreat.

'Of course. But you'll understand that I'm required, nonetheless, to make the request, Sir. I hope that with rest and good medical care Lady McCartan's condition will improve. I'm sure it's a very anxious time for you both.'

He stood and crossed to the door leading to the hallway.

'Good day. Thank you for your co-operation and for your valuable time.'

Chapter 23

'We have him. We have him, Boss.'

Pat Mossop's face was lit with excitement as Swallow arrived back at Exchange Court. In one hand he held a telegraphed message that he stabbed at with the index finger of the other.

'Who've we got?'

'Spencer, Boss. We've located him.'

'Timmy Spencer? McCartan's coachman?'

'One and the same. He's in a monastery in Tipperary. This just came in to the ABC room from the RIC in Roscrea.'

'Are they sure?'

Mossop handed him the telegrammed sheet.

'See for yourself, Boss.'

The message, from the District Inspector at Roscrea to 'The Superintendent' at Exchange Court, was succinct but persuasive.

Sir,

Reference DMP circular and photograph seeking information on whereabouts of Timothy Spencer, native of Cork City, believed to be armed and suspected of involvement in crime. I beg to report that subject has been identified by a member of Dunkerrin station party to whom Spencer is known personally at location two miles distant from this office.

Subject is staying at Mount Saint Joseph Abbey, a foundation of the Cistercian fathers, situated in the area of Mount Heaton. Subject is resident at the abbey guest house which is frequently used by persons in distress or who have an addiction to alcohol and where the monks render whatever assistance may be possible.

I believe subject is unaware that he has been identified. Constables have taken concealed positions close by the monastery grounds in case subject attempts to leave location. I await your instructions in this matter.

Yours faithfully,
Edward Fleury (DI)

'What do want me to do, Boss?'

Mossop's excitement when things started to come right in an investigation sometimes reminded Swallow of a small boy in a toyshop. He hopped from one foot to another, with eyes twinkling in anticipation.

'What time is the next train to Roscrea?'

Mossop grinned.

'I knew you'd ask that, Boss. It's the four o'clock from Kingsbridge. I've got Swift and Vizzard standing by and there's an arrest warrant on the way from the Bridewell as we speak.'

'And I knew you'd have the answer, Pat.' Swallow laughed in response. 'It's best we go down ourselves and not leave the job to the RIC. It's our case and they're more used to prosecuting farmers for having unlicensed bulls than dealing with armed robbers.'

'I've requested a car to be here for three o'clock,' Mossop said. 'It's about two and a half hours from Kingsbridge to Roscrea. So I'll message the DI in your name. They'll probably be there to meet us at the Roscrea station.'

He handed Swallow a letter as he turned to the door.

'And there's something in here from Horseman, Boss.'

Swallow opened the envelope with his name on the front.

The goods are to be returned tomorrow evening (Friday) with regrets that they are unsuitable for use by this firm. I will meet the vendor at the previous location at 8.00 pm.

Horseman.

The timing was good, he calculated. In fact, it could hardly be better. Even if he was obliged to overnight in Roscrea, he could be back in the city on a mid-morning train. That would leave time to put in place any last arrangements for his plan to derail Polson's scheme.

He scribbled a quick note for delivery to John Mallon.

Chief,
The word from Horseman is that nothing will happen until tomorrow (Saturday). I have plan for after that. Am now on the way to Co Tipperary with arrest party in relation to McCartan case. When arrest of suspect is effected I will ABC details.
Yours faithfully,
J. Swallow (Det. Inspr.)

Before the police sidecar ordered by Mossop drew up at Exchange Court, Swallow repeated the standard check, required by regulations in anticipation of an armed arrest, with the three G-men.

'Firearms?'

Each detective drew his Webley Bulldog revolver from its shoulder-holder, showing fully-loaded chambers to the man next to him. Swallow drew his own firearm and displayed it to Mossop.

'Ammunition re-supply?'

Each of them displayed a metallic clip containing six rounds of .44 ammunition.

'Accoutrements?'

Four pairs of rigid, steel handcuffs appeared.

It was a time-honoured routine that some G-men complained of as archaic and unnecessary, but older denizens of Exchange Court remembered the unhappy fate of a colleague who found that he had forgotten to load his revolver on the night he stumbled upon a group of Fenians planting explosives on the Belfast railway line. When he called on them to put their hands up, one of them produced a pistol and fired. When the G-man tried to fire back, the hammer clicked on an empty chamber. The second shot from the would-be dynamiter took him in the chest and lodged in his spine. The man was paralysed from the neck down for the rest of his days and discharged on pension.

Roscrea would be the sixth stop on the train's journey from Kingsbridge terminus to Limerick. The magnificent terminus, designed by English architect, Sancton Wood, in the style of an Italian *palazzo,* was busy, with two trains recently arrived from Waterford and Cork, disgorging hundreds of passengers into the concourse. The carriages on the four o'clock, however, were pleasantly uncrowded and the four G-men had no difficulty in finding a spacious booth in a second-class carriage close to the buffet and bar.

Swallow and Mossop were well accustomed to armed arrest operations. Tom Swift, with five years of service in G-division, had sufficient experience to know more or less what was involved. Johnny Vizzard was the novice and was beginning to show his nervousness.

'Will this fellow try to use the gun … if he has it, that is?' the young G-man asked nobody in particular, as the train chugged out of the city's drab suburbs and into the rolling grasslands of west County Dublin.

'He might,' Swallow answered flatly. 'But with luck we'll take him by surprise and there won't be any real trouble. The one thing we don't want is a young man dead in a religious monastery. He's a criminal now, with a long record. But with a policeman's bullets in him, he'll suddenly be transformed into a hero and a patriot. There'll be ballads about him fighting and dying for Ireland.'

Vizzard laughed nervously.

'Aye, that's the way it happens, alright.'

He was twisting a blue cotton handkerchief fiercely between his fingers.

'Come on,' Swallow said, rising from his seat. 'It's a long journey and a hot day. I'll stand ye all a drink.'

The buffet bar was busier than the relatively small number of passengers might have suggested. A cluster of men with craggy, sun-burned faces and strong southern accents took up one end of the bar. Cattle-dealers, Swallow reckoned, heading back to Limerick after disposing of their fattened animals, now destined to be shipped to Liverpool, at the auction pens on the city's North Circular Road. Two or three others in business suits, gathered by the doors that connected theirs to the next carriage, were probably sales representatives, he guessed.

He ordered whiskeys for himself and Swift. Pat Mossop took a pint of porter. He usually chose plain rather than stout on the grounds that it was a penny cheaper, but as Swallow was buying he went for the stronger brew on this occasion. Vizzard did not drink alcohol and settled for a lemonade. They stood back from the bar and surveyed the countryside, now flying past as the train gathered speed. Soon they were passing through Swallow's native county of Kildare. He attempted to orient himself towards his home village of Newcroft. Somewhere over there to the south were the fields he roamed as a boy and the comfortable public house from which his mother and father made a modest living, sufficient to put his sister Harriet through teacher training college and him through medicine, had he not drunk his way to failure.

He had little sense now of ever having been that young boy. That whole world was gone, disappeared. As was the world he had moved through, when he was supposed to be studying to become a doctor. The memory of those two years at the Catholic Medical School on Cecilia Street, more than a quarter of a century ago now, was a blur of roistering, drunkenness and hopeless incapacitation. With Maria and the baby there had been a chance, perhaps, to create, finally, a place or state of contentment and happiness. But the baby was dead. And the distance between himself and Maria seemed to grow now with each passing day. Their world together had been a happy one for a time that seemed cruelly short. Would a day come, he wondered, when it too would seem as distant and unreal as that Kildare childhood, or the two years in medical school?

He brought himself back to the present and tried to identify landmarks between the stops. After Newbridge, he could see the distant outlines of the Curragh Camp, said to be the biggest military installation in the Empire. The low prominence of the Hill of Allen sat to the north. Next he identified the round tower of St Brigid's abbey and the squat outline of the cathedral at Kildare town. Then the train was skirting the flanks of the wide, boggy lands that stretched away, ablaze with yellow furze, into King's County. He could identify the rocky promontory of Dunamase topped by its ancient fortress, once the stronghold of the powerful O'Moore clan, close to the town of Maryborough. To the south, the low Slieve Bloom range ran, hazy blue, to the horizon.

They resumed their seats after one drink. The job they had ahead of them would require full alertness and clear heads. Even with the one whiskey, Swallow felt himself becoming drowsy in the warmth of the evening sun, coming through the carriage windows. He might even have been dozing lightly when the train slowed on the approach to Roscrea but he had come to full wakefulness before it came to a shuddering halt and the door was opened.

'Inspector Swallow?'

The dark-haired young man in a well-cut tweed suit who stepped forward to greet them as they alighted on the platform could not have been more than twenty-seven or twenty-eight. He held out his hand in greeting.

'Edward Fleury, DI. You're very welcome.'

Swallow decided the accent was Ulster. Rural Ulster.

'I've a car to take us down to the barracks.'

Dublin's police operated out of stations. The RIC had barracks. And Roscrea's barracks, a three-storey granite construction in the town's main street, with loopholes and steel shutters on the windows, lived up to the name. Swallow was struck by the long terraces of small, neat houses, built in uniform style as they crossed the small market town.

'Army housing,' Fleury announced, answering Swallow's unasked question. 'This is one of the best recruitment areas for Her Majesty's forces. Munster Fusiliers mainly. A few Leinsters too. The wives and families are well housed and well looked-after while the men are away.'

Once they reached the barracks, the young district inspector led the four G-men to his private office on the first floor.

'We're away from prying eyes here,' he told Swallow. 'The walls have ears and eyes around here. The news about four bobbies of some sort arriving on the Dublin train will be all over the town by now. So the quicker we move to get a hold of your Mr Spencer the better.'

He crossed the room, opened the door to the adjoining office and called a name that Swallow could not catch.

The tall man in civilian attire who came in was heavily set and probably aged around fifty.

'My Head Constable, Jerh Sullivan,' Fleury said. 'He's in the picture about why you're here.'

Sullivan nodded in greeting.

'Thanks, Sir. You're very welcome here. I'll show the gentlemen the lie of the land, so.'

He took a ruler from Fleury's desk and pointed to an ordinance survey map on the wall.

'The monastery is two miles to the west. Technically it's in King's County and you're in Tipperary here, but it's in our district. It's about half an hour to get there by car. Your man is staying in the Guest House. I know the layout quite well so I can bring you to the door. But the monks retire early. They'll be in their dormitories by now. So the place will be quiet and the horses and cars would be heard approaching. We'll have to leave the transport about a quarter of a mile away, outside the gates and go in on foot. I've got four men out there in concealed positions already and I've another six available for the arrest party.'

He turned to Fleury.

'That's all in accordance with your instructions, Sir, I believe.'

Head Constable Sullivan was a man one would be glad to have along for this kind of a job, Swallow reckoned. He liked his confidence, his easy presentation of detail and his respect towards a superior officer who was probably young enough to be his son.

'I'm sure that'll be more than adequate,' Swallow said. 'Do you know if he's armed?'

Fleury shook his head.

'We don't know. One of Head Sullivan's constables happens to have a brother who's a monk in the abbey. He went to visit him early this morning and he recognised Spencer having breakfast in the guest house refectory. He knew him from an investigation in Galway a couple of years ago. Arson and cattle rustling. He wasn't convicted because his barrister persuaded the jury he was political. You have a warrant, by the way, haven't you?'

Swallow pushed the warrant, issued just hours earlier, across the desk.

'There it is. All in order. But is there an issue about church sanctuary? If we go in to make an arrest are we likely to have a hundred angry monks at our throats?'

'I don't think so,' Fleury smiled. 'That's a bit of a myth. In fact, the abbot has called us out there once or twice to remove some troublesome characters who'd moved into the guest house. But I think it's best if we leave off the uniforms and do this job in mufti. The abbey is a curiously peaceful place, I find, even though I'm not of the same church. So the less show the better.'

'All that makes sense,' Swallow agreed. 'It's possible, maybe probable, that he has a gun. There was a gun in the robbery that we're investigating. It wasn't fired but we'd be best to assume it's the real thing and be prepared.'

Fleury had three cars available to transport them to the abbey, an official horse and trap and two short charabancs that carried his own men as well as the G-division detectives.

Sullivan's constables were all in plain clothes as well.

'No benefit in making a show of force or anything like that. The main things is every man is briefed on the job and has his revolver,' he told Swallow. 'We'll have a few Lee-Metfords as well but they'll stay in the well of the car unless they're needed.'

The Lee-Metford, newly issued to the RIC to replace the Martini-Henry rifle, Swallow knew, was a formidable weapon, capable of firing a full magazine of heavy .303 rounds quickly and with great accuracy. Hopefully there would be no need to deploy them on this occasion.

'You and I can travel in the trap,' Fleury said to Swallow. 'I'll tell you a bit more about the district as we go.'

The countryside between the town and the abbey was mixed farming land, some under tillage and some supporting small flocks of contented-looking sheep. Most of the dwellings they passed were single-storey, thatched cottages but here and there a few more spacious, two-storey houses stood facing the winding, hedge-lined roadway.

'It's quiet enough here now,' Fleury said, pointing across the farmland. 'Most of the bigger estates have been broken up. A lot of the tenants have bought out their holdings, thanks to the Land Acts and that's taken the heat out of things. You can see that some of them are doing better now. They're getting good prices for mutton, milk and even eggs. So they're starting to build good new houses, as you can see. But just a few years ago, before my time, all of Tipperary North Riding was troubled territory. There's a long tradition here of shooting policemen, not to mention land agents, bailiffs and estate managers.'

'So, how long have you been in the police?' Swallow asked.

'I'm six months out of the Depot Cadet School.'

Swallow laughed.

'You're not serious? You give the impression of being accustomed to command for a lot longer.'

'I'll take that as a compliment, Inspector,' Fleury grinned. 'I did a few years in the army with the Enniskillings before I went to the Depot. My family has a good business in Omagh so my father bought me a commission. I could have stayed on. I was gazetted for promotion to major. And I enjoyed seeing a bit of the world, Singapore and South Africa. But I met a lovely young woman, got married and we've got two young children now, a boy and a girl. Families don't like the separation that comes with military life. So the RIC seemed a good option.'

The driver hauled the trap to the side of the road under a copse of beech. The charabancs, travelling a few yards back, came in behind. Swallow could see the grey outline of the abbey's buildings, perhaps a quarter of a mile away, through the trees.

The men dismounted from the charabancs and gathered in a circle around Sullivan. He pointed to a raised hedgerow running from behind the trees.

'The ditch there goes all the way to the monastic enclosure. We'll have cover almost as far as the guest house itself. There's men in position at the gates but there's three doors to the building so we'll need to split up. The main front door and the back door will be locked but the third door is always left open. That's to conform with the monastery's tradition of hospitality.'

'To be clear, now,' Fleury told the group, 'this is a DMP arrest, so Inspector Swallow and his men are in the lead here. We're in support. Is that clear to everyone?'

A murmur of understanding went around.

'You've all seen the photograph of the man we want,' Fleury said. 'So we don't want any mistakes. And we don't want any shooting unless it's absolutely necessary in self-defence. He may be armed. But even if he is, he's got to be given every opportunity to come in peacefully. I don't want anybody getting trigger-happy.'

There was another brief murmur.

'So, I'll lead the party through the door that's kept open,' Swallow said. 'Detective Sergeant Mossop and Detective Vizzard will cover the front door and Detective Swift will go around the back.'

'I'll be with Inspector Swallow,' Fleury said. 'Head Sullivan, where do you think you'd best be placed?'

'I think I'd best go in with you, Sir. I know the layout and the routine of the place. There'll be a monk on duty, if that's the term, to receive visitors in case they arrive late at night. He'll probably be in a bedroom, a cell they call it, at the top of the first flight of stairs. In all probability he'll know me and I'll ask him where we can find Spencer. There's about twenty rooms there, mostly with two or three beds in each. But they won't all be occupied.'

They moved off in single file, sheltering behind the ditch until they came to the point where it ended, just short of the monastic enclosure. Fleury silently indicated left and right to tell the parties to cover the front and back doors.

'That's ours,' he whispered, pointing to the side door. 'It's closed but it won't be locked.'

Swallow stepped from the cover of the ditch, walking briskly to cover the open ground. Fleury, Sullivan and the RIC men followed.

Perhaps ten yards from the door, he heard one of the constables shout from behind him.

'Look there. Look … the window.'

Halfway along the side of the guest house, a ground floor window had been flung open. Swallow glanced around in time to see the back of a man as his feet hit the ground. Then he was running, first across the gravel pathway that circled the house, then across the green sward, leading to fields beyond.

Fleury reacted immediately.

'Secure the house,' he shouted to Sullivan. 'I'll have him.'

Then he was sprinting over the pathway and into the meadow-grass, shedding his jacket as he ran, without slackening his pace.

Swallow threw his own jacket to Sullivan.

'Hold that. I'll follow the DI.'

Then he was running too. The ground sloped away at first and then levelled out. By now, the fugitive had reached the boundary fence that separated the monastery grounds from the farmland. He was fast and fit, no doubt. Swallow saw him vault the five-bar gate into the field. But Fleury was lithe and athletic. He too vaulted the gate, just a few seconds behind. By the time Swallow reached it, his own breathing was laboured so that he had to climb the bars, losing more time.

Now the land sloped downward again. A broad pasture, dotted with sheltering beech ran down to a river, where he could see cattle drinking. For a brief, unreal moment, he allowed himself to think how lovely it was, with the slanting sun silhouetting the contented animals at the riverbank. It could be the perfect scene for an artist.

Then he heard a shout and turned to see three of Fleury's constables coming up fast, revolvers in their hands. As he started to run, he heard shots from behind and felt the RIC men's bullets whistle past his head.

He turned again.

'Stop firing,' he shouted. 'Stop the bloody firing. We don't want him dead.'

If they heard him they took no notice. One man stopped, took an aiming stance, gripping his gun with both hands and fired twice at the fugitive again. Swallow saw him start to reload. He had to have fired five shots already, emptying his gun.

But Fleury was gaining ground. His quarry was almost at the river now. Swallow could see no way across other than a wooden bridge, perhaps a hundred yards downstream. The fugitive would either have to jump in the water or try to gain the bridge. He halted for a moment, unsure, and then decided to try for the bridge. But the moment's hesitation was enough for Fleury to close the gap between them.

Swallow saw the young DI barrel into the man, rugby-style, knocking him backward towards the river bank. They were both scrambling to their feet as he came up the last few yards to them. He heard Fleury call something he could not catch and he saw him step forward, hand outstretched towards the young man, now panting with laboured breaths.

He could hear the pounding feet of the RIC men coming up behind. There were more shots, two, maybe three from the constables. He saw the young man's right hand come up, pointing the black revolver at Fleury.

He shouted.

'Get away. I don't want to …'

The rest of what he said was indistinguishable. Fleury stepped back, arms raised. Swallow scrabbled at his shoulder holster to reach for his own weapon. Grasping the butt of the Bulldog he was close enough to see the young man's finger squeeze the trigger and to feel the shock wave as the heavy lead slug blasted from the barrel.

He was on the gunman even as he saw Fleury, in his peripheral vision, falling backward. He smashed the heavy Bulldog down on the man's face, his other hand fastening on the smoking gun. Now they were both on the ground, with Swallow on top. He brought the Bulldog down with full force a second time on his adversary's head. A third blow across the bridge of the man's nose brought the sound of cracking bone and a jet of bright blood. He heaved and squirmed, trying to get out from under the weight and to break Swallow's grip on his gun hand. But Swallow was heavier and stronger and held firm. Then there were other hands grasping at the man's wrists. A constable's boot came down hard on his neck, pinning him to the ground. Another boot drove into his side several times. Swallow felt himself being lifted to his feet as the prisoner on the ground succumbed to the accumulation of punishment and stayed still.

A hand touched his shoulder.

'Easy, now, Sir. We have him. Are ye hurt?'

Without answering, he turned to where Fleury lay on the meadow-grass, a constable kneeling beside him was whispering the Act of Contrition into his ear.

The right side of the young inspector's forehead was a bloodied mess of bone and brain, his eyes were wide open, staring at the evening sky. Swallow reckoned he had probably been dead before he hit the ground.

'I know he wasn't a Catholic like the rest of us,' the constable said apologetically, rising to his feet, pale and trembling, 'but sure, it can't do any harm, can it?'

'No,' Swallow told him. 'No, no harm at all.'

Chapter 24

Saturday, June 8th, 1889

John Mallon held his head in his hands.

'Jesus Christ, Swallow. This isn't good. Not good at all.'

'It isn't, Chief. I don't know what to say. We played it absolutely by the book. Fleury had a good plan. He seemed to have covered every eventuality. I can only guess that someone spotted us either in the town or as we travelled out into the country and passed the word along that there was a posse of peelers on the move. It's strong Land League country around there, the police aren't loved.'

'What happened then? Not the official version. The real story.'

'The truth is that the bloody peelers lost their heads. Fleury would have had Timmy Spencer if he'd had a few more seconds. Then they came up behind him, blazing away with their revolvers. I saw one fellow stop to reload. The marvel is that we weren't all killed. If they'd kept to their orders Spencer might never have produced the damned gun at all.'

'And the official story?'

'Oh, the usual. Warning shots were fired in the air.'

Mallon nodded slowly.

'That's a fact. The RIC Inspector General has been on to the Chief Commissioner, as you'd expect. That's his account too and they'll stick to it. The IG's fairly upset about Fleury. He thought highly of him, saw him destined for higher things.

He had managed to get on speaking terms with the local Irish language enthusiasts and the Gaelic games fellows. He was even taking lessons in the language. Then he loses his life to a little gouger like Spencer. There's a young widow there with two small children as well.'

'I know, Chief. He told me about them. I think his own family are more than comfortable, though. So they should be well provided for, at least.'

'That's some small comfort, I suppose. Presumably in all the circumstances you didn't get a chance to question Spencer about the McCartan case? Robbery's a small issue compared to murder.'

'No, Chief. But they're bringing him to Mountjoy later on today. We'll interview him as soon as he's lodged in there.'

'You look absolutely exhausted,' Mallon said. 'I'd strongly advise you to get some sleep before you do anything.'

He knew he needed a change of clothes, a shave, a good wash and a rest. The events of the previous evening and night were blurred with lack of sleep. He and Mossop had accompanied Head Constable Sullivan and the RIC men who had taken their slain inspector to the local infirmary where a young intern doctor on duty pronounced him deceased and at Sullivan's request reluctantly conducted a swift *post mortem* examination.

'Isn't it fairly clear what happened?' the doctor asked testily. 'The man's been shot.'

'It mightn't be so clear in a courtroom in three months' time,' Sullivan answered firmly. 'Your conclusions will probably be needed in evidence.'

The doctor shrugged and gestured to Fleury's body.

'Very well, if you insist. The man suffered a considerable trauma. It's consistent with a bullet wound. There's a wound to the right hemisphere of the head,' he told Sullivan. 'It wasn't very close, because there's no powder scorch on the skin. The bullet passed right through. It took a portion of skull away and a large amount of brain matter. Death would have been instantaneous. I'll do measurements , write it up and you'll have it in the morning.'

Swallow was not unimpressed. The young doctor seemed to know something of the relevant medical jurisprudence, notwithstanding his tender years. Perhaps he had more experience of dealing with gunshot wounds in this unsettled rural area than if he had been doing his internship in the city.

As they left the hospital, they sawTimmy Spencer, surrounded by armed constables, being treated by a nurse for the injuries to his head and face from Swallow's Bulldog Webley.

Later, as darkness fell, an undertaker arrived to prepare Fleury's body and to transfer it to the house in the centre of the town where he had lived with his family. The undertaker recommended that the coffin be closed because of the gross disfigurement of the head and face. Nobody disagreed with him.

Head Constable Sullivan had left it to a senior sergeant to have the local courthouse opened and to bring Spencer before a magistrate, to be charged with the murder of District Inspector Edward Fleury.

'You'd better go along there and give your evidence,' he told Swallow. 'You're the arresting officer.'

The courthouse was surprisingly spacious, with a mock Grecian façade and a well-appointed interior. When Swallow got there it was already half full with uniformed RIC men, some press reporters and a large number of townspeople who had gathered there as the news had spread of Fleury's death and the arraignment of the accused man.

Swallow gave evidence of arrest at farmland in a location the name of which he could not pronounce but which seemed to satisfy the magistrate who, according to Sullivan, was unhappy at being called from his manor house, some three miles away, at dinner time. The accused man stood steadily enough in the small courtroom, handcuffed to two RIC men, his face swollen and heavily bandaged.

'You're a DMP man?' the magistrate nodded towards Swallow.

'Yes, Sir.'

'What are you doing here in Tipperary North Riding?'

'I was pursuing inquiries in connection with serious crimes in the Dublin Metropolitan police district, Sir.'

'Hmm. And I suppose you wanted to question this man?'

'Yes, Sir.'

'Are you willing to tell us what these serious crimes amounted to?'

'I'd prefer not, Sir.'

The magistrate seemed relieved that he was not going to be unnecessarily detained by a narrative in which he had no real interest.

'What do you say to the charge?' he asked Spencer.

'I didn't kill anyone, yer honour.'

The magistrate looked exasperated.

'Enter that as a not guilty plea,' he instructed the court clerk.

He remanded Timmy Spencer to the custody of the Governor of Mountjoy Prison. The sergeant rose to say that as the last train of the day had already departed for Dublin, it would be necessary to hold the prisoner overnight in the police station. The magistrate nodded curtly and rose from the bench, signifying that the brief hearing was concluded.

The Roscrea police station on the main street was fervid with activity. RIC men from outlying stations had travelled into the town on bicycle or on horseback as the news of Fleury's death spread around the district. They milled around the front door and in the day room, smoking and conversing in hushed tones. Curious townspeople mixed with them, expressing shock and sympathy. A couple of newspaper reporters from *The Tipperary Vindicator* and *The Nenagh News* moved through the crowd, taking notes.

It would be Sullivan's unwelcome task to break the sorrowful news to Fleury's widow, still happily unaware of what had happened to her husband.

'The County Inspector's on his way from Thurles,' he had told Swallow before the court hearing. 'He should be here in about an hour. We'll go down to Mrs Fleury together. I'll get the minister from Saint Cronan's to come with us. That's where the family worship. I can't think of a harder job than what I have to do now. She's a gentle lady. A great wife and mother. And they were very close.'

Swallow's mind ran briefly to the night at the Rotunda Hospital when he had to tell Maria, who was heavily sedated but still in pain, that their baby was dead.

'There's nothing harder than bringing bad news,' he said simply. 'I don't envy you that task, Head.'

'Maybe when you're done at the courthouse you might want to come to the house to express your condolences,' Sullivan suggested. 'And you'll need billets for the night for yourself and your men, so I've sent a message down to the hotel to open up a few rooms. It's comfortable and they'll do you a good breakfast in the morning for your journey.'

Sullivan had allocated his own office at the RIC station to Mossop and Swift to enable them to compile a report for early transmission to Mallon in Dublin, providing them with paper, pens and ink.

'I know you fellows in the Metropolitan have these type-writer machines,' he apologised. 'They have them in Thurles but I'm afraid they haven't got out as far as Roscrea yet. I've arranged with the postmaster to have the telegraph office open for you with an operator. He'd normally close down at six o'clock.'

'Here's the story for the Chief, Boss.' Mossop handed him a single sheet of foolscap. 'I think it's all there, short of what's happened down at the court hearing.'

Swallow scanned the document slowly and carefully. As he expected, Mossop had compiled a succinct and accurate narrative of the day's events. He handed it back to him.

'I wouldn't change a word there, Pat. Just add in that the accused is remanded to Mountjoy and that we'll be on the first train back to the city in the morning. Then get it off on the telegraph.'

It was almost dark by the time he left the station to walk the short distance to Rosemary Square, in the centre of the small market town, where the Fleury family lived. Knots of people were gathered on the pathway leading up to the house and in the neatly-tended front garden, filled with summer flowers. Mostly they seemed to be men of consequence in the town. There were bowler hats and umbrellas, stiff collars and gold watch-chains. Through the open front door he could see that the hallway and front rooms were filled with people.

He pushed his way into the crowded sitting room on the right where Sullivan and two or three others seemed to have formed a protective ring around the young woman in a navy blue dress who sat weeping in an armchair that was much too big for her slight frame.

Sullivan stepped forward and placed a hand on Swallow's arm.

'This is Inspector Swallow, from Dublin, Ma'am,' he said quietly to the woman. 'He was with your poor husband when he died.'

Swallow reached out to sympathise. Her hand was cold as ice in spite of the warmth of the summer night. She looked up at him without focusing and opened her mouth as if to say something. But no sound uttered. He recognised the symptoms of shock.

'I'm very sorry indeed for your loss, Mrs Fleury,' he said quietly. 'Your husband acted with great bravery.'

She drew her hand away and stared away towards the window.

'Yes … I'm sure he … he did,' she said, after a long silence. 'Where … did you say you met my husband?'

'Ah, on police duty, Mrs Fleury,' he said tactfully. 'I had the privilege of knowing him as a fine officer.'

'What about the children's supper?' she looked at him quizzically. 'They should be in bed, you know.'

'The children are being looked after, Mrs Fleury,' Sullivan told her. 'They're gone above to my house and my missus will take care of them, never fear.'

There was no reply. She put her hand to her mouth and held it there with the tears flowing down over her fingers.

Sullivan caught his eye and nodded towards the door. They stepped out of the room into the hallway.

'The poor creature is overwhelmed,' Sullivan said. 'Her brother's a doctor over in Mountrath. He's just arrived now with his wife. So I'll ask him to give her something to help her rest. We'll start moving this crowd out of here to give them some peace. You can't do any more than pay your respects as you've done. Will you go down to the hotel and I'll be along in half an hour? We could probably both do with a couple of drinks.'

It was a long and a late night after Sullivan joined the G-men at the hotel bar. The big head constable had held his emotions together until he got a few pints of Rathdowney ale and three or four Cork whiskeys inside him. Two of his sergeants joined them at the bar. The RIC men were in disbelief at the events of the day. They were emotional about their DI. Edward Fleury had clearly been a popular and respected young officer.

The drink flowed and stories about policing were told until the small hours, some of them probably true, most of them well embellished in the telling, and a few, Swallow recognised, absolute invention. Finally, the exhausted barman retreated to his bed, leaving it on trust that the night's quota of alcohol would be paid for in the morning.

The first train to Dublin would depart from Roscrea station at seven o'clock. Mossop, Swift and Vizzard went to their rooms to snatch a couple of hours of sleep but Swallow stayed at the bar with Head Constable Sullivan until the thin light of dawn appeared outside the hotel windows. The hotel delivered on the good breakfast that Sullivan had promised and the G-men dined on generous helpings of porridge, followed by bacon, sausage, pudding and eggs, all washed down with strong tea.

There was an open car to bring them to the railway station. The RIC driver shepherded them through to the platform even as the train came into sight down the track. As the G-men boarded, an escort party of uniformed RIC men with carbines at the slope took the handcuffed and bandaged Tim Spencer down the platform to the last carriage, *en route* to Mountjoy Prison.

Strangely alert, in spite of the excess of alcohol and lack of sleep, Swallow itched to go down the train to question him. But it would be an unacceptable crossing of professional boundaries, he knew. Spencer was the RIC's prisoner now. He was going to be made amenable for the murder of one of their own. The investigation of a suburban Dublin robbery, regardless of the prominence of the victim, was a trivial thing by comparison. He settled back into his seat and started to doze as the train picked up its rhythm.

When he felt himself being shaken by Pat Mossop he realised he must have actually slept for most of the journey. They were steaming into Kingsbridge Terminus. The RIC had two open cars waiting to take Spencer and his escort to Mountjoy Prison. And there was a DMP open car to take Swallow and the G-men to the Castle. John Mallon would want a full and immediate briefing.

His head pounded and his stomach was heaving from the previous night. But it was warm and comfortable in Mallon's front parlour and he realised that he had dozed off again, having recounted the events of the previous evening.

Now Mallon repeated his earlier exhortation.

'Go home, Joe. Get some rest for a while.'

'I'm ... sorry, Chief.'

Mallon recognised his embarrassment and his hesitation.

'If you don't want to go to home, why don't you take a bed upstairs here for a couple of hours? You can wash up and shave later. I'll get someone to run up to Pim's to get a fresh shirt for you.'

He glanced at his pocket watch.

'Take a couple of hours. Sure, Mrs Mallon will put your name on the pot for dinner around one o'clock. We can leave other business until then.'

He was more than glad of the offer. He climbed the stairs wearily and slept solidly in the back bedroom of Mallon's house until a hard thumping on the door woke him almost three hours later.

The housemaid called through the door.

'There's a shirt for ye out here, Sir. An' there's hot water an' a razor an' soap.'

The hot water was reviving and he felt better for shaving away two days' of unkempt stubble. The shirt, procured from Pim's store, behind the Castle on South Great George's Street, was fresh and cool against his skin.

'You look a lot better,' Mallon told him as they sat to the table.

Dinner was a hearty Irish stew. As soon as he got some of the tender mutton, potato and carrot down, the nauseous effects of alcohol poisoning in his stomach started to abate.

'Thanks, Chief. I feel it.'

'I've a bit of good news,' Mallon said.

'That'll be welcome.'

'I've managed to get a bit of money together to see if we can keep Captain O'Shea quiet. It's less than I'd hoped for but it'll probably be enough to make him happy for a while anyway. It's about £3,000.'

'That's quite a feat,' Swallow said. He meant it. The Under-Secretary for Ireland, the top public official in the land, was paid £1,500 a year and that was an impressive sum.

Mallon sliced a floury potato on his plate.

'As I'd hoped, there are business people around who daren't support Parnell in public but who don't want to see him brought down. So they've been willing to contribute. It's all on a confidential basis, of course. Although at the rate O'Shea gets through cash, it won't last too long. I messaged Mr Parnell and he's very pleased. The money should be lodged to his account at College Green on Monday morning.'

He forked a portion of potato into his mouth.

'What news from our friend at *The Irish Times*?'

'The last I heard from Dunlop was just before I went to Tipperary yesterday. He says they'll be notifying Polson this afternoon that they won't run with it. So he'll be looking around to find a new outlet to publicize the scandal.'

Mallon frowned.

'The last time we spoke, you seemed to think you had a way of dealing with that, although you were being very mysterious about it.'

Swallow chewed on his mutton for a moment.

'I did, Chief. And I was. And by tonight I'll know if it's going to work.'

Chapter 25

Every prison had its own particular smell, Swallow had long concluded, having visited almost every penal institution in Ireland, as well as a few in Britain, in the course of his work. It was a product of what the authorities decided to put into the prisoners' diet, the substances they employed in order to maintain some sort of hygiene, the type of work that was done inside the walls, the age of the buildings perhaps, and something else that was elusive and indefinable.

The smell of Mountjoy Prison on the city's North Circular Road had many ingredients, he knew. These included boiled vegetables, animal fat, dank water from the nearby canal, human waste, sawdust from the prison workshops and strong disinfectant. The intangible element, he had decided, was the anger of youth.

Mountjoy was Dublin's local prison, where unruly young men served generally short sentences, sometimes no more than a few months. Convicts, those serving three years or more, went to Kilmainham or Maryborough. But for many of the young offenders, Mountjoy was a revolving door. Petty thieves, alcoholics, vagrants and ne'er-do-wells rotated in and out through its steel-studded door. The pent-up resentment and frustration of several hundred young men, doomed to a repeating cycle of arrest, imprisonment and release, injected something that was almost poisonous into the air of the place.

It also operated as a remand prison where men accused of offences were confined awaiting trial. Technically, prisoners on remand were innocent and benefited from a somewhat more benign regime. They got marginally better food, more of it, and larger cells where possible. They could wear their own clothes rather than prison greys and they were excused work.

But when Swallow and Mossop arrived at Mountjoy in the afternoon, the cell they were shown into by a senior warder to interview Tim Spencer was a cramped, cold space at the end of the prison's A-wing.

'We've no remand cells free at the moment,' the prison officer told them as they crossed the circle to the A-wing. 'They're full of politicals. We have to treat them with kid-gloves, you know. So your man has to put with what we can do for him. I'm sure you're not too sympathetic anyway.'

Tim Spencer was sprawled, motionless, on his bunk, his head still heavily bandaged. He turned slowly to sit up when he heard the door being unlocked to allow Swallow and Mossop to enter.

When Swallow introduced himself and Mossop, he spat contemptuously on the stone floor at their feet.

'I know who ye are. Ye tried to kill me back there in Tipperary, didn't ye? I know yeer type, useless, lazy cafflers. What d'ye want with me, now? I've said me piece already to the bloody peelers.'

Swallow turned to the warder.

'We'd like a bit of private time with the prisoner, if that's alright.'

'It's fine. But be warned, he's dangerous, this one. Had to be restrained when the RIC fellows were questioning him earlier. We don't like to use the handcuffs when a man's in a cell. But sometimes you have to. So be careful. I'll be outside. Just bang on the door when you're done.'

Immediately the iron door clanged shut, Swallow stepped across the cell, lifted Spencer from the bunk, took him around the throat with both hands and pushed him hard against the wall.

Mossop stepped forward, alarm on his face. He spread his arms wide.

'Easy now, Boss. This isn't right. That man's hurt already.'

Swallow relaxed his grip and moved back a step.

'Alright, Pat. Alright. But he needs to change his attitude. The reason he's hurt is because he pulled a gun to shoot a policeman.'

He jabbed a finger towards Spencer.

'We'll start with you showing a bit of respect, you little tramp. Don't make the mistake of thinking we're like the harmless country peelers who were in with you earlier. We're G-division. We can bloody well do what we like to you. You're not our prisoner so we won't be held answerable for whatever state you're in. Do you understand?'

Spencer drew himself painfully from the floor, leaning with outstretched arms to reach the edge of the bunk. A trickle of blood came out of his mouth and down his chin.

He made an attempt at speech through bloodied bubbles.

'Y ... you ... c ... can't ... do ... this. It's not right.'

Swallow took the Bulldog from its holster. He drew back the hammer and pushed the barrel against Spencer's forehead.

'I can fucking shoot you now, Spencer, and save the Crown the expense of a trial. Nobody would even ask me to explain myself. Although I wouldn't have any difficulty persuading a coroner that I shot you when you tried to get hold of my revolver. Now, will we try to start our conversation again?'

Mossop tensed himself, ready to grab at Swallow's gun-hand, if necessary.

Spencer nodded wordlessly and slowly pulled himself to a half-sitting position.

'Them peelers said they'd see me hang and to admit what I done. But I tol' them I wasn't admittin' to anthin' at all. So wha' ... what do ye want wi' me?'

'We're not concerned with you shooting that RIC inspector,' Swallow said. 'That's not our particular problem. We want to talk to you about the robbery at the McCartan house where you worked, at Templeogue Hill. There's a fortune of money and jewellery gone from that safe and it's my job to get it back to its owners. And that's before we start talking about the violence done to Sir John McCartan and his wife.'

Spencer visibly flinched.

'I'm not talkin' about McCartan or what happened out there. I was gone … I was gone to Cork when that happened.'

'Yeah,' Swallow said mockingly. 'We heard you were gone to Cork to bury your mother. God help the poor woman, rearing a son like you. But I understand she's in fine health.'

He let the Bulldog's hammer down gently and lowered himself on to the wooden chair beside the bunk.

'Look, Spencer, you know you're going to go to the gallows for shooting Inspector Fleury and there's nothing I can do about that. But I can try to get you more comfortable quarters and better food if you co-operate. Like I said, we're not here to talk to you about the shooting of the RIC man.'

'An' like I said, like I'm after tellin' ye, I didn't shoot him. I fired a shot but 'twas just to stop him comin' at me.'

'Well, it did that surely,' Mossop said sarcastically. 'His poor wife and the little children he left behind know all about it.'

'Look, I was in th' army,' Spencer wiped away more bloody bubbles from his mouth. 'I fired wide. I know how to shoot. I didn't know who them fellas were or why they were comin' after me. 'Twas self-defence.'

Swallow holstered his gun slowly.

Something about the way that Spencer spoke had struck a questioning note in his head. He knew that certain shift in tone or delivery from innumerable interrogations he had conducted with hundreds of suspects in the past. Often, there is a change in the way a subject delivers himself when he has nothing more to say. It may mark the point at which he has gone beyond caring whether his questioner believes him or not. Spencer's defiance and contempt were suddenly all gone. Now Swallow knew he was looking at something between despair and indifference.

It was just possible that the man was telling the truth. He had certainly seen him produce a gun and fire one shot as Fleury closed with him in the meadow by the river. But there had been a fusillade from the RIC men's revolvers as they closed in to where he had been cornered by Fleury. Where the shots went nobody would ever be able to say.

And the round that had killed the young DI had passed through his skull and was lost somewhere in the ground. There was no forensic evidence available to prove anything one way or another.

'I didn't know them fellas after me was peelers,' Spencer said quietly. 'How could I have? Sure weren't they all just dressed ordinary?'

'So who did you think they were?' Mossop asked. 'The Salvation Army?'

Spencer pushed himself up to a fully sitting position on the bunk.

'Look … you know enough about me … a man like me makes enemies. Lots o' them. That's why I was hidin' in the monastery.'

'A man like you doesn't usually spend a lot of time in monasteries,' Mossop answered. 'How did you even know about the place?'

'A few hard-drinkin' men from back home went up there for the cure,' Spencer said. 'They said it was an aisey place to spend a bit o' time. The monks kinda take pity on the likes o' me. Nobody else does.'

There was something about the way Spencer expressed himself that almost elicited a sense of sympathy in Swallow.

He caught Pat Mossop's expression and knew that something similar was going through his mind.

'I can't promise you anything, Spencer,' he said after a few moments. 'It's going to be up to a judge and jury to decide if they believe your story. But I'll be the main witness. And I suppose it's just possible that I might be able to save you from the rope if I give my evidence the right way for you.'

Timmy Spencer reacted sharply. He seemed suddenly alert.

'How d'ye mean? What are ye sayin' to me?'

'I can tell the court I saw you raise your gun to shoot Inspector Fleury. Or I can say that I saw you threaten him … that I saw you pull the trigger, but I can't be sure if you actually hit him. There was a lot of lead flying from his own men. The bullet that struck him wasn't recovered because it passed right through his head. How can anyone say who fired the shot that killed the poor man?'

'Would … would that get me off?' Spencer asked.

Swallow shrugged.

'I don't think you'll walk free. But it would probably make the difference between a long sentence and being hanged. Being locked up is better than being hanged, I'm sure you'll agree. There's always parole. You could be out in a few years. You can plead that you didn't know Fleury was a policeman. In honesty, I'd have to testify that I didn't hear him identify himself as such when he had you cornered at the river. With some juries and maybe if you have a very good barrister it might work.'

Spencer nodded enthusiastically.

'But that's it. I know I didn't hit him. An' I didn't know he was a peeler. That's the God's honest truth of it. I thought them fellas were gangsters after whatever they thought I had.'

'You mean what you got out of the robbery at Templeogue Hill,' Swallow said.

'I might,' Spencer said cautiously. 'And I mightn't. There's nothin' to connect me to that.'

'Come on, Timmy,' Swallow said mockingly. 'Come on now, you know what I need from you, now, if I'm going to do what I can to save your neck.'

Spencer sighed. It was almost a groan.

'Alright. But there's more that you don't know about,' he said slowly. 'There's somethin' you haven't even guessed at. It's a lot more important than who robbed oul' McCartan and his missus. I can give you the case o' yer life. Ye'll be promoted and well rewarded. You'll be grateful for the day you met Tim Spencer. But I'll need a few more guarantees from you.'

Chapter 26

'Jesus, Mary and holy Saint Joseph.'

Swallow had rarely seen John Mallon show anything that might be remotely described as shock. There had been some occasions. The most memorable was on the May morning, seven years previously, when news had come through to the Castle that the Chief Secretary, Lord Frederick Cavendish, and the Permanent Under-Secretary, Thomas Henry Burke, had been assassinated in the Phoenix Park.

Mallon prided himself as always having the latest and the best intelligence on every political faction, every pressure group, every fanatic, moving or active in or around the city. And indeed his network of informants had given him regular reports on the people leading the Invincibles, who had carried out the assassinations. But they had not warned him about the gang of misfits and half-wits they had recruited to carry out the most spectacular political crime that Ireland would see throughout the Land War.

When he and Mossop had heard the astonishing tale that Timmy Spencer had to tell, Swallow realised that he had a timing problem. The information they had elicited from Spencer was crucial and ought to be reported without delay to their superior. Once Mallon was apprised of what McCartan's coachman had revealed, it would be essential to take immediate follow-up action. But at the hour that Swallow was making his way with Mossop back to the Castle from Mountjoy, he knew that Andrew Dunlop at *The Irish Times* was preparing to tell Reggie Polson that the newspaper was not going to publish any report about Captain O'Shea's intended divorce petition.

Swallow's plan, however, in order to have Polson abandon the idea of going to any other newspaper with his tawdry story, required that he should be present when the newspaper man and the security agent would meet.

'Take me through this slowly, Swallow, so I can be sure I've got it all right,' Mallon said. They were in the front parlour of the chief's house. Mallon's office staff rarely worked on a Saturday afternoon and he was usually to be found at home at that time.

'Timmy Spencer's story is that McCartan murdered Sarah Bradley, the housekeeper,' Swallow told him.

'Spencer says that Lady McCartan had hired Sarah Bradley herself. She's a member of the Presbyterian faith and she wanted a housekeeper of the same faith. Mrs Bradley told her she was also Presbyterian but Spencer says he thinks this was a convenient fiction.'

'That happens,' Mallon interjected. 'Religion is an easy badge to change.'

'But once she got settled into the house she somehow started to take over her mistress's place,' Swallow continued. Lady McCartan's health was deteriorating and Sarah Bradley started to take control of money in the house. After a while she didn't live or sleep in the servants' rooms any more. She took her meals with McCartan and according to Spencer she started wearing the wife's clothing and jewellery. Spencer says he could see the changes in John McCartan. He seemed to be increasingly influenced by Bradley. He handed over all sorts of responsibilities to her. She even had the keys to his private desk and to the house safe so she could pay the household bills and the other servants' wages.'

Mallon nodded.

'It wouldn't be the first time I've heard of that kind of thing either. There's been a few cases like it in England. Usually there's an affair of the heart going on. And then the master of the house or his mistress murders the wife. Sometimes they conspire to do it together.'

'Fair enough, Chief. But if Spencer's story is true, McCartan seems to have had second thoughts. He seemed to realise that this woman was taking over their lives. He says there was an almighty blow-up in the house one night. He was out in the stables but he heard screaming and shouting across the yard. He says he heard McCartan saying, "you will get out." Then he heard Sarah Bradley answering, "I will not." He says then he heard one of the dogs barking and howling and then there was silence.'

'I know it's early in the day,' Mallon interjected. 'But I think we need a drink.'

When he had poured two Bushmills he took his seat again.

'Go on.'

'The following evening McCartan calls Timmy Spencer into the house and tells him he needs to go out in the trap. He says that someone has poisoned the dogs and he wants to get rid of their carcasses. So Spencer asks him why doesn't he let him just bury them on the land? Oh, McCartan says, because they're poisoned and he doesn't want to have poison in the ground. There's cattle grazing there on the land around the house.'

'So then Spencer brings the trap around to the back of the house. Inside the back door there's a roll of carpet roped up tight with something ... or somebody ... in it. McCartan tells him to give him help to get it into the trap. So he does and then McCartan drives away. Three, maybe four hours later, Spencer hears McCartan drive the trap into the yard. He has to get up, stable the horse and clean up the trap. The carpet is still there but there's nothing in it.'

Mallon sipped at his Bushmills.

'Maybe it really was the dogs. Did Spencer see a woman's body?'

'No. But it only makes sense for McCartan to drive off on his own with whatever he has in the carpet if he's trying to conceal things from Spencer. If it was just to dispose of a couple of dead dogs, he'd have sent the coachman to do it.'

'Fair enough.'

'At all events, according to Spencer, Sarah Bradley wasn't ever seen again. Spencer says the maid, Cathleen Cummins, told him that the room she'd slept in was kept locked.'

'It's circumstantial,' Mallon said. 'But it's damned suspicious. Is Spencer willing to swear to all this?'

'He's a Corkman, Chief,' Swallow laughed. 'They do nothing for nothing. But I think I can do a deal with him. He could hang for Fleury's murder but if I give the evidence that I truthfully can, I think he'll get off that. He might get off with manslaughter and he'll surely go down for possession of a firearm with intent. That will draw a stretch of a couple of years.'

'That's an interesting trade-off. His life for his evidence against McCartan,' Mallon mused. 'I've met McCartan many times. Like yourself, I've crossed swords with him in court. I never thought particularly highly of him so I never wanted the Crown brief him for us. But I wouldn't have taken him for a wife-killer.'

'Ah, there's more, Chief. Spencer wants a written undertaking from you that he won't be prosecuted for anything to do with the robbery at McCartan's or for helping or concealing McCartan's killing of Sarah Bradley. If he gets that he'll make a sworn statement.'

'Well, he doesn't want much, does he?' Mallon countered sarcastically.

'He knows how to play his cards, alright. He may not have had much schooling but he's a smart lad. He's not impressed with the word of a mere detective inspector. But he thinks you'd be a reliable ally. I told him that if we can recover the money and jewellery taken at McCartan's we might be able to do something about dropping any robbery charge. The truth is that we haven't any direct evidence linking it to him anyway.'

'That's a fact,' Mallon nodded. 'But if McCartan murdered this Mrs Bradley, shouldn't we have a body?'

Swallow downed the rest of his whiskey.

'There's the last bit of the jigsaw, Chief, I think.'

'How so?'

'According to Spencer, the cook at Templeogue Hill, Mrs Quinn, asked him the next morning about the master going off on his own in the trap the night before.'

'She knew about it too?'

'In a roundabout way. Her husband was walking home from The Morgue, that's the public house on the Blessington Road, after a few pints.'

Mallon's tone was impatient.

'Yes, yes … I know it.'

'And he tells his missus when he gets in that he's just seen Sir John in his trap down beyond the bridge, just halted there, in the shadow of the trees.'

'So?'

'That's the point at which the Poddle comes up over ground. It's not protected or fenced. A man could roll a body in there without much effort and be fairly sure it wouldn't ever be seen again.'

'Jesus Christ.'

Mallon grabbed at the Bushmills bottle.

'Jesus, Swallow. I didn't intend to have more than the one. But I need another after that.'

He poured for both of them.

'What we know about Sarah Bradley matches everything Harry Lafeyre has been able to tell us about the remains we took from the river,' Swallow went on. 'She'd probably accumulated the diamonds and sovereigns over various prior employments before she came to the McCartans. I'll wager that the set of keys we recovered down there will fit some of the locks at Templeogue Hill.'

'It's a hypothesis,' Mallon agreed.

'There's one other small detail that might tie in,' Swallow said. 'Harry Lafeyre found animal hairs, probably a dog, on the ligature around the neck of the skeleton in the Poddle. He thinks it was probably used as a lead or a tether.'

He raised his whiskey glass to Mallon.

'So Chief, how are we to feel about laying a charge of murder against one of the princes of Dublin's business community, a QC and a leading member of the Corporation?'

Mallon gulped down his own drink and reached again for the bottle.

'This has to be handled carefully. Very, very carefully. It's dynamite.'

He offered the bottle to Swallow.

'No thanks, Chief. It's been a hell of a week and it's been a long day already. And I've an important job ahead this evening.'

'What's that?'

'You're better not to know too much, Chief. But I'm hoping that at the end of it, Mr Reggie Polson won't be so anxious to do business with the newspapers.'

Mallon grimaced.

'I won't ask any more questions, so. I'd like to think about McCartan overnight, Joe. Maybe even until Monday. Spencer won't be going anywhere. We've a lot of problems right now. Not least keeping Parnell where he needs to be. If we lay a murder charge against a man like that we'd want to be damned sure we're right and that we can prove it. It'd be a sensation and one hell of a challenge with the resources we have. We'd make a lot of powerful enemies. I always try to avoid the mistake that Napoleon Bonaparte made.'

'What was that, Chief?'

'Making too many enemies by invading too many countries at once.'

Chapter 27

The Burlington bar was decently busy but not full. Some of the early evening patrons who had come for a few drinks after leaving the banks and insurance offices along Dame Street had repaired to the restaurant, leaving perhaps half a dozen tables peopled with serious drinkers who would probably still be there at closing time, Swallow reckoned.

Billy Gough, the manager, had promised there would be an alcove table reserved for him from nine o'clock. It had to be in direct line of sight of the bar counter, Swallow insisted. Gough was as good as his word. When Swallow took his seat he was looking directly at the long, polished mirror that ran behind the barmen's serving space.

The barman on duty was a recent hire. But he had served Swallow before and he knew him. And he evidently had his orders.

'With Mr Gough's compliments, Sir.'

He deftly landed the large Tullamore on the table and poised the soda syphon over it.

'A splash, Sir?'

Swallow nodded.

'Thanks. A good drop.'

The Tullamore's light taste, with the effervescence of the soda, was refreshing after the heaviness of Mallon's Bushmills.

The new electric lights, recently installed in the bar, had been switched on when Dunlop walked in, shortly after nine o'clock. He spotted Swallow and dropped himself into a chair opposite.

'I was half-expecting you wouldn't be here,' he said. 'Our correspondents down in Tipperary have been filing reams of copy about the shooting of the district inspector at Roscrea. And you're all over the story. By the sound of it you were lucky not to get killed yourself. So what happened?'

Swallow gave the newspaperman an attenuated version of the shooting and the arrest of Timmy Spencer.

'So you believe the attack on McCartan and his wife was an inside job. Is this Spencer fellow the ringleader or was he just a foot-soldier?'

'I'm still not sure about that. By the looks of it, he probably provided the key to let the gang get in through the back of the house.'

'So now he's above in Mountjoy on a murder charge,' Dunlop mused. 'His prospects wouldn't seem to be very positive, then?'

He motioned to the barman, mouthing the word 'Jameson.'

'That's an understatement.'

Swallow did not offer the journalist any account of his interview with Spencer in his cell or of his claim that McCartan had murdered his housekeeper.

'Do you know McCartan?' he asked.

'I do,' Dunlop said. 'He's a rather opportunistic Parnellite, I'd say. A difficult man. Pressmen find him singularly unhelpful. Aggressive even. And he's not even a particularly successful barrister. He's more of a businessman. And his success with that is due to his wife's money and connections, as I understand it.'

The barman deposited his whiskey on the table.

'We can talk about this again, if you like,' Swallow said. 'What time did you tell Polson to be here?'

Dunlop drew his pocket watch, glanced at the dial and grunted.

'I said half-nine. He should be here fairly shortly now.'

'What's he expecting to hear?'

'I didn't show my hand. I just said I'd have the editor's answer for him. I told him the editor was very interested in the story, which isn't untrue. If anything, I'd say he thinks we're going to publish. So he's in for a bit of a disappointment.'

'Any doubts or questions about what we're doing?' Swallow asked.

'Not a one. Let's just get on with it.'

Swallow raised his glass and clinked it against Dunlop's.

'Here's hoping this works, so, Mr Dunlop.'

Almost on cue, Reggie Polson appeared at the door. He glanced around the bar, surveying the tables and the patrons. When he saw Dunlop and Swallow he crossed the room and took a chair between them in the alcove.

'Inspector Swallow, Mr Dunlop, good evening to you both. You know each other, I gather.'

'You could say that,' Swallow told him. 'For rather a long time. We have a good working relationship, if I may use the term.'

Polson seemed momentarily nonplussed.

'I should have assumed that. This is a small city. Police and newsmen have to rely on each other in certain circumstances.'

'We do, indeed, Mr Polson,' Swallow said. 'We do. Now may I order you a drink? Scotch and soda, I believe?'

The barman was already on his way across the room with Polson's order.

He directed a short splash of the syphon into the Scotch.

Polson raised his glass.

'Thank you, Inspector. That's kind of you. Now, if you don't mind, Mr Dunlop and I have some private business to discuss.'

Swallow smiled coldly.

'Actually, Mr Polson, your business with Mr Dunlop isn't private any more. It would be more accurate to say now that Mr Dunlop and I have some business with you.'

Polson's eyes narrowed aggressively.

'I think you'd better be careful, Swallow.'

'Oh, I'm being very careful, Mr Polson. Very careful indeed. So careful that I've had photographs of you taken with a hidden police camera, located over there behind the mirror.'

He pointed to the shining glass behind the bar.

Polson flexed in his seat. His eyes darted momentarily to the mirror. But he made no attempt to move.

'What the devil do you think you're playing at? I've told you I'm here to meet Mr Dunlop. Now clear off, before I'm obliged to make you.'

He drew back his jacket to show the stock of his revolver.

Swallow put his hand to his head to scratch his right ear. It was the signal to Pat Mossop and Johnny Vizzard in the next booth to step out behind Polson. Vizzard jammed the barrel of his Bulldog, covered with a red flannel kerchief so it was not visible to the rest of the bar's clientele, against the back of his head. Mossop's left hand went firmly on Polson's shoulder while his right hand reached over and deftly lifted his weapon from its holster.

'Now, Mr Polson,' Swallow said, still smiling, 'there'll be no need for any of that kind of talk. Mr Dunlop and I need to explain some things to you.'

The two G-men retreated to their alcove table as Dunlop put a large envelope on the table and pushed it towards Polson.

'There you are, Mr Polson, or more correctly, Mr Smith. I'm returning your material that you so kindly offered to *The Irish Times* and I'm telling you that the editor has decided it won't be published in our columns in any circumstances.'

Swallow leaned across and grasped Polson's wrist as he reached for the envelope.

'Or anywhere else.'

'You're making a serious mistake, Swallow,' Polson hissed through clenched teeth. 'And I hope you're not doing the same, Mr Dunlop.'

Swallow relaxed his grip on Polson's wrist.

'No. You're the one who's made the mistake, Mr Smith. I believe that was who you were known as in your time in Madrid? You made the mistake of telling me in your drunken state, here in this bar the last time we met, that you were there last March when Richard Pigott supposedly committed suicide in the Hotel Los Embajadores.'

Polson snorted.

'I deny it. Casual bar talk. You had a lot of drink taken on that occasion yourself, Swallow. This is nonsense. And my name isn't Smith. Whoever he is.'

'I can help you there, Mr Smith, or whatever your real name is,' Dunlop intervened. 'You may remember a correspondent in Madrid by the name of Cornelius Clarke. You briefed him on occasion, and drank with him a lot, when you were supposedly an attaché at the British Embassy there, although, of course, the entire press corps knew you were an intelligence agent.'

'Yes. An Irishman with common sense and loyalty, for a change. It was a pleasure to know him.'

'You're not very good at reading people's loyalties, Polson,' Swallow said. 'Cornelius Clarke is a loyal Irishman, like myself. And he will testify that you were at the Hotel Los Embajadores and present when Pigott was shot. And I'll testify that you told me the same thing here in the Burlington Bar a few days ago. It's not easy to dismiss the evidence of a distinguished correspondent and the evidence of a senior detective inspector when they're saying the same thing. You're looking at a possible murder charge, Mr Polson.'

'Don't be ridiculous,' Polson gulped at his Scotch. 'I was a diplomat. I've got absolute immunity for anything I did in Spain.'

'Well, that's true,' Dunlop said. 'It's interesting, mind you, that you're not denying anything. You're merely saying you can't be held to account.'

Polson shrugged.

'Suit yourself.'

'You can be assured that I will, Mr Polson, and so will my newspaper. We are preparing a series of detailed articles, revealing how a British security agent was involved either directly or indirectly in the murder of Richard Pigott in Madrid. The articles will go on to reveal that, yes indeed, the agent in question, yourself, operated with a pseudonym, under the cover of diplomatic immunity from the British Embassy and that he briefed international correspondents misleadingly and deliberately to the effect that Pigott had taken his own life.'

Polson shifted uncomfortably in his chair. Swallow saw the scar on his face make a little twitch.

He realised he was actually enjoying this.

'I think we'll all have the same again,' he intervened cheerfully, raising a hand to the watchful barman.

'That will just be the first article,' Dunlop went on. 'On the second day, we'll explain to readers why Her Majesty's government, having promised Richard Pigott a great reward for bringing down Mr Parnell, then authorised its secret agents to silence him. The reason, of course, being that Pigott was going to reveal who it was that set him up to forge the letters supposedly linking Parnell to violence and terrorism. That trail, of course, would lead right back to the Cabinet and maybe even to Lord Salisbury himself. I daresay the government could fall.'

The barman delivered the fresh round of drinks wordlessly.

'Then, in the third article,' Dunlop continued enthusiastically, 'we shall reveal that the agent who was responsible for Pigott's assassination is currently working in Dublin Castle in the office of the Assistant Under-Secretary for Security, Mr Smith-Berry. We will say that he is working under the name of Reginald Polson but that he has had a number of earlier aliases, stretching back to other murky assignments in Cairo and elsewhere.'

He paused to shoot a jet of soda into his whiskey.

'Now, of course, each day's article will be accompanied by a stereotype illustration of this man, Polson, or whatever he calls himself, based on the photographs being taken of you, even as we sit here, by Inspector Swallow's colleagues on the other side of that two-way mirror behind the bar.'

He tasted his drink.

'Ah, that's good. I was never one for soda. I prefer still water. But I must say this is very refreshing.'

'So,' he resumed, 'by the second day of publication, of course, there will be uproar in Westminster. There will be extraordinary pressure on the government, sustained by our many colleagues in Fleet Street who delight in scandal and all its details. They'll demand an inquiry, of course. I'd expect resignations will be demanded, starting with your boss, Mr Smith-Berry, certainly extending to the Home Secretary and possibly the Prime Minister. You're going to become quite famous, Mr Polson, or should I say, infamous, if only for a short while. And, clearly, your career in the service of the Crown will be at an end.'

'Ah, that mightn't be such a problem, anyway,' Swallow interjected. 'Considering how they dealt with poor Pigott once he became a problem, they'll probably send someone to do much the same to you. So you won't have to worry about making ends meet for very long. You'll be dead.'

Polson had paled. He sat silently, staring into his Scotch.

'You bastards,' he said finally. 'What do you want of me?'

Swallow realised he was enjoying it so much that he was tempted to string out Polson's evident agony for a while longer. But he resisted.

'I'll come directly to the point, then, Mr Polson. We want you to help us look after Mr Parnell and to keep him in position for as long as he wants to be the leader of the Irish people and of the Irish Party at Westminster. If we have your assurances on that, I'd venture to say that Mr Dunlop and his editors will be able to find some way of filling those columns with newsprint other than the story of your life and times, illustrated, of course, with your likeness each morning.'

'Oh, I'd be delighted, I'm sure,' Polson hissed sarcastically.

'Good,' Swallow said. 'So, there'll be no more stories going to newspapers or periodicals about Mr Parnell's private life or about Captain Willie O'Shea and his wife. And there'll be no more details being passed to journalists about any possible divorce proceedings involving Parnell or O'Shea or Mrs O'Shea. Is that understood?'

Polson nodded without enthusiasm.

'I understand. I'm a realist. But it's not possible for me or anyone else to prevent O'Shea going ahead with a divorce petition if he wants to. If there's a petition lodged in the courts, that'll be a matter of public record and the newspapers will report on it.'

'That's undoubtedly true,' Swallow said gravely. 'But I have it on good authority that Captain O'Shea won't move any petition, for the time being anyway. I believe he may have, well, had a bit of good luck and that his immediate financial needs are being met.'

'If that's the case,' Polson said, 'then you've won this round. Believe me, there's nothing personal in this for me. I don't give a tinker's curse about Parnell or O'Shea. I'm just trying to do the job I'm paid for. And inadequately, at that.'

Swallow wondered if Polson was angling for a personal payoff as well. If he was, he was barking up the wrong tree.

'Now, there's a couple of other safeguards to this new understanding that we have between us, so I'd just like to explain what these are,' he said. 'You might have an idea that you could solve the problem you now face in the same way you dealt with poor Pigott. You might even make arrangements for me, or Mr Dunlop, or even both of us, to meet with, shall we say, some sort of accident.'

Polson swallowed a mouthful of Scotch.

'Perish the thought that anything untoward should befall either of you.'

'Quite. So, you need to understand that full copies of what Mr Dunlop was to have published about you are lodged with several sympathetic colleagues of his in various newspaper offices, and not just at *The Irish Times*. If anything were to happen to him, the material would be in print instantaneously and not just in Dublin either.'

He gestured across the room to where five men had occupied a table shortly after Polson had entered the bar. Even at that distance it was evident that they were not typical of the Burlington's clientele. Two of them wore cheap trilbies. One had a workman's cap on his head. Another man sported a loud, checked waistcoat. Another was wearing tight, scarlet trousers, with a glass-studded belt. An improbably bright diamante tie pin glittered on the silk shirt-front of the tall, swarthy man sitting in the centre of the group, nursing what looked like a very large Cognac.

Swallow signalled to the tall man to join them, drawing a fourth chair around the table.

'Now, Mr Polson, I'd like to introduce you to an individual who is, shall we say, well-known to the police here in Dublin. This is Mr Charles Vanucchi. Charlie, this is the gentleman I spoke to you about.'

Vanucchi placed his Cognac balloon on the table and stretched a hand across to greet Polson.

'I'm pleased to meet 'cha, Mr Polson. I've heard a lot about ya.'

'Tell Mr Polson about yourself, Charlie,' Swallow said, sipping again at his own whiskey.

'Well, I suppose, the truth is, Mr Polson, I'm what ya might call a hardened criminal, a ruthless killer, in fact. Actually, I'm not all that ruthless at all, compared with them characters over there. I only kill for personal reasons, like if someone has insulted a friend, or if they get in the way of my business. Now, some o' them fellas over there just kill because they like doin' it.'

He jerked a thumb over his shoulder at his four companions, drinking at their table.

'Them lads really are ruthless. They'd kill quick as look at ye. Me, like I say, I generally need a very good reason. And my good friend Detective Inspector Swallow here says he might give me that reason in respect of yerself.'

He gulped at his Cognac.

'My friend, Detective Inspector Swallow, has told me that you might want to cause him some harm, like, to get him out of the way. Now, I've given him an undertakin' that if any mishap should befall him, I'm not going to be hangin' around waitin' for some court or some judge to say you done it. I'm goin' to seek ye out and kill ye meself. Or mebbe send some o' the lads over there to do it.'

He jerked his thumb over his shoulder again towards his companions.

'One other thing, Mr Polson. You might think that you'd be safe by puttin' a lot o' miles between yourself and Dublin. But think about me name – Vanucchi. The Vanucchis come outta a stretch o' land between Naples and a little town called Ercolana, just a bit to the south of it. There isn't much in the line of career opportunity around there so we've spread all over the place. I've got brothers and first cousins and cousins to the fifth degree all over the bloomin' world. So if one Vanucchi, say in Dublin, needs a job done in, say, New York, or Capetown, or London or Cairo, or anywhere, it's not a problem. An' we're all more or less in the same line o' business. Do ye get me drift?'

Polson maintained his composure rather well, Swallow thought, in all the circumstances.

'I don't know anything about you or your family or what line of business you're in,' he told Vanucchi coldly. 'And I don't care. I've given an undertaking to these two gentlemen and I will honour it. You don't need to try to scare me. You couldn't anyway.'

He faced back to Swallow.

'I doubt if you play tennis, Mr Swallow. But if you did, you'd know there's a score in the game known as "advantage". It puts one player seemingly in the lead. But that lead can be as easily lost as it can be gained. You have the advantage now, Mr Swallow. But this isn't the end of the game, not by a long way. You Irish have a saying that it's a long road without any turning. Believe me, this road has many turns ahead. And you won't like some of them.'

Swallow grinned.

'No, I don't play tennis, Mr Polson. But I've a bit of an interest in an old Gaelic game called hurling. It's coming back into popularity now around the country, not that you'd know anything about that. It's played rough and fast and players can get hurt. They have a saying in hurling, "if you can't get the ball, get the man." I think it's fair to say that in this game now, we've got the man.'

Chapter 28

Sunday, June 9th, 1889

He slept fitfully in his underclothes on the first floor dormitory at Exchange Court and woke to bright daylight streaming through the un-curtained windows. He drew his watch from his jacket, at the end of the bunk. It was gone eight o'clock. The other sleeping spaces were empty. If there had been others there overnight, they were gone by now. He had no idea what time he had finished at the Burlington Bar or reached Exchange Court, but he had the clearest recollection of insisting to the others in the bar that, no, he was not going home to Grant's. He was in no fit state to face Maria or to engage in the difficult conversations that he knew were now unavoidable.

It had been a late night, or more accurately, an early morning in the Burlington Bar. Once Polson had departed, he and Dunlop had been joined by Mossop and Vizzard. Then Hogan, the photographic technician, emerged, declaring himself exceedingly thirsty, from his confinement in his concealed vantage point behind the bar. The G-men had to show appreciation in kind to Charlie Vanucchi and his toughs for their supportive appearance. And the criminals, in order to maintain their own dignity, felt they had to reciprocate. Dunlop ordered repeated rounds from the barman, hoping out loud that the newspaper would cover his not-inconsiderable expenditure. When it came to the official closing time of half-eleven, the manager, Billy Gough, designated the entire party as hotel residents, extending their entitlement to stay and drink all night if they wished. Then he joined the company himself.

Swallow was bombarded with questions about the shooting of DI Fleury and the arrest of Tim Spencer. Fleury was RIC rather than DMP, but he was a policeman. And an Irish one. A brother-in-arms. Every G-man knew that his story could be their own, in any given set of circumstances. They wanted detail. Could he have saved himself? Did he leave a wife and children? They lauded Swallow for bringing the assassin down. It was Charlie Vanucchi who put the question that the G-men wanted to know but were reluctant to ask. Could Swallow not have shot Spencer first, since he was so close? He gave a vague answer that told the drinkers he did not want to discuss that aspect of the incident.

He hauled himself to his feet and made his way to the washroom at the end of the dormitory. What he saw in the mirror was unflattering. His eyes were bloodshot, his hair unruly and he needed a shave. The clean shirt that Mallon had procured for him thirty-six hours previously was rumpled and grimy on the floor. The washroom had a Vartry water connection so he ran a tap to splash his face and head. It was sufficiently icy to numb the pounding in his temples, at least temporarily. Someone had conveniently left a razor on one of the washstands and he began scraping away most of the dark stubble around his cheeks and chin.

He knew it was Sunday. He realised he would be expected at the morning crime conference. He might even have to chair it. Because it was Sunday, the numbers present would be fewer than during the week and it probably would not last very long. But the G-men working on the Poddle murder case, as the newspapers had started to refer to it, as well as those still investigating the McCartan robbery, would report developments, if any, and they would need to be tasked for the day.

He knew he had to report to John Mallon on the apparently successful outcome of the encounter with Reggie Polson the previous evening. The chief of detectives could not know any details, but it was important that he should be able inform Parnell as soon as possible that there was no imminent threat of O'Shea's intended divorce petition being publicised.

He tried to order his thoughts as best he could while working with the razor. He needed to talk to Mallon about how best to proceed after Timmy Spencer's claims concerning the disappearance and murder of Sarah Bradley. First he would need Mallon to do a letter for Spencer, assuring him that his demands for immunity would be met. Then, assuming that his boss was willing to go along with that, he would have to take a formal statement from Spencer in Mountjoy. Once that had been completed, he knew, the standard investigative processes would have to be put in train. There would be a thorough search at Templeogue Hill. That would require a warrant. And manpower. The set of keys recovered from the Poddle would have to be tried in the various locks at the McCartan house. And McCartan himself would have to be questioned after caution. His reaction, Swallow knew, was likely to be explosive.

The pounding in his head re-started as he began to apprehend the complexities of the day ahead.

Discretion would have to prevail at the conference, he knew. It would be sufficient for the attendance to be told of the circumstances that had led to Spencer's arrest. They would have already learned the main details from the newspapers, at all events. But he would reveal nothing of Spencer's allegation of murder against McCartan and the probability that his victim, Sarah Bradley, and the woman whose remains had been taken from the Poddle were one and the same. If Spencer's information turned out to be wrong, or if Mallon decided against doing the deal he was asking for, the investigation would be stalled, probably permanently.

To his surprise and relief, Duck Boyle was at the rostrum in the Parade Room, ready to chair the conference. Any appearance by Boyle on a Sunday was a rarity. Usually, it signalled that something to his own advantage was in the offing. Swallow did not much care. The presence of the rotund superintendent meant that he would be spared the responsibility of chairing the conference with the devils of last night's drink pounding away in his head.

The conference, as he had expected, was brief, with a limited attendance. Fewer than a dozen G-men and some uniformed constables were gathered at the top of the room.

'Gintlmin, we'll show our appreciation, in the customary way, of Inspector Swalla's great work in Tipperary,' Boyle called out, as Swallow took his seat.

There was sustained clapping and cheering as Boyle reached across to shake his hand.

'An' in acknowledgin' Inspector Swalla's courage an' his quick actions, we'll also remember an' respect our RIC colleague, Edward Fleury, who gev his life in th' execution of his duty. So we'll all stand for a minute's silence.'

In fairness to Boyle, Swallow reflected as he stood in the hushed Parade Room, he could mobilise a sense of propriety when the occasion demanded it.

Pat Mossop looked a lot better than Swallow felt. He gave a coherent summary of a few snips of intelligence that had been gathered for the murder book over the previous twenty-four hours. A jeweller in Kingstown had reported that some gold half sovereigns had gone missing from their display case. One matched the date of one of the coins recovered from the river. A detective would visit him on Monday morning to follow up, checking any possible connections to known criminals. Information had been received about a woman who had gone missing from her home at Swords, a small village, north of the city. Because her husband was away, working in Scotland, her disappearance, around April, had not been reported. The RIC at Swords were making further inquiries.

The main focus of interest was the arrest of Timmy Spencer, although the robbery at McCartan's now seemed almost unimportant relative to the murder of a police inspector. Questions came to Swallow from the floor one after another. How did the RIC locate Spencer? Had he any political connections? Where did he acquire the firearm he had? Had he admitted to the robbery? Who were his accomplices? Where was the cash and jewellery taken in the raid?

He tried to adhere to the truth as closely as possible but he knew he was being disingenuous. A constable visiting the monastery had recognised him by chance, he said. Spencer had not been involved in any political crime that could be identified. But he was known to keep company with some low-level members of the Fenian Brotherhood in certain public houses in Cork. And he was known to have boasted to others that he was a sworn Fenian. He would be questioned more closely on these matters later in the day. No, he had admitted nothing, which was true. Nor had he identified any accomplices. There was no knowledge yet of where the proceeds of the robbery might be hidden.

'You'll understand that the murder of District Inspector Fleury has to be given higher priority than our robbery investigation,' he explained to the conference. 'We've had to step back to allow the RIC to do their work first. They've been questioning him about what happened in Tipperary. I don't honestly know if he's made a statement yet. But I'm planning to question him this afternoon at Mountjoy and I hope I can learn the answers to some of this when I do.'

Heads nodded and there was a murmur of comprehension across the group.

'There's nothin' much else can be done here, so,' Boyle announced. 'It's a grand, sunny mornin' out there so we'll all go about our business and resume our deliberatin' here tomorra' at the same time.'

He beckoned to Swallow as the detectives and constables started to file out the door.

'I'd add a word o' sincere personal congratulation, Swalla'. Knowin' you, I'd say you wanted to take this Spencer fella alive and at least that's come to pass. It won't be any comfort to the poor RIC man's wife and family but it'll give his colleagues satisfaction to see him at th' end of a rope.'

'He'll get a fair trial,' Swallow said tactfully. 'And a chance to say his piece. That's more than Fleury got.'

'Tell me,' Boyle leaned forward conspiratorially, 'did ye make any progress in that matter of McCartan and his carry-on with the housekeeper?'

'I'm working on it,' Swallow told him. It was not an untruth. 'I don't think you were far wrong in your information, Super. If I get anything solid I'll fill you in.'

If McCartan was indeed linked to the death of the woman found in the Poddle, he reminded himself, he would be required to report back with any developments to Boyle anyway. As superintendent of the B-division, where the remains had been retrieved from the river, he was technically in charge of the case.

When Swallow stepped out into the Lower Yard the morning air was filled with an irresistible aroma of frying bacon. He crossed to the police canteen and ordered black pudding and fried eggs. He took three thick slices of soda bread, slabbed with butter and washed the lot down with two full mugs of tea. The hot food and the sweet tea started to tackle the poisoning in his stomach and he started to feel half-normal again. The pounding in his head started to recede and he reckoned he was in a fit state to present himself to John Mallon.

Mallon was dressed for Mass when Swallow got to his house. Every Sunday, with his wife and children, he walked from the Lower Yard to the Roman Catholic parish church of St Nicholas of Myra on Francis Street. Husband and wife dressed impeccably if conservatively for this weekly ritual, knowing that every eye was upon the powerful chief of detectives as he led his family to their customary place at the front of the congregation.

'You don't need to know the details of how it's happened, Chief,' Swallow told him as they sat in Mallon's parlour. 'But

Reggie Polson won't be doing any business concerning Mr Parnell with the newspapers in the foreseeable future. I can't say the issue won't arise at some point. But we wanted time and I'm fairly sure we've got it.'

'I can hardly imagine how that might have come about,' Mallon said cautiously. 'But I assume it has something to do with the wretched condition you're in yourself this morning. You look as if you've been run over by a steam train. Twice.'

Swallow was a little taken aback. He had convinced himself that he had sufficiently recovered from the night before and attended to his appearance to pass himself off reasonably well.

'That's a fact, Chief,' he admitted. 'It was a challenging night. But it was in a good cause.'

Mallon grinned.

'Fair enough. Now, I've thought about Spencer and McCartan and what to do. I've decided that I'll give Spencer his letter of comfort. I can't say I like the idea but a lot of this job is about compromises and trade-offs, isn't it? We can't turn a blind eye to murder and even if it means that we make a new lot of enemies we're going to have to go after McCartan. You're fairly sure, aren't you, that Spencer is telling us the truth on this?'

Swallow nodded.

'I am, Chief.'

'In that case we'll need a warrant for the search at Templeogue Hill.'

'I guessed that's what you'd do, Chief. In conscience, I can't say that it was Spencer's shot that killed Fleury. And if it's a choice between clearing up a robbery or a murder, the murder has to come first. As soon as you can let me have the letter for Spencer, I'll go back to Mountjoy and take his statement.'

'You'll have to put Doyle in the picture,' Mallon said. 'That means you'll have to move quickly then on McCartan. Doyle won't be able to keep the story to himself. And anyway, it's his division so it's his case at the end of the day.'

'I understand, Chief.'

'It'll be best to question McCartan at his house, in the first instance. There'll be enough of a stink doing that but it'll be less so than if you take him to the station, either at Rathmines or here. Which of the magistrates do you think we should ask to do the warrant for a search? It needs to be someone who isn't connected to politics or the law and who can be relied upon to stay quiet.'

'I can get Dr Lafeyre to do that, Chief. He holds a magistrate's powers ex-officio. Once I'm done at Mountjoy I can go to his house on Harcourt Street and swear in front of him.'

'Good idea. And put maybe half a dozen men on standby to search the McCartan house.'

He stood and reached to a side table.

'Here's your letter for Spencer. Now, I'm going to Mass with Mrs Mallon. Parnell is crossing from Holyhead tonight on the mail boat. I'll arrange to talk to him as soon as he disembarks in the morning.'

He turned for the door.

'It'll be a long day and probably a late night for you, Joe. You can tell me it's none of my business if you like, but I take it that you won't be going home to Thomas Street and Mrs Swallow?'

Swallow realised he had not thought that far ahead. In fact he had hardly thought about Thomas Street and Maria at all since the shooting of Edward Fleury.

'Probably not, Chief. I'll take a bunk in the dormitory.'

'You're your own boss in such matters,' Mallon said, not unkindly. 'But it's time you put first things first. And your home and your wife should come first. You shouldn't be in that dormitory tonight.'

'I know that, Chief,' Swallow acknowledged. 'But I need to be in a better state in my mind to go back to Maria. I need to be able to give her my full care and attention if we're to make a go of things again.'

'Fair enough,' Mallon said. 'God knows, I'm not one who particularly leads by example in this, but I'd suggest you cut back on the Tullamore for a bit. The bed is upstairs again for you here tonight, if you want. But when we get these jobs out of the way, I want you to take a bit of leave and look after things at home.'

'I appreciate the concern, Chief. I genuinely do. And it's a lot more comfortable upstairs here than in the bunk up there at the office, so I'll take you up on that offer. I'd be glad if you'd extend my thanks to Mrs Mallon as well.'

He was tempted to climb the stairs to the quiet bedroom at the back of Mallon's house there and then. He could sleep for a couple of hours. But he knew he could not be certain that he would wake when he needed to. And if he was going to sleep anywhere on this Sunday morning, he told himself, it should be at home in Thomas Street, with Maria. He wondered what she would be doing at this time. Sunday mornings at Grant's were quiet and unhurried. It seemed an eternity since he had left the house, unable to find the necessary words to comfort her in her distress. He should be going back there, he knew. But he would have to be in better shape and in a clearer, less distracted state of mind, if he was to avoid making a bad situation worse.

Chapter 29

Swallow went to Mass at the Franciscans on Merchant's Quay. Mossop was Church of Ireland and had gone with his family to service at St Audoen's, as was his weekly custom. Swallow told him to be at Exchange Court after service to accompany him to Mountjoy, he would need a good notetaker in Timmy Spencer's interrogation. Then he sent a message on the ABC to Mountjoy police station, situated beside the prison, requesting the governor to have a room made available.

The Franciscans did the kind of Mass he liked. There was no sermon as such. His friend Friar Laurence, who had performed the marriage ceremony for himself and Maria a year previously, was the celebrant. After communion, he turned his back to the altar and addressed the congregation in a way that made Swallow want to stand up and cheer.

'It's a beautiful, summer day, my dear people. So I'm not going to keep you in here. Go out and enjoy it.'

He made a blessing with his hand in the sign of the cross.

'Oh, I nearly forgot. Do unto others as you would have them do unto you. That's what Jesus had to say on the Mount. That's all I have to say too. God bless you.'

In other circumstances he would have gone around to the friary, behind the church, to talk to Laurence and spend a little time with him. The elderly priest was passionate in politics, a fervent Home Ruler and Land League supporter. Swallow might even have confided in him and sought his advice about the difficulties that had arisen between Maria and himself, but the day ahead was already full. He filed out of the church along with the rest of the congregation and made his way back to Exchange Court to rendezvous with Mossop.

They took a northbound tram from Westmoreland Street to Mountjoy. Sackville Street was quiet, its shops and offices shut for Sunday. Even the flower sellers at Nelson's Pillar were having their day off too, although a small queue of people, some with children, had formed in the sunshine to climb the one hundred and sixty-eight steps to the viewing platform at the top of the monument, erected by public subscription to honour the victor of the naval battle at Trafalgar eighty years previously. In happier times, on a fine Sunday like this, Swallow remembered, he had climbed it with Maria. It was the best threepence-worth of a view that anyone could have, they had laughingly agreed later when they took afternoon tea at the Imperial Hotel. The great sweep of the bay stretched to the east, from Howth to Killiney. The mountains rolled away to the south towards Wicklow. The great central plain of Ireland lay to the west, shimmering in a green haze. Away to the north they could make out the peak of Slieve Foy in the Cooley Mountains.

The interview room provided by the governor for the questioning of Timmy Spencer at Mountjoy was not unpleasant. It was located to the front of the prison, close to the governor's own office. Its two windows were high and barred, but they faced to the south, receiving good light from the day outside.

With Spencer seated across the table, Swallow gestured to the two prison officers who had brought him from his cell, to remove his handcuffs. The bruising across the prisoner's face where Swallow had hit him with his Bulldog was turning from black to a mottled blue and yellow.

'Is the grub any better, now?' Swallow asked him, after the officers had left to take up their positions outside the door.

Spencer seemed to be in good spirits.

'Not great now, but there's a bit more of it. It's better than the army. Not as good as down in the monastery. I wouldn't mind a few pints of porter though. Murphy's, if you can arrange it. I wouldn't touch that Guinness stuff.'

'That's not within my gift,' Swallow smiled. 'But I have something else for you. Can you read, Timmy?'

'Enough.'

Swallow took Mallon's letter and pushed it across the table. Spencer opened the envelope and read the single sheet, topped with the crown and the insignia of the Dublin Metropolitan Police, slowly and carefully.

'That's what I want, alright. You're a man of your word, Mr Swallow,' he said finally.

'Now, Timmy,' Swallow said, 'you're going to give me your statement about the murder of Sarah Bradley. Sergeant Mossop here will take it down and you'll sign it. But before we do that you're going to give me all the information I need about the robbery at Templeogue Hill and the other robberies that you've been involved in around Dublin. I want to know who else is involved, where I can find them and I want to know where the cash and valuables are that were taken in these jobs. You have a written promise there from Chief Superintendent Mallon that you won't be prosecuted for any offences to do with them.'

Spencer shifted uneasily in his chair.

'And you're going to swear that I didn't shoot that peeler down in Tipperary?'

'I can swear that you aimed wide. I can swear there were shots flying around from his own men's guns. I can swear he didn't say he was a policeman and that you had no way of knowing who was chasing you.'

'That's the truth of it, Mr Swallow,' Spencer said. 'I thought it was one of the gangs from here in the city. They don't like the idea of anyone operatin' in their territory. I know they were lookin' for whoever was doin' them robberies all over the place. There was even goin' to be a reward from yerselves for whoever could finger us. That's why I took off for Tipperary and stayed in the monastery. Like I told you, I knew a few lads from Cork who'd gone up there for a cure from the drink.'

He paused for a moment.

'Do you think they'll believe ye when I'm tried?'

Swallow shrugged.

'I don't know. There aren't any certainties. But I'm the best hope you have of avoiding the gallows. The only hope, I'd say. You'll be put on trial. Maybe for murder, maybe for manslaughter. If it's manslaughter and you're convicted you'll do time. Anything up to ten years, I'd say. But you might get off. It depends on the jury and what they think of you.'

Spencer was silent again.

'I'll tell you what you want to know so, about them robberies,' he said finally.

He turned to Mossop.

'Write down these names. Richard Walsh. Tommy Dillon. Andy White. Jackie Doolan. They're the lads in the robberies.'

'I need addresses,' Swallow said.

Spencer laughed uneasily.

'They're all together. Portobello cavalry barracks. That's where I did my own time, serving Her Majesty's Empire, and all that. Walsh and Dillon are grooms there in the stables. White's a farrier. Doolan's a sergeant, looking after the officers' horses.'

Swallow felt like kicking himself. It was all so simple and it all made sudden sense. G-men had worn out their boots, tramping around the city, checking boarding houses and dives to find some trace of the housebreakers who were not part of any of the usual criminal gangs. Nobody had thought of checking the various military barracks, half a dozen in all, dotted around the capital. The Military Police were generally well up to any anything of a criminal nature going on among the ranks. They had to have nodded in this case.

'Who's the main man, then?' he asked. 'Who came up with the idea?'

'That'd be Jackie Doolan. He'd know the houses likely to be worth a job. Then he'd roster the others so they'd all have their passes on the one night. They'd leave the barracks at different times and then they'd meet in a house off Clanbrassil Street to change out of their uniforms into mufti. They'd head out to do the job and they'd be back at the house in a couple of hours, change back into uniform and be back in the barracks before lights-out.'

'How would Doolan know what houses were going to be "worth a job" as you put it?' Swallow asked.

'Same way as he knew McCartan's would be a good mark. There's coachmen and stable lads all over the city who're out of the regiment. Like myself. You get an honourable discharge and it's easy enough to get fixed up with a job. I had my discharge papers and I, well, equipped myself with a couple of references. McCartan thought he was lucky to have me.'

'So, you're saying these fellows tip the word to Doolan? Did you do that with McCartans?'

'Yeah, Doolan keeps in touch with them all. His lads, as he calls them. They'll fill him in on what's in the house. Is there silver? Or good jewellery? Cash? How many servants? Is there a dog? What locks are on the doors? All the details that you'd need to do a job. Then there's a few quid in it for the information.'

'Where's this house exactly that you've told us about, near Clanbrassil Street? Who lives there?' Mossop asked. 'We need details.'

Spencer shrugged.

'I don't know the address but I could bring you there. I was only there the once. That was when they – we – did the job on old McCartan's place. Doolan's brother lives there. If he owns it or if he's lodging, I don't know.'

'That's where the loot is, I assume,' Swallow said.

'I'd say so. When we did the job at McCartan's that's where we brought what we'd got. Doolan gave each of us twenty pounds and handed everything else over to the brother.'

'What's the brother's name?' Mossop asked.

'Bartholomew. "Bart," for short. Bart Sullivan.'

There was something familiar about the name, Swallow told himself.

'Would we know him?' he asked Spencer

Spencer laughed.

'You should. There's a third brother. He's a bobby.'

Chapter 30

There were six G-men available, waiting beside three unmarked side-cars in the Lower Yard, ready for the raid on McCartan's. The drivers, also in plainclothes, stood gossiping and joking and occasionally grooming their patient horses, standing in line inside the Palace Street gate. Swallow and Mossop would travel in the first car. Shanahan and Swift would come behind. Vizzard and Feore would bring up the rear.

Swallow reckoned the right hour to reach Tempelogue Hill would be around nine o'clock. The household would not have retired to bed. The roads around the house would be quiet, with few passers-by likely to see the activity and possibly alert the neighbours that something untoward or unusual was happening. There would still be sufficient light in the evening for at least a preliminary search of the house. In any event, Mossop had provided every man with a Bullseye lantern for the illumination of any dark spaces, such as cellars or attics.

Harry Lafeyre had been taken aback when Swallow presented himself at his house on Harcourt Street, with a request that he sign the search warrant for the McCartan house in his capacity as a magistrate.

'I'll do it, of course,' he told Swallow. 'But you'll need to tell me what evidence you have to suspect him of murder. He's not the most pleasant of men but he's highly respected and well-known.'

Swallow handed him the signed statement that Timmy Spencer had made under caution earlier in Mountjoy.

'Read that. It's not conclusive, but it's enough to justify a search and putting questions to him. The physical descriptions we have of Sarah Bradley match what you were able to tell us about the woman in the Poddle. And we have evidence, admittedly at second hand as of yet, that McCartan was down where the river flows across open ground the night that Bradley disappeared.'

Lafeyre spread the statement on the surgery desk and read it slowly and carefully.

'I agree. It certainly justifies suspicion,' he said when he had finished. 'He heard what he describes as a heated argument between McCartan and the housekeeper. He heard the dogs snarling or barking. And he saw McCartan load what he says was Sarah Bradley's body into his trap and drive it away. Down here at the end, he says he hasn't been threatened or offered any inducements to make this statement and that he's doing it of his own free will. I suspect I could cause you difficulties if I were to press you on that, Joe.'

'I'd argue that offering to turn Queen's evidence is a well-recognised ground upon which to offer immunity to someone who's been involved with others in a crime. It's been done a score of times that I can recall over the years. We did it with the Maamtrasna murders. We did it with the Invincibles.'

'That's true,' Lafeyre agreed. 'Mallon's supporting you on this?'

'Of course. But I'll put all my cards on the table to you,' Swallow said. 'Spencer hasn't been threatened. It's quite the opposite, in fact. He's facing a murder charge and he's going to be hanged if he's convicted. But I'm not sure he actually shot Fleury, the RIC inspector. My evidence would honestly be that he fired a shot but he didn't want to kill the man. At least three of Fleury's own men were blazing away. It's at least possible that he was shot by one of his own.'

Lafeyre frowned.

'Are there forensics? Can they identify the gun that fired the fatal shot?'

'I'm afraid not, it passed through. It could be anywhere in a wide area of rural North Tipperary.'

Lafeyre reached to the inkstand, drew out the quill and signed the warrant with a rapid flourish.

'You'll take something since you're here? A glass of wine? Or something stronger?'

'I'd welcome a pot of tea, if that can be arranged.'

Lafeyre pulled on the bell-cord by the fireplace. After a brief interval his housemaid appeared.

'We'll have some tea please in the parlour,' he told her.

They crossed the hallway when they heard the clinking sound of china being laid in Lafeyre's parlour a few minutes later.

'You're being very temperate, Joe,' Lafeyre said casually, dropping sugar lumps into his teacup.

'Ah, I think I've been overdoing it a bit.'

Lafeyre nodded.

'Lily tells me you and Maria aren't doing so well. Has that anything to do with it?'

'Well, you know, things haven't been good since she lost the baby. She doesn't seem to have a lot of heart now. Or energy.'

He poured tea into his cup.

'I think I've tried everything I can to get her back to her old self. But it's not working, really.'

'There are physical side-effects of a miscarriage that can be distressing for a woman,' Lafeyre told him. 'And there are emotional side-effects. There are a number of medical men around the city who specialise in what the French call *les maladies mentales*. Someone might be able to help. Would you like me to raise that possibility with her?'

Lafeyre meant well, Swallow told himself. But he felt himself disquieted at the suggestion that Maria might require anything more than time to recover from the loss of the baby.

'No, thank you Harry. I think we can get the better of the situation between us. At least I hope so.'

He finished his tea, took the warrant and walked back to Exchange Court along St Stephen's Green, North King Street and South Great George's Street. The tea had been soothing and refreshing and had cleared his head. Now he had to concentrate on the business in hand.

Chapter 31

Swallow knew minutes after he had entered the house at Templeogue Hill and presented an outraged and astonished Sir John McCartan with Harry Lafeyre's warrant, that a disaster of his own making was unfolding before him.

He had deployed Vizzard and Feore to the rear of the house in accordance with standard procedure, while he and Mossop climbed the granite steps to the front door. Mossop rang the bell-cord while Shanahan and Swift stayed out on the gravel driveway, watching the windows to the front. When Cathleen Cummins, the maid, answered the bell, he and Mossop had stepped smartly into the vestibule.

'We need to speak with Sir John,' he told her. 'Tell him it's police business.'

Before she could answer, the door to the drawing room opened and McCartan stepped into the hallway.

'Inspector? What on earth do you want at this hour? We're about to retire for the night.'

The tone was both interrogative and irritated.

Swallow stepped forward and handed him the warrant.

'As you can see, Sir, this is a warrant, duly signed by a magistrate. It authorises me and my colleagues to search this house to seek and secure any evidence that may relate to the suspected murder of one Sarah Bradley at a date unknown. I hope we'll have your full co-operation.'

McCartan took the warrant in both hands to read it in the dim light of the hallway. Then he seemed almost to stagger, as if he had been pushed. He backed towards the drawing room door through which he had come. Swallow and Mossop followed.

The room was darker again than the hall. It succumbed earlier to the onset of dusk since its windows faced east. After a moment in which their eyes adapted to the gloom, they saw McCartan's wife half-rising from an armchair beyond the fireplace.

'Who are you?,' she called sharply. 'And what right have you to barge in here? This is outrageous …'

McCartan raised a hand to check her.

'Leave this to me please, Dorothy. These are policemen. There isn't any danger.'

He turned to face the G-men.

'How dare you? Hasn't my wife been through enough? Haven't we been through enough recently? What is this preposterous charge about Mrs Bradley being murdered. It's utterly ridiculous. She's actually in Belfast.'

Swallow prided himself on his capacity sometimes to pick up a tone of untruth in a spontaneous response from an interviewee. There was none of that in what McCartan had just said. It was his first intimation that all was not going to go well.

But he knew he could not allow himself to be deflected from following procedure.

'I need to warn you, Sir,' he told McCartan. 'You're not required to say anything if you do not wish to do so. But anything you say after this point may be taken down and given in evidence. Do you understand this caution?'

McCartan snorted.

'Good God, man. What d'you take me for? I'm a Queen's Counsel. I have no idea what this is about or why you're doing it. But I'm telling you now that at the end of this, you and whoever put you up to it will pay a heavy price.'

Swallow faced Dorothy McCartan.

'I'm sorry about this, M'am. I'm Detective Inspector Swallow and this is Detective Sergeant Mossop. There are a number of other police officers with us. We have authority to search the house as we have reason to believe that a serious crime may have been committed and that we may find evidence here. I've just showed your husband the magistrate's warrant.'

As he spoke, he could hear the other G-men in the hallway. Earlier he had sketched the layout of the house as best he could from memory and from the information given by Timmy Spencer. Now each man was going about his pre-allotted search tasks. His would be to locate and search the room that had been Sarah Bradley's.

McCartan had more or less recovered his composure. He handed the warrant back to Swallow and walked over to where his wife now stood.

'I told you previously that my wife is not in good health. I'd like to take her to her bedroom. I assume you don't intend to search there.'

'By all means let the lady go to her room, Sir,' Swallow answered. 'But I suggest she might be prepared to vacate it for a while later. It's not impossible that my officers will have to search there too.'

McCartan took his wife's hand and led her from the room. Swallow could hear their slow footsteps, ascending on the stairs as the sounds of the G-men searching came from the rooms close by.

'You can start with these,' he told Mossop, gesturing to the finely crafted, French cabinets, nestling in the alcoves between the fire-mantle. 'Any papers, documents or objects of interest. Put them out for examination. I'll get busy upstairs in Sarah Bradley's room.'

He climbed the stairs to the landing. The housekeeper's room should be at the end of the corridor at the rear of the house. The door, as Spencer had told him, was firmly locked.

He returned to the landing and called downstairs for Shanahan.

Shanahan had been apprenticed to a locksmith in Francis Street before joining the police and he still had some skills of the trade. Before they set out from the Lower Yard, Swallow had given him the set of keys recovered from the Poddle along with a copy of Hogan's photograph of them laid out individually against a foot rule.

'Your job is to try every key in every lock in the house,' he told him. 'That includes interior and exterior doors, cupboards, desks, wardrobes, safes. Anything with a lock on it. Then mark and number every match on the photograph.'

It was both a pragmatic utilisation of Shanahan's skills and a gesture of absolution from Swallow for the G-man's earlier failure to ascertain how the gang had gained access to the house.

'I need you up here to open a door for me,' he called to the G-man when he appeared at the foot of the stairs. 'Bring up the keys.'

Shanahan climbed to the landing to meet him, the key ring in his hand. Swallow knew from his expression that something was wrong.

'There's none of these fitting any of the locks, Inspector,' he said apologetically. 'I've tried every one of them in the back door, the front door, the kitchen doors and the out offices. There's a few locked cupboards in the pantry or larder or whatever it is. I've tried the small keys on them. There's not a match to be had anywhere.'

Swallow felt his heart sink. If none of the keys matched, the whole basis of the investigation and the search of the house was breaking down. If Shanahan was right, whoever the keys belonged to, they did not apparently belong to anyone resident in the McCartan house. The hypothesis that the remains recovered from the Poddle were those of Sarah Bradley would be in ruins.

'Are you sure?' he asked Shanahan unnecessarily. 'You've tried them all?'

'Absolutely, Boss. But I'll try the upstairs rooms anyway. You'd never know.'

None of the locks on the first floor responded as Shanahan tried one key after another. At the locked door of the housekeeper's bedroom, there was a faint click and a partial engagement between key and lock but no more.

'No good there,' Shanahan muttered. 'But the tumblers are loose. It's an old lock and I can manage it, I'd say.'

There was a sliver of space between the bolt and the receiver. Shanahan slid a penknife blade into the space and pushed to the left with one hand while rotating the key with the other. There was another click, this time louder and more decisive. He grunted, then smiled with satisfaction as the bolt slid back and he turned the handle.

Swallow was unsure what he expected to find in the room that had been occupied by Sarah Bradley. Evidence perhaps of violence? Signs of the struggle that Timmy Spencer claimed to have heard the night she disappeared? Traces of a clean-up after a crime? Or perhaps he had expected to find the room as Sarah Bradley might have left it before she met an unexpected end, with clothing and other personal effects indicating an unplanned failure to return.

The room told him nothing, other than that it had not been occupied for a long time. The air was musty and fetid. There might have been the faintest, lingering scent of some stale perfume. A scattering of dead flies lay across the window sash. The single, iron-framed bed, with a damask cover, had been made up with sheets and pillow-cases. The wardrobe opposite the bed was quite empty as was the small chest of drawers under the window. The ewer and bowl on the washstand were both bone dry.

As he stepped out into the corridor again, John McCartan appeared on the landing.

'Inspector Swallow, I'd like to speak to you please,' he said calmly. 'Can we go downstairs?'

Swallow followed him silently down the staircase into the drawing room.

'May I take it that we won't be disturbed here by your men?' he asked. 'I presume they've finished searching this room.'

'Yes, Sir,' Swallow nodded. 'I hope your wife is not unduly upset.'

'She's as you might expect in the circumstances. But she's resting now. How much longer will this search take?'

'I can't really say. We'll finish as quickly as we can, but it's a big house.'

McCartan indicated to him to sit.

'I'm outraged beyond words at what has happened here this evening, Mr Swallow. I have to tell you that I am rather struggling to contain my anger and not make things worse for my dear wife. And I will require some time to decide how I will deal with this appalling intrusion into our lives and this misuse of police powers. But I assure you, the consequences will not be pleasant for you, and possibly for some of your superiors.'

'It's understandable that you should feel angry, Sir,' Swallow said. 'But I have to do my duty.'

'You've also to use your common sense and your intelligence, Man. What is this nonsense about Mrs Bradley being murdered?'

Swallow knew he was on the backfoot.

'The police have reason to believe that she was. And a witness saw you leave this house in darkness with what might have been a body, wrapped in a cover.'

McCartan gave a low laugh.

'My poor dogs. Poisoned by a farmer, I believe. I've just become sure of who did it.'

'What did you do with the dogs?'

'I drove out to the mountains beyond Rathfarnham and buried them close to one of the paths where I used to walk with them.'

'Why not have your coachman or someone else do it? It must have been quite a laborious task.'

'Those two dogs were very loyal to me, Mr Swallow. Burying them was a job to be done by the master that loved them, not by a servant.'

'You were at The Morgue, the public house at the Templeogue bridge, that night.'

'I was. As you said, it was a laborious task. I rarely visit licensed premises. But that evening, I felt I needed a brandy. In fact I had two.'

Swallow was momentarily silent. Unusually, he realised he was unsure how to pursue his line of questioning.

McCartan leaned forward in his chair.

'Mr Swallow. I will eliminate any doubt or suspicions you may yet entertain. But I require your absolute assurance of total confidentiality.'

'I can give you that, Sir,' Swallow answered.

'I have a letter from Mrs Bradley posted and dated from Belfast just three days ago. I can assure you she is alive and well.'

'It's not that I doubt you, Sir,' Swallow lied. 'But it would be helpful if I could see that letter.'

'I think you probably know why I would hesitate to do that, Inspector. Mrs Bradley's time here was not the most tranquil. She left quite suddenly and after a great deal of unpleasantness. The content of the letter would be, well, sensitive.'

'Again, I can guarantee you that it would kept be in my absolute confidence.'

McCartan was silent for a moment.

'Very well.'

He drew an envelope from his pocket. It bore a Belfast stamp, dated June sixth. It was addressed to Sir John McCartan QC, at the Dublin Law Library.

'Read it, Mr Swallow.'

Swallow spread the single sheet on his knee.

St David's,
Cliftonvale Avenue,
Belfast,
Co Antrim.

Dear Sir John,

Thank you for arranging to forward my belongings.

I am very sorry that my departure from my post at Templeogue Hill had to be so sudden. Clearly, my efforts to be a suitable housekeeper to your home were not in keeping with your wishes or expectations, or indeed, with those of Lady McCartan.

When Lady McCartan offered me the position, I was aware that it would pose particular challenges, given the state of her health. I took up the post with the best of intentions. However, I realise now that in your view, I assumed responsibilities and duties that were not appropriate to my station. I very much regret that you saw these efforts on my part as unwelcome and, indeed, at odds with your own requirements for the smooth running of your household.

I will not deny that in my time at Templeogue House my respect and affection for you personally grew considerably. You, in turn, expressed affection and sentiment for me which, while flattering, was far from appropriate and which could only give rise to the greatest scandal had it been allowed to develop in any way. For my own part, I wish we had met in different circumstances. I also wish I could have been of more assistance to you in the particular difficulties and responsibilities you face. But this was not to be.

Thank you for forwarding the payment due to me for the last month of my service.

As you will see from the address here, I have found suitable employment in Belfast, at the house of a gentleman who is prominent in the commercial life of this city.

I remain, respectfully yours,

Sarah Bradley (Mrs.)

He handed the letter back to McCartan.

'Thank you, Sir. I appreciate your confidence. The letter appears to be self-explanatory.'

'It is, Mr Swallow. I allowed a certain foolishness to overtake my common sense in relation to Mrs Bradley. My actions and my disposition raised hopes in her that could never have been realised and in the end matters became quite acrimonious. It was quite impossible that she should stay on and so her employment here had to come to an end.

'You'll understand that I shall need to verify the authenticity of the letter by having the Belfast police speak directly with Mrs Bradley herself.'

'I suppose you will,' McCartan said wearily. 'Do what you must. All I would ask is that for Mrs Bradley's sake you do it with more tact and discretion than you have displayed in this house.'

Swallow knew that his words were formulaic. An attempt to stage a dignified withdrawal in the face of a catastrophic mistake. He had no doubt whatsoever that when Belfast CID would visit the address given on Sarah Bradley's letter, at G-division's request, they would find her alive and well.

Chapter 32

Monday, June 10th, 1889

Swallow and his raiding party of G-men had returned to the Castle shortly before midnight. The search at Templeogue Hill had yielded nothing of significance. Conversation among the dispirited G-men was muted as the side-cars made their way back through the quiet suburbs into the darkened city. They dropped Pat Mossop off by his house on Wexford Street. Mick Feore suggested that a few late-night pints in an obliging hostelry might be in order once the horses were stabled. The idea was taken up with weary assent rather than the enthusiasm of men who have just attained a coveted goal or prize. Swallow decided to adhere to his new-found temperance. He parted from the others in the stable yard and made his way quietly to his bedroom at Mallon's house.

When he woke in the morning, John Mallon had already left the house for his office. He drank two cups of tea in the kitchen, declining the cook's offer of breakfast and set out to report to his boss. He was not looking forward to it. Had there been any positive result from the search he would have made out a late-night briefing note and left it on the desk for Mallon's clerk to find first thing in the morning. When bringing disastrous results it was better to go face to face with the chief of detectives and recount the unhappy story in full.

Mallon did not beat around the bush when Swallow finished his account of the night's work at Templeogue Hill.

'I'm going to have to shift you, Joe. There's no way around it. There'll be calls to have you sacked, reduced in rank, suspended, all of these. The lawyers will be outraged. The business community too. There'll be protests and petitions to the Commissioner. It's bad enough that people like the McCartans should be attacked in their home in a well-policed city. But then to have them treated like criminal themselves by the police, it's more than the great and the good of Dublin can tolerate.'

'I know that, Chief,' Swallow said apologetically.

'If I move you over to office duties for a bit and if I do it quickly, it might die down. If we manage to recover the cash and jewellery taken from them it'll weigh to our benefit too. We can call in a few favours from our friends in the newspapers to put a positive gloss on things.

'Do you think Spencer genuinely thought McCartan had murdered Sarah Bradley at the house?' Mallon asked. 'Or was it a way of walking us into trouble?'

'I don't know, Chief. On balance, I'd say he genuinely thought McCartan had done for her. He's not too swift in the head. I doubt he'd have the imagination to come up with a plan like that.'

Mallon stroked his beard reflectively.

'Maybe. Sometimes the most dense ones are also the most cunning.'

'What do you want me to do about taking in these cavalry lads over in Portobello Barracks? And what are we going to do about Stephen Doolan's brother's house being used as a depot for stolen property?'

'I don't think you've been listening to me, Joe.'

There was more than a hint of exasperation in Mallon's voice.

'I want you to do nothing. When you walk out of here now, I want you to lose yourself for an hour or two. Go to the Dolphin or someplace and have a good breakfast. Come back when you've done that and go straight across to the Chief Commissioner's office. I'll have told them you need a desk and a chair and a bit of peace and quiet for a while. Harrel has a few jobs he wants done. Paperwork for a while.'

'Understood, Chief. I'm sorry.'

'You needn't worry. I'm quite capable of taking charge of things,' Mallon said affecting a patient tone. 'Remember, I did your job for a lot of years. The first thing I'll do is have the RIC detective office in Belfast establish that Sarah Bradley really is alive and well and where she claims to be. Although I doubt that McCartan was telling you anything other than the truth.'

'Unfortunately, I doubt it too, Chief.'

'Then I'll have a message sent to the Military Police office at Portobello. With luck, the four characters identified by Spencer will be in the cells there in an hour. The army doesn't hang around waiting for evidence or that kind of thing. I'll go down to the crime conference now in a few minutes and I'll get Mossop to organise a few of the lads later in the morning to get over there and start questioning them.' Swallow told himself that Pat Mossop would do it right. But interviewing the suspects in Portobello should rightly be his job.

'That's good,' he told Mallon, trying his best to sound disinterested. 'Mossop is well ahead on this already.'

A disquieting thought occurred to him.

'Do you think the fellows in Portobello might have taken off by now? They'll have heard that Spencer is in Mountjoy and they'll know there's a good chance he'll put the finger on them.'

'I'm ahead of you there,' Mallon said with a satisfied grin. 'As soon as I knew what Spencer told you, I got a message to the GOC, Ireland. There's been a "confined to barracks" order in force all across Dublin for the past 24 hours. I asked the GOC to impose it in all barracks so as not to set off alarm bells with the fellows we want in Portobello. Nobody's going in or out at any military installation in this city until it's lifted.'

Swallow reminded himself he should never underestimate John Mallon.

'I know it's not my business now, Chief. But you know this could go very hard with Stephen Doolan. He's one of the most solid skippers in the force. If it turns out his brother is the main man in a crime gang, it'll be difficult for him. And it'll be worse again if it turns out that his other brother's house is being used to move stolen property. It's hardly possible that he's known about this, is it?'

Mallon grimaced.

'I'd have thought Doolan would be the last man who'd likely turn a blind eye to something like this, even if there was family involved. He's got, what, maybe twenty or twenty-five years' unblemished service? He can retire anytime he wants. But who knows? I'll have a warrant to search the house this morning. We'll probably have to question him, at the very least.'

'Well, that's that, then, Chief,' Swallow said. 'I'm truly sorry. I know I've presented you with the biggest foul-up that G-division has encountered in a very long time.'

Mallon shook his head.

'No. This can be dealt with. If we box clever, it'll be stormy for a bit, but then it'll die down. We're left with an unsolved murder, a body in the Poddle and all that. But even murders get forgotten about.'

He gestured to the selection of morning newspapers spread on his desk.

'Crime is important. But it's far more important that we keep Parnell where he should be. That's out of the newspapers, at least insofar as his private life is concerned.'

He stared hard at Swallow.

'And that, it seems, is what you've managed to do, Detective Inspector Swallow. I can live with an unsolved murder and an angry Chief Commissioner. But I wouldn't want to be trying to keep the madmen in check without Parnell's calming influence. God knows how you did it, but I don't need to know.'

Chapter 33

At some point during the afternoon he realised that he had not responded to old Ephram Greenberg's request to visit him again in Capel Street. He had some new information, according to the message left by Katherine Greenberg at Exchange Court, concerning the diamonds and gold coins that had been recovered from the Poddle.

The day had been punctuated by news of dramatic developments which he followed from his sedentary location in the office of the Chief Commissioner. News of crime or advances in an investigation travelled quickly around the police offices. Clerks in adjoining departments liked to show colleagues how much they were in the know by being the first with confirmation of a significant development, an operation in one of the divisions or an arrest. Gossip and chat was shared in the canteen in the Lower Yard and in the many licensed premises frequented by policemen in and around the Castle.

His station in the Chief Commissioner's office was far from unpleasant. He was accommodated in a small room that had a desk with a capacious drawer, two chairs, a coat-stand, a waste-paper basket and a tall, wooden filing cabinet. Its solitary window faced west into the stable-yard. Thus, while the view was not particularly uplifting, the light was good.

The clerks in the Chief Commissioner's office were pleasant and welcoming to him. Police clerks, he knew, fell into one of two categories. There were career clerks, men who had chosen to work indoors, usually at an early stage of their careers. These were generally better educated than the average policeman and they had an allowance that boosted their pay somewhat. Mostly they had the rank of sergeant, which gave them a little more money again. The other category included men like Swallow, as he now found himself. These were not in their roles by inclination but because fate and circumstances dictated that they should not be at work in the divisions or in contact with the general public.

The task allocated to Swallow by the superintendent who acted as the Chief Commissioner's personal private secretary was to work on perfecting the text of the forthcoming Annual Report on the Dublin Metropolitan Police for 1888. It was due to be forwarded to the Chief Secretary for Ireland not later than the thirtieth of June, as required each year by regulation. There were two principal objects in the task, the superintendent explained. First, the narrative had to be proofed for grammatical propriety. Second, the columns of statistics had to be checked for numerical accuracy. In no circumstances was there to be any departure from the sentiments so carefully articulated and set down by the Chief Commissioner himself. The formulaic style and presentation, sacrosanct over decades, had to be strictly maintained, right down to the assurance, at the conclusion of the report, that its author had the honour to remain the obedient servant of its distinguished addressee.

Two hours later, when he had managed to find no more than a couple of misplaced apostrophes, a clerk from the Weights and Measures office next door came by to tell him that four cavalrymen were in custody at Portobello Barracks in connection with the robbery at Sir John and Lady McCartan's. An hour later, the same clerk came by to tell him in shocked tones that one of the cavalrymen was a brother of Sergeant Stephen Doolan in the A-district.

And when he broke from his paperwork to have his mid-day meal at the canteen, a sergeant from the ABC telegraph office told him a message from Belfast CID had confirmed that Mrs Sarah

Bradley, the subject of an earlier inquiry from G-division, had been located, alive and well and employed as housekeeper at the home of a Belfast bank manager on Cliftonvale Avenue in that city.

In the mid-afternoon, while he was cross-checking the total number of offences under the Street Trading Acts detected and prosecuted during the year, the door was opened by none other than John Mallon himself.

'You're gainfully employed, anyway, I see,' he said gruffly.

'I could give you an argument on that, Chief. But I won't.'

Mallon took the straight-backed chair in front of the desk.

'There's a few developments that you might be interested in.'

'Always glad to keep up with the news,' Swallow quipped. 'But you'd be surprised how well it travels in here anyway.'

He was glad to see his boss. It made his new surroundings in the Chief Commissioner's outer office less unfamiliar.

'I went out to Salthill this morning to see Mr Parnell. The funds to persuade O'Shea to stay quiet came through earlier so he was mighty relieved. And I told him that you had somehow persuaded the people in the security section in the Upper Yard to abandon their attempts to get the newspapers to run with the story about the divorce petition. He asked me to convey his particular thanks to you for that. But he's a strange man. First, he was pleased. Then he told me he'd almost prefer if it was out in the open.'

Swallow was moved.

'You can understand how he'd have mixed feelings, in a way. It can't be great living that sort of a double life. But it's kind of him to send that message. I only did what any Irishman concerned for the good of his country would do.'

'The fact is, you did it,' Mallon said, 'whatever it was. I don't suppose there'd be any connection between it and the fact Mr Reginald Polson, a member of the Assistant Under-Secretary's department, was noted by our lads on the North Wall, going aboard the Liverpool steam-packet later in the morning, with all of his luggage?'

'Ah, I wouldn't know anything about that, Chief. But it wouldn't surprise me greatly that he'd want to move on. He told me he found Dublin very dull entirely.'

Mallon face was impassive.

'Really? That's a pity.'

'The other thing I want to tell you is that the search team down at what we were told is Stephen Doolan's brother's house on Clanbrassil Street has struck gold. Literally. The place is like an Aladdin's cave. It's crammed with jewellery, watches, gold and silver ornaments and so on. They're still trying to count all the cash they've recovered. It's under floorboards, in boxes in the attic, under the beds, everywhere.'

'Well, that's a bit of good news, for a change. Do they know if any of the McCartans' stuff is in that haul?'

'Subject to confirmation from the McCartans themselves, it looks positive. There's rings, pearls and watches that match the descriptions they gave us.'

'So there may be a God in Heaven, after all. And maybe he occasionally takes pity on poor *policemen* down here.'

Mallon smiled.

'And there's one other bit of intelligence that you might be glad to know too. Stephen Doolan hasn't been on speaking terms with either of his brothers for years. There's nothing so far to suggest that he suspected either of them to be involved in crime.'

'I'm glad to know that. I'd have been astonished if he was aware of anything like that without doing something about it. But obviously he's a bit unfortunate in his choice of brothers.'

Mallon stood.

'He is. I'm personally going to take the stuff recovered at Clanbrassil Street that we think belongs to the McCartans and bring it out to Templeogue Hill myself. It might just be possible to put some sort of a curtain around what's happened. What the French call a *cordon sanitaire,* I believe.'

'How could you do that, Chief?' Swallow asked. 'He was furious beyond words, threatening every sort of punishment on me. I know he's a bit mercurial and he can blow hot then blow cold. But in fairness to him, I've given him adequate reason to be angry.'

'I can't deny that,' Mallon acknowledged. 'But I've been making my own inquiries. It's known that he acted very foolishly in allowing Sarah Bradley to more or less take over his house, humiliating his wife and taking charge of the household as if she was mistress of the house. There's little doubt a relationship or a dependency grew up that was, at very least, inappropriate.'

'All of that may be true, Chief. But how does that help us?'

'Ah, well. There's a vacancy coming up shortly on the bench. It's in the High Court of Justice, in fact. Sir John has expressed an interest in the appointment and, of course, it's in the giving of the Lord Lieutenant.'

He grinned mischievously.

'As it happens, I'm having a private lunch with the Lord Lieutenant next week and I expect we will discuss it, as we discuss all sensitive appointments. It's important that the judiciary have the full confidence of the police. And it's important that appointees to the bench are men of absolute propriety, with good judgment, not given to foolishness or indiscretion. Of course, it would be fatal to the ambitions of any would-be member of the bench if it became known that the police had good reason to consider him as a murder suspect, notwithstanding that they found they were mistaken.'

'Are you serious, Chief?' Swallow was incredulous.

'I believe that Sir John might think it better all-round if there were not to be any publicity about what happened at Templeogue Hill last night, or why it happened. It wouldn't help his standing among his legal colleagues or among the judiciary, whose distinguished ranks he is keen to join. Indeed, if the Lord Lieutenant were to hear about these things, it would be catastrophic to his ambitions. So I think I can mollify McCartan by explaining that the over-zealous officer who raided his house has been transferred to desk duties. And he'll be pleased to know that I intend to speak so highly of him to the Lord Lieutenant over lunch.'

Swallow spent the rest of the afternoon trying to tot numbers of offences reported and detected across the city's six uniform divisions, checking them against the totals recorded by the Chief Commissioner's own clerical staff. However it was inordinately difficult to concentrate.The audacity of what Mallon was planning to do scrambled his thinking. When he found that someone had incorrectly totalled the numbers of persons charged with being drunk and disorderly in a public place and when he rectified the error, he marvelled at his capacity to keep simultaneous processes running parallel in his head.

Most of the Chief Commissioner's staff worked regular hours and started to shut their offices from half-past five or so. He had finished all his long tots and cross-checks by then but he lingered on almost to the hour, poring over the introductory text. Finding no further stray apostrophes, he folded the file, locked it in the drawer, descended to the Lower Yard and exited the Castle by the Palace Street gate, just as the Angelus bells started to ring across the city. He crossed Dame Street into Parliament Street, now shaded from the sinking sun, and crossed the bridge named in honour of Henry Grattan, who had briefly secured an independent parliament for Ireland a little more than a century ago, onto Capel Street.

All the shops were shut now, their proprietors and assistants either retired to private quarters on the upper floors or to the more cramped rooms at the back of the tall, elegant houses. The dark roller-blinds were down behind Greenberg's plate-glass windows, protecting the valuable displays both from the evening sun and the eyes of would-be snatch thieves and predators. The shop doorway, as always when the business day was done, was sealed off from the street with a heavy, wrought-iron grille.

The private entrance was a separate, narrow doorway where the house adjoined its neighbour. He hauled on the bell-cord and heard a faint, distant tinkle from the top of the narrow stairs inside. The Greenberg's elderly housemaid who opened the door to him was from some remote village in Poland and in spite of having lived for decades in Dublin spoke little or no English. But she knew Swallow was always a welcome visitor to the house and smiled wordlessly before preceding him laboriously up the narrow stairs to Ephram's first-floor parlour.

The old dealer was seated at the long mahogany table that sometimes doubled as his work-top. The remains of his supper lay on a tray beside him, chicken bones and some scraps of red cabbage on a plate, with a half-consumed glass of dark red wine beside it. Swallow was surprised to find him already in a dressing gown as if preparing to go to bed.

His eyes lit up when he recognised his visitor.

'Joseph. You're very welcome. Come in, come in. Take a seat here and join me in a drink.'

The elderly maid, anticipating her master's wish, had already procured another glass from the cabinet and placed it on the table beside him. Ephram reached slowly across for the opened bottle of strong, Lebanese *Syrah* and half-filled the glass. Swallow noticed that the old man's hand had a distinct shake that he had not noticed on previous visits.

'The usual, Joseph. The very best from the Bekaa Valley.'

The voice was a little weaker too.

Swallow had abjured alcohol for more than twenty-four hours and felt the better for it. But it would be offensive to refuse to drink with Ephram, he told himself. And wine was more or less safe, not having the potency of whiskey. He raised the glass in appreciation.

'Thank you, Ephram. Here's to your very good health.'

The wine was good on his palate.

'If I had known you were coming, I would have delayed my supper and we could have dined together. You have not eaten?'

'Thank you, Ephram, but I'm not hungry. I looked after myself in the police canteen earlier in the day.'

'That's not proper food,' Ephram gave a little snort. 'Katherine told the cook earlier to prepare cod in white sauce for her own supper. She always makes a good deal more than is needed so I know there will be plenty for you. It's always very appetising, I promise you.'

As if on cue, the door opened and Katherine walked in, carrying two cloth-bound ledgers.

'Mr Swallow,' she smiled brightly. 'I heard the bell but I assumed it was one of the men from the Synagogue come to visit my father. They are all his friends and they like to have conversation with him. You are very welcome, as always.'

She was in the working uniform of a city businesswoman. The long, dark dress, buttoned to the neck and without adornment of any kind, was severe but also flattering. Katherine had recently started to gain a little weight and her slightly fuller figure sometimes reminded Swallow of her late mother, Miriam.

'We've got very formal, haven't we?' he quipped. 'What happened to Joe?'

She laughed.

I'm sorry. Of course. You're very welcome, Joe. It's just that I've been in the shop all day, dealing with customers. I have to adjust my disposition and my terminology now that the day is ended. And I need to change out of this drab attire.'

She put the two ledgers on the table.

'These are up to date, now Father. Everything up to close of business today is there. But I don't want you to check them until tomorrow. The doctor wants you early to bed for a while. Will you promise me?'

Ephram sighed.

'I know. I know. Yes, I promise. I'll go up after I've had a short conversation with Joseph. But I want you to give him supper before he goes. He hasn't eaten and I told him that you had ordered the cook to prepare that nice cod she bought for you in the market this morning.'

'Of course, I will,' she smiled again. 'You have your conversation together and I'll have the table prepared in the dining room.

I'm looking forward to supper myself and it will be very nice to have company.'

When she had left the room, Ephram poured more wine for them both.

'Katherine works very hard now, because I can do so little in the business,' he said. 'I don't have the energy that I used to. The brain is still good and I can advise her on buying and selling, but even going up and down those stairs now is difficult.'

Swallow nodded.

'You know I did some medical training before I joined the police, Ephram. So I can offer some advice to you, as well. My advice is, listen to what your body is telling you. None of us can do everything we did when we were younger men. We all know that. At least we can't do everything as well or maybe as quickly. So don't ask unreasonable things of your body. Treat it kindly.'

Ephram smiled.

'That's good advice, Joseph. And it's flattering to hear myself compared in any way to a young man like you, in your prime. We both know I'm old enough to be your father. Maybe even your grandfather. But my worry is that when I am gone, Katherine will be alone in the business and alone in life. She should have married, you know. There were several very suitable young men of our faith who could have been a good husband to her and whom I would have been very happy to see come into the business. But she would have none of them. Now, I fear it is too late.'

He sipped his wine.

'Now, let me tell you something that I think might be of help to you. You brought in some stones and some half sovereigns the last time you called here. You told me in confidence that they might be connected with the finding of that woman's remains in the underground river at Essex Street and you asked me if there was anything I could tell you about them.'

He pointed to Swallow's glass.

'Drink up, Joseph. I do not intend to leave an unfinished bottle behind me when I go upstairs.'

Swallow obeyed. The wine was getting better as his taste buds adapted themselves to it.

'Two days ago, an old friend of mine who is in the same trade in Manchester was visiting Dublin to buy some rare books that a gentleman had been offering for sale in his house in Merrion Square and he came to visit me here after he had concluded his business. So, we had dinner together and drank some wine and we exchanged all the news about the trade. Who was doing well, who was doing not so well. What the coming fashions were likely to be for art and jewellery. You can imagine, yourself. Any business runs on knowledge and judgement.'

The old man's voice seemed to strengthen as he relished the telling of his tale.

'So, then this friend of mine told me about another man in the business, also in Manchester. A man called Harden. Daniel Harden. I know him too. He was in business here in Dublin for some years before he went to Manchester. He told me that Harden had suffered a heavy loss last year when a woman in his employment stole a collection of precious stones and gold coins from his house. I gave nothing away, of course, but I questioned him closely to find out what I could. What he described as having been stolen from Daniel Harden seemed remarkably similar to what you found in your search of the river.'

'We circulated details of that to all the police forces in the Kingdom,' Swallow said. 'Manchester Police would have notified us if there was a match.'

'Ah, yes, of course,' Ephram's eyes lit up as he delivered the concluding element of his narrative. 'There is another piece to the jigsaw. The police in Manchester would not have been told about the theft because Harden is not an honest man. He is what you call a "fence". A man who receives stolen property and pays the thief perhaps a fraction of what the goods may be worth. He was not in a position to go to the police because he got them from a thief and who knows where the thief got them? My friend told me this.'

It was plausible, Swallow told himself. If the woman who robbed Daniel Harden wanted to put distance between herself and her criminal employer, crossing the Irish Sea to Dublin would be a good option. Who could say what mishap might have befallen her? And it was entirely possible that it was her bones that had been taken from the Poddle. They had investigated every other reported disappearance in the city without success. But if the dead woman was not from Dublin in the first place that would explain why nobody in the city was looking for her?

'Can you find her name?' he asked Ephram. 'If this is the same woman then it may be that we can trace her movements. She would have needed some place to stay if she came to Dublin and she must have had contact with some person or persons. We might yet be able to find why and how that body ended up in the Poddle and maybe even yet make someone amenable for it.'

'Ah, I doubt it, Joseph,' Ephram said wearily. It was as if the effort of relaying his story to Swallow had exhausted him.

'My friend recognised my interest in what he had said and he seemed to think that he had told me too much already because he was very anxious to change the conversation,' he went on after a pause.

'I know there would be little point in my asking him for any more detail. I could guess his identity. But I am so long gone from Manchester that I know only the older men in the trade. There are now many younger dealers in business there whose names I do not even know. And I doubt if Daniel Harden would be very co-operative if you sent your colleagues in Manchester around to his house to talk to him.'

'Perhaps you're right,' Swallow said. 'There comes a point in any enterprise when it's probably wiser to step back. Maybe it's best to let it go.'

At all events, he told himself silently, he was no longer on G-division's investigative strength. Since his interview with Mallon earlier in the day, he was a desk-man. A pen-pusher. A glorified clerk. And Mallon had made it very clear that he was to stick to clerking.

The old dealer's eyes were starting to close and his head was nodding.

Swallow reached across the table to ring the small bell beside Ephram's now-empty wine glass.

After a few moments, the elderly maid came into the room.

'I think Mr Greenberg needs to retire,' he told her.

Ephram rose from his chair, took maid's extended arm and shuffled with her towards the door. He half-turned as he stepped out to the landing.

'Good night, Joseph. Stay and enjoy your supper. And I hope you will call again soon.'

He refilled his wine glass, emptying the last of the Lebanese *Syrah.*

He was listening to Ephram's slow footsteps on the stairs as Katherine put her head around the door.

'Supper is on the table in the dining room,' she said quietly.

He rose and followed her across the wide landing. The Greenbergs' dining room was at the back of the house, with three tall windows in the Georgian style, looking west across the city. Now the evening sun filled the room with a warm, pink glow, bathing the Chippendale furniture and damask wallpaper and glinting off the polished silver on the two sideboards. The walls were hung with good paintings of the Irish and British schools. Swallow could identify a Faulkner watercolour and what was either a Maclise or a work copied expertly in his style, probably by one of his students. To the right of the Carrara marble fireplace he recognised a still life, depicting fruit on silver and silk, the painting in oils for which Katherine had been awarded a distinction the previous season by the arts committee of the Royal Dublin Society.

'Please, won't you sit, Joe?'

She gestured him to the table where two places were set with crystal wine glasses, fine china and ivory-handled cutlery.

'You like my Father's *Syrah,* I know,' she said. 'So I have another bottle.'

She poured the wine into the goblet by his hand.

'Enjoy the wine and the sunset for a few minutes,' she said warmly. 'I'll just need to attend to the food because the cook is gone and the maid will be busy with my father upstairs for a while.'

He sat back in the chair and sipped at the wine, watching the shadows deepen beyond the big windows. The sinking sun silhouetted the great dome of the Four Courts across the rooftops and caught the shining granite of the Wellington Memorial in the Phoenix Park away to the west. Beyond the Park, the eastern fringe of the central plain of Ireland was already a carpet of darkening blues and greys.

He tried to imagine what might be happening now at Grant's on Thomas Street. He could not count how many nights it had been since he been there with Maria, waiting to retire contentedly to the big bedroom on the second floor, or watching protectively as she presided over the business of the two bars, supervising the barmen and greeting the customers with a familiar word and a smile. Monday would be a quiet night usually. They would be lighting the lamps shortly. First, in the select bar and then in the public. The regulars would have started to arrive by now too. A few old pensioners from the Royal Hospital would have their usual corner of the public bar. Shopkeepers from James's Street, Francis Street and from Thomas Street itself would be gathered in the select bar to swap information at the end of the day's trading. There would be clerks and brewers from Arthur Guinness's at Saint James's Gate. Some of the excise men from Power's distillery on John's Lane would probably be there too.

A sense of sorrow started to well up inside him. It had been gathering all day, even as he had sat in the Chief Commissioner's outer office, cross-checking statistical totals and hunting stray apostrophes. Sorrow seemed to reach into every part of the world around him. It was connected to so many failures and so much sadness. The loss of the baby. The life that would never be. The world that he and Maria had hoped to build together. His inability now to reach Maria in her grief. His own failure to take control of his life and to take the decisions that were necessary, not just for himself but for Maria also.

And there was just too much wickedness. A clutch of bones reclaimed from the river, all that remained to testify to the life of an unknown woman, brutally cut short, for reasons unknown. She must have been somebody's lover, daughter, mother perhaps. A brave young police inspector, shot dead in a Tipperary field, leaving a wife and a young family. A statesman, desperately striving to secure the right for his compatriots to rule their own country, being harried and hounded for his courage.

He brought himself back to immediate surroundings as Katherine came back into the dining room, carrying a silver tray, laden with two steaming plates of fish, a dish of small, new potatoes and another of green beans, flavoured with something that was familiar from the many times in the past that he had dined with the Greenbergs. She placed his roasted cod, topped with its creamy white sauce, on the table in front of him and took her own place opposite.

The fish was perfect, firm but moist and very slightly crisped on the surface. The white sauce complemented it perfectly. The new potatoes were fresh and sweet and the green beans, flavoured with he knew not what, were delightful to the palate.

'You must be hungry, Joe,' Katherine said. 'There's a second helping in the oven if you'd like some more.'

'Thank you,' he smiled. 'One gets quantity rather than quality at the police canteen. But this provides both. It's excellent.'

'Surely you don't eat at the canteen very often? I believe you told me that your wife employs a very talented cook at your house.'

'She does. Carrie is a real jewel. But sometimes, well, it's not practical for me to eat there. Police hours are irregular. And running a busy public house sometimes gets in the way of Maria's mealtimes as well.'

Katherine picked silently at her food for a moment.

'It must be nice, all the same, to have the companionship and the affection when you do manage to co-ordinate your movements and you can be together.'

'Yes,' he said. 'But married life has its ups and downs too. You know we lost a child that Maria was carrying. That hasn't been easy.'

'No, obviously, I've never experienced that kind of loss. But I can imagine.'

She poured more wine for them both.

'I have learned to live with loss of a different kind,' she said quietly. 'It's not as acute as yours, I'm sure. But it's real to me.'

'I'm sorry to know that. I always think of you as very confident and at ease with your circumstances.'

She laughed but without humour.

'Ah, that's what the world sees. A clever, capable Jewish girl, well-set to take over the family business. Understands the fine art and jewellery trade and knows how it works. In fact she's quite good at business. Paints a bit herself, too. A talented amateur.'

'You're being a bit hard on yourself. A lot of people would envy you.'

She raised both hands and gestured around the room.

'Look at this. It's a gilded cage and I chose to enter it. I've got an old man upstairs who's coming to the end of his days. He wants the business that he and my mother built up together to stay in the family, as he puts it. But I'm an only child and I feel I have to honour that. If I didn't, I'd sell, pack two trunks and move to London, or New York or Paris. Wouldn't that be exciting?'

'Will you consider yourself bound to the business even after your father is gone?' he asked.

'Yes, unfortunately. People would consider that foolish. But I've given him my word. He had this idea about children and grandchildren coming along to run it in future generations. It was a big disappointment to him that I never married, so I want to leave him with part of his dream. The Greenberg name will stay over the door for my lifetime, at least.'

'You could marry yet, Katherine. You could have children.'

She shook her head and laughed again.

'I'm past marriage age for a Jewish girl, Joe. When you're on the wrong side of thirty, any self-respecting young Jewish man will think of you as an old maid.'

'Would you have to marry within your faith?'

'Actually, I couldn't give a hoot about my faith.' She snorted disdainfully. 'But I haven't met any man that would interest me, within or without it.'

She paused.

'Except one or two that are already married.'

Already warm from the wine and the heat of the evening, he felt himself blushing. Katherine's affections for him had been apparent since she was a schoolgirl and he a young constable whose beat brought him each day through Capel Street and past Greenberg's Fine Art and Jewellery. He had been a regular visitor to the shop and to the private quarters upstairs. He would have long conversations with her father, while her mother would feed him delicious *speck* and kosher bread and strong Arabica coffee. But he could honestly say that although he was flattered, he had never done or said a single thing that could be construed as encouraging her.

'That's unfortunate,' he said after a moment.

'Oh, don't misunderstand me, Joe. I'm not unhappy for myself about not marrying. Although I worry about how I'll manage the business on my own after my father is gone. It would be better to have someone in it with me who could share the responsibility.'

'I can understand that,' he said.

'You know, if things were different, you and I could be excellent business partners,' she said suddenly and urgently.

'You've got an eye for good art and I think you have a sense of what the trade is about. And I daresay the financial rewards would be better than police pay.'

They sat in silence for a short while, staring at their empty plates.

'Will I open another bottle of wine?' she asked eventually. 'It's such a short night. It won't be easy to sleep.'

'No, thanks. Not for me, at any rate.'

'I think I'll have another glass anyway.'

She rang the small bell on the table. On cue, the maid came through the door with an uncorked bottle of *Syrah*. Then, without instruction, she went along the room, lighting the oil lamps one by one, creating soft, yellow pools of light.

When she had gone, Katherine poured more wine for herself. She gestured towards Swallow's empty glass but he waved the bottle away.

He knew the last thing he needed was more wine. It would be no more than a brisk walk in the warm summer night to Thomas Street and the air would counter the effects of what he had already taken. He wanted a clear head tonight. There were many things he needed to say to Maria and, no doubt, there were things that she wanted to say to him. Things that both of them had put off and avoided for too long.

He pushed his chair back from the table.

'Thank you for a very good supper, Katherine. Thank you also for the very flattering suggestion about the business. However it's not something I could consider. I'm sure there are quite a few people who could meet your requirements, but I'm not one of them.'

She nodded.

'I understand, Joe. Now, it's time for you to go to your home.'

He stood.

'Yes, it is. I'm going home to my wife. I'm overdue there.'

Postscript I

December 22nd, 1890

Dublin's winter had arrived with a singular viciousness after a deceptively mild November. The weather in those mild, dramatic and sorrowful days, however, had not by any means been the principal subject of conversation in the coffee shops, the offices or the public houses.

The topic on people's lips, in the newspapers and indeed at public gatherings was the sensational developments at the Law Courts in London where Charles Stewart Parnell had acknowledged that for years there had been an illicit relationship between himself and Katharine O'Shea, the wife of Captain Willie O'Shea, and that he was the father of her three children.

O'Shea had filed his suit for divorce, naming Parnell as co-respondent, almost a year previously. So the fact of his allegations had already been in the public domain. But had not the leader of the Irish Party, the champion of Irish nationalism and Home Rule, repeatedly assured his colleagues, his supporters and even his friends in the press that O'Shea's charges were false? He would be exonerated, he insisted. And did not everyone testify to his honesty, his righteousness, his integrity? If Parnell said the charge was false, who would challenge him?

They had tried to break the 'uncrowned King of Ireland' before, with arrest, imprisonment, fines and most recently with Pigott's forged letters, purporting to link him to violent crime and incitement. But he had confounded his enemies at every turn and most of his supporters confidently expected that he would do so again this time. Few had been prepared for this extraordinary about-turn. After the hearing, he let it be known that he had decided not to challenge the accusation because he wanted to be free to marry Katharine. The court granted Captain O'Shea's application, giving the lovers that freedom. But there was a sting in the tail, with their two surviving children being placed in O'Shea's custody.

Swallow had never seen John Mallon so gloomy.

'They'll never forgive him,' he said, shaking his head as in disbelief. 'He chose Kitty O'Shea over Ireland's cause. That's how it's being described out there in the streets. An Englishwoman to be placed ahead of Home Rule. He saw off his external enemies, but he's left himself wide open to the enemies at his own back. Christ, how could a man be so stupid?'

Mallon had produced the customary bottle of Bushmills in his front parlour. The Monday evening outside was bitterly cold. Flurries of snow whipped around the Lower Yard leaving small accumulations on the windows' sills and in the doorways. Darkness had descended before the offices had closed for the day, leaving it to the gas-lights to mark the outline of the buildings.

It had been a tumultuous five weeks since the conclusion of the divorce hearing in the London Law Courts. The publicising of the affair had brought angry denunciations from the Roman Catholic bishops, including the powerful Archbishop William Walsh of Dublin. More seriously, Protestant church leaders in England also denounced the adulterer whose parliamentary party was in alliance with Gladstone's Liberal government at Westminster. Gladstone had reportedly informed Parnell that he expected him to fall on his own sword and resign the leadership. Otherwise, he warned, the government would collapse, he would not be re-elected as Prime Minister, Salisbury's Conservatives would be back in power and any prospect of achieving Home Rule for Ireland would be lost.

At first, it had seemed that it would be possible for Parnell to defy them and hold on. On November twenty-fifth the party's members at Westminster re-elected him as party leader. But when Gladstone's threats became public, a second ballot was called for. After a week of intrigues and machinations, a majority of the Irish Party members walked out, led by North Longford MP, Justin McCarthy, renouncing Parnell and founding a new party, to be known as the Irish National Federation.

'At times like this, I thank God for Bushmills, even if it is a Protestant whiskey,' Mallon said grimly. He poured two generous measures.

'That's it now,' he said, affecting a false nonchalance. 'We can all relax. No more talk of Home Rule. The politicians have sunk their own boat. The agitators and the gunmen and arsonists now have a clear field. Mark my words, Swallow. Give it just a few years, maybe a decade or so and the hard men will be in the driving seat. It won't be Home Rule. It'll be open revolution. Thank God, I won't be the one to have to deal with it. I'll have taken my pension and gone back to Armagh.'

Swallow did not much care for the Bushmills and Mallon knew it. But he drank it out of politeness and respect for his boss. He tried to be positive.

'We got a year, Chief, maybe two, paying off O'Shea and blocking the attempts by the crowd in the Upper Yard to leak the story to the newspapers,' he said, taking a mouthful of the dark spirit. 'And things are quietening around the country. The crime figures are way down. Farmers are getting good money now for crops and animals. It mightn't be as bad as you think.'

'I saw a letter in one of the newspapers during the week, saying the Land War is over,' Mallon mused. 'It's abated a lot, I know. But not absolutely. The bitterness and the anger are still there in the countryside. Hard to blame people, I suppose. And there's all sorts of new influences and threats astir. This Gaelic games thing is going to be powerful. There's a new Gaelic League that's supposed to be for cultural activities, but I tell you it's going to subvert the schools and the colleges. The government is going to give a lot more authority to local councils and, I promise you, they're going to be taken over by people with no loyalty to the Crown. England is slowly losing Ireland. It's only a question of when the process will be complete.'

He topped up his own whiskey, looking disapprovingly at Swallow's still almost-full glass.

'I've been meaning to ask you, how are you now after the Spencer verdict?'

The other topic of public conversation in recent weeks had been the unexpected acquittal of Timothy Spencer for the murder of District Inspector Edward Fleury in Tipperary, more than a year ago.

The case for the Crown had first begun to look doubtful when Spencer's counsel told the jury that there was no way of knowing who had fired the fatal shot that took the young policeman's life. No fewer than three of the RIC constables at the scene had agreed that they had fired their revolvers as they closed with the fugitive in the monastery field. Since no bullet had lodged in the dead man's body and no bullets had been recovered at the scene, it was impossible to say whose shot had killed him.

But when Detective Inspector Swallow took the stand and testified that he had not heard Fleury or any of the others call out to identify themselves as police, the possibility was planted firmly in the minds of the jury that Spencer may have thought he was acting in self-defence against criminals from his past life.

Spencer testified in his own defence, stating that he had retreated to the monastery for safety and rest. When a party of armed men in plainclothes arrived, he feared for his life and fled across the fields. He had no idea they were policemen. When he found his way blocked off by the river he turned to face his pursuers and, he admitted, he drew his gun and fired once over their heads to deter them.

'Three or four of these men were carryin' guns and there was shots bein' fired at me all the time,' he said plaintively. 'But I never fired at annywan.'

Mossop gave evidence that when Inspector Swallow handed him the firearm that he had taken from Spencer he opened the breach and found that just one round had been fired. In considerable degree, defending counsel told the jury, this corroborated the accused man's evidence.

'I've always been a proud Irishman,' Spencer said when his counsel asked him to outline his political convictions. 'I'm bound by oath not to reveal anny more. But I can tell ye I'm not a criminal. Annythin' I done, I done for Ireland's cause.'

It was not open to the jury to bring in any verdict other than 'guilty' or 'not guilty' of murder, the judge explained. Whether through error or because conviction for murder had seemed certain to the law officers, no fall-back charge had been notified by the Solicitor General or counsel for the Crown. There were gasps of dismay from family and colleagues of the deceased inspector in court when, having retired after two days at hearing, the foreman of the jury said it was their unanimous verdict that Spencer was not guilty. When Spencer walked free and the courtroom started to empty, there were hisses and catcalls from the public gallery to Swallow.

'Shame.'

'A disgrace.'

'Call yourself a policeman?'

'Traitor.'

Later that evening, he had gone to The Brazen Head with Pat Mossop and Mick Feore. They had finished a few quiet pints and were about to leave when an inebriated Timmy Spencer appeared at the door of the public house. He focused bloodshot eyes on Swallow.

'Ah, there's the man,' he slurred. 'A rare man, Mr Swallow. A peeler that keeps his word. Ye said you'd give your evidence, straight up. And so you did. Fair dues to ye. Ye done me a great favour.'

'I told the truth, that's all,' Swallow said sharply. 'You got no favours from me, Spencer.'

Spencer stumbled a little. Pat Mossop stepped forward and steadied him so that he leaned against the wall.

'Ah, but didn't I do you a li'l favour?' Spencer wagged a wavering finger. 'Didn't I tell ye how to find them robbers that yer G-men were lookin' for? Ye hadn't a clue, had ye? But it was Timmy Spencer that put ye right. An' all four o' them now doin' long stretches in Maryborough prison.'

Swallow reached out suddenly and took him by the shirt.

'I'd advise you to say no more, Spencer,' he hissed, forcing him hard against the wall. 'What's done is done. People have ears and they listen very carefully, even to a drunk. So shut your mouth unless you want some of them here to give you a watery end in the Liffey.'

He relaxed his grip. Spencer laboured for a few moments to regain his breath.

By now, the customers in the bar realised something was going on between the G-men and the drunken man who had appeared in the doorway. Most of the clientele were content to watch curiously from their stools by the bar but half a dozen or more had moved forward to form a threatening phalanx.

Swallow heard someone mutter.

'Bastards. Bloody G-men. Lave the poor man alone.'

Mick Feore stepped forward, arms outstretched.

'Easy now, Men. There's nobody in trouble yet. So let's keep it that way. We're just having a few words here with this gentleman and then we'll be on our way.'

Feore grasped Spencer by the collar and propelled him through the door, into the street. Swallow and Mossop stepped out after him into the night air.

'Have you some place to go, Spencer?' Swallow asked. 'Have you a bed for the night?'

Spencer grinned stupidly.

'Ah, don't worry about me, Mr Swallow. I'm used to roughin' it.'

'Have you any money?'

'Not a bob. I sort of … celebrated earlier.'

Swallow dug in his pocket and found a half crown.

'Here,' he handed Spencer the silver coin. 'Get up to the night shelter and get off the street. That'll see you right for a bunk and a hot meal.'

Spencer looked at the half crown and then pocketed it. He leaned forward to Swallow, raising his hand to cover his mouth.'

'C'mere for a minnit. There's somethin' I want to tell ye that'll be between us.'

Swallow inclined his ear.

'Go on.'

Spencer steadied himself.

'I've been a bit less than honest wid ye,' he whispered. 'I'm tellin' ye now, I shot the peeler. I might as well tell ye the truth now. I went for the heart, fair and square. But it was the head that got it. Lucky for Tim Spencer, I s'pose.'

He laughed and stepped back.

'I'll pay ye back yer half crown whin we meet agin, Misther Swalla'. I'm a man o' me word, as ye know.'

He had never told anyone what the drunken Spencer had whispered in his ear that night outside The Brazen Head. There would be no benefit in anyone knowing that his evidence had resulted in the acquittal of a man who should rightly have been convicted and hanged.

Was that truly the case though, he often asked himself since. He had given evidence based on what he believed he had witnessed. It was entirely possible that Timmy Spencer did not really know himself, either, what had happened. It would not be out of character if he were to claim to Swallow, once he had been safely acquitted, that he had aimed to kill Fleury. He could do it simply to be mischievous, to see if he could disquiet and torture the man who had, after all, apprehended him that day in the monastery field in Tipperary.

He had considered confiding in John Mallon. It would have been something of a relief, he knew, to share the burden of doubt with someone whose judgment he trusted. But he could identify no compelling reason to do so. He could live with his own doubts. It would be impossible either to prove or disprove the truth of what Spencer had said. It was best to leave it and move on.

'I'm fine with it,' he told Mallon. 'Every fibre in my body resents the idea of a gangster like Spencer going free. Once he started playing the Fenian card to the jury I reckoned that he was going to get off anyway. But I'm at ease in my conscience. That's more important.'

'Of course,' Mallon nodded. 'Conscience does make cowards of us all. That's Shakespeare, you know. Hamlet.'

He bristled slightly. Where did cowardice come into the equation?

'I know, Chief. I went to school too.'

Mallon was momentarily embarrassed, realising his faux pas.

'I'm sorry. There wasn't any implication in that. The phrase just came into my head.'

'Ah, I understand. I'm a bit sensitive probably. I've been locked up in the bloody office for over a year, filling out forms and shovelling paper. I miss the job. The real job.'

Mallon did not answer immediately.

'I know it goes against the grain. But it had to be done. It wasn't easy to persuade McCartan to let everything drop, even if he wanted to be a judge and even if he needed me to speak for him. I had to make it clear and assure him that you were being punished.'

Swallow grunted.

'Well, I'm being punished alright. And he's got his job in the High Court. Is there any chance I can get out of the bloody office and back to some real work?'

He had long given up hope of ever escaping the drudgery of the Chief Commissioner's office.

'I'd say we should leave it until the New Year,' Mallon answered. 'Then maybe around St Patrick's Day you should come back into G-division. As senior crime inspector.'

'Are you sure, Chief?' he asked cautiously.

'There's a bit of context. We've a good bit of change coming up in the force shortly. The chief superintendent's job in the uniformed divisions is going to be filled. It's been left vacant now for more than three years. There'll be a lot of competition for that and I'd put my money on Duck Boyle. He's got all the right connections in the Masons and his brother an archdeacon. It's not just a coincidence that he got appointed to the B-division right here in the centre of the city after just a year in charge out there in the E.'

Swallow understood. The B-division covered the Castle itself, the City Hall, the banking and insurance district and the exclusive, residential areas of the Georgian quarter. The superintendent of B-division was always first among equals in the rank.

'And there's talk, only talk mind you, at this stage, of raising my post to Assistant Commissioner, to reflect the expanded workload of the division,' Mallon continued.

That would be significant, Swallow knew. No man who had risen from the ranks, much less a Catholic farmer's son from Armagh, had ever made it to the dizzy heights of commissioner in the DMP.

'It would be an appropriate way of acknowledging your work, Chief,' he said simply.

'That means they'll need to appoint a new detective superintendent here,' Mallon said. 'It'd be good to have you back in position since you're the obvious man for the job.'

In spite of lack of enthusiasm for Mallon's Bushmills, he allowed himself a deep draught. And then another.

'I'm going to have to take that on board and think about it, Chief. Stepping into John Mallon's shoes isn't an ordinary challenge.'

Mallon smiled for the first time that evening.

'I'll take that in the spirit it's offered. But you're not an ordinary man, Swallow. Think it over. It's an opportunity that mightn't come your way a second time.'

He finished his drink and bade Mallon good night. The snow outside was heavier now, forming white patterns on the kerbstones and lodging in the ironwork of the Palace Street gates, now shut for the night. A few light flakes lodged on the helmet and the moustache of the uniformed constable who stepped away from the glowing brazier in the sentry box to open the wicket gate so he could exit the Castle.

'Good night, Sir. Bad night if you're going any distance.'

'Thanks,' he smiled, as cold flakes landed on his own nose and cheeks. 'I'm only going up the street. Stay warm yourself now in that box.'

The bells of Christ Church rang nine o'clock as he passed the City Hall into Lord Edward Street. The cathedral's granite bulk offered some shelter from the wind driving the snow up from the river. Once he passed into Cornmarket it whipped against his ears and face, even stinging his ankles through his woollen trousers.

Ordinarily the shops along Thomas Street would be shut at this hour, but with three days to Christmas, the hours of commerce had been extended and the street was marked out along both sides with light that caught the snowflakes as in a child's kaleidoscope. The bright windows of the butchers and the grocers and the fishmongers and the bakers were filled with tempting seasonal delights. The pitch of animated voices, punctuated here and there with loud laughter and even the occasional snatch of a song, flowed out from the busy public houses.

When he reached the end of Thomas Street, Grant's was busy too, as he would have expected. He could see through the plate-glass windows, even before he went through the door, that both bars were humming. Dan Daly, the head man, was in the select bar pumping the tall, brass handles on the syphons that drew pints of strong, black porter out of the kegs in the cellar below. The two curates in the public bar were engaged in the same industry although neither of them could touch Dan's ability to have as many as a dozen perfect pints on the go simultaneously under the taps.

Swallow could not say with certainty when exactly things had started to come right again at Grant's. At some point Dan Daly had shed his air of despondency and grievance and become his old self again, going about his work contentedly and without complaint.

Maria's sense of melancholy dissipated gradually and she recovered her *joie de vivre* and her sense of fulfilment in running the business. She started to socialise again, meeting with Lily and Harriet for lunch from time to time in Wicklow Street or Grafton Street. In the summertime, she would sometimes plan a picnic on his leave days, packing a basket to be taken on the train to Kingstown or even sometimes as far as Bray. His work in the Chief Commissioner's office was repetitive and unexciting. But it had the advantage of regularity, with fixed hours, and they could plan outings together. In the autumn, they started going to the theatre two or three times a month. Maria's favourite venue was the Queen's Royal on Great Brunswick Street and they had seen every production there up to and including the Christmas pantomime.

Lily's marriage to Harry Lafeyre on Midsummer's Day in June had been some sort of a turning point, he knew. The ceremony was held in the beautiful Byzantine church, built on St Stephen's Green, to serve the adjacent Catholic University. Friar Laurence from the Franciscan house on Merchant's Quay performed the ceremony and the newly-wedded couple led their guests across the sun-drenched square from the church to the United Service Club for the reception.

Lily had asked Maria to be her matron-of-honour. At first Maria was reluctant and spoke only of her doubts and apprehension about her role and about the day itself. But as the date drew nearer, Swallow noticed that her fears started to give way to anticipation and then to excitement. She delighted in going through the details of all the preparations with her sister and in the visits to the dressmaker and to the shops where all the perfect accessories for the big day had to be selected and ordered. She looked very beautiful in the elegant gown of cream satin that she and Maria had designed together, commissioning one of Dublin's most celebrated dressmakers to bring it to reality. At the reception in the club's magnificent function room, gaily decorated with flowers, Maria seemed to laugh and enjoy herself again as in the early days of their relationship.

It had been a gradual process, he knew. He also knew that much of her restoration was attributable to the changes in himself and in his working regime. Within a few weeks of being assigned to the Chief Commissioner's office and being relieved of investigative duties, some of the former warmth in their relationship had started to come back. He began to understand that what he had taken as a reverse was in fact a blessing. John Mallon had done him a very great favour, without realising it.

He drank alcohol less frequently and when he did he drank less of it. His work routine meant that he could go home to Maria most days to join her for the midday meal. And it meant that almost every evening he could come home to Thomas Street. They would take their evening meal together and then take turns at being a presence downstairs, mingling with the clientele, supporting Dan and the other barmen and keeping a watchful eye on the evening's trade.

When he first came back to Thomas Street in June, after being moved from investigation duties, he realised that his clothes and personal effects had been transferred from the main bedroom he shared with Maria to the smaller room that he had originally occupied as a lodger and which was still referred to by the servants as Mr Swallow's room. He was briefly angry. But he accepted that it was not unreasonable. His comings and goings had been utterly unpredictable. It was upsetting and disruptive to Maria, already stressed after the loss of the baby. Eventually, as the pressure of his caseload mounted, he was spending more nights in the dormitory at Exchange Court or in Mallon's house than in his own home. He knew that it was a disastrous regime in which any relationship was bound to wither.

They continued to occupy separate rooms for almost two months after his return. Then one evening, when he came home from work, he found that everything had been moved back again to the main bedroom.

'No point in having the maid make up two rooms every morning, is there?' Maria said drily.

They were sitting to their evening meal in the dining room on the first floor.

'No, I suppose not,' he answered, unsure of how to respond.

Suddenly, Maria giggled.

'Ah, you know that's not why I did it.'

She giggled again.

'Sure, it'll give the servants something to talk about anyway, the mess you always leave our bed in.'

Now, coming up to Christmas, it sometimes seemed to him as if the past year and a half was a blank. It might not have happened at all. The loss of the baby was always there but it lessened in intensity. Maria's melancholia gradually became a distant, if unpleasant, memory that could still cause him pain. She had rediscovered her life and they had recovered their lives together. He felt as if he had somehow diverted off the highway of his own life for a time but then re-joined it.

He had expected to see Maria when he entered the select bar, stepping in from the snow. On a night as busy as this, with Grant's abuzz with pre-Christmas cheer, she would usually be on hand, conversing and chatting and making sure the regulars got their favourite tipple 'on the house' to mark the season.

He brushed melting snowflakes off his coat and pushed his way through the drinkers to the public bar. She was not in there either. Familiar faces nodded and smiled, wishing him good cheer and the blessings of Christmas.

'A merry Christmas, Mister Swalla'.'

'Season's cheer, Joe.'

'Beannachtaína Nollag.'

'Happy Christmas and many of them.'

He nodded back and mouthed greetings and salutations in return.

'You'll be lookin' for herself, Mr Swalla'?'

Dan Daly, as if sensing his concern, had followed him through from the select bar.

'I am, Dan. Is she alright? Is she above?'

The head barman smiled.

'Ah, don't fret now, Sir. She's gone upstairs. She said to tell you to go straight up when you came in.'

He took the stairs two at a time. There had to be a reason why Maria was not downstairs two nights before Christmas.

She was sitting by the coal fire in the parlour with the heavy, brocade drapes drawn across the windows, blocking out the winter cold from the street. Four lamps were burning, dispensing an even pattern of yellow light across the Persian rug and throwing shadows against the wall on either side of the mantle.

'Joe,' she called as he entered the room. 'You're home. I was worried about you when I saw the snow starting to come down.'

He kissed her cheek and took the chair opposite.

'Don't be foolish, my love. It's only a few flurries. It'll be gone by morning.'

He struggled out of his overcoat and sat again.

'It's busy below. I thought you'd be down there but Dan told me that you'd come upstairs. Is there anything wrong?'

'No. But I wanted to be here where we could be on our own as soon as you arrived. I've something to tell you privately.'

He held his breath, fearing for the worst.

'I was at the doctor earlier,' she said.

'Why?' he asked urgently. 'Why didn't you tell me? Is everything alright?'

She smiled.

'Everything is fine. But we're going to have to prepare the nursery for a new arrival in our lives.'

Postscript II

December 26th, 1890

Officially, the public houses were closed on Saint Stephen's Day, the first day after Christmas. Bar staff who had worked tirelessly through the festive season were given two full days to rest, to be with their families and to enjoy their own celebrations.

Unofficially however, many houses were serving regular customers and friends. The front doors might be shut but those in the know went behind the premises to find their entrance. A back door would open briefly after a signal, perhaps a sharp knock on a side window or a rap on the door itself. And because all the barmen were gone for their well-deserved holiday, the publicans and members of their family would usually be found serving behind the bar.

So it was at Grant's on Saint Stephen's morning. The first customers, a pair of pensioners from the Royal Hospital at Kilmainham, had tapped on the back door with their walking sticks shortly after eleven o'clock. Maria had decided to open only the select bar, leaving the public bar unattended and she ushered the two elderly men inside to be served by Swallow. There was a steady stream of customers during the morning and they took turns behind the bar.

Shortly after noon, Swallow opened the door in response to a quick series of taps on the window. He was a little surprised to see Duck Boyle on the step, arms wrapped around himself in his heavy overcoat to counter the cold.

'Let me in there, Swalla', like a good man.'

The corpulent superintendent was across the threshold and into the back hallway before Swallow could say a word.

'God, there's a wind out there that'd take the skin off yer face,' Boyle wheezed. 'Compliments o' the season to yerself an' all in the house.'

He stamped his feet to shake off the overnight snow.

'You're very welcome, Super,' Swallow said. 'And the compliments of the season to yourself. Come on into the bar and I'll get you something to take the chill off you.'

Boyle crossed into the select bar and pushed open the door of the first snug beside the counter.

'Ah, that's grand. All to meself,' he said, finding it empty. 'Mebbe you'll join me yourself for a while if you're not too busy. Would yer missus be alright to look after things on her own fer a bit?'

Swallow looked to Maria who had immediately apprehended the situation in her head. Duck Boyle was not a regular visitor to Grant's. He was here for a purpose beyond merely having a drink on the house, although that might be a minor consideration also. She nodded in affirmation as Swallow silently pointed first to himself and then to the door of the snug.

'There you go, Super,' he planted a large Powers whiskey, Doyle's favourite tipple, on the snug table. Against his better instincts, given the relatively early hour and the prospect of a long day ahead, he had poured himself a Tullamore.

Boyle raised his glass.

'Here's to yer health, Swalla' and to all of us for the New Year. 1890, what? Hard to believe. A new decade. The very last wan before we're into a new century.'

The superintendent appeared to be in an uncharacteristic philosophical mood. Swallow had never known Duck Boyle to ponder very much upon the future or, indeed, to reflect very much on the past.

'I have a bit o'news, Swalla', somethin' you prob'ly wouldn't have heard over the past couple o'days, what with it bein'

Christmas an' you sort of isolated annyway, over there in the Chief Commissioner's office.'

It was true, Swallow had to admit to himself, that with the passage of time and as he became more acclimatised to conditions of greater domesticity and regularity, he had become considerably disengaged from the daily round of crime news.

'So what's that, Super?'

'I'm on the brink o' solvin' the murder case in the river.'

'The woman we found in the Poddle?'

'That's it exactly.'

'So what's happened?'

'Well, you'll recall that Dr Lafeyre had spotted the couple a' gold fillin's in the dead woman's mouth. Now, Tim Hogan, the photographic technician above in the RIC Depot took pictures, as ye know, of every part o' the skeleton, includin' the teeth with their fillin's in gold.'

'Indeed.'

'Now, them pictures was circulated to all the police forces in the Kingdom. An' it seems that there's a fellow in the Manchester CID who was apprenticed to a dentist before he joined the force. He takes an interest in these matters an' when he saw the pictures sent over by Horgan from Dublin, he recognised somethin' unusual and familiar about them.'

'Go on.'

'Ye prob'ly don't know this, but Manchester seems to be very advanced in matters of dental medicine. They set up their own dental college there a few years back and it seems to be more than well regarded.'

He drank from his Powers.

'So, the gold was put into the cavity in layers, it seems. He could spot that in a way now that an ordinary person wouldn't. He calls it foil. Them fillin's usin' foil are sort of brighter than other gold fillin's. But it's a fairly new way of doing the job. It used to be done with a very fine wire. So he talked to a few o' the dentists teachin' at the college and a few practicin' dentists around Manchester to see who was usin' this new technique and one o' them looked at the pictures and said he thought them fillin's might actually be his own work.'

Swallow's mind went back to Ephram Greenberg's information from his fellow dealer in Manchester. The location tallied. He started to sense that what was unfolding in Boyle's narrative might actually amount to something concrete.

'The CID man asked this dentist if he could identify the individual from his patients' list. It took a bit o' work but eventually he narrowed it down to two or three women of the right age from around Manchester. He had them checked out one by one and all were accounted for except one.'

He reached into his pocket to find his notebook.

'Margaret Ryan, aged thirty-four, believed to be a native of Dublin. A cook and housekeeper, a widow, it's believed, with a couple of young children taken away an' put in an orphanage. She was in the employment of one Daniel Harden, a dealer in jewellery and fine furniture with a domiciliary address at New Gardens Street. Now, here's the thing, Swalla'. Mr Harden seems to be, in the phrase, well-known to the bobbies in Manchester. He's got convictions for receivin' stolen property, for sellin' on stolen property and for serious assault. He's understood to be a native of someplace in Ireland too but nobody seems to have any idea what place.'

'So what connects her to the bones found in the Poddle?' Swallow asked cautiously, sipping his Tullamore.

'Manchester CID picked up a whisper that for some reason she left Manchester in a hurry and went back t' Ireland. An' Harden sent a couple o' fellas over here after her. Hard men. Manchester CID have their names. The intelligence is that she'd taken somethin' from Harden. Somethin' valuable, obviously. An' he wanted it back. The two toughs kem back to Manchester an' the word is that they found Margaret Ryan but they didn't get their hands on whatever it was they were after.'

Some mental image of an unknown Margaret Ryan swam into Swallow's mind. It became easier to imagine the bones in the Poddle as the remains of a once-living person when one had a name. Margaret Ryan. He could not allow himself to imagine her brutal end when the thugs sent to follow her from Manchester failed to find the treasure she had secreted in the belt she wore about her. At some point her ordeal had come to an end. But whether she was alive or dead when she was put into the dark waters of the Poddle was anybody's guess.

He had to remind himself that Boyle had never learned about the diamonds and half sovereigns that Lafeyre had found in the belt. That information had remained confidential to himself, Lafeyre, Mallon, Chief Commissioner Harrel and, of course to Ephram and Katherine Greenberg. To this date, as he understood it, they remained in the big evidence safe in Harrel's office in the Castle.

'Do we know where she went when she came to Ireland?' Swallow asked.

'Not a clue. We're workin' on it. But it's more than a year ago. So the chances are slim that we can locate her track now at this stage.'

'How are you going to proceed from here?' Swallow asked.

'We're goin' to send a couple o' G-men over to Manchester with the skull of our woman so it can be formally identified by the dentist fellow. They'll take that bunch o' keys ye found in the river too. My hunch is they might fit into doors and locks in this fella Harden's house. Then we're goin' to have Manchester CID take in the two heavies that he sent over here. They prob'ly did for her and dropped the corpse into the Poddle somewhere. Most likely we can get wan o' them to turn Queen's evidence agin' t'other and hopefully agin' Harden himself.'

He threw back the last of his Power's.

'Now, Swalla', whaddy think o'that?'

Swallow knew what Boyle wanted to hear. And he saw no reason to deny him.

'That's great work, Super. Sure, I managed to make no progress at all when I was working on the case. You'll get great praise from the Commissioner when he hears what you've managed to do. And you'll get great notice in the newspapers too. Sure, they were all full of the story, "woman's bones in underground river" and all that at the time.'

'That's very true, Swalla'. But of course I'm indifferent to all that publicity stuff. It's not what a good policeman should be thinkin' about. Of course, if this comes to a successful conclusion, there'll be praise for every wan involved. Mebbe even promotion, if ye understand what I'm sayin' now.'

Swallow understood perfectly. It was important to Boyle that he should get as much credit as possible. There was a post at the rank of chief superintendent coming up. He had the right connections to work on his behalf. A notable success in crime detection would weigh even more heavily in his favour. But it was also important that he could put himself forward as the genius of the successful investigation. Swallow knew he was being invited to write himself out of the script.

Why not, he asked himself? He had thought about Mallon's offer to restore him to the G-division crime office with a view to facilitating his own promotion. But it no longer had the appeal it once had. He would be happy to step back and let Boyle take centre-stage. And it would be more than churlish, he told himself, to make anything of the role of the unknown Manchester CID man who had assiduously trawled through local dental records and finally matched the skull in the Poddle to the missing Margaret Ryan. No doubt, if the investigation came to a successful conclusion, his work would be acknowledged by his own authorities there.

Across the counter, he saw Maria, smiling and laughing with the regulars, as she dispensed their drinks and listened to their banter. She looked happy and well, at ease with the world. In a couple of hours, they would see the last of the customers off the premises, close the select bar and climb the stairs to the peaceful home that they had learned to share together.

'You're right, Super,' he said. 'There's a lot of other things to think about.'